THE DAYS AFTER THAT NIGHT

SINMISOLA OGÚNYINKA

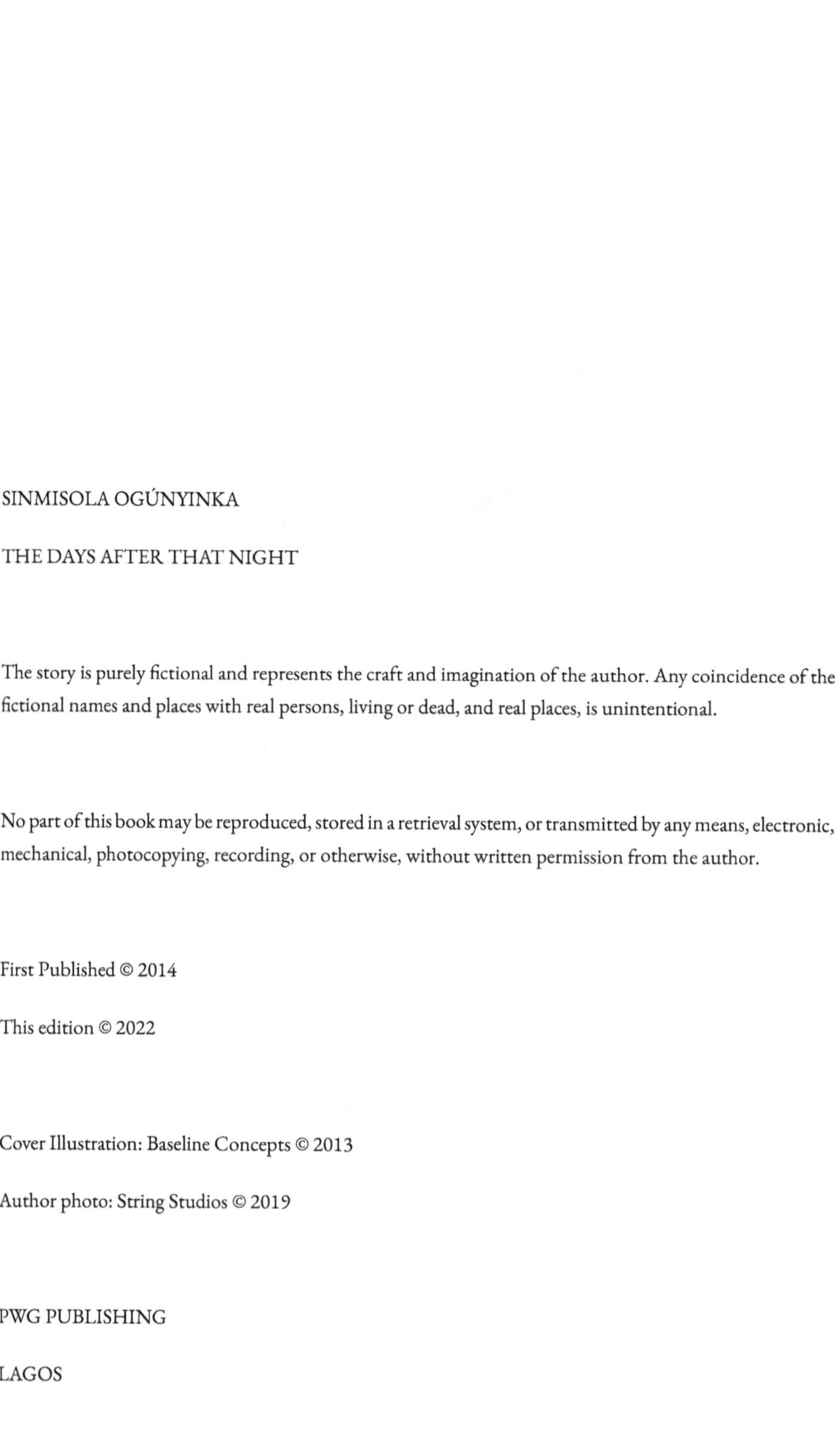

SINMISOLA OGÚNYINKA

THE DAYS AFTER THAT NIGHT

The story is purely fictional and represents the craft and imagination of the author. Any coincidence of the fictional names and places with real persons, living or dead, and real places, is unintentional.

Cover Illustration: Baseline Concepts © 2013

Author photo: String Studios © 2019

PWG PUBLISHING

LAGOS

DEDICATION

All my friends from Ijaw (Ee-jaw) kingdom *and*

Their excellencies Donald and Onari Duke, leaders I greatly admire.

THE DAYS AFTER THAT NIGHT
WINNER - NIGERIAN WRITERS' AWARD 2017
(FAITH-BASED CATEGORY)

When Ijaw women battle, even their men stand aside

CHAPTER 1

On the 31st of December, in the year 2003, at precisely the twenty-third hour, Ebisine Francis George gave up the ghost.

Tonbra sat with her hands folded in her laps, in the doctor's office. She couldn't feel sorry for the way she must look, knowing she'd not had a bath in more than 24 hours. How much longer would she wait for the verdict? The white t-shirt she wore looked limp and dirty, awful, just the way she felt. The constant jerking of her head toward the door at every imaginary movement mirrored her hope. And fear.

Tonbra's thoughts wandered to the young man seated across from her, whoever he was. He couldn't be a doctor, or he probably could be. It didn't matter. He seemed concerned. She reckoned he came for check-up as well, from the conversations that drifted above her head.

Whatever.

New Year's Eve of 2003 forever would haunt her memory, after Ebisine's condition got worse. His system reacted to a strong antibiotic after two previous ones failed and he slipped into a coma. All that information came from the whispers she couldn't help but latch on to.

Otherwise, no one said anything.

Tonbra believed in God. She believed God would save her, and her loving husband.

Such an honest, God-fearing, God-loving gentleman didn't deserve to die. A man with so much unique ability and prospect in life...couldn't die. She believed it beyond reasonable doubt.

"He'll be alright, I'm sure," the young man said.

If her mind tuned in to count, that could be the hundredth time in the last hour.

"I'm sure." She cleared her throat and nodded, glad she didn't have to force any smiles or anything.

The man didn't smile either. He must understand the dilemma she faced. Her eyes darted again to the NSH-branded wall clock. 3a.m. She could only thank God for little mercies because she would have been stranded with her sick husband if this man hadn't come in at the time he did.

Only members of staff of NNPC (Nigerian National Petroleum Corporation) or any of its subsidiaries or joint venture companies used NSH, NNPC Staff Hospital, except with a guarantor. Desperation had brought her here. Convinced she would get sympathy because she had no money, and no guarantor, she'd come. The stranger signed as guarantor.

She'd never seen him before, and still didn't know his name. He looked not much older than her, but her mind drifted away... Only Ebisine's health mattered at the moment.

On New Year's Day people met new people, and celebrated. Would she celebrate later in the day when the doctors patted her back and hailed her bravery and strength, and Ebisine, fresh out of the coma?

The door opened, and the doctor walked in with a work-weary gait. His head was full of grey hair, and wrinkly jowls complemented his pot-bellied mass. One or two nurses had assured her of his expertise, a consultant and specialist in the area of blood infection. One of the best, the young man earlier told her. She searched his face for any signs. Not one.

The doctor took his seat and placed a sheet of paper on his desk. Tonbra looked at it. Her eyes shot up and she screamed a shrill sound that rent the walls of NSH. "Yeeee!" She slid to the floor.

***

The doctor leapt to his feet, swift for his frame, the same time Dini, did. "Dini! Help her," the doctor said. "Lie her down."

Dini caught her before she hit the floor, and with male strength, which many underestimate, carried her. She weighed almost nothing in his arms. He placed her on the examination table with care, despair at his shameless notice of the outlining of her bosom beneath the rumpled t-shirt. Could she have picked this shirt on purpose, with the print, 'hell is real,' in bold print on the front? He didn't think so. She would give every batting of her lovely almond eyes to have it taken off.

Earlier, he'd noticed a lot more about her.

Dini squeezed his nose in a knowing manner. "Didn't make it?" He pulled on his moustache. His hand roamed to his recent goatee, and he twisted thoughtfully. He needed a shave.

The doctor shook his head and returned to his seat. "There are papers for you to sign as guarantor. You knew the implications, didn't you?"

"I get the body as well?"

He looked at the document the doctor dropped on his desk. The death certificate. As guarantor for the deceased, he'd sign for and take the body. And clear the bill.

Tonbra Ebisine George came to, disoriented and seemingly unaware of her surroundings and circumstance. She sat up, her beautiful eyes stared at the doctor and Dini helped her back into her seat.

"I am sorry, Mrs. George," the doctor said. "He didn't make it."

How many times would a man his age and status, mutter those same words? Words that would now form the future for the young widow. And forever change her life. She looked hopeless and Dini's heart bled for her.

"Hey." She gripped her stomach. "Who will care for this baby in my stomach? God. Why! God o! Tamara!" She spoke a string of words in her mother-tongue for a while, and then went from that to complete loss of control. She wept then wailed, then went calm, and still.

Sighed, prayed, rained curses on the devil then burst into tears again.

The two men watched her manifest as she wished. She could not be consoled at this point. The need to vent became primary.

"It's not true. I want to see him." She stood. "I want my husband! I want my husband!"

Dini blocked her exit and turned to the consultant. "Doctor, can she be calmed down?"

The doctor called the nurses' station.

"I want my husband. Let me out!"

"Doctor? She needs some drug or something."

"Going by what she said, Dini, she may be pregnant. I won't want to give her anything just now."

Pregnant?

A nursing sister with a figure-hugging uniform walked in to render assistance. Tonbra got a bed in a private ward and a harmless dose of antidepressant to make her sleep.

Hence began the year 2004 for Tonbra Ebisine George and Dinipre Brisibe.

CHAPTER 2

No one showed up to help. It could be due to the time of year. No one wanted to be called up on New Year's Day to come and comfort the widow of the dead. So, Dini could not leave the bereaved woman alone.

He collected the death certificate, signed off all the necessary documents, and settled the bill with his staff credit card. He was glad to leave to the staff house after all the stress. His room beckoned, and he embraced the anticipated rest with relish.

He didn't live in Warri and didn't choose to spend the New Year here. But giving in to his superstitious beliefs to have his overdue medical check-up before the year ran out, he arrived at NSH. As fate had it, his arrival at the hospital coincided with the same moment the ambulance with Ebisine's unconscious body blasted in.

Plans to go home to see his mother now truncated, he faced another task, being an ally to a stranger. Home held more appeal. His mother missed him and made no pretences about that. Working two months offshore on ExxonMobil's platform made him long for land, and home, and mother. With colleagues taking advantage of his single status, he'd backstopped for a couple of married men, and ended up working three months at a stretch.

It happened often. As a specialist in his field, energy and earth resources, Dini worked away from home for several months without a break. He enjoyed much of it. His job summarized his life.

At about 4a.m. on the 1st of January, back from the NSH, Dini's head hit his pillow and he slept off.

The incessant ringing of the phone on the bedside table woke him up. The annoying sound snapped him out of a dreamless sleep and he sluggishly stood, rubbing his eyes, yawning and grappling for the phone. He guessed who. Right. Erebi.

"Hello?" With one hand to the phone, and the other busy with his pyjama, he walked to the bathroom and relieved himself.

"Why? Dinipre Oyinkuru Brisibe! Happy New Year, first of all. Where are you? When are you coming home?"

"Hi, Sister. Happy New Year."

"Mama is worried, of course. We all are. I've been calling your line since. You didn't pick up."

Dini groaned. He could feel her frown. Erebi, so like their mother, overacted at times. "I just woke up. I'm sorry." He walked back to the room and picked up his Kelvin Klein watch, 11:45a.m. "Good God."

"What's that?"

"I just checked the time."

"We thought you would wake up very early and come since you said you couldn't make it again yesterday."

"I just woke up, Sister." He yawned and heard the loud complaints from his mother and others in the background. His sister's voice seeped through as she explained the situation to those on her side of the phone.

"So, when do we expect you now? Are you sure you're alright, this boy?"

"Have I lied to you before?"

Erebi screamed and they both laughed. "Many times. Too many times."

"I won't come today. I'll be home tomorrow."

Erebi raised her voice. "Hey—"

Dini cut her. "See, I'll explain better, but I need to help a young widow arrange for her husband's burial today." No point concealing matters. It may only make things worse.

"A young widow?"

"See, I have to go now. I'll come home tomorrow. Just see how you'll explain that to—"

"Talk to your mother."

For another ten minutes, he spoke with his mother, explaining what he already said, why he needed to stay back in Warri. Mama complained he didn't have anybody in Warri, how then would he spend the first day of the year, alone. Erebi and her family would go back to Lagos on the 2nd and so would the others. Would he come this late in the festivities? The whole village would be so boring without him— on and on and on. He hung up after a deadlock with a headache.

Dini washed up and went back to the hospital. Mrs. Ebisine George sat stiff on her bed in the private room. Her glazed, swollen eyes seemed calm. He noticed to his consternation he found her beautiful eyes alluring, seductive.

She looked at him, when he walked in, and then looked away. Had she expected her husband to walk in? Her expression said so. He felt sad for her. Though he didn't like the way she seemed to look through him. His friends thought he cared less about his appearance, but he had never lacked female company, and that had satisfied him. For the first time, he truly wished she

would not see him as short, lanky, and from the last time he looked in the mirror, bushy. He wanted this one woman to like him.

He took the only seat in the room, and for a moment, respected her silence. "How are you?"

"Fine, I guess." She looked at her hands, and tears filled her eyes.

He had never found himself in this condition before. The broker in bereavement. Words eluded him. "I have made all the arrangements. Would you want him to be buried here in—?"

She shook her head. "His family expects me to bring him home. Isaba. That's where we're from. Everyone's at home now for the festive—"

"Of course. I made arrangements for an ambulance to go anywhere you wish. And I wasn't sure you had a car. Do you have a car?"

Her eyes shot to his and large tears dropped from those gorgeous eyes. She did not bother to wipe them. She only shook her head again and looked away. He wondered how beautiful she would be at other more cheerful times. Her fair skin looked pale. Her facial features, all small, complemented her big almond-shaped eyes, and wide mouth.

He marvelled at how her rather prominent forehead balanced out high cheek bones, and thick but well-shaped eyebrows. Her medium-length hair scattered, cluttered, and limp, hung around her face. Still, going by her features, any man could easily fall for Mrs. George.

"You have a car for as long as you wish and a driver as well."

"Thank you."

They lapsed into a long period of silence.

"I told him it is dangerous to follow the militants so close without government backing," she said as though from a distance. "Did you know him at all?" She turned to look at him.

"No." He shook his head. "I never met him." He didn't even know what the man looked like. He hadn't seen his face...hadn't looked at the corpse either. He couldn't bring himself to. Only fate got him involved at all.

"For the past three years, Ebisine worked closely with the recent upheaval in some of the troubled areas of the Niger Delta. Contending for the CNN award for best African Journalist drove him into the most dangerous spots to cover the news." She stared into space.

"It's a noble cause."

"Until then, he had worked for Delta State Daily. Ever ambitious, the pace of the media house proved too slow for him, and he went freelance. He is a very stubborn man. So, determined." She sobbed. "So hardworking."

Dini didn't have a clue as to what to do. It disturbed him the way she referred to the dead man in the present. A gas or oil pipe, he understood. She wasn't an engine with parts, or men missing their wives. Those he dealt with often. He had on his hands a broken woman who probably thought her life just ended.

Her slender shoulders sagged, and she sniffed. "I told him not to go with the militants. And see what has happened in the end."

He didn't know what happened to her husband, except that an infection refused to respond to treatment. And now he was dead.

"You need to be strong."

"To be strong? How?"

"For the burial. And. Your—your baby."

She burst into tears, heaving and sniffing. Indecision and confusion warred within Dini... a weeping beauty eluded his thought process. His hand twitched in anticipation of a touch, a pat, but he held back. What could he say, or do? Nothing occurred to him.

When she pulled herself together, he stood. It would be good to get home to Apoi.

Give Mama a pleasant surprise and see Erebi and the other family members.

He understood Mama's reasoning. Sounds of glee and joy permeated the airs during festive periods in Ijawland. Everyone came home. Everyone.

"I have to go now, but please, don't hesitate to—"

She looked up at him, her eyes sucked him in, and he sat down. He couldn't leave her like this.

"I'll be fine. You have done more than enough."

He couldn't leave her alone. He stuttered a protest from his chest, a groan that couldn't be put in words. Why didn't anyone in either her family or her husband's know she would need help? He clenched his teeth, and hands, in a bid to control an outburst of anger and frustration.

She looked at her hands and shrugged, the gesture tore his heart apart. "I'll be fine."

"Look, I'll stick by you till at least, you get to your family. I'm not rushing anywhere."

He knew he'd said and done the right thing when she didn't comment again. He stood once more. "The ambulance and the car are waiting for us. Whenever you're ready."

Chapter 3

The youths gathered on the outskirts of Isaba. Many wore dark clothes. Some wore rags. They held guns and machetes, small and big knives, and chanted war songs. It looked scary to someone who had no prior knowledge of a custom that encouraged this ritual for every young person brought into the land in a box.

Tonbra sat beside Dini as still as darkness. She'd found out his name along the line, sometime. He had been so gracious to continue to help. Giving the Toyota Camry with the driver, and the NSH ambulance, more than compensated if he left but he stayed. Even without giving these, she appreciated his being there. He'd stepped in when she needed help the most.

Thank God for the Camry. Or else she would have had to hop from taxi to taxi to get her kids, pick her clothes and a few other things, and then head for Isaba. A family car of their own topped the list of purchases for the year for Ebisine and he worked his life away to achieve it. Literally.

And then Dini volunteered to follow her. As though he saw the great fear in her eyes when he stood to leave. It terrified her to be alone. No words could express her gratitude at this trying time in her life.

The period of year did not help matters. Everyone in her family had left town to. Everyone in her family had left town to celebrate the Christmas and New Year in the village. She'd stayed back so Ebisine could travel with her and the kids. Instead...

The day he arrived almost unconscious, she'd asked her neighbour to keep her children. Timi, at age six, replicated her at that age, with fair beautiful skin, large almond-shaped eyes and long, dark hair. Pere, three, looked more like his father. She'd picked them up on the way out of town, amidst sympathies from her neighbour. Now she sat with the two, who obviously now understood Daddy would never return.

Dini had looked surprised when she got to her house to pick her children. She didn't blame him. Many people never believed she was married not to talk of being a mother of two.

Dini knew how to care for children. From nowhere, he produced sweets and a card game, which took their minds off the sad news their mother a little earlier incoherently and tearfully broke to them.

Tonbra did not understand why the man escorted her to Isaba. Didn't he have a family? Probably he didn't. In her work as a legal secretary, she met many estranged individuals who had no one. Maybe Dini fitted that class of people. Since the beginning of the journey, he spoke little, only assisting the children to sit well, and then play a little. She knew nothing about him.

But he qualified to use NSH, which meant he had a good job, well, that was the popular opinion. So how could he not have family?

Tonbra turned to look at him beneath the dark sunglasses she had found when she went to her house to pack. The man stared out at the landscape as though he'd never seen it before. It left her wondering about his identity. Why be so helpful? Where did he come from? She knew she should be ashamed she took no interest in him all the while he offered his assistance, but that could be excused. Ebisine just died!

She couldn't think straight. Her mind clogged with thoughts and words and fears and so much… too much to bear. If she tried to sit down and think about her situation, she would run mad. On reflex, she rubbed her hand over her stomach. Ebisine's seed grew in there. She wished she hadn't argued with him about her pregnancy. She would remove it. Quietly abort and face a future raising two children alone. She had no choice.

An involuntary sob escaped from her lips and everyone turned to look at her. Timi grabbed her hands and squeezed and began to cry. Because Timi cried, Pere cried as well. She hugged both of them, refusing, unable to look at the stranger in the car. The angel.

Sometime between the day of Ebisine's arrival and now, she concluded he couldn't be human. He had to be an angel. Though he looked none of an angel.

His profile matched average and she disliked fair-skinned men. She liked her men, tall, dark, handsome, just like Ebisine and most unlike this Dinipre. She loved muscles and this man had little or none. Short, average, bushy? He looked rough and unattractive. Maybe if he visited a barber shop, he would look nice. She did notice he had a remarkable mouth, fuller upper lip, covered by thick moustache.

An angel, she expected, would be personable, charismatic, dominating physique— Not this hairy for one. Dark, sleepy hair covered his thin arms, and his face down to his neck. Too much hair, she thought wearily.

He leaned over and short of touching her face, patted Timi's back. "It's okay. Don't cry," he said softly. "Mummy will be okay."

She looked at him from under her thick dark glasses, assessing, though her tears spilled unrestrained. She shameless took advantage of the opportunity to study him. The concern on his face caught her attention. Even

Ebisine never showed such empathy for anyone. Oh Ebisine! Her life revolved around his existence. And would now be wrapped around his death.

The ambulance in front slowed down, and so did the Camry, thus drawing their attention away from her tears, to the mob ahead.

Dini gasped, and she turned to him. "It's customary," she mumbled. "The youths mourn."

He nodded. "I know."

The youths raised their guns and fired in the air. They jumped and screamed, and the females let out air-rending shrieks. The ambulance came to a complete stop and the youths danced around it violently.

The Camry driver turned back and Dini waved his concern off. "They're harmless. Just follow the ambulance." He turned to look at Tonbra who now wailed. "He must have been very important."

She wished to tell him Ebisine had no status of importance in Isaba. The customary display by the youths affected all indigenes within certain age grades, but her throat clogged, and she choked on her own tears. No one in Ebisine's family had attained any achievements. His parents had spent the last twenty years in the village, after retiring from civil service.

Though respected in their own circles they represented nothing more. Ebisine had died as he had lived. Struggling. Unknown. Irrelevant.

After a few minutes of the ritualistic dance around the ambulance, the youths climbed into the bed of a two-cabin truck and led the party to Ebisine's family compound. There the wailing took another turn. As soon as the vehicles parked, Tonbra stumbled out, held her children in a death-grip, and wailed.

***

People flocked around her, screaming in a dialect common only to the clan. Dini couldn't even pick a word of what they said. He found a seat in a corner of the frontage and watched in shock. The ambulance driver felt just as left out in the strange ways of the indigenes. With the Camry driver, a stranger as well, they sat through the wailing ritual which went on for hours. The village wailers cried and screamed, and kept quiet at particular intervals, as though rehearsed.

Dini's attention went back to Tonbra, now draped with a black wrapper, signifying her mourning had officially begun. Instead of wearing any other colour, she would tie that wrapper till she had black mourning clothes because of the age of the deceased, he knew that much about the tradition.

At sundown, the mourning party dispersed and Tonbra went into the house with her children. Some youths removed the casket from the ambulance and took it in.

Dini turned to the two men. First to the ambulance driver. "I'll give you some money to return tomorrow." He addressed the Camry driver. "But you'll stay with me till I leave here." Both nodded. He gave the ambulance driver some money and then turned back to the Camry driver. "We may sleep in the car tonight."

"No problem, sir."

"We'll stay in the ambulance and you can have the Camry to yourself," the ambulance driver said.

"Thank you." He looked round the compound. Nothing seemed to be happening except the occasional wailing and sighing, which punctuated the night sounds. "Find something to eat and I'll see you in the morning."

The ambulance driver frowned. "What about you, sir?"

"I'll be fine, thank you."

The two men nodded and walked into the night. Dini walked back to where he had been seated and gazed into the descending darkness.

They found him the following morning. The ambulance driver bade him farewell and left and the other driver went to sit in his car, waiting for the unknown.

Dawn turned to day. Visitors trooped into the compound, weeping, and groaning, and speaking the dialect. Tonbra finally came out of the house and expressed surprise to find him seated outside. To give her some credit, she showed remorse, and he cherished her brief grimace more than the painful experience through the insect-biting, sleepless discomfort of the night.

"I'm really sorry I—left you out here."

"It's alright. I understand."

She looked round and then turned to him. She looked depreciated. She sucked in her breath, and batted sunken eyes. Her protruding forehead and gaunt cheeks made her eyes look ready to pop out. Her fair nose had a permanent tint of reddish pink, evidence of her continued crying. He would hug and cuddle her but he couldn't. Not here. And she would not understand. For now, being a stranger created the barrier.

"You can come in for a few minutes. My parents-in-law are awake, but the ceremonies will not start till a bit later." She turned and faced the front door of the old-style bungalow. He followed.

"Ceremonies?"

"Burial meetings and rites," she said so softly he almost didn't hear. "He may be buried today."

That's fast, he thought, but then, what would they keep the corpse for?

She led him down a long corridor with rooms on either side till they stopped in front of one. She turned to him and put her index finger on her lips. "Shh." Then she opened the door and tiptoed inside.

In a couple of hours, it would be noon, but the sun had risen early today. Rays of warmth and light seeped into the room, contending with the drawn striped curtains. Dini adjusted his eyes to the near darkness of the room and found the children fast asleep on a king-size bed.

Two chairs loaded with clothes rested against the wall on one side of the congested room. Tonbra carried the clothes off one and dumped them on the other. Dini could almost hear the groaning of the second chair as some of the newly dumped clothes fell off the chair. Tonbra ignored them. She made no move to draw back the curtains or switch on the lights, so he simply took the seat she had cleared.

"Why are you doing all this for us—me?" she whispered. "You said you don't know my husband. And I don't know you either. Why are you helping us?"

The question hit him in the bottom of his belly. He thought he had a straight answer but for the first time since coming into the room, he cherished the darkness. He hesitated because he found it hard to explain. How would he tell her this transcended help—and edged on a weird yearning to be near her? That the attraction he felt toward her, though they knew nothing about one another, reached to the deepest part of his soul.

Dinipre Brisibe compromised in love. The four-letter word meant nothing more to him that any other word with those same alphabets, juggled and used with other alphabets. His heart remained his. Of course, he had dated all sorts of women, white and black, but none of those relationships amounted to anything. None of those women touched a part of him—like this.

"I thought you left yesterday—"

"I couldn't leave you like that." He scratched an insect bite on his arm and rubbed it with the pad of his thumb. "I wanted to be sure you're alright."

She raised her voice a little and then as though remembered the sleeping children, lowered it. "I am at home now. My family is here. I am as alright as I can be."

Her voice carried such force, he flinched in the dark. He jerked to his feet. "Well, I should be on my way then." His voice, as hard as hers. He did not fault her. He would be curious as well, especially since he refused to explain his motives.

He froze when her hand shot out and grabbed his in a firm grip.

"I am not ungrateful," she said, her whisper fierce. "If not for you, how would, what would—" Her voice broke into a sob and he sat down.

He reversed her hold and rubbed her soft hand with his. "I'm sorry. I should have explained."

"He has almost nothing—" she sniffed. "You see." She dragged in a long deep breath, her gaze intent. "So stubborn and has nothing."

He tried to read her rigid frame. Her brittle voice slashed through his emotions, adding effect to the shivers initially caused by their first contact.

"After the November 99 massacre at Odi, Ebisine took leave of his job without permission, to cover the news. His boss was very upset with him.

"He refused to apologize and was given three months' suspension without a salary. I was almost due for Pere, and we needed all the money we could get. Though I was working, it wasn't enough.

"House rent was due—we didn't have a family who could really help." She tried to remove her hand from his, but he wouldn't let her. "This is the first time someone would help without—any reason."

"I understand," he mumbled.

Not quite, he thought. All his life, people had been eager to help him. People warmed up to him. People loved him. Did people who got no help at all really exist? Ebisine George, for one.

"Ebisine emptied our account in those days. We lived from hand to mouth—" she swallowed. Again, she tried to remove her hand from his. "A few months after his punishment had been served, he resigned and went freelance." She walked to the window but didn't open the curtains. He followed her and stood close behind her and kept his hold on her.

"What happened to him? How did he get sick?"

"He went to cover some news about a negotiation between government officials and the militants in Rivers State. When the deal went sour, the government officials covered the backs of their own, their press men—Ebisine got caught in a shoot-out. He got hit. Some fishermen found him the following day by the river side, alive but almost dead." She hiccupped, breathed in and continued, "They took him to a police station at night, and dumped him there—" She paused for a long time. "And ran away. The police thought he was an armed robber—"

"My goodness!" The man must have suffered a great deal. Poor fellow.

"He was shot in the leg. Thank God he had a form of ID. They finally brought him home. We took him to a private clinic. They said they would amputate him but needed to treat the infection which had spread—you know the rest of the story."

He needed to confirm. "They couldn't control the infection, right? He slipped into a coma." He hated to say it. "He died."

"Ebisine would have preferred to die than to be amputated." She heaved a heavy sigh, and turned, falling into his arms. "Please hold me." He did, and she burst into tears, heaving and sobbing. "Ebisine is everything to me. Everything. I love him so much."

"Shh. It's okay," he whispered.

It felt so good to hold her. He felt selfish, enjoying her moment of pain so unashamedly.

He patted her back till the tears subsided.

She sighed and moved away from his hold. "I'm sorry. I'm sorry but you have to leave today. No one will understand what you're doing with me at this time, except we lie. And I don't want to lie."

She fidgeted with clothes long fallen on the floor, and turned around, her eyes darted toward the door.

"I know. Can I pray with you? Are you a believer?"

She nodded.

"Can I hold your hands?"

She didn't respond so he took her hands and held on firmly while he prayed a short prayer for comfort, hope and succor.

"When is the burial?"

"I don't know yet. His family will decide. But today, maybe—I hope."

"I'll come and see you afterward. You need to be strong."

She stared at him. He felt she understood his motive, but he needed to lay a foundation. "When I decided to help your husband, my motives were pure. But after I saw you, met you, everything changed—I'm sure you understand?"

Now accustomed to the dimness in the room, he searched her face. At his confession, her head jerked up and her lovely eyes doubled in size. Her lips tremulous, and seducing him beyond reason, he took an uncertain step backward.

He needed to leave so he would not make a fool of himself. He turned and strode out of the door.

He beckoned on the Camry driver. They had a journey of a couple of hours ahead and he couldn't wait to get home, shower and rest. And see his family after three months.

Just before he got into the car, he turned toward the direction he assumed was of the room he just left. He couldn't decide if he was right and if so, if she stood at the curtain and peeped but he needed to pause for her before he got in the car. He gave a slow nod and then turned to the car.

She didn't need him now. She would later. And he would be there for her.

CHAPTER 4

He got in as Erebi and her family prepared to leave and took them all back indoor. Mama did small traditional dance steps around him, laughing and clapping. Though Dini worked offshore and had his own accommodation in Lagos where Erebi also lived, he spent most of his time onshore with Mama. Somehow, she would lure him to visit and he would end up spending more than half of the time.

He'd developed a love for his land and his people in the process and as soon as he arrived, word went around. Dini had a lot of money to throw around by virtue of his job, and status as a single man, and he threw much of it around the land of Apoi. He financed several projects to improve the lot of the people, like the primary health centre and a block of flats providing free housing. His scholarship scheme helped more than twenty kids, and at different levels of primary and secondary, and tertiary education.

Dini had returned from Texas, the previous year, a doctorate degree holder. At the age of twenty-nine years old, he'd gotten the degree in one of the best universities in the world, University of Texas at Austin (UT), and returned home to an enviable job with the NNPC, Nigeria's central parastatal for oil and gas.

The pride and joy of his people, his community organized a grand party to welcome him home. Being from a humble background seemed rather than not, to whet his unlimited appetite for knowledge. His principal in Arogbo Community High School, a one-hour trek from his native village of Apoi, had described him as the Einstein of Arogboland. Later in UT, a professor of chemical engineering would call him a genius.

On his return from the states, he renovated the old family house, and added rooms so each of the siblings could have private and comfortable accommodation when they visited. The old bungalow, now a one-story building had eight rooms' en-suite, four downstairs, and four up. Dini and Erebi had a room each downstairs, and dedicated two rooms to their mother, while the four younger children took the rooms upstairs with a six room

boys' quarters constructed for additional family members.

Before long, the compound filled up with people paying homage. Some brought fruits and wine, and palm wine, gifts and food items, many came with requests. The compound hummed with activity and Mama played hostess, entertaining with the gifts brought.

Erebi managed to steal Dini into his room. In her early thirties, the three-year gap in their ages seemed non-existence by virtue of their close relationship.

Erebi hugged him.

"Goodness, sis, I missed you." He pulled back and assessed her.

She looked good and he told her as much. He tickled the cute dimple on her cheek and they both laughed. She swatted his hand away. "Tobi is taking good care of you. Someone may think you're a whitey with your skin so radiant."

"Ah, Dini, where's this compliment coming from?" She giggled like a teenager. "Trying to bribe after disappointing everyone."

"I'm sorry." Dini scratched his head. "The past two days have been horrid." He smiled and hugged her again. "But I'm glad to be home."

"We'll soon leave so we don't get to Lagos late. You know Tobi can't drive at night."

"Your husband should get his eyes checked." Dini slumped into one of the three chairs in the room. "Having a dark bunch of six-pack muscle without good eyes is close to zero."

Erebi laughed. "Thank you. I like his six-pack."

"He's not getting any younger, big sis. Before you know it, he's fifty. That's like half of his time spent."

Erebi sighed and took a second seat. "You know all you men are the same. He will never listen. He thinks his eyes are twenty years younger than they are."

"And you women, you know how to twist us around your little fingers," Dini said. "You see, I am right. Twist him into getting his eyes examined."

Erebi laughed and clapped. "You sound like some twisting is going on in your life as well. Mama wants to carry her grandchildren o."

Dini laughed. "You've given her four. Your sister Yinla is doing her bit with two already."

"One!"

"But she's heavy. What's the difference?" He laughed more. "Except she's expecting more than one?" His eyes widened.

Erebi laughed. "You can never change, and you know your mother. That's me and Yinla's allocation. Your slot is vacant."

"She talks about it every time I come home. Does it never expire?"

"Your wedding day is the expiration day."

"She sent you to me, right?"

"No. I'm just preparing your mind."

"Funny, sis. You're on your own agenda." He stretched. "Wow. What a day?"

"So how did you spend watch night? Where did you go?"

"How many times will I need to say this?"

"Of course, you must tell Mama about it."

He stood. "So wait till when I want to tell Mama."

"I'm leaving in the next five minutes. Tell me, my friend!"

Dini laughed and sat back. "I was on a rescue mission." He narrated his ordeal in detail, including all the nitty-gritty.

"So, you had a maiden-in-distress and you really went to the rescue. What should we call you now? Captain Nigeria or Superman?"

"Captain Ijawland may suit me right."

Erebi sighed. "Poor lady. I can just imagine how she'll be feeling now."

Dini sighed. "You should see her when I left this morning. She was—lost." He shook his head. "It tore my heart into two."

"I hope you're not having any feelings for her, the way you're looking. Dinipre Oyinkuru Brisibe!"

"I won't say anything till you see her."

"Means you're going back to her—tomorrow?"

"No. I'll give a week, maybe two."

Erebi shook her head. "It's too soon, Dini. And I don't think she'll want any relationship now. She'll mourn at least for one year—"

"I'll wait for her. Erebi, she needs me. And I know I love her."

Erebi's eyes widened, and she pushed the nearest part of Dini's body to her, which happened to be his knee. "No! A widow with two kids—who you say is pregnant?"

"Well, she insinuated she's pregnant. It doesn't show."

"No."

"No? Why? What's wrong with her? You won't even know she's ever been married if you see her."

Erebi's eyes widened till Dini thought they would pop out and wished he could explain and make her understand.

"Mama can never accept her for a daughter-in-law. With three kids? What happened to all the young, beautiful girls—?"

"What happened is that I don't want any of them, Erebi." Dini gripped her two hands and looked at her. "I want to give it a try. And I want you to support me. Believe me, I'll make the right choice."

Erebi held his gaze for a while and then looked away. Their relationship transcended that of siblings. They behaved like Siamese twins. They acted like soul mates. Even Erebi's new family and Dini's job did not reduce the intensity of their closeness.

She took a long, deep breath and looked at him. "I trust you."

"Thank you." Dini only then realized he had been holding his breath, and he released it. "I needed to hear that."

She stood. "Take care of yourself." She pulled him into a hug. "And don't tell Mama about this Tonbra yet, till you're sure."

"Of course."

She preceded him out of the room and joined the party in the large sitting room. The family soon bade Erebi's family farewell and the hum in the house continued as Dini fraternized with his kinsmen.

At sundown, Mama organized dinner for her children and their friends and other family members in the house. She delayed Dini's meal, and instead, called him into her room, which he had expected anyway.

He loved and cherished the relationship he had with his parents. Before his father died, they had maintained such closeness rare for a man like Oyinkuru Brisibe, his father.

His mother had been the pillar of the family. She was strong, hardworking, and ready to protect her family. Working the farm to support her husband, much as was the tradition of most farming families, added a major part to the growth of their family. Now though she still insisted on going to her farm, not because they would not eat if she didn't do it but because she couldn't stay idle.

Mama in her youth, had been a village belle, and young, strong, and dark-complexioned Brisibe, a few inches taller, had stolen her heart before she celebrated her sixteenth birthday. They'd had many children, some died but now in her early fifties, and without a husband, her 5'4 frame, average size, and fair complexion from where Dini took his colouring, looked fit and firm. She had long, dark hair now sprinkled with gray, and her somewhat weathered face had small cut marks on her cheeks and forehead.

Dini stood at the entrance for a moment, just admiring her.

"I serve your food alone for reason." Mama motioned him to the bed, where she was already seated. "I want us to eat together."

He lazily took the seat offered. "That's great, Mama."

He meant it. He loved to chat with his mother. She was a sensitive woman and much as she had her usual concerns about his welfare and future, she knew her admonitions could turn to harassment, and knew when to stop.

She walked to where the door stood ajar and called out a name he wasn't familiar with.

A voice from within the house responded and she closed the door and returned to her seat.

"They bring food just now." She looked at him with fondness and smiled. "Doh!"

"Oh Mama, I missed you." He took hold of her wrinkled hand and squeezed it. "And I've missed your food. Hope you cooked this one."

She laughed. "So, you know I no prepare the lunch?"

He had taken his bath as soon as he arrived earlier in the day, and then had some pounded yam before attending to guests and then seeing Erebi off.

"Your food is special. No one cooks like you in the world. Even when I was in Texas, I missed your food."

The door was pushed back gently, and a young lady brought in a tray of food. She placed it on a table cleared for that purpose. She opened the dishes and the sweet aroma of native food filled the room.

Dini took a long deep breath and laughed. He spared a glance at the dark-complexioned teenage girl. She smiled and turned to leave the room.

"Oyinemi, come greet my son," Mama said.

The young lady turned back and squatted in front of him. "Doh. Welcome."

"Thank you." Dini smiled, and motioned her

to rise. "Who's she?" He turned to his mother.

"She's Oyinemi, daughter of Tebekaemi Salpon." Dini frowned. "You not know him. He is palm wine tapper but after falling, he no work again."

"Oh, I'm sorry about that." Dini looked at Oyinemi. Her face was delightful. Young, innocent, and pretty. "Please stand up." She stood but remained in the room. He noticed immediately her average height, about two inches shorter than him, and her full youthful face, lovely round eyes, and chubby cheeks.

"How's he now?"

Oyinemi looked at Mama who responded. "He still no work. He break his leg. Oyinemi and her brother, Opuowei join their mother to tend farm when they are not in school."

"Huh, I was going to ask about school."

"Yes, my son. She and her brother in school because of you." Mama had a hint of pride in her voice.

"That's good." Dini smiled at Oyinemi.

Mama looked at him. "Oyinemi is eighteen and just finish secondary school."

"Hope she'll continue?"

"She wait for your scholarship," Mama said teasingly. Dini's eyes widened. "Then she will continue."

Oyinemi went all the way down on her knees and her young face burst in a feast of joy.

Her laughter was contagious, and Dini and Mama laughed along with her.

"Get up, Oyinemi. You can go," Dini said and smiled.

She looked at Mama who nodded and she left the room.

"She like school. Her mother ask me take her as my child. Marry her to my son—just take, she say."

"That is ridiculous. Why would a mother say that?"

"Oh, you don't know? People dash me children since you travel to America." Mama laughed heartily and stood to dish the food.

"Well, I think I can understand that. If the child is yours, then the child is my sibling as well."

"Of course. I tell Oyinemi's mother she keep her daughter, I have enough." She dished a hearty portion and gave him. He made a satisfying sound and Mama laughed. "But the girl come to help me all the time. She will make good wife, I'm sure." She looked at Dini.

He shrugged. "I guess. She's very pretty at least." Mama arched her eyebrows knowingly and Dini laughed. "She's definitely too young for me."

Mama laughed. "I think out of all people you send go school in this village, they are most grateful."

"I'm glad to be useful." Dini took a lump of the starch with the soup and heaved a heavy sigh. "This tastes so good, Mama. Thank you."

Mama joined him on the bed and they ate together. When they were through, Mama took the plates from him and returned them to the tray.

"Oyinemi say she want be teacher. If she can go university, she can be teacher, I think?"

"You think right, Mama. She'll take an education course and that settles it," he said. "Thank you for that delicious meal."

"Anything for my first son. Now what keep you away on New Year Day?"

"Long story, Mama. I had to help a patient in the hospital. And the man ended up dying."

"Eh! Shame? How his family?"

"They've taken him home for the burial."

"What sad way to start year. Thank God you're here. Hope you go stay long—as usual?"

"Mama, I have a lot to do in Lagos. And I may need to go to Warri—"

"What in Warri? You only go hospital in Warri! You sick?"

"Well, that will soon change. I met a woman there—"

Mama jumped to her feet and did a little dance. "What her name?"

"Not so fast, Mama. She's gone to her village and will be back in about a week or so. That's why I need to go there and see her."

"Hey, what you doing for me here? You go Warri tomorrow if you like." Mama laughed. "Hey, my Lord!"

"Yes, we thank God, Mama. Oh!" He laughed and shook his head. "You're wonderful."

Chapter 5

He saw her two weeks later. He'd deferred his trip to Lagos and travelled from Apoi to Warri. His scheduled trip back offshore was from Lagos so he decided to go to Lagos in the last week.

He had to visit Warri twice before she returned. He hadn't gotten her cell number so he couldn't call to check. On both occasions, he'd chartered a vehicle because he didn't have the Camry, a company vehicle, at his disposal anymore, and his car was parked in Lagos.

Tonbra looked harried for a moment and hesitated at seeing him. His heart skipped several beats on seeing her. She had lost even more weight, and her fair complexion looked pale. Her hair was stiffly pulled back and bound with invisible bands. She wore no jewellery. Her large eyes looked eternally sad and did not even light up on seeing him. She wore a long, drab black dress, which hung loosely from her shrunken shoulders down to her ankles.

He refused to be discouraged. "It's been so long, Tonbra. How are you?"

"I just came back yesterday."

He leaned against the doorpost and stared at her, his heart thudded in his chest. Would she refuse him entry? "I came twice before. Your neighbours told me you were not back."

"I just came back yesterday," she said just as blandly as she said it the first time.

He looked at his shoes for so long, it surprised him she still stood there when he looked up. "I want to enter your house."

"My husband's sisters are here. We came back together."

He shrugged. "Just let me in, Tonbra. I am a friend of your family. I did my part in helping to save your husband's life, without even knowing him. Or you."

His words seemed to jolt her. As though she'd been woken up from sleep, she jerked back and he walked in.

He first noticed the tiny space inside. The sitting area had two sofas better placed in a room twice the size. Her two children were sprawled on each of the sofas.

A huge, well-arranged, bookcase against the wall had all manner of books. That bookcase took almost all the available space against the wall facing the sofas. At the close end of the wall, a 21" television set was squeezed in place on a stand that must have been bought with it. The stand had two other layers and a CD rack, full and spilling to the carpeted floor. The layer next to the TV shelf had a DVD player. The last layer had some more CDs and magazines.

A door led out of the sitting room to what Dini found to be the kitchen because he could sneak peek a tabletop cooker. By the door, a dining table against that side of the wall, gave room for just four chairs to be pushed in.

Another doorway demarcated by a floral curtain led to what Dini assumed to be the rest of the house.

To give credit to Tonbra, the house was clean, and besides the scattered CDs and magazines, looked neat enough. A sad note of mismatch stamped the room with the wall painted a dirty blue, a brown carpet, cream and green curtains, and sofas that looked blue-black. Obviously, all had been procured at various times and periods, sporting different levels of wear and tear.

Family pictures lined the walls. Ebisine and Tonbra in their wedding outfits. With the children, alone, and together. The walls were crowded with wall frames. They obviously liked pictures in this family. Dini had never been one to hang things on the wall.

For the first time, Dini got to see the profile of the man he helped. The couple differed. Clean opposites in fact. He was at least a head taller than her, dark chocolate complexion, and on the hefty side.

In one of the pictures, he had a huge, gapped-tooth smile. Dini reluctantly observed he had a smooth oblong, clean-shaven, and handsome face. Absently, he rubbed his chin. Thank God he'd shaved, and now he had only the moustache, which helped to bring out his diamond-shaped face.

Tonbra carried Pere up and asked Dini to sit. She passed through the curtain-door and disappeared into the house. He didn't sit but instead, walked to the bookcase. It was, as he had guessed, full of Ebisine's books. Catalogues on the Nigerian civil war, histories of wars in Africa, and several special- interest topics lined the shelves.

"Ebisine was working on his first book, before he—when he—"

He turned and looked at her. She had dropped her son inside. "What was he writing about?"

He thought he saw a glimpse of a smile, or maybe his imagination was running riot.

She shrugged and took a seat on the sofa where Timi still lay. "Do I know?" Then she chuckled. "Poor dear. He's been writing a book for as long as I knew him." She looked at him with a sad smile. "He had this idea that writing a book would boost his career, but he just couldn't do it."

"I think it's a talent. I couldn't even read a book that was not academic, not to talk of write one." He walked down the stretch of the bookcase looking at the books. "He does have an impressive collection though."

"Sometimes food on the table took the brunt," she muttered but he heard her. He turned to face her. "Of course—Ebisine loved his family. But his passion consumed him."

"I can't fault a man who believes he can through his career provide a better life for his family. Sometimes, the line between obsession and passion becomes so thin, we cross it."

"My husband jumped right over into his death." She looked at him with her eyes so clear, it was the blue sky before the storm.

He took the few steps to the second sofa and sat, aware of the two sisters somewhere in the house, who'd probably not heard Tonbra had a guest, or were being rude, or polite, as the case may be. Whichever way.

"We need to focus on your future now. Your kids. Your baby."

Her eyes flared and he wondered what he'd said to annoy her. It lasted just a moment and then she relaxed. He found it hard to read her thoughts, and he was exercising the kind of patience he'd not known he had.

"And you need someone who can be there to help you through this initial period of pain and anger, and confusion, and sadness."

"I don't even know you—you just came out of nowhere."

"Do you believe God sends help in time of need?"

"Of course, I do, I'm ever grateful for helping my hus—"

"But I don't believe the help was for Ebisine." He lowered his voice. "He died."

"What are you trying to say? My husband

hasn't been dead for a month."

He retained the quiet tone. "God sent me to help you. And I'm not going to take that lightly, Tonbra." Her mouth popped open to speak but she closed it back. "I don't take it lightly. I know it's so incredibly soon. No one will understand it now, but I need to be close. I want to be your friend at this time. I defi—"

She sprung to her feet cutting him off. "Oh, Toru, and Grace, this is, Dinipre. He—he was the one I talked about—" Her words hung in the air.

He hadn't noticed the two sisters when they came in. He turned in his seat and stood. He didn't know which was which, but the sisters looked a lot alike. A lot like their brother. Same dark-cream chocolate complexion, same oblong face. The one had long hair extensions which she let free. She looked young, in her twenties, and wore some make-up and loop earrings. The other looked much older, probably older than Ebisine. She had skin-cut hair. They were both slightly taller than Tonbra. Slightly taller than him. Neither wore anything that looked like mourning clothes.

Dini nodded at them together. "Please accept my condolences."

"I'm Grace." The older extended her hand and Dini took it. She held on to his hand though the handshake was meant to be over. "Tonbry told us how you tried."

Toru nodded slowly. "Even with the ambulance and the hospital bills."

Dini tugged his hand and Grace released it. He brushed the hand over his close-shave haircut self-consciously. "I wish we were meeting under more pleasant circumstances."

"We want to thank you." Grace perused Dini. "We learnt you worked at the hospital, NSH."

"I work offshore, actually. For NNPC. I supervise on platforms of joint-venture companies."

"Really?" Grace went to sit on the sofa he'd been on, subtly inviting him to do the same.

He took the cue and followed suit. He knew he wouldn't have much of a choice anyway. "I had a friend who worked for Shell. And I succeeded in sneaking on one of the platforms once." She winked and giggled. "For a few hours only, though. The security was something else." She shook her head. "We were checked several times before entering the platform."

"I wonder how you could have even gotten in the helicopter at all."

"I had to be passed off as crew."

Dini shook his head. "Too close a call. It could mean the whole platform. You know, what if you were a suicide bomber or something—"

"With that security? We were almost stripped at the airstrip. In fact, I told myself, I'd never subject myself to that sort of thing again."

Tonbra and Toru sat on the other sofa and listened to the conversation.

Grace became a self-appointed hostess and by the time he was forced to leave, hours before he planned, she had worn him down. Dini gathered she was indeed Ebisine's senior by ten months, unmarried and available. She worked as a nurse in Benin but took compassionate leave to be with Tonbra.

During the conversations, Dini also gathered Toru was twenty-three and a fresh graduate from University of Benin, awaiting her national youth service call-up letter, and Ebisine came from a large family. And so did Tonbra though her family would not come round just yet. Which he found so strange. Both ladies would be with Tonbra for at least two weeks.

The information left him aching. But then, what had he expected. He made it clear he also intended to hang around for a week or so and then go back offshore. That piece of information seemed to excite Grace.

He finally stood to leave, realizing the ladies would not give him and Tonbra any more privacy, and he preferred not to over-stay his welcome.

"Please can I see you for a minute, Tonbra?"

She followed him out of the house. He'd hired a small golf car and driver for the day. He walked to the car and got into it, summoning her to follow suit. She hesitated and then got into the back seat with him, but with her feet outside the car.

"You'll need some money—"

"No. I can't. I can't take money from you."

"Of course, you can. I didn't want to discuss money with you in front of your sisters-in-law."

"Well, I'm sure they're both peeping and wondering what you're telling me now."

He brought out a bundle of crisp five hundred naira notes from the back pocket of his jeans. "Take this."

Her eyes bulged. Her face came to his with a frown and she shook her head, eyes searching.

He picked her limp hand from where it lay on her lap and pushed the money into it.

Tears sprang to her eyes.

"Look, stop crying, please." He pulled some cards from his shirt pocket and picked one out. "Here's my card. My number is on it. Call me anytime. Anytime of the day or night. I'm in Warri till end of the week. I'll go to Lagos for a week. Then I'll go back to work. Call me anytime you need me."

He brought out a pen from his shirt pocket and a small piece of paper. "I'm staying at Asia Rooms. It's a small getaway guest house owned by a friend. Here's the address." He scribbled on the paper, and then brought out a Nokia phone. "Give me your phone number."

She looked at him till large tears dropped from her eyes. Her lips trembled. He reached to her and cleaned the tears with his hands.

"Please stop crying."

She cleaned her face and sniffed. "I don't have a phone."

His mouth dropped. "You don't?"

She shook her head.

"Wow." He sighed. "Okay. I'll get something for you."

She shook her head again. "You're doing too much."

"Not when I'm glad to be doing it. And definitely not when I have the capacity to."

"It's obvious you have a lot of money, but I can't take things from you. I'll be lying if I tell people you're just an ordinary friend—"

"But I am still an ordinary friend. And I will continue to be. For now."

"But the relationship will change. Then you will make your demands and I will not be able to pay back." She pushed the money and slip of paper to him.

"Give me some credit, Tonbra, please."

Maybe the convincing way he said it made the difference. And then she needed what he had to give and couldn't care if he called in the favours or not. Well. Without a word, she picked the money and the note.

"Thank you." She got down from the car.

He bent to get a last look at her. "Take care of yourself."

She walked away.

Chapter 6

With her back so stiff, she feared it would snap. She strode back into the house. Goose bumps covered her neck and arms. She heard the car zoom off and let out a single breath. This couldn't be happening. She couldn't be clutching a bundle of money in her hand right now.

How stranger could fate deal with her? No one ever gave her money.

She walked straight to the room she had shared with her husband till the day he died, and shot the bolt of the door, to be sure no one interrupted her. The children had at some point during Dini's visit, gone to the neighbour's house and would be there till she called for them. She knew Toru and Grace would have seen her enter the car with Dini, and would want to know what transpired, and she needed to gather her thoughts before she faced them.

She knew what a bundle of five hundred-naira notes meant but still, she counted it, and swallowed hard.

Dare she say she had never before handled, never touched fifty thousand naira at once? It might be ridiculous but so true. She and Ebisine had struggled all through their married life. Many times, she felt guilty for not doing anything to add value besides the job she did at a local law chambers as a secretary.

The job afforded her to meet many people in high positions in the society, but the remuneration didn't measure up. Ebisine however thought the contacts and exposure would pay off one day, and the low salary would mean nothing then. How wrong he was. She realized he had been wrong about many things. So full of his knowledge, his thoughts, his ways. So full of zero.

Still she loved him beyond measure, beyond recognition, beyond thought. In his gross self-containment and ignorance, he dominated her life, and her very existence. Anything he wanted, she did. His overwhelming influence directed her every thought and action, and now, she found herself lost.

"Oh Ebisine, how could you leave me? Just like that? Just like that?"

She hugged her pillow and punched the bed and muffled the sobs that

came from deep in her belly. She could never love another man. Never. She would never love another man.

Ebisine had taken her to that height and dumped her defenseless. She ought to be angry with him. Instead, she felt hopelessly devoted.

To raise the money for Ebisine's treatment Tonbra had sold everything valuable in the house including her phone. They had taken him out of the private clinic because she couldn't continue to pay. Why had this Dini not come along then? Why didn't God bring him a week, or a month or a year earlier?

She looked at the money on the bed and heaved. She still wanted money. In fact, now, she needed it. She didn't have a kobo left.

There was no food in the house, and she had been praying God would send a helper. She had thought her boss, a big-time lawyer in town, would rise up to the occasion but not a single person from her office had showed.

But God had sent a help.

Well, not in the form she expected. A suitor. A chuckle escaped her lips. What an irony. Ebisine's body wasn't cold yet, and someone already wanted to fill in the gap. God forbid. She had to make it clear to Dini she would never marry again.

Which brought her to this pregnancy in her belly. She had to remove it. She'd wanted to when she first discovered and would have. Ebisine had been upset with her, first for getting pregnant, and then to want it removed.

"I have accepted this is God's gift, why can't you?" he'd said.

"We can't afford to have another child. As it is, we can't even feed the ones we have."

"Slight taken," Ebisine said, and turned away from her. She hated when she made him realize how inadequate his efforts were.

She had turned to pleading with him not to get upset and thus ended the argument in his favour. As usual. Still she'd gone to find a doctor secretly, hoping she could get it done and then feign miscarriage.

It didn't work. The only doctor who agreed to abort the child asked for thirty thousand naira. Thirty thousand!

Thirty thousand.

Tonbra gripped the five hundred naira notes on her laps and shut her eyes. She could do it. She had the money now. Before she would think of the many other things needed to do with the money, she got to her feet and found her scarf. She tucked in the money in her purse and opened the door. Toru and Grace, slightly bent over her keyhole, jumped back when the door opened. Tonbra looked at them with disgust.

Grace sneered, hissed and clapped her hands. "What does that man want? Was that money he gave you? Tonbra Ebisine George! Your husband never begin rot, you don dey follow man!"

"Excuse me." She squeezed past the two and headed out.

"Hey, Tonbiri!" Toru marched after her. "Come back here."

The house was tight. The corridor between the two rooms could not take two people side by side, so they had to file after her. Tonbra hated the house as much as she hated her sisters-in-law. They'd formed the habit of remixing her name from the very first day she met them. She hated it.

"I'm going to the market. He gave us money for food—which obviously no one in your family has."

Grace followed closely. "Tonbarara!"

"He's trying to help us." Tonbra wailed.

Tears, which seemed to be just beneath her eyelids, flowed and the two ladies who'd caught up with her in the tiny parlour, stopped short.

They exchanged hard-staring for a moment and then she turned and left the house. She hated them. She hated Ebisine's family as much as she loved their son. Throughout her seven years of marriage, he had stood between her and them. She had cringed when the two sisters volunteered to follow her and help with settling back.

Help. How ironic. They all arrived together just the day before, and all the two had done was either sleep, or chat with one another. They would be with her for two weeks. She had devised a way to cope with them, she would hide behind her grief. She could only do so much to prevent them from hurting her.

She took a taxi and stopped at the market. Dini's gift had come at the most appropriate time. The little food they brought from the village just finished that morning, and she'd hoped to get a little loan from her neighbour till she could resume work the following week. Well, God stepped in right on time.

God.

She'd cursed God several times for killing Ebisine, her lifeline. Yet she knew God had not forsaken her. Or how else could one explain this coincidence called Dinipre Brisibe?

"God, I'm sorry." She closed her eyes for a moment and took calming breaths. "I am sorry." The second apology was for the abortion she had to do after leaving the market, not because she wanted to keep the baby, no.

Her apology went for the sin of taking a life.

She pushed it off her mind, knowing it would depress her to do it after careful thought. Already, that small voice had reminded her, this was the last thing Ebisine left with her. And she had screamed back in her head, "Burden. Liability." And that had silenced the voice.

Not only would she remove this baby, she would remove her womb as well. Be sure she never had a child again.

She moved into the market, feeling heady. No more thoughts. No more thinking. She bought a few items, meat, vegetables and soup ingredients, starch, rice, yam, plantain, and beverages, milk, sugar.

Her heavy bags didn't stop her decision to head for Dr. Finidi's house. She hefted her load out of the taxi and walked to the doctor's front door.

He was home. The forty-something year old was clean-shaven, with dark-complexioned, tall, lanky good looks. He showed her where to keep her bags and led her into his office. There were movements from within the house, but she saw no one. Finidi had converted part of his residence to a clinic so he could see private patients at home.

He directed her to a seat. "You are very lucky. I just came in."

Tonbra sat down and without pleasantries, went straight to her reason for coming. "I want to do the abortion now."

The doctor arched his eyebrow. "How far gone are you?"

"It's about 13 or so weeks now."

Finidi stood. "Get on the table. Let me examine you."

She did. After the examination, and certain questions, he asked her to return to her seat.

She straightened her dress and did.

He took his seat behind his crowded desk.

"Mrs. George, you're at least seventeen weeks." He looked at her. "Five weeks into the second trimester."

"I have the money you asked—"

"What of your husband?"

"Doctor, I want to do this now. I—"

"You don't understand. You came the first time at barely four weeks. I need your husband's consent and—"

"My husband is dead."

"What? Oh my. What happened?"

He looked genuinely sorry, and Tonbra softened her voice. "It's the reason why I can't have this child. I can't cope with three. Two is more than a burden. I told you so when I came."

The doctor sighed. "Please accept my condolence."

"Thank you, doctor." She paused and then looked at him. "Can we do it now?"

"There are documents for you to sign. And your fee is seventy-five thousand."

She jumped from her seat. "Seven—you told me thirty thousand."

"At three weeks plus, I could even do it free. Not in the second trimester. Sorry, madam."

Tonbra looked at her options. She'd spent almost ten thousand in the market. She hoped to keep the rest for other needs since she wasn't going to ask Dini for any more money and didn't think he would give any more either. School fees were due. Definitely Pere would not go back to school as things stood.

"Doctor, please. See, I have only forty thousand here, please."

"No, madam. You're hitting on twenty weeks. I don't even do anything later than fourteen. As it is, you'll need to sign my legal documents, agreeing you'll not harass me if anything goes wrong." He stood. "I'm sorry."

"Doctor, you don't understand. I want to die." She sobbed. The tears dropped from her eyes in uncontrollable torrents. "I want to die, please." She went on her knees. "Doctor, instead of refusing to do this for me, kill me. Kill me."

CHAPTER 7

Tonbra was sick when Dini called on her the following day. So sick her sisters-in-law did not allow him to see her. He didn't see her the day after either. On the third day, he brushed past Grace and walked into the house.

"She can't die in the house. If she's so sick, she should be in the hospital."

He couldn't contain the anger threatening to burst at the seams of his emotions. With the house so small, he had little trouble locating the room. He knocked gently and opened the door. She was cuddled under sheets while her children played a form of game on the limited floor space.

He noticed Grace had not followed him, neither did Toru. Well, better.

He entered and assessed the situation. The kids looked up when he walked in, smiled and continued their game. Timi seemed to be having a hard time teaching Pere the game but didn't look about to give up.

Tonbra, though covered, looked very much alert. She raised her head to stare at him, surprise registered in her expression, but she didn't say a word. He took the couple of steps to the bed and sat beside her. He touched her forehead, and looked round the room, seeking ventilation. The room had only one set of curtains, and it was drawn back to let in some light and air. Still the room needed more air to help her temperature go down.

He turned to look at her. "How are you?" His voice trembled in trepidation, his heart ached with compassion. How could he have been so foolish to let those ladies fool him the two previous days? "You need to go to the hospital."

She shook her head, tucked in the wrapper around her, and shook her head again.

"I can't let you stay like this. You've been sick for two days. I—"

"I'm fine."

He checked the time. "It's past ten o'clock. You can't be fine and still be in bed this late in the morning."

"I can be."

He sat on the bed. "Tonbra, please. Look, do you want to kill yourself?"

"Yes. I want to die."

He shut his eyes tight and fought raging emotions. "I can't let you die."

He pushed the wrapper away and shocked to discover she wore nothing underneath, flung it back over her. Shock and shame overwhelmed him, and he stood.

"Okay, I can't get you out to the hospital, but I can be of use to you. What have you eaten today?"

She pulled the wrapper over her head. "Nothing."

Frustrated, he dragged his hand over his hair, face and neck. He turned to Timi and squatted close to the girl and her brother. "What is wrong with Mummy?"

Timi looked at him with a frown as though a little annoyed for being interrupted. "Nothing." She resumed her play.

Dini walked to Tonbra. The wrapper vibrated, giving off the impression she was sobbing or shivering. He opened the door and went to look for Grace or Toru.

Both ladies were crammed in the cubicle-size kitchen. He stood in the doorway for lack of space to accommodate him in the kitchen.

"Please, excuse me."

They both looked at him, hissed and continued with what they were doing, basically chatting.

"I know I shouldn't have pushed you to enter your rooms, but I am worried for Tonbra."

Grace turned to him again. "She is fine. Sick before but fine now. You saw her, didn't you?"

"She's crying again."

Toru turned on him, her eyes flared. "Her husband just died. She cries every day and night."

"Look, Dinipre, give her time," Grace said with maternal concern. "She'll be fine. Trust me. It's normal for her to be like this."

Dini sighed. "Okay. Thanks." He left them and returned to the room.

Tonbra was still immersed in her wrapper but all calm, and quiet.

He resumed his seat next to her but moved to her feet this time. He tapped her and she groaned. "Can I see your face, please?"

She pushed the wrapper off her face but kept her eyes closed. "Timi is not in school today."

"She has not started."

"Schools have resumed—"

"She has not started."

"Why?"

She shrugged. "I don't know."

"Oh, Tonbra." He covered his face with both hands and sighed.

"Just go away. Leave me alone." She began to heave heavy sobs. The children ignored her but Dini moved closer and gathered her in his arms.

"It's okay, darling. It will all be alright. I'm here, love. It's well." He continued to coo in her ears till her crying subsided. He continued to hold her for a long time.

"I know how this can be like." He pulled back and looked into her swollen eyes. He also knew when to retreat. He'd overstayed his welcome. He cleaned the residue of tears from her face.

"I'm leaving for Lagos tomorrow."

It gave him tremendous joy when she shuddered and looked up into his eyes, the fear and confusion he'd seen before, back.

"I have to do some things in our office. And I'm scheduled back offshore," he said, gazing back into her sad eyes. Could joy ever be seen in them? "That's why I need to be sure you'll be fine."

She rested her head on his chest. "I'll be fine."

"How much do you pay for the children's fees?"

"Only Timi is in school." She drew back, and holding the wrapper around her, leaned against the wall, away from him.

Her withdrawal displeased him. "You may need to put Pere also. You should get a job so you won't be alone too much."

"I have a job."

"Oh, that's very good. So both of them have to go to school." He picked up a small bag he had carried into the room. "I got you a phone." He placed the bag beside her.

"Oh, thank you."

"I stored my number in it already." He sighed. "And I've saved your number as well. Give me your account number so I can pay into your account from time to time." He brought out his phone and poised to type.

"I don't have an account."

He gasped. "You don't?"

"Well, the only account I have is joined with Ebisine." She shrugged. "And there's no money in it."

"How do you get paid in your office?"

She sneered. "Peanuts. I earn twenty thousand naira and the cashier pays it in cash."

"Oh-kay." He stood and removed his wallet and sat back. "We can do something temporarily." He pulled out a number of cards from his wallet and selected one. It was a debit card. "I have some money in this account. I'm sure it can cater for the kids' school fees, and you'd have some change left for housekeeping. Take some after that and open your own account. The password is 1912, my birthday and month."

He extended it to her, but she didn't take it. He looked at her and found her eyes glued on him. "Come on."

"This is too much. I can't take your ATM card—"

"You keep saying that. You can't, you can't, you can't." He laughed. "You can. Now, take it, come on. Please." He waved it toward her. "Please. Do you want me to beg you all the time?"

She worked her jaws and swallowed. "What do you want from me?" she whispered.

He lowered the card and sighed. "I want to give you time to get over your loss. But sincerely, eventually, Tonbra, I want to marry you."

***

He left the following day as he'd said, and Tonbra heaved a heavy sigh. He had begun to rankle. His love, written all over him, could not be reciprocated, and she hated herself for that. Hated him for offering it when she could not give back. She was indebted, and that made her unhappy. But she couldn't deny the so-needed gifts he gave.

After his declaration of purpose, he had

spent the rest of the day with her. He was domesticated. He prepared lunch for everyone and even Grace and Toru warmed up to him. The children as well. He joined them in front of the house and played ball with them, promising to replace the jaundiced ball they had.

After he left, she took the courage to check out the box he'd left on the bed, the phone. It was the beautiful Nokia 7650, a camera phone.

She yelped in delight and then covered her mouth. This was obscene. How could he try to buy her? She picked up the ATM card. It was still rare. Few people, mostly the rich, could use the card. She tucked it into her bag and visited the bank the next day.

Tonbra wasn't accustomed to bank runs. As things stood, she never had enough money to do anything. The salary she received in cash was dispensed for the many immediate needs. She tried to make sure there was food in the house so once the salary came in, she shopped for food. Ebisine would take whatever remained for all their other concerns and add whatever little he had to it. Life had been hard.

She wasn't sure of what to do with the card and she went to the customer service desk.

The lady looked suspicious after she narrated her story and then took the card from her and went into some other office. After a while, she returned with the card and asked Tonbra to follow her. They went into the manager's office. The man behind the seat wore a stiff dark suit and blue shirt with a grey tie.

His tone and look depicted firm professionalism. "You say your fiancé gave you the card?"

She stared at the manager. "Yes."

"And he didn't teach you how to use it?"

How would he have? The question irritated her. "He doesn't have ATM machine in his house."

The manager arched his eyebrow. The customer service lady hissed. "There is a lot of money on this card, so we're going to call the owner of the account to confirm it is not lost," the manager said softly.

Tonbra sat back and folded her arms. "I'm waiting." She expected the man to ask for Dini's phone number, he didn't.

He picked up the telephone on his desk and dialed a number scribbled on a piece of paper. He began to speak almost immediately, and after the pleasantries, introduced himself and stated his matter. Then he kept quiet for a long time. Then he thanked the person on the other side and hung up.

"We have the confirmation we need, madam." He looked at Tonbra. "He did mention that you'll need to open an account. Er, please bring the account forms."

"That's if I want to open account in your bank after you called me a thief."

"It's procedure, madam. We protect our clients, and you will get that protection as well."

"I don't want to open here."

The manager looked at her and smiled politely. "He asked me to open for you. Didn't you discuss the bank with him before coming?"

"You just accused me of stealing his card."

"We did not. And we're sorry you feel bad, but we have to follow procedure."

She shifted in her seat and rolled her eyes. "Okay."

He looked at the lady again. "Please bring the forms." Then he turned to Tonbra. "I will personally assist you to withdraw." He stood. "Shall we? The ATM machines are at the entrance."

She followed him. "I want to know how much is in the account before I withdraw."

"No problem, madam."

At the ATM machine, he took her through the process. A shiver ran through her body when she discovered Dini had almost half a million naira in the account. Timi's school fee was only fifteen thousand. If she added another fifteen for Pere, she would only need another ten to run the house for now.

"How much do I need to open the account?"

"For a savings account, the minimum you need is N1,000.00 only."

She juggled in her mind. He had given her fifty thousand, just this week. She didn't need any more money besides the school fees. If she took ten for exigencies, five would suffice to open the account.

She withdrew forty-five thousand naira from the account. This could be a test from the Dini, and even if they ended up not getting married, she didn't want him to think she stole from him.

Marry! She could never love any man again. She would not marry Dini. At the right time, she would have to make that clear to him. And to God, she hoped he would never think of her as a thief, taking all this from him when she surely knew she would not marry him.

CHAPTER 8

He called every day. From the day he left till he returned three months later. And Tonbra found herself looking forward to hearing Dini's voice.

What a wonderful man. A man in love. He told her he loved the way she laughed. And even the way she cried, which had reduced considerably. Timi and Pere loved him and talked with him over the phone. He made sure he credited her account every month with fifty thousand after he collected his ATM card from her. More than they needed.

When he returned, he acted love stricken. Besides being reserved, especially about public appearances, she did everything with him. He had a whole month, and he spent it with her. Her stomach had grown beyond measure and he took pleasure in feeling the baby. With the pregnancy, he told her she was the most beautiful pregnant woman in the world.

Though they attended her church together, she refused to introduce him to anyone, pleading with him to give her more time. He accepted. After all, she was just in the fourth month of her widowhood.

He had planned to leave from Warri back to his base, but had to see his mother first, as was his tradition. He planned the trip a week to the end of his visit, and tried to persuade her to go with him, but she refused.

***

The trip home as usual, was refreshing for him. He took time to rest and to familiarize himself with the events at home, and in the family. The elderly man coordinating his scholarships, his principal in high school, and the same man who recommended him for the scholarship to FUTA, spoke highly of the program. Three of the students on his scholarship scheme had just finished secondary school, including Oyinemi, and were about to sit for JAMB, and other examinations that would qualify them for entry into university.

He returned to Warri, a couple of days before going back offshore, to make arrangements for a taxi driver to work for Tonbra.

"I don't want to hear that anything happened to you while I'm away. I should leave a car for you, but you can't drive." He winked at her. "Though that must change once you offload this truck."

She still had two months to go but he cut his offshore duty to six weeks so he could be back to stay with her. Since they were not married, he couldn't register her in NSH as a wife, so he paid the regular fees for non-staff. But it meant little to him. He couldn't imagine her being cared for by any other healthcare facility.

Dini returned offshore but as usual, called every day. The taxi driver he employed did a good job. The man took the children to school and Tonbra to the office and back every day. He did some domestic chores for her as well, but as the expected day neared, Tonbra had to employ a nanny to help with the children and do housekeeping.

Dini arrived two weeks to the expected date as he'd said and stayed at the Asia Rooms.

Daily, he spent his day with Tonbra and her kids. Timi was preparing for her end of session examinations and Dini derived great joy helping with her revisions.

Tonbra wanted to work till the last day but Dini pressurized her to start her leave a week earlier.

"It's a precious week. My boss will not let me stay a day after three months of maternity leave—"

"Then you quit the job. What's he paying you?" he countered, and she kept quiet.

She commenced her maternity leave, and spent most of the day, being spoiled by Dini. He waited on her, hand and foot. Asia Rooms was not far from her residence and he kept a close watch on her progress.

Two days to the expected date, Tonbra went into labour and on the 5th of July, in the early hours of the day, she gave birth to a bouncing baby boy.

Dini couldn't contain his excitement, despite himself. He had never had such an experience before. He trembled as he walked into the delivery room, minutes after the baby was born.

"Ebisine wanted another boy."

Tonbra's first words tore at his heart, but he smiled to encourage her. It hurt that she didn't say anything about what he had wanted. He had wanted a girl, anyway. It now made meaning to him she had never spoken about the sex she preferred.

"We thank God you're fine, and baby is fine."

She smiled weakly and her eyes drifted shut. He squatted beside her and held her hand.

He loved this woman. There was sweat on her face and he wiped it with his bare hand.

She smiled. "Ebisine. That will be his name. Ebisine Francis George." After a while, her breathing evened out. She was asleep.

Dini hated the name. He hated the fact that the child would bear his late father's name.

But he played along with Tonbra. He had a name for the baby but kept it to himself. In his mind, he reserved the name for the child Tonbra would bear for him. Then he would have a say. For now, he could not contest, and the child belonged to the dead man.

Dini returned offshore a week later, displeased. Much as he struggled to keep a straight face, celebrating the late Ebisine was difficult for him.

The whole family came to visit in the tiny house, going in and out, bumping into one another. They made blind comments about how the baby was a replica of his late father.

Ebisine's mother came to do omugwo, and made it clear her son had reincarnated.

Tonbra's mother came as well. Sisters and cousins and brothers and uncles were all over the place. Though Dini did not fit in, and was not recognized, he paid the bills. Food and drink were in excess. Tonbra never introduced him. Not even as a friend. He tried hard to understand.

He decided to go back through Lagos so he could stay in his house for a few days and catch a breath. His younger brothers used the four-bedroom condo while he was away, but he liked to stay in once in a while, to have a feel of his own place. He also needed to talk to Erebi. She had always been his close ally and he needed to get encouraged on this one.

Dini drove his 2002 Toyota Camry into the garage of Erebi's Aguda house, and parked right behind her Toyota Corolla, before turning around to the back of the house.

Erebi was in the kitchen as he had expected. Her job as head teacher of a multi-racial school in Lagos afforded her the time needed to keep home and house, and care for her four children. Her husband, a chartered accountant worked as a partner in a thriving accounting firm, and not as lucky with his time.

He gave her a half-hug. "Hi."

"You too," she said. "Welcome. I wasn't expecting you till later. For dinner."

He checked his wristwatch and shrugged.

Five o'clock. "I thought I'd come for your company. Join you to make the dinner."

They shared a laugh.

"You always did like the apron, didn't you?"

Erebi burst into laughter and Dini joined in. "I know what you're thinking," he said. "You can never forget, can you?"

"Why you like the apron so much? I can never forget."

They laughed together. When he was a boy, Mama had been in the kitchen, cooking, with Erebi helping. Dini had insisted he wanted to help and reluctantly, Mama had agreed. When he thought his mother and sister were not looking, he'd dipped his hand in the hot pot of soup to steal meat and screamed in pain. That was how they knew what he'd been trying to do. He'd been three years old.

Hoping to be able to hide the meat before getting caught, he'd asked that Mama give him an apron like the one Erebi tied, a makeshift wrapper Mama ensured anyone working with her tied.

"I don't need aprons now. I eat what I like, when I like."

Erebi placed a tray of vegetables on the kitchen table to pick them. Without asking, Dini joined in.

"Did you see Mama on this trip?"

"Why are you asking that question? She tells you everything."

Erebi laughed. "Well, you're right. She said there's a woman in your life who's taking you away from her."

Dini exclaimed. "Is that what she said? O gracious goodness."

"Is it the same woman? The widow?"

"Your mother told me never to visit her again if only I will build my relationship with a woman and get married. She wants to carry babies." Dini sighed. "Now I'm building a relationship, she complains the woman is

taking me away from her. You can never satisfy women."

Erebi laughed. "You know your mother."

"Well, I checked on her on the way here yesterday," he said, and laughed. "I know she won't forgive me if I don't."

"Ha, thank God. I've not spoken with her since yesterday morning." Erebi nodded toward her set of knives and Dini removed one for her. "Thanks. So, is the woman the same one?"

"Yeah."

"Hey, I know that tone. What's wrong? Are you still with her?"

Dini struggled with how much to tell and decided to spill the beans. "Well yes, but I want you to listen carefully before you react."

"This must be serious." She dropped the knife on the vegetable and turned to him. "Tell me everything."

"She just had a baby. Last week."

"A baby?" Erebi's eyes widened. "For you or the late husband?"

"She was pregnant when the man died, Erebi. I thought I told you. I didn't care then but it's hard." He swallowed. "I don't know how I feel. I thought I'd love that baby as my own.

I thought I did."

Erebi covered his hand with hers. "I understand."

"Tonbra has named the new baby her late husband's name—"

"No! Ha, she shouldn't do that. Huh, the child should have his own identity, please."

"My thoughts exactly. I even had a name I wanted to give him."

"Keep your name for your own child."

Dini smiled. "That's what I decided." He exhaled. "I love her, very much. It amazes me how much I love her, but I don't seem to feel loved by her." He shook his head. "Profoundly grateful yes, but that emotion—"

"You can't blame her, Dini, it's too soon. Maybe you're rushing her."

"Her house was full of people, coming to visit the baby. Some come to greet her about the death. She didn't acknowledge me. Not even privately to her mum or sisters or brothers. I don't feel right about that."

"Give her time. I know how you feel but I tell you, it will be strange if she can just switch to loving you like that." She snapped her fingers up in the air, making a sharp, cracking sound. "I'm sure she'll come around and show you all the affection you deserve."

"I do hope so, sincerely."

"What about the other kid? You did say she had a son or is it a daughter?"

"She has two already." His face brightened up. "They're wonderful. I tell her I could fall for her only because of her kids. My God. I miss those babies."

Erebi smiled. "How do they take you?"

"They love me as well. I know that. You know children—they can't hide their feelings."

"Yeah, you're right." Erebi gnawed at the insides of her cheek.

"If she showed half the emotion her children showed, I won't even notice—it's bad."

"Grief has a way of changing people, you know. Mama was torn when Papa died, and you know, I learnt a lot of lessons then."

"Did she resist the people who tried to help her?" Dini needed to know because he'd been away at UT.

Erebi looked at him and shook her head. "No. But it was different. Papa was old. Mama didn't have young children." Erebi lowered her gaze and said softly, "She wasn't pregnant."

"You're right, aren't you?" Dini mopped imaginary sweat from his face. "I should be patient."

"I don't know if Mama will like the idea that she has three kids, though."

"We'll cross that bridge when we get there." His phone rang. He picked it and looked at it for a long moment.

"Why don't you want to pick the call?"

"It's a text message."

"Oh."

He looked up and shut his eyes tight. Erebi gripped his arm and shook him gently. "Who is it?"

"Tonbra."

"I hope she's alright?"

Dini opened his eyes and swallowed.

"What did she say?"

He looked at the phone again. "I miss you." He looked at Erebi. "Like air."

CHAPTER 9

Mama did not like the idea undermined her feeling a hundred times. Mama detested the idea.

On his return back offshore, Dini spent his usual three months, and then got a letter sending him for a six-month course in Russia. He was given a week to prepare for the trip. He took a quick decision. He wanted to marry and relocate Tonbra to Lagos. He asked Erebi to hint Mama.

Tonbra had agreed but on the condition that it would be a secret marriage. She agreed to move to Lagos, and live in Dini's house, and it would be easy to find a school for the kids since the new session had just resumed.

Erebi knew Mama would not take a soft landing with the news. But she didn't prepare for the frenzy Mama went into. She had her strong reasons. The woman still mourned and would for another three months. She had three children. What names would the children bear? Besides, Dini didn't know her well enough.

Despite all the protests to Erebi, Dini

brought Tonbra and her children to meet Mama, in transit to Lagos where they'd agreed to do a registry marriage. The wine-carrying ceremony would have to come after Dini's return from Russia.

He had pleaded with his sister to be in attendance to break the fall when it came, and so they arranged to visit on a Saturday. Erebi arrived the day before to be sure Mama was prepared for the visit.

Dini had seen his mother in a lot of moods, but never so quiet and reserved. Mama welcomed Tonbra with a hug and a mumble, and that was it. She had prepared starch with *oguro* native soup, one of Dini's favourite meals. The children loved the meal. Mama carried the baby while they ate and afterward, Tonbra breast-fed him.

Mama sat opposite her and watched, which made Erebi and Dini uncomfortable. She never kept quiet with guests.

"What his name?" Mama said. She had not said a word since they came in more than an hour earlier, after her sullen greeting.

"Ebisine."

"Your husband name?"

Dini opened his mouth to protest and closed it right back when Erebi shot him a hard look.

"Yes, Mama."

"Change the name."

Dini arched his brows. "Mama?"

"Is his only name?"

"Francis."

"Hmm." Mama turned to Dini. "Is the name you give him?"

"I—" What could he tell her? He didn't even know who had told her Ebisine's name. Erebi, no doubt. "It's—uh—still the family name of the—uh—late um—"

"You don't give name." Mama folded her arms and stared into space with this infinite

sadness on her face that broke Dini's heart.

His mother had been a pillar in the family, holding things together with her life on many occasions. He had always vowed to make his mother happy. Obviously, she struggled with the decision he just took about Tonbra, and it was painful to watch.

He exchanged glances with Erebi, but no help came from there. He looked at Tonbra whose eyes pleaded with him to rescue her. He didn't know what to do or say. Anything he did now would mean a lot. He looked at Mama. Her hands were folded across her chest, and she bit her lower lip. Oh dear.

The silence elapsed till Tonbra finished breastfeeding Ebisine. Mama reached out and kept the baby on her shoulder to belch. Within seconds, a large sound that broke the ice came from the baby.

Mama laughed. "Hmm, opuobori."

All of them laughed at once. The reference to an elephant was as exhilarating as the way Mama said it.

"Boys can eat so much," Erebi said. "My sons showed me pepper. Mama, did Dini eat so much as a baby?"

The question might have eased into friendly conversation but the smile on Mama's face froze. "Dinipre not his father."

They all went silent after that.

Till Dini stood and told Mama they had to get going. Mama again hugged each of them with a soft greeting.

"Erebi, I'll see you tomorrow when you return," he whispered into Erebi's ears. For the first thirty minutes into the drive to Lagos, no one said anything.

Tonbra checked and saw the babies were fast asleep at the back. "Mama doesn't like me."

"She doesn't know you."

"Oh, but she doesn't like what she's seen so far—she could hardly respond to my greeting."

Dini tightened his hold on the steering. A strange anger rose from within him. "You can't blame her, can you? You are not so friendly yourself."

Tonbra turned to look at him. "What do you mean by that? How was I unfriendly?"

"Maybe it's not what you did, but what you are." He raised his voice. "Maybe your spirit emits unfriendliness. Maybe you're so d—consumed by your grief you feel nothing for anyone, and Mama saw through you."

"How dare you talk about my grief? What do you know about my grief?"

"That's the point. Do you even see me at all? You're so blinded by you, your feelings, your children, your grief! You don't care a d—about others. You don't care about me." He shouted at the top of his voice. "You don't know what I know or don't know. All you see is what you can get."

She raised her voice to match his. Her voice trembled as though she would cry but she controlled it. "Then what are you doing with me? What do you want from me?" She hissed. "After all I've been through all you can say is that I am selfish. Do you know what they call me in Ebisine's family just because I am with you?"

"What do they call you?! Tell me if I care."

Her voice dropped. "Whore. Whore." And then she burst into tears.

The sobbing shook her whole being. The baby sleeping against her bosom stirred. Dini glanced quickly at the back and noticed Timi had come awake.

"I know that is what your mother thinks too. And your hypocrite sister."

"How dare you, Tonbra? Just shut up 'cause Timi is awake."

"I don't care. I don't care." She screamed. "You don't love me. I hate you too. I hate you."

Dini desired from the bottom of his heart to respond but Timi began to sob. He clenched his teeth to control and abide the hurtful words. Tonbra continued to speak, saying the most awful things he had ever heard in his life. How he was nothing to her and his family was nothing and she wanted to go back to the life she had in Warri. Thank God her things had not yet been moved, and the rent debts had been cleared by 'God's infinite mercy.' She talked and talked and talked.

And finally fell silent, and asleep.

***

They got married in a quiet ceremony the following Tuesday. Erebi attended as a witness, and Tare, Tonbra's youngest sister, who had just finished secondary school, and travelled from Bayelsa State to live with

Tonbra. She had told her mother about the marriage but warned her not to let anyone else know about it. Timi wore a lovely grey dress like her mother. Pere and Dini wore grey suits.

To maintain their testimony, Dini had opted to stay in his sister's house till after the marriage. Arriving Lagos from Apoi, he had dropped Tonbra and the children at his house and after seeing to their comfort, gone to Erebi's house.

His two brothers had cleaned the house and prepared food for the arriving party. Dini introduced them to his new family. His brothers moved to the semi-detached boys' quarters where they didn't need to have any contact with the main house.

Dini was due to travel the day after his wedding and had made adequate arrangements for the upkeep of his new family. Being away for six months would give some other people jitters but not Dini. His bank had been detailed to transfer a hundred thousand naira every month to Tonbra's account. He had made adequate arrangements for all his concerns as well, his mother, brothers, and his scholarships.

His efficiency in planning and attention to detail about their needs was meant to be enough reason for the grudge between him and Tonbra to crack up. It didn't. As he took his vows and looked into her eyes, he realized he would never be able to stop loving her. And it scared him.

Since their arrival on Saturday, she had shunned him, even though he was upset as well, and had ignored her. But after church on Sunday, he decided to appease her. His effort yielded no result until Tuesday after taking his vows. She smiled at him and got all the love and encouragement he needed.

No apologies rendered for all the horrible things she said to him, but for peace's sake, he let it go.

Erebi was radiant. She invited the family to a wedding dinner in her home. Though Dini initially resisted, it could not be helped because Erebi had invited as many of their friends and family members as she knew in Lagos.

When she'd returned from Apoi on Sunday, she had been too tired to talk. Dini had spent the whole day Monday with Tonbra in his house and returned late. There had been no talk. As soon as the party began to wind down, Erebi excused him. It had to come at some time.

They went up into Erebi's guest room, where they were sure not to be disturbed. Erebi closed the door quietly and turned to him. "You're horny."

Dini took a moment to assimilate the accusation and laughed. "Goodness, Erebi. You never cease to amaze me. Can you imagine? You won't kill me one day."

"Admit it." Erebi laughed. She sat at the edge of the dresser and smiled at him.

He folded his arms across his chest, looked up as though in thought, did a little drama like thinking about it. "Yeah, the anticipation is a bit

challenging." He shrugged and laughed. "We've been in a Christian courtship." He sighed. "Huh, it'll be over soon."

Erebi clapped her hands and laughed. "I was right."

"You're always right."

"She's a beautiful woman."

Dini sighed and sat on the bed. "I'm glad you think so."

"She is. And I think she loves you too. She kept glancing your way, and with that sweet smile."

"Huh. Thank God. What can I say?"

"She'll make a good wife."

"Erebi, I know there's more to this talk than how lovely Tonbra is. What happened after we left Mama?"

"The strangest thing, Dini." Erebi shook her head. "Mama went into her room and covered her head with her wrapper."

Dini stilled. "She wept?"

"No. But she refused to get up or eat anything."

"My visit made her lose appetite." He jerked

to his feet. "Now my visit is unbearable."

"She's worried for you. You know her. She's thought of you in twenty years' time already."

"And what does she see? Doom? That Tonbra will leave me? She won't."

"She didn't talk to me." Erebi sighed. "The day before, she accused me of setting her up—she said I betrayed her. So, she sees us on the same side."

"So, when she covered her head, what did she say?"

"Nothing."

"Nothing?"

"I sat with her and explained all over again how you met and didn't want to leave for your course without marrying, and how Tonbra's mourning meant you couldn't have a large ceremony."

"And?"

"She didn't say a word. Not a grunt. Not a sigh. I left when I got tired." Erebi shook her head. "The following morning, she behaved as though the previous day never happened."

"This is bad."

"She'll get over it."

"You think so?"

"You see, the day before, while reacting, she said Tonbra would not be able to have a child for you till at least two years from now."

Dini chuckled. "Is that her problem then?" He sighed.

"Can you blame her? She wants to carry your baby."

"And she will. I really was shocked at her behaviour. Huh, I know Mama."

"I hope Tonbra didn't feel too bad."

"That's a story for another day. Now I know Mama's concern, I feel better." He stood. "The next time you see her, help me tell her to calm down." He stretched and winked at her. "I have to leave now. I don't want it to be obvious my wife is horny too." He laughed and headed for the door.

Erebi laughed and followed him.

At the door, he turned and hugged her. "Thanks for the beautiful party."

CHAPTER 10

2009

Mama entered Dini's Victoria Island residence and walked straight to the huge family portrait, which hung facing the front door in the lobby area, where two porch seats, separated by a huge Arabian flowerpot, were placed on a fancy rug. Tonbra's pride, soft shades of gold, cream and red defined the room.

For a moment, Tonbra stood in the parlor, hid from her sight, curious as to what the older woman would do.

Mama stopped and fixed her gaze on Dini. He hadn't changed a bit. He wore a simple-cut blue kaftan. His smile reached to the soul. Mama's hand shot forward to touch his face, but she held it back.

Her gaze flipped over Tonbra and the two older children and rested on 5-year old Ebisine's face. The boy was a delight to look at. He had the most fascinating features just like his late father. He wore the same kaftan with Dini, and Pere. He had a sweet smile on his face and rested his head on Dini's chest.

Mama looked at Tonbra. She looked none of a mother of three, and all of a beautiful young woman. She had maintained herself well, and she looked happy as well. She wore a pink and blue skirt and blouse that matched Dini's blue, the same as what Timi wore. Her face was made up lightly, her mouth curved in a soft smile. Mama glanced the other two children but left her gaze on Dini.

Enough, Tonbra thought. "Mama! Welcome."

Tonbra walked into the room, and Mama turned to look at her. The older woman assessed her bright yellow sleeveless blouse and white three-quarter skirt, and beautiful silver slippers. Tonbra beamed.

A smile broke on Mama's weathered face, and she received Tonbra's hug. "My daughter."

"Dini told me his driver will bring you today."

She collected Mama's handbag, and with a proud gait, led her up three steps to the large sitting room professionally designed with a large red fibre rug in the middle of the gold and cream French marble floor.

Gold leather sofas formed a curve around the room, facing a huge mantle-place, where several framed family pictures were arranged. On the wall ahead of the mantle-place, a 64" Samsung TV bracketed the wall. A home theatre was placed on a lone shelf beneath the mantle-place with the speakers hung on the four corners of the room.

More family pictures hung on the wall, with beautiful original artworks, and fancy lights. Golden curtains with lace trimmings draped four floor-to-ceiling Victorian windows.

Tonbra's gaze followed Mama's. Since the last time Mama visited, the house had been redecorated twice.

A uniformed man walked in with two bags. "Put them in Mama's room."

"Yes, madam."

"I hope he drove you well, Mama?"

"Hmm. I sleep on the road."

Tonbra chuckled. "That means he drove well."

The driver went in the direction of a room just by the corner off the sitting room. On his way out he stopped in front of Tonbra. "Mama

brought some yams and fish, and palm oil and palm fruits, and some oranges and pawpaw and—"

Tonbra turned and hugged Mama on the seat. "Ha ah, Mama! What for?"

"You Lagos people no eat well. All the food I see for your market is old and rotten," Mama said.

"Ma-a-ma!" Tonbra laughed and turned to the driver. "Hand them over to Deborah. She knows what to do with them." The driver gave a small bow and left.

Tonbra turned to look at Mama and smiled. "So, how are you? I hope everyone at home is well."

The elder woman sat back and sighed. "As well as we be. And, how are you? And children?"

"We're fine, Mama, thank you. Just missing Dini more and more."

"Huh, now he will soon come?"

"You know that's how it is. When it gets closer, it will be more difficult to wait." Tonbra sat forward. "Oh, see me!" She turned toward an exit of the sitting room. "Deborah!"

A voice answered, "Yes, madam."

"Bring water for Mama." She sat back. "I will have some starch prepared for you just now."

"I no eat. Nowadays, my stomach take small. After good breakfast, I eat early supper and finish."

"Mama, are you all right?"

"I'm fine. Is old age."

"Oh, Mama!" Tonbra laughed. "You're not even sixty yet. You're still young."

Deborah, a plump, dark-skinned, twenty-ish lady, wearing a maid's uniform, brought a jug of cold water and a glass with ice cubes in a separate bowl on a tray, and set them before Mama.

"Thank you, my daughter."

Deborah curtsied and left.

Mama served the water without ice and took a long sip before sitting back. "Dini go be back this evening?" It was a rhetorical question, but Tonbra nodded all the same. "Hmm." She finished the water in her glass and kept it without refilling. "When will children come from school?"

"Pere and Ebisine close by 2. Timi gets home by 4."

Mama looked at the large-faced table clock on the mantle-place. It was close to 2. "Ha, they soon start coming, and then you no go have my time." She rested back her head and closed her eyes.

Tonbra touched her forehead gingerly. "Are you feeling well?"

She opened her eyes. "I am fine. I am very fine. Tired."

Tonbra stood. "Let me help you. Your room is ready."

Mama patted the space where Tonbra sat. "Sit down. Let me talk first."

Tonbra lowered herself. Mama had never had cause to 'talk' to her. Ever since that first time they met, the relationship had been cordial. She had even begun to be fond of her mother-in-law. And to trust her.

All through the rough times she'd had with her family and Ebisine's, Dini had been a sure pillar behind her. His family had been supportive as well. Contrary to the first impressions, they were now her closest allies.

"Hope all is well, Mama." She didn't know what to expect.

"I want ask you that question, my daughter." Mama's brows furrowed. "I know is not my problem, but if there is problem, there are thing we do."

"I don't understand, Mama."

"After your last baby, I expect you wait one or two year, and then have baby. This is five year now." Mama sighed simultaneously with Tonbra but continued to speak. "I no want ask Dini, so I no upset him more. But there are thing men use when they no able to impregnate woman—"

"Mama—"

"I know it be very embarrassing for men.

You can tell treatment to him. I can, but his wife—"

"Mama, no—"

"For one, you give him very hot bath, or if he like, very cold bath—you even add ice block to—"

"Mama, wait!" Tonbra sat forward and clasped her hands in her laps. "Dini is not the problem. Dini does not have any problem that I know of."

"Maybe he no want tell you."

Mama stood and walked to the room separated for her from the day they bought and moved into the six-bedroom triplex. The house had been redesigned to accommodate a bedroom downstairs so Mama would not need to climb up. She'd also have easy access to the kitchen, the laundry, a private sitting room, and a prayer room.

The master bedroom, Timi's room and the boys' room, were on the first floor, with a family room, and a study. The last floor, which had two rooms shared by the servants, also had a kitchenette and a sit-in space. All the rooms in the house were en-suite.

To accommodate guests when need be, Dini had carved out a guest chalet with two rooms at the side of the house, barely distorting the large green area and architectural aesthetics of the half-acre compound.

Within a few minutes, Mama came back, her jaw set. In her hand she held something round, wrapped in banana leaf.

Tonbra jumped to her feet. "No, Mama. We can't have this in the house, we are believers!"

Mama sat down, and with her lips pressed together, an opened the leaf. Tonbra stared at her, aghast.

"Mama—"

"This is just herbs I prepare myself. It no do with your church!"

"But I can never take it! Dini will never take it!" She leaned over to look at the slimy concoction. "God forbid this." It gave off a funny, herbal smell and looked brownish.

"What our men do is mix with palm wine—"

"Dini will never take palm wine! Mama, didn't he tell you he recently became a deacon in our church?"

"Do you eat vegetable?"

"Yes, of course, Mama."

"This is just like vegetable. I remove juice from it such way that you put in drink, or turn in starch—"

Tonbra shook her head. "Oh Mama, please. I can never, never give this to my husband to drink or eat!"

"Some man chew solid. One, two month their wife get pregnant."

Tonbra shook her head viciously. "No, Mama. No way. Please. Don't do this to us. Don't, please. Dini is happy as he is. He is content." She looked at the older woman and the funny, pasty stuff on the banana leaf. "We will never resort to this." She turned and half-ran from the room.

***

Dini came back from his trip to the Netherlands, fagged out. It had been an intensive one week of training and getting trained. The Universal Gas Confederacy was an organization of privately-owned companies seeking to tap into gas energy. As an energy expert, Dini had been invited to an

international summit as a faculty member, while also attending a course. The days had run into late nights.

Ever since he returned from the Russian course five years earlier, he had grown in his career, and become the youngest energy expert in the country. At the course, he had performed so well three countries had offered him jobs in their power sector. His own country had taken him out of NNPC and given him a job to head the technical team in Nigeria Gas-Energy Corporation (NGEC), an organization under the presidency, set up to provide the overdue constant power supply to the African nation with the largest population. It had established him in Lagos because of the easy access to local and international flights.

Though his offshore duties were rare now, he still hardly stayed at home. Any opportunity to be with his family, he grabbed with both hands.

He particularly wanted Mama to visit. She hated to leave her home. As his career boomed, her importance in the village increased, and she even got conferred with a chieftaincy title. Mama now had a portfolio in the Kalasuwea's cabinet, as Iyalode, the highest title conferred on a woman. And she took it seriously. Since his traditional marriage, which was a carnival, just as Mama wanted, she had visited only a couple of times.

Close to 10p.m., Dini walked into his house. Tonbra was waiting. He pulled her into a warm embrace and kissed her hungrily.

"Thank God, I'm home." He pulled back and looked into her eyes. "How's my baby?"

"Fine." She shrugged. "You must be famished."

"I couldn't eat over there. I miss your cooking."

She pulled him toward the dining room, an elevated area off the sitting room, designed to host at least twelve people at mealtimes. He followed obediently.

"How's Mama? She should be asleep now, I guess?"

"Hmm. Mama!" Tonbra pulled back a seat for Dini, and then took her seat. She opened a dish Dini knew she must have just put food in, because his favourite rice meal, coconut rice let off steam.

"She's here, isn't she?"

"She is."

"And?"

She served the food. "After your meal, we'll talk about Mama."

Dini frowned. "What's wrong with Mama?"

She placed the plate in front of him. "Nothing."

"I can't eat now. There's something wrong, what is it?" For effect, he pushed the plate away.

"You don't have to worry about Mama, she'll be fine. I—"

"Did you see her after she came in?"

"Yes."

"Talk to me, Tonbra."

He made to stand but her hand gently rested on his. "She was talking about having more kids."

Dini sat back and sighed. "I thought she was sick or something."

She moaned. "That was what I thought at first, as well. She was so—so morose. She brought—things."

"Things?"

"In some banana leaf. Brownish thing. She said I should mix it in palm wine—"

Dini chuckled. "Mama! I hope you made it clear that wasn't an option."

"I did." Tonbra leaned closer to him. "I tried to make her understand we are happy as we are."

He looked at her thoughtfully for a moment, smiled and continued to eat. "We are, aren't we? I'll see her before I go to bed."

"Isn't it late? She would be asleep."

"Mama won't sleep till she sees me tonight."

They talked at length about his trip. She updated him on the events on the home front. He drank a glass of water after the meal. "That was delicious, baby. Thanks love." He gave her a peck and stretched.

"I'll clear up while you see Mama."

He stood. "Okay love."

Tonbra touched him gingerly. "I wanted you to know that, she was er, a bit upset I didn't take the charm from her."

"She was?"

She stood to her feet and held his hand. "I couldn't bear the thought of what she was saying—I walked out on her."

"You did."

"I know I was wrong. But the mere suggestion upset me. She refused to eat since then. All she's taken is just water."

"I'll talk to her." He patted her cheek. "Don't worry."

"I'm sorry. Just that—"

"I know how you feel, of course." He gave her another peck and left to Mama's room.

He knocked on the door and Mama asked him to come in. Dini had supervised the designing to ensure it had enough space, big and well-furnished with a king-size bed, and an elaborate dressing table with stool, and full-length mirror. A fine blend of beige and brown colours matched the bedspread, curtains and carpeted floor.

Mama sat on the only single couch in the room. Her bed looked like it had not been slept in.

Dini squatted in front of her and she patted his shoulder. "Mama."

"My son. Ado o! How are you?"

He smiled into her face and pulled her into a hug. "I hope the journey was smooth."

"I should ask you. How your journey?"

"I'm fine, Mama." He sat on the edge of the bed. "Tonbra said you've not eaten."

"I go Erebi house and eat."

He arched his eyebrow. "Huh! She didn't tell me you went out."

"She no know. I just take taxi."

"Mama, don't do that again. Huh! I'm sure Erebi didn't know you just left like that."

"I no tell her. She go make big issue I had to tell her important talk."

Dini smiled. "You went to report us."

Mama smiled, but her wrinkly eyes looked lost. "I no live here."

"Mama, I think Tonbra made our stand known—"

"Before I talk about her, call her. Let her come hear."

Chapter 11

Mama convinced him to call Tonbra to the conversation. She didn't want to be misquoted. She made him realize the discussion centered on her reason for the visit. She had no plans to stay any longer than two days.

Dini reluctantly went to fetch Tonbra. He'd had a long tedious day and wished he could just go to sleep. After early morning meetings, he'd caught an afternoon flight out. Thank goodness, he hadn't checked anything in or he probably would still be in the airport! He could excuse himself from this and Mama would have no choice but to let it wait but he didn't want it to wait.

Several times, Mama had teased about a new baby, but bringing charms into the house would, could not be accepted.

Tonbra had cleared the table and gone upstairs already. She was in the bathroom, about to do her facial wash when Dini walked in.

He sounded resigned, even to his own ears. "Mama wants to talk to both of us."

Tonbra's hands on the facial wash tube froze and she turned to him. "You're tired, and this can wait till tomorrow." Her eyes showed none of the calm in her voice.

"I want this done now. I want it settled now. If it means she'll get upset, then now than later."

She reached out and touched his cheek.

"You've never had to face Mama on this issue—are you sure you want to, when you're so tired."

He removed her hand from his face. "Let's go." He turned around and left the room.

Tonbra joined him downstairs. He felt it would look odd if they went into Mama's room separately, and so waited for her to come down.

"We have to present a united front," he said and held out his hand to her. She took the hand, with a smile of gratitude and relief.

After a brief knock, they both entered the room. Mama remained as he had left her, which meant she had been waiting. Dini sat on the spot where he'd been, and Tonbra sat beside him.

"Thank you, my son." Mama looked at Dini.

"I know you be very tired. And I think you go ask me to wait till tomorrow. But since you are here, I want thank you." She stood and went to her dressing table. The banana leaf was wrapped and left in plain view.

She picked it and went back to sit down. "This is what I bring your wife, Tonbra." She lifted it toward him. "She reject it. With anger."

"Mama, I am glad she did. I would have been very upset too. We are believers in Jesus. We don't mix our faith with herbs and divination."

"This is herb not divination. If I get the thing here, I will turn in front of you." She looked at Tonbra. "Don't you eat vegetable?

This just like leaf." She turned to Dini. "When you small, this is what I give you to cure everything. From my farm." She divided her gaze between the two of them. "Do you take honey?" They nodded. "There is honey. Small pepper too. You no know roots of emi, and erunje but you know aloe vera. This is the thing I mix here." Her voice rose slightly. "Will I harm you, Dini? Will I harm your woman you love and marry?"

"Mama, of course not. We didn't think you wanted to harm us—"

Mama went on her knees. Dini and Tonbra leapt to their feet and drew her up. "Please, Dinipre Oyinkuru Brisibe, I beg you on grave of your father and grandfather, no allow me see shame."

"How?" Dini tried to hide the anger rising in his voice. He couldn't. "What is the meaning of this, Mama? In what way have I ever done anything to shame you? I am a happy and content man. I have a wife, and a good job, beautiful children—"

"Hey uhn! Dini, wait." Mama sat back. "Wait there. Where your children?"

"Mama, please, don't harass me tonight. I have three children. They give me immense joy. I am a fulfilled man."

Mama turned to Tonbra. "How many children you have?"

Dini walked to the dressing table and leaned over it, his trembling hands shook with rage.

"Three, Mama."

"And where their father?"

Dini swung around. "Mama!"

"Dini is their father. That is what we have chosen to tell them. What we have chosen to stick to."

Mama looked at them. "Why their father name different from Brisibe?" The horror and shame on Tonbra's face mirrored Dini's.

"Who told you that? Who is trying to destroy the joy and peace in my home, Mama?"

"No one. I am not fool! Your children tell me, Tonbra. I ask them when you get angry and go your room. They all tell me Francis George their father name. I wonder how you lies to those children! And you call yourself children of Jesus!"

"Enough, Mama! I will not allow you to upset us anymore."

Mama did not seem fazed by his outburst. "Dini, please. This herb go help your strength. It go help you. I know men who use and their life never remain same. Just one child is what I am ask for. One that I call my own!" She shuddered.

There was cold silence.

Tonbra reached out and collected the leaf. "He will use it, Mama."

Dini turned to her, his mouth dropped open. "What are you saying?"

Mama looked at the two, a trace of uncertainty crept into her facial lines.

"Mama, I will ensure he uses it. God help me. Dini, please let's allow Mama to rest. And you've had a long day too."

***

Dini was fuming when they got back into their bedroom. He pulled off his shirt and stomped into the bathroom. He stood under a cold shower, getting cleaned up, and cooled down at the same time, and watched with great annoyance as Tonbra carefully placed the banana wrap on her dressing table, and then walked into the bathroom to finish off her facials.

He was bursting at the seams with a desire to speak, and lash out at her, but promised himself he would not let it out. If she wanted to play, then he would watch her make him play.

After a soothing shower, he wore his night boxers and slid under the sheets. He thought sleep would come within minutes, but he felt Tonbra's hands on his belly. He groaned, turned, moaned, and then succumbed to her loving.

Afterward, they cuddled.

"You don't expect me to use that thing, do you?" he said into her hair. "Why would she bring something for me alone, anyway? I don't understand her."

"She knows I'm fertile but she's not sure you are." She snuggled closer and spoke into his neck. "Of course, you'll use it. Will you tell her you didn't?"

"I'm sure you're joking."

"I don't think she came to joke."

"She raised important issues, you know." Dini sighed. "Mama may not be schooled, but she's the smartest illiterate I know."

"We talked about this before."

"Timi knows I'm not her father and is matured about it. But Pere and Ebisine—they can't continue bearing their father's name, Tonbra."

"We've talked about this several times. Why are you bringing it up again?"

"Because it has come up again."

"I want to sleep, Dini." She yawned. "Maybe we can talk about it in the morning." She closed her eyes.

Dini knew the exact moment she slept off. Probably ten seconds after she spoke, before he could coordinate his response. She was right. They had talked about this but did they settle it? The children bore their father's name. Even Tonbra had turned her middle name to George.

Being referred to as Mrs. Tonbra George Brisibe distressed Dini greatly but his wife had chosen to stick to it. They had lied to the kids that George was the grandfather's name and Brisibe was the great grandfather's name—bla bla blu.

Dini hated the lie. Once upon a time, he had wanted another child too, but had come to discover Tonbra couldn't have any more children. There had been a medical explanation – secondary infertility. Initially he had tried to convince her to go through treatments but with time, had settled down to the fact that 'they' and not 'she' had three children. Only that there were three people in the 'they.' One, dead and gone.

Dini couldn't find sleep though the cool bath refreshed him. Everyone had overlooked the fact that Tonbra didn't get pregnant because after all, there were children in the family.

Obviously, he had been wrong. Mama was watching. She overlooked nothing.

He thought people didn't mind. Tonbra didn't mind, and he had trained himself not to, either. Had thought Mama didn't. How wrong? Probably Erebi was not as complacent as he thought as well.

Abruptly, he got up. It was after midnight. He knew Erebi would be asleep, but he had to talk to her. Mama had gone to see her. He wanted to know what they discussed.

The phone rang out twice before a drowsy Erebi picked up. "Dini. Hope nothing."

"I need to talk to you about why Mama came to see you."

"Mama. What's wrong with her?"

"Nothing."

"Look Dini, can you—Oh my. Hope all is well. Where are you?"

"Erebi. I'm sorry. Nothing is wrong, really." He heard rumbling in the background and Tobi's voice. "I'm sorry to disturb."

"Hold on, please."

He heard voices and then a door closed.

"Yeah, Dini. What's going on?"

"Mama—can I confide in you, Erebi?"

"Of course, you can. What did Mama do?"

"No, well, nothing. I want to know what she came to do in your house today."

"To visit."

Dini could almost see the nonchalant shrug. Nothing in the voice gave anything away.

He had no reason to suspect Erebi was hiding anything from him. "She said nothing? Told you nothing about me?"

"She seemed distracted. But no, she told me nothing about you. Why? What happened?"

"Can I confide in you, sister? Can I tell you something?"

"You're asking for the second time and making me uncomfortable." She yawned. "What happened?"

"Mama talked about having babies. Me and Tonbra."

"What? She did?"

"Yeah. She thinks I need some herbal remedy or something."

She chuckled. "I'm sorry, Dini. She told you that?"

"Tonbra was there as well. She didn't give Tonbra anything—"

"That figures. Tonbra has three kids."

"Yeah, but Tonbra is the reason we don't have any kids. There's nothing wrong with me."

"Oh. Does she know?"

The concern in her voice sent chills through Dini. "We know. We accept. We are fine by it.

We have three kids," he said rapidly.

"But Dini—"

"Tonbra must never know I discussed this with you, please. This is our secret. She'll be devastated. Please."

"I understand. Dini. I do."

"It alarmed me that Mama would—go to this extent."

"I knew she wanted you to have your own kids but—"

"I have my own kids!"

"You know what I mean, Dini. I thought it would be nice as well, but then—" He could feel that shrug again. "I felt—See, it's none of my business."

"I hope it stays that way. We are happy. Our kids are doing well."

"I respect you for protecting Tonbra this way." Erebi yawned again. "I mean, not letting anyone know she's the problem."

"Well, it's not confirmed. We just assume. I did all the tests, and I'm fine. She—she didn't want to do any tests and—see, Erebi, we are fine. Honestly."

"Well—"

"If Mama ever talks to you about this, please. Let her understand. This is our decision. My decision."

"Dini—"

"We are fine."

***

Mama decided to return home the following day.

Her decision displeased Dini as much as the discussion they had the previous night, and this made him more loath to let her go back with public transportation. Just returning from a trip and going to the office the following day, he needed his driver. Yet he couldn't watch his mother enter a taxi back home.

"I'll come and see you soon," he mumbled after she reluctantly sat at the back cabin of his Toyota Tundra.

"Okay, my son," she mumbled in response.

He knew she wasn't happy as well, or she would have stayed for another day. Well.

He called another driver from the office to

pick him up, and promptly made himself forget all about the troublesome visit.

CHAPTER 12

Erebi had a monthly habit of visiting hers, and Tobi's mother. She made sure it fell on the second weekend of the month so she would not miss the thanksgiving service on the first Sunday in her church. If she would wait to see Mama on her monthly visit, she would need two weeks. She couldn't wait.

Especially after she went to Dini's house after her school hours to visit and discovered Mama had left. Reluctant to ask Tonbra what happened, lest she disclose what she'd discussed with her husband in the night, and not willing to disturb Dini at work, she took a quick decision and called Tobi. She had to go to Apoi that evening.

It was late she knew, but she planned to stop at Akure, spend the night, and take the first bus to Apoi the following morning. Tobi concurred. She didn't bother to tell either Tonbra or Dini.

She arrived Apoi before 8a.m. Mama ran out in the open, tying only wrapper. "Hope all is well."

"Mama, ado o! All is well."

"How Dini? Tobi?"

"They are fine, Mama. Let us go in." She ushered Mama inside. "I left very early. I am hungry."

Mama looked at her, and sighed. "There is cold pap and fresh vegetable soup I make last night."

"Ha, that will be okay. I'm fine with it."

Erebi found the food in Mama's kitchen and dished some. "Should I bring some for you?" She turned, raised her voice and discovered Mama had followed her into the kitchen.

"No."

Mama hovered around as Erebi ate, and then asked to sleep. Unknown to Mama, Erebi found herself too nervous about what she had to say. How she would say it? She was excited and anxious at the same time. Till she arrived Apoi, she had mixed feelings. One voice had told her categorically to steer clear. This was none of hers or anyone's business as Dini had said. Yet, her

stomach turned each time she thought of everything.

She had watched Dini live his life for Tonbra and their kids. Her kids. It was never a secret who owned those children. Tonbra told them stories about their real father all the while. Though Dini turned deaf ears, he couldn't deny he knew he was an outsider, a lunch ticket and roof over their heads. Erebi never spoke about it. But over the years, she had grown distant from her brother so she would not be tempted to interfere.

Now she felt a need to do something.

"I wanted to know what happened between you and Dini. I was at his house to visit you yesterday and told you had gone."

"Is why you travel all the way, risk your life, leave your husband and children?"

"Mama, is it not important?"

"Why you no call?"

"Well, I felt it was important to come and see you about it."

"You wrong. I'm send you back to your family today."

"Ha ah, Mama. Is that what I get for all my trouble?" She finished up her meal.

"Yes o, Erebi. This not how I teach you."

She wanted to open the can of worms and snicker when Mama exclaimed. She wanted to prove to Mama she did the right thing. That she had secrets Mama would beg her for. She didn't like the way Mama chided her over her trip, which would bring the good of Dini, and ultimately, the whole family.

"Mama, I just wanted to show I care—"

"By risk your life? When you rest small, come and go back. And no try this again. Are you small child?"

This is our secret.

The words came back to her, coupled with the scowl on Mama's face. It really was not her business. She stood and packed the empty plates to the kitchen. As always, there were young people in the house, helping Mama. One of them took the dirty plates from her.

Till Erebi returned to Lagos later in the day, and related what had happened to her husband, she didn't believe the trip had gone the way it did. That Mama had pushed her out was incredible. And that Mama had not said a word of what she discussed with Dini taught her another lesson about loyalty.

***

Three months later, Mama returned to Lagos, and this time, to stay with Erebi. In the last three months, the tension had built up between Mama and her older children. Even the younger children felt the heat.

As Iyalode of Apoi, Mama had extensive roles, which meant she had to meet people and settle conflicts daily. Now she had to take this duty back home to resolve the conflict festering under her own roof, starting from the day Dini brought Tonbra home.

Erebi received her well. A trained teacher, she displayed finesse in the art of diplomacy. But all the cool and calm entendre came crashing when Mama opened up in her blunt manner after dinner.

She hadn't travelled all the way to hide her heart from either Erebi or her husband. After the sumptuous meal they served her, she called husband and wife to her guest room.

She brought out a bottle with a liquid similar in colour and smell to the paste she had given Tonbra three months earlier.

"Erebi." She looked at Tobi. "My in-law." She lifted the bottle up. "This what I give plenty men in Apoi to drink. They no waste time, their wife conceive and have baby, boy, girl, even twins." Mama kept it on the floor. "What is there? Emi, erunje, aloe vera, honey and other small herb." She divided looks between the couple. "It is not charm. Many of my friend come from Arogbo, and other towns, Ondo, Akure, the story is same."

She fixed her gaze on Tobi. "The last time I come Lagos, I no want tell you why I come. I know Erebi was angry, but I think why give them this trouble? But I no go keep this anymore."

Erebi sat forward and frowned. "Mama, what is it?"

"I cannot, God forbid." She snapped her fingers and turned it over her head three times. "I cannot charm my own son." She put the bottle to her mouth and took a healthy swig. "This is just herb."

Erebi exchanged glances with her husband. "What are you talking about?"

Mama related the incidence of her last visit to Lagos. When she finished, the couple sighed and shook their heads.

Erebi finally found her voice. "I'm sure Dini would have taken it." She shrugged. "These things have their ways of working."

Mama shook her head. "No. He no take it."

"Mama, these things have their ways. People's body systems work differently."

"If he did, she go be pregnant by now."

"Maybe she is and they just didn't tell you yet," Erebi said.

A shadow of doubt flashed across Mama's face and for a moment, it seemed she would capitulate.

She sighed and bit the bottom of her lip. "No, she is not." Her eyes darted between Erebi and Tobi. "I go there before I come here, to be sure. She no get or I go know. Even if she get one day old in pregnancy, I go know."

Tobi's eyes lit up for a strange moment and he opened his mouth, then closed it right back. Mama turned to him and arched her eyebrows.

"Maybe she's the one who needs treatment," Tobi said softly. "Maybe she can't get pregnant."

***

Erebi brushed her teeth with Sensodyne and did her routine facial scrub before Tobi walked into the bathroom. She turned to look and smile at him.

"Erebi?"

"Hmm?"

"Do you think Mama is sincere?"

"Mama?"

"About her motives. I'm talking about her motives."

Erebi shrugged. "What's on your mind?"

"The things she said. What she wants us to do." He shook his head. "She's your mother and you know her better than I do."

"Mama has six children, darling. She loves all of us." She shook her head. "At least she tries. But you know Dini is just so special. So special—" Her voice trailed off.

"I understand."

"He has affected so many lives. Everyone has something to say for him, even me." Tobi nodded his head but said nothing, so she continued. "Mama feels he should be happy. And I think in her own estimation, having your own children is one of the joys of living."

"And Mama is right. Children are a joy."

"She believes Dini is not happy like this, not having even one child of his own."

"What do you believe?"

"I—"

"Because what you believe is going to determine if we can carry out Mama's request or not."

"Well, I disagree with Mama. I think Dini is a very happy and content man."

"He loves his wife, that I know."

"He does, with his life. He loves her children too." Erebi paused. "What's that look on your face?"

"The look, love, is confusion. That's why I asked you if Mama is sincere."

"Mama has always been a sincere person. She does her things without ulterior motive."

"Not hatred for Tonbra?"

"I don't know but I don't think so, dear."

"She went to the house today, knowing Dini will not be there. Told a small lie about going back today and then comes here and asks us to—"

"No, she's not like that."

"Well, you said you disagree with her."

Erebi folded her arms across her chest. "I do. But I also understand her plight and I sympathize with it."

"I'm not saying this to argue, I just want to know what to do. What we'll do." He rubbed his face. "We have to decide."

"We told her, yes. So, there's nothing to discuss, really."

Tobi rubbed his jaws and shut his eyes for a moment. He drew her into his embrace. "It's so confusing, honey. To compromise a brother who trusts us—"

She snuggled closer. "For his own good."

"When we are not even sure it's what he wants."

"You make it sound as if we want to poison him."

"My point is that, funny enough, I agree with Mama." Erebi's eyes widened. "I do." He chuckled. "I don't think your brother is as happy as he makes out."

"You're wrong." She shook her head. "He's in love with his wife and her children. He loves his job. He loves his life."

"The children bear their father's name."

Erebi jerked out of his embrace as though he had torched her. Her back straightened. "They don't!"

"They do. Dini told me."

"I can't believe that. They—"

"Or let me say, he gave me their birth certificates when he wanted me to open accounts for them with my bankers. Erebi love, they all bear their father's name."

"Of course, that would be on their birth certificates."

"On their school report sheets too?" He arched his eyebrows. "The account was a special one for students. I opened for our kids and thought it would be good for his as well. He was travelling and wanted to do it immediately, so I offered to help. Part of the requirements for the account is proof that they were in school."

Erebi shook her head and let out a deep sigh. "Incredible."

"Dini was embarrassed when I reacted to it. I didn't mean to make him feel bad, but I was shocked. That was when I saw it."

"Saw what?"

"Infinite sadness. It's always there. Behind his smile. Look at his eyes. The sorrow behind his eyes."

CHAPTER 13

Oyinemi Salpon, by no special design of hers, left the school premises last. The Standard Education Centre Akure (SECA), sandwiched between two residential buildings behind Oceanic bank on the busy Oba Adesida high street in Akure, had become her second home, the staff and students, her second family. But being the last to leave, besides the reason that she loved the school, bordered more on her one-room accommodation being in one of the buildings beside the school.

The Standard Education Centre had been started long before Oyinemi had any form of education. Seeing the passion of the founder, one of her lecturers at FUTA, she had grown to love the school and vowed to work there as a volunteer. Her services however didn't go unappreciated though by a small stipend.

Oyinemi had graduated top of the course the lecturer took because she had a special passion for her course of study, adult education. She had gotten a job and opted to defer her youth service till she felt she could be posted right back to Ondo state, a feat many told her was impossible for the dual reason of being an indigene and having finished her university education in the state.

Oyinemi loved to teach and had a talent for it. As a child, she would gather the children in the neighbourhood, and play school. There was no doubt in her mind she would eventually stand in front of people and impart knowledge. As she grew up and saw the level of illiteracy amongst her people, she chose adult education as her field of specialization.

Oyinemi identified with the vision and mission of SECA. She lived and breathed it. She had only been out of the university for less than a year but was perhaps the most valuable staff the organization had. Her working hours were ridiculous. She started work at the school at 12noon and sometimes did not lock up till close to midnight. The office though opened at 8a.m. by the secretary, Yemi, so enquiries could be made. Yemi had normal working hours, from 8am to 4pm, and she took her break for one hour at the same time

Oyinemi resumed. Sometimes, like today though, Tari would wait for her.

Binatari Ekiye, Tari as he was fondly called, worked with Oyinemi. A young average height, thick-set, dark-complexioned trained teacher, during the day, he taught biology at the Federal Government Girls' College. In the evening, three days a week, he taught basic science at SECA.

Because of the nature of the job, very few teachers signed up for fulltime like Oyinemi. Most of the subject teachers especially, worked part-time. The first time he saw her, he fell in love with her. At least, he told her so. Over the months, he set out to prove it.

Oyinemi liked everything about the young man. He was hardworking, devoted to the students he taught, jovial and fun to be with, and good-looking. Above all, he was a teacher, and he shared her passion to educate the world.

Knowing they had a date after the last set of students left at 8pm, Oyinemi put away her scripts and notes and locked up. She was eager for this date. Tari had told her he needed to have an urgent discussion with her. Like all spinsters in love, she expected it would be the day. The proposal should come today.

She passed through the single toilet cubicle that served all the teachers, both male and female, and touched up her face. Being so close to the teachers' room, she made it her duty to see the convenience caused no inconveniences as par smell or dirt.

Her lipstick had faded, leaving only a thin pink line along her lips. She cleaned it off and applied a fresh layer of pink. It suited her dark complexion. She dusted her face with brown powder and lined her eyes with a black pencil. She smiled, satisfied.

In her school days, she had learnt a little about make-up and had earned some income doing make-up for others. It still served her purpose. As an amateur artist, she made a little income on weekends, doing facials for brides. She had always hoped that one day, she would have the opportunity to sit still and have her face made up on her wedding day.

She walked to the staircase, which led down to the lobby, where she knew Tari waited for her. He stood by the secretary's desk, studying what looked like his teachers' manual. The federal government had recently published a new curriculum for schools, with many changes and improvements that needed getting accustomed to.

Oyinemi studied him for the umpteenth time, without his knowledge. She loved to look at him when he wasn't aware of her. He rated high in good looks by all standards. Conservative in his appearance and ignorant of his appeal, he wore common clothes usually.

Now clad in brown corduroy jeans and a striped polo shirt with predominant cream and navy lines, he looked ordinary, like he looked most of the time. He wasn't tall by masculine standards, just a couple of inches taller

than her female average. He had dark, hairy and shiny skin, just the way she liked it, and he kept his haircut low and neat.

As though sensing her presence, he arched his neck up and caught her gazing at him. His face broke into a smile to expose a neat set of well-maintained teeth. Her heart skipped a beat, and she smiled.

"I hope I didn't rush you," he said, closed the book in his hands without taking his eyes off her, and took two steps forward.

She shook her head. "No. I'm ready." She walked down the stairs.

He held out his hand to her and she placed her hand in his. "You look so beautiful, Oyinemi." His eyes looked over her with admiration.

She wore a pink and black block dress and matching black peep-toe shoes. Her jewellery was small but complementary, and she carried a big black bag.

"Thank you." She smiled at him. "Where are we going?" She locked the front door and put the key in her bag.

Tari didn't have a car, but he had called a cab. He had never done that before. Definitely, this was the night.

"Sunview."

She gaped in delight. Sunview hotel was one of the best in the state. And one of the costliest as well. "I wanted to take you somewhere—special."

"Thank you. Sunview is definitely special."

Oyinemi grew increasingly nervous. She wanted this. Since the day her feelings for Tari started to change from colleague to friend to something more than friend, she'd wanted this. He fitted her speculations to the tee. Yet, she had butterflies in her stomach. What if he said nothing? Would she be able to bear the disappointment? Would she disgrace herself? Start to cry, beg, or propose in turn?

Her mother had always said she was too strong-willed. Too determined for a woman. Going after what she wanted no matter the cost! But it was the same determination that had taken her thus far. She would not have been able to get into primary school without it, farming and selling so just she could buy school uniforms and books, and feed herself. Her determination served her well.

The taxi driver drove into the magnificent premises of SunView hotel. Oyinemi had visited the hotel as a student of FUTA, attending parties but never after her graduation. She noted the driver had gone to the parking lot after dropping them at the entrance. How much Tari would have invested in this date?

Previously, they'd gone out to smaller hotels and restaurants or sit-outs, fast food joints, never anything so impressive. He must know the areas in the hotel well, as he led her to the restaurant. To her delight, dinner was buffet. It took all her in-built graciousness not to let out a delightful yelp.

A starched waiter led them to a cosy table for two and took their order for drinks. Tari made small talk, and after the drinks were served, led her to the food. Much as Oyinemi loved good food, her stomach was too nervous, and she feared she would not be able to eat. She took a small serving of fried rice with chicken, and coleslaw and felt gratified Tari's plate looked just as flimsy.

They ate over small talk, never broaching any topics that led directly to them or the future.

After the meal, he took her back home.

Oyinemi held on to her own, sure though that after he left, she would cry herself to sleep. He walked her to the door. As she had thought, the taxi driver had waited till they finished their dinner, and now still waited in front of SECA building.

She occupied a room on the first floor of the 2-storey building that housed several one- and two-room accommodations. They climbed the stairs and walked to her door.

She inserted the key into its hole and turned it but stopped short when Tari cleared his throat.

"I can't come in," he said. "I'm sorry. The taxi."

"Of course." She half-turned and looked at him but was unable to maintain his gaze, afraid he would see how sad and agitated she felt. "I enjoyed the night very much. Thank you."

She waited for him to turn and leave. When several minutes had passed awkwardly, she looked at his face. His eyes were affixed on her.

In barely a whisper, at that very moment when she raised her eyes to look at him questioningly, he said, "Oyinemi, could you ever—marry me?"

Chapter 14

One of Erebi's favourite TV shows, Newsline, aired every Sunday night. From the time she discovered it with Frank Olize anchoring, and on to Abike Dabiri, she never missed it once. For her, the Sunday night NTA network program was one of the pleasures of life. Everyone who knew Erebi, knew she loved it.

She settled cosily in her parlour and while her last child, eight-year old Biye, sulked as she finished off her pending homework, Erebi tuned in to the show just in time. She didn't recognize the new anchor, a middle-aged man with a delightful face and a slur that reminded her of the renowned Frank Olize. Anyway.

The top story featured the CNN/African Union of Journalists' African journalism awards. Erebi nearly turned to another channel, disappointed the first segment of the program covered the awards extensively. She had no interest in journalism in the least.

She turned to Biye, who sat close to her feet, and checked on the girl's assignment.

Before she knew it, she abandoned her program and concentrated on looking through all her daughter had been doing, till Biye shrieked.

"Mum, look at Timi's daddy!"

Erebi's head came up just as the camera panned a table where Dini and Tonbra sat. "Ah ha, what are they doing here? Maybe his office." She gave the homework book to Biye. "Finish up that math and don't get me angry."

Biye quietly returned to her work, and Erebi fastened her gaze on the screen.

The awards held little or no interest in a while. And then the posthumous award to Ebisine Francis George for journalistic research in conflict resolution came up. And to receive the award, Tonbra was called upon. Dini stood amidst the applause, looking so proud of her.

Subconsciously, Erebi slapped Biye hard on the back. "Go and call your daddy! Run!"

Biye shrieked on the impact of her mother's slap but ran all the same, out of the room, shouting "Daddy! Daddy!"

Tobi had dozed off in bed when he woke up with a start on impact of a hit by Biye. He jumped up before knowing why and raced after his daughter to the parlour.

"What?!"

"Watch!" Erebi did not take her eyes off the screen.

Tonbra looked so beautiful, she took your breath. Her slim shoulders were clad in a beautiful small-sleeved silver dress that curved over her tall, slim body, and reached her ankle. The neckline though looked decent. Simple white gold jewellery graced her ears and neck, and wrists. She heaped her hair amidst extensions in a tight and neat wrap on her head, and her make-up looked to have been professionally done.

She looked graceful, a delight. She accepted the award and took the podium to give a small acceptance speech.

"I want to thank you all for giving this award to Ebisine Francis George of blessed memory, a man I love with my whole being. If he were here today, he would have felt so grateful to you all for giving recognition to all the work he had done but I am, on his behalf.

"Especially I want to thank CNN, and the AUJ, organizers of this prestigious award. My husband's very good friend and former colleague, Ebele Azikiwe, who worked tirelessly to ensure Ebisine's work did not disappear after all these years. I know how much we spent in time and funds to bring him here, Ebele, thank you. I want to thank my family who stood by me through—"

"I have to get this recorded—"

"Sshhhh!"

"—my children. Ebisine will live forever. Thank you very much!"

Tonbra raised the plaque above her head and a loud roar of applause went up. Again, everyone in the hall stood for her as she walked back to her seat. Dini hugged and kissed her.

"The children are there as well!" Erebi jumped to her feet. "Tobi, what was that? And those children were there to hear that crap!"

"Will you let us hear this thing?" Tobi snapped. He sat forward and held his head with both hands.

"Ah! No."

"Settle down, this woman. No, what?"

The next award came up, also posthumously and then the awards rounded up. Onyeka Onwenu began to sing her new remix of *One love keep us together*. Tobi sat back in the couch and closed his eyes as Erebi paced, agitated. She didn't even notice Biye had abandoned her homework after calling her father.

"A man she loves with her whole life! How could she say that in that place? She didn't even acknowledge Dini!"

"You don't know that!" Tobi said defensively. "When she was appreciating family, you didn't let us hear. You were ranting."

She threw up her hands in the air. "Well, we would have heard his name over my ranting!" Tears stung her eyes. "She has no regard for Dini. She had always just been using him!"

"Don't talk like that." Tobi dragged his hand over his face. "You'll just whip up unnecessary sentiment and upset yourself for no reason."

"That kind of occasion and they never mentioned it to us."

"Well, it doesn't concern us, does it? We're not the dead man's family, are we?"

"But Dini is?" She cried. "I'm going to call Dini!" She bent over the stool beside the couch and picked up her phone.

Tobi sat up and raised both hands in protest. "Wait. Now calm down, will you. Let me think this through before you make any calls and upset everybody."

"See how beautiful she looked!"

Tobi arched his eyebrow but said nothing.

"See how radiant she looked. Did you ever see Tonbra so—full of life—peace or joy?"

"You're upset," her husband said, and stood abruptly.

"What are you going to do?"

"Sleep. I'm beginning to have a headache so I'm going to push all this behind me and get some sleep." He stretched. "And I advise you do the same." She gawked at him. He walked to the TV and switched it off from the wall. "I'm sure we'd be able to think better in the morning." He walked out.

Her mouth dropped open and she blinked. She returned into her seat and stared after him. Just like that?

She looked at the phone in her hand and dialed Dini's number. He picked up on the third ring. "Sis!"

His cheerfulness rankled. "Hello, Dini." Her voice was hoarse, much as she tried to sound normal. "I just saw you on TV."

"TV?"

She thought she heard his voice go dull but wasn't sure. "Yes. The awards."

"Oh really!" He chuckled. "That was months ago. Are they just showing it? My phone won't rest tonight then. This happened when it was aired as a news item at the time."

"Well, on Newsline. I'm just seeing it."

She must have sounded so bad on the line. He paused for a long moment. "Are you upset about it or something?"

"I don't know, Dini." She rubbed her temples with her other hand and bit her lower lip. Was something wrong with her? Why couldn't these men

see what she saw? "I saw a lot that displeased me."

"Like?"

"Wait, Dini, are you trying to pretend or something? A lot was wrong with the whole thing."

"If I saw anything wrong, would I be asking you? Obviously, this call is not to congratulate me or Tonbra!"

Erebi gasped. "Congratulate!" Was he teasing? He sounded serious. His voice had an edge, as though he was getting upset as well.

Upset?! For what? "You—they—she was called Mrs.

Ebisine Francis George!"

"And so? That was her name!"

"No longer her name, Dini." She felt as though her bones would come apart. What's wrong with him?

"What is your problem here, Erebi? What is making you so angry?" He definitely sounded angry now. "The man is dead, and I am not in competition with him!"

"Right. Tonbra is your wife. She is Mrs. Dini Brisibe!"

He kept quiet for a long time. Just as she made to speak, he sighed and spoke softly. "Point taken. Thanks for noting it."

"Is that what you're going to say?"

"What do you want me to say, Erebi? They called her by her dead husband's name who they were honouring, I let it go. He's not married to her anymore, I am."

"Are you?" The tears which she had held back fell. She took several deep, calming breaths. "She said he lives forever, she said she loves him with her whole being—" She choked when she tried to continue. "She refers to him in the present!"

Dini continued to be quiet on the other side of the line.

"You didn't hear the things she said, or you won't be so complacent." She liked the word. She sniffed. "Yes, complacent is the word." She continued when he still said nothing. "She didn't even acknowledge you. Someone who didn't know would think you were probably her brother in that place. No mention of any Dini Brisibe anywhere. After all you've done for her. Are you still there, Dini?"

"I'm hearing you."

"See how elegant she looked. So beautiful. Her eyes glowed. You could see she was so happy. I have never, never seen her look so happy with you!" She paused and drew in her breath. She had so much to say. "If not for you, where would she be today? Where would she be?"

"You tell me, Erebi!"

"I don't know. She could be anywhere. But she's with you, spending your money. She spent your money to make sure her dead husband got this award! Or which job does she have? Which money does she have?"

"She has her own money!"

"Which you gave her?"

"Yes, I give her an allowance. Is there anything wrong in that? Do you think I give her money and then do an audit? She has a d—right to her money!"

"What do you get in return?" She didn't think to stop shouting at the top of her voice. She just needed to drive this into his brain. "She can't even give you a child! One child!"

"You're prying, Erebi! This is none of your business! What my wife does or does not do for me is none of your frigging business!"

Dini had never sworn to her before. Hardly ever raised his voice, but not now. He was yelling. And he'd sworn twice in quick succession. It slowed her down, somewhat.

"She's using you, Dini Oyinkuru Brisibe." She hiccupped. "She's using you, and when she's done, only that dead husband of hers and the children she had for him will inherit everything you've worked all your life for!"

Dini's teeth must have been clenched when he spoke, but he had lowered his voice. "You're insulting me, Erebi."

"Is that how you see this? Prying and insulting?"

He sounded rigid. "Yes," he bit out. "Yes, Erebi. Don't call me again. Don't visit me if you think I made a mistake marrying the woman I married. I love her, she loves me. You probably have no idea what that means—"

"Dini?"

"But I have had enough of your interferences. I want peace in my home, and I have it. And you or Mama or anyone else will not destroy what I have laboriously built for myself. This is my life."

"Dini."

"Back off!"

Her mouth dropped open, and she didn't realize he had hung up on her. Dini?

"Dini? Hello? Dini!" She jumped to her feet and noticed Tobi stood at the entrance.

The weight of the anguish rolled over her and she burst into tears. She staggered toward her husband and he pulled her into a tight embrace, rubbing her back and murmuring assuring words to the crown of her head.

"He said I should never call him again. Never visit again!" She sobbed. "She has ruined him. She has ruined Dini."

***

Dini lowered his shaking hand as calmly as he could and replaced his phone on the bedside stool. He doubted if sleep would come tonight. He had said a lot of things he probably shouldn't but all well. He did not need his

sister bad-mouthing his wife.

Tonbra looked at him for several seconds after the explosion and then snuggled close, wrapping her arms around him.

She buried her head in his chest. "Thank you."

Her appreciation irritated him. After all, Erebi was still his sister. "For what?" He pushed her arms out of his body and turned away from her. "I need to sleep. I have a long day tomorrow."

"Jealousy is eating her alive. She'll be carcass by the time it's done with her!" Tonbra hissed and turned to her side of the bed. She fell asleep within minutes.

Dini turned slowly to look at her sleeping profile. Erebi was right. At least one child would have made everything easier.

CHAPTER 15

Dawn broke over Apoi with birds fluting in the star-apple trees in the Iyalode's compound. Erebi's monthly three-day visit ended today. She stretched to her feet and rubbed her eyes over a yawn. She didn't know what woke her up so early. She checked her wristwatch and exclaimed. Barely 6 o'clock! She had slept late and fitfully in the night and hated to wake so early. She would be leaving Apoi for Lagos today and wanted to be strong for the journey.

She sat up and walked into the bathroom to wash her face. Maybe an early morning walk would help? She felt a headache coming. She needed to have a clear mind. She wore her previous day's clothes, and slippers, and slipped through the back door.

The cool morning air refreshed her dreary nerves. Erebi took several calming breathes and strolled down the street to her old primary school. Over the years, Apoi had metamorphosed from a village to a beautiful country town. She was ever proud of her hometown.

Thoughts of Apoi took her mind back to Dini. As one of the driving forces behind the growth of this ancient and legendary town, he had given so much to it, and what did he have? A wife who exploited him on all levels.

Tonbra was a beautiful woman, who, no doubt, had a strong hold on her husband. Erebi didn't have a problem with that. Her problem was on what Tonbra use that hold for, to benefit herself and her children alone. And her late husband.

Since the days after her encounter with Dini two weeks earlier, she had been moved to do some findings of her own about the awards, and discovered that not only had Tonbra spent hundreds of thousands of naira to advance the research her late husband worked on, she had started a foundation in his name. The foundation gulped hundreds of thousands on a monthly basis on similar researches and sponsoring journalists in the field. To cap it up, the monetary reward that accompanied George's award had now been fixed in an account for his children. To care for the children in case

Dini finally threw her out! Erebi thought wryly.

It was too much to bear, yet she felt helpless.

This visit to her mother should have been uneventful except that she couldn't lie to Mama she used the herbs for Dini. Mama's eagerness to entertain and chat with her tore at her heart.

But how could she prepare kunu or zobo and give to Dini to drink? Whilst heavily laced with Mama's fertility potions. Mama told her the herbs were harmless, even to children, but she couldn't do that. She couldn't invite Dini for lunch or dinner and lace his juice—

Yet her conscience refused to vindicate her.

She wanted to do something. She wanted to leak the secret between her and Dini, especially since Dini tried his best to cut her off. She had called several times and he, each time, refused to pick her calls or return them. Twice she visited him when she knew he would be home, and he refused to see her. Even Tonbra snubbed her!

When she arrived, Mama's excitement and charity had driven her close to a confession that she didn't have the nerve to lace her brother's drink, even if it was for his own good!

And close to confessing it was futile. Dini didn't have a fertility problem. Tonbra did, funny as that seemed.

She entered one of her former classrooms and absently sat down. The furniture was new. Recently, the Apoi Youth Association, which she and Dini belonged in, did a general overhaul of the schools in Apoi. She ran her hands over the smooth surface of the desk in front of her and wished life could be so smooth. Why did good people marry bad people?

Because right now, nothing could convince her Tonbra was not evil!

She didn't know how long she stayed there but the sun had come up when she finally stood and made the short trek back through footpaths discovered several decades ago.

It took less than ten minutes to return to the house.

Mama and her maids were busy making food, sweeping, cleaning and generally preparing for the day. The old kitchen, situated at the backyard, was still being used despite the fact that the modern one had been carved into the main house. There, Mama stirred vegetable soup over a large charcoal burner.

She looked up, and without smiling, enquired where Erebi went to. "I went for a walk."

She'd had a near-quarrel with Mama the previous night and some strong statements had been made.

Mama straightened. "I'm sorry for the thing I say to you yesterday."

The words surprised, and softened Erebi. After all, they both wanted the best for Dini. "I'm sorry too, Mama." She turned back toward the house and then stopped and turned to Mama who was staring at her. "When you finish cooking, I want to tell you something." She turned back and rushed into the house.

She got in the bathroom and had a quick bath. She planned to leave after breakfast as she normally did and though what she had to tell Mama could boomerang, she would face it off.

Mama, being her usual self, hid anxiety if ever she had one, and insisted Erebi had breakfast before saying what she had to say.

One of Mama's maids cleared the plates and Mama led Erebi back into her room, closing the door firmly. She sat on the edge of her bed and looked at Erebi. "I trust my girl with information, but I no know what you have to tell me—how is important."

"Mama," Erebi took a deep breath. "I know I may be wrong telling you this. I mean," she paused. "I promised Dini it would be between us—" Her voice trailed off and she battled with the decision to speak out. Mama characteristically remained quiet, allowing her to decide.

"The first time you came up with this—herb drink thing. I spoke with Dini." She shrugged. "Well, Dini spoke with me!" She sighed. "There's nothing wrong with Dini, Mama." She looked at Mama to gauge her reaction. There was none. "If they don't have kids, it's because of Tonbra!"

Mama kept quiet for a second longer than necessary. She then sat up and cleared her throat. "Dini tell you is not the problem?" Erebi nodded. Mama sighed and sat even straighter. "I want you tell him to come see me."

Erebi shook her head vigorously. "No, Mama, he mustn't know I told you anything!"

Mama furrowed her brows. "He no go know." She reached out with a heavily beaded hand, a sign of her traditional authority, and squeezed Erebi's hand. "Okay, tell him call me."

Erebi lowered her gaze and fought tears. "He won't pick my calls. He won't even see me!"

"Why? What happen?"

Erebi, despite herself spilled the whole tale, taking pride in the fact that she did not break down and weep in the process. Afterward, Mama kept quiet for such a long time. Then she patted Erebi's hand and smiled.

"Our people say that woman who is sweeping floor do not turn her buttocks only one way. Erebi, go back to Lagos. You have do your part."

Erebi stood. "I can call Tonbra and ask her to tell him," she said. "At least she still picks my calls, though she's very cold."

"Do that. Tell her I tell her husband call me. Today."

Erebi knelt down in respect and Mama said a word of prayer over her. She quietly left the room, not sure she had done the right thing.

***

Mama remained in her room long after Erebi had gone. She knew. She had known all the while Dini was fine, but she just couldn't understand the mystery behind their inability to have a child. How would Tonbra be the reason when she had three kids already but then in Mama's years of experience, women and even men end up all sorts. She believed every woman had a destined number of children. Surely, Tonbra had used up all her chances.

That left Mama with only one option.

She called on Mebi, the latest girl in her employ. Mebi was on scholarship under Dini's scheme, and had come to live with Mama, after her mother, her only surviving parent, died. One of five children, Mama had accepted all, but only Mebi stayed with Mama. The other four siblings went to live with Mama's four younger children. Mebi, a gangly teenager, the oldest of the children, was eager to serve and could work like a horse.

"Go Salpon compound. Ask the daughter to see me before she travel."

Mebi curtseyed and ran off to do Mama's bidding. Oyinemi Salpon had only visited Mama the previous day. It was her norm, anytime she came in from Akure to visit her parents. But yesterday, she had come with news. Someone wanted to marry her. A teacher like her in the city of Akure. A Mr. Binatari Ekiye. Well.

Meanwhile, Mama got busy. She stood on her side table and pulled open her old trunk box, which she kept on her wardrobe. There was very little in the box, a few old clothes and articles of interest. She found what she sought easily and took them out. They had the musty smell of 'house' but then, she expected as much. The heavy velvet wrapper had been in the trunk box for five years. The other fabric though not as expensive, a cheap wax textile, had more worth more than the velvet. It had been a gift from her own mother.

Mama laid the two pieces of clothing on her bed and then went into her kitchen to prepare a rich plantain pottage meal with plenty of fish and bush meat. By the time she finished, Mebi was back with Salpon's daughter, Oyinemi.

Mama led Oyinemi into her room with the food on a tray.

"Let us eat," Mama said softly. It was significant in their culture for Oyinemi to eat from the same bowl as Mama, especially because of her chieftaincy title.

Oyinemi hesitated, a look of confusion on her face. Slowly, she washed her hands in the water bowl, and took a small portion, following Mama who used her hand to eat. She chewed carefully on the food.

When the meal finished, Mama pushed the tray aside and looked at Oyinemi. "I need your womanhood."

CHAPTER 16

Dini walked into the building of SECA purposefully.

The ancient building had been renovated several times though it still showed signs of age with some cracks on the wall, and paint peeling. The old signboard did nothing more than occupy space because SECA didn't need it anymore. It did not only have a name in Akure, it had become a landmark.

When he'd been a student at FUTA, the building had been used for something else, but shortly before he graduated, the school had moved there.

The reception area was small, and a middle-aged receptionist sat on an electric typewriter. A typewriter in this day and age! She looked up from running her fingers over it at an amazing speed and smiled at Dini.

"Good evening sir."

Dini returned the smile. "Good evening. I'm asking for Ms. Salpon."

"She's teaching a class, sir. Can you wait for her?"

Dini checked his wristwatch. Six o'clock. "Huh, I guess I'll just leave a note for her." He brought out a pen from his shirt pocket and got a piece of paper from the receptionist. The message was simple. Mama had asked him to stop by on his way to see her and tell Ms. Salpon, the time is ripe. Whatever that meant.

On the phone, Mama had sounded convinced Ms. Salpon would understand the message clearly. He wrote the note just as plainly and simply as that and folded it.

"Ah, here she comes," the receptionist said.

Dini straightened in time to see the legs alone, half-hidden from his view by the design of the staircase. She wore red slip-ons. Her legs were slightly bowed. They joined the rest of her body via a shapely hip-side, a small waist and correspondent small bosom. She was dark in complexion, milk-chocolate rather than dark. She wore a cream and red polka-dot dress that flattered her figure. She knew how to dress. Her hair was woven in tiny locks, a style that left some falling over her forehead.

She was a pretty woman. Beautiful round eyes, full lips, pointy nose, chubby cheeks, thick well-shaped brows.

Dini smiled at the thought of noticing so much about her. Especially when he realized he'd seen her before. Mama had introduced her to him once. Ah, yes. She still looked as youthful.

"Oh, hello." He pasted a smile on his face. "I was just dropping a note."

She went down almost to her knees. "A do o! Welcome sir!"

"Please, rise, my sister," Dini said. "I'm sorry to disturb you. I was leaving a note."

"No disturbance, sir. Let me see you out."

She led the way and Dini disturbingly noticed the slight sway of her hips. He quickened his steps and moved ahead of her to where he parked the Tundra. At the truck, he turned to her and handed her the note he'd written.

"Mama said you'd understand perfectly."

She opened the note, read and grimly nodded. "Thank you, sir."

Dini wished she would disclose a bit of the meaning behind Mama's message, but her face was totally shut off.

"What do you do here?"

She seemed taken aback by his question.

"It's an evening school. Adult education."

"Yeah, I know. I mean, are you a teacher?"

Of course, the receptionist had told him she was teaching. Ah, Dini, he sighed. He wanted to make conversation with her. Know her better.

Dini, remember Tonbra? There's a Mrs. Dinipre Oyinkuru Brisibe in Lagos.

"Yes, I am. I teach English, and Civic Education."

"Really, interesting." He leaned against the chassis and folded both his legs and arms. "Is the school doing well?"

She shrugged. "Better than many others."

Her dress had small sleeves and she began to rub her arms as though cold, though the weather was fair.

"Are you cold?"

"No, not at all, sir. Thank you."

She still had not smiled. In fact, she looked sad.

He straightened. "I'm sorry to keep you. You must be busy." She nodded. "I'll be on my way then." He opened the door and got in. "Will you be coming to the village, as well?" He wanted to know.

"Yes. For the weekend."

He smiled. "We may see then. I'll be with Mama till Sunday." It sounded too much like an invitation. But she still did not smile.

She stepped back and he closed the door. He manoeuvred the truck back on to the road and waved. She didn't wave back, and he wondered what troubled her. He didn't remember much about her, but she had been one of the many students who benefitted from his scholarship scheme. He was glad

she made it through.

She was awfully shy though. He liked her. Very lovely to behold. Of course, she looked nothing like Tonbra. Tonbra had a model's figure, and a fair complexion. Even after three children, her stomach remained flat, her skin, firm and well-nurtured. This Ms. Salpon however was something else. She looked homely, like a wife. A real wife.

"Oh, Deacon Dini Brisibe!" He groaned and pushed both women out of his mind.

***

Dini didn't know what Mama wanted him to spend two nights for but it had been long since he did. And he welcomed the change from the hustle and bustle in Lagos. Besides, he missed Mama's food. Most importantly, he deserved the rest. In the past few days, things had been strained between him and Tonbra. Her involvement with her foundation took all her time and energy, and the strained relationship between Erebi and his family generally made him feel alone.

Recently, he became more involved and committed in church, but the new relationships he developed here didn't make up for his family. He had few friends, mostly his colleagues and career associates. His closest allies remained Tonbra, Erebi and other members of his family. Now one part of the family was estranged, and the other part seemed to do nothing to help.

In those days when his father got upset with anyone in the family, Mama always stood as advocate. He'd subconsciously expected as much from Tonbra but that didn't happen.

Instead of advocating for Erebi, Tonbra advocated against.

The journey to Apoi was smooth and he arrived in good time. Mama ran to meet him and hugged him. He had told her he would be late because of the office and she had calmly accepted. She prepared kalabari fulo and Dini ate till he couldn't stand straight. When last did he have real native food?

Home sweet home.

Afterwards, one of the girls prepared a warm bath for him and he promptly went to bed after the relaxing bath. Early the following morning, Mama woke him up before dawn to talk to him.

He'd suspected there was more to her invitation. He'd even suspected what the topic would be.

"Thing no go well in Shabomi," Mama said, taking him unawares at first. Shabomi was the seat of the king of Apoi.

"What's the problem?" He sat up and rubbed sleep off his eyes. "Is the King Kalasuwea alright?"

"Oh, I guess he is, Dini." Mama sat up. "Is his Iyalode is not well."

Dini frowned. "What is wrong with you, Mama?" Perhaps he had been wrong about this visit. "I've never known you to be sick?"

"My sickness is of soul and not of body, Dini. And I am afraid, it may last take my life!"

"Never, Mama! We still need you for many many years. What sort of ailment is this? What can we do to speed up your healing?"

"You. You be the sickness!"

He didn't get it. "Me? Mama, how?"

"I have six children and all produce."

Dini took a deep breath and laughed. "Oh Mama! That?"

"Yes, Dini. Is killing me!"

"You can't die, Mama. I see at least forty years more in your eyes!"

"Dini, is not joke!" Mama was so close to tears, the smirk on Dini's face disappeared. "Look, Tonbra can never give you child. I know."

Dini stood. "No, Mama. I won't take that."

"Women have destiny to born a number of children. After having six of you, I never carry again!"

"Mama that is old wives' fables. My wife will give me children when God decides to favour us!"

"That is the old woman tale you talk, Dini. This has nothing to do with favour of God. She have finish the number of children God give her. I don't know if is three or if she abort some but—"

Dini shouted. "Give me a break, Mama! Tonbra never had an abortion! She never could!"

Mama lowered her voice. "Dini, I no have anything against your wife. I love her." She lifted her hand to him, beckoning him to her. "I love Tonbra. Is not her fault. Is because I love her that I'm going about this in way she will not know."

Reluctantly, he took her hand and went back to sit on the bed beside her. "Mama, I want to have a child of my own, more than you can imagine. But I love my wife, and I believe God will answer us one day—"

"Is she believe God with you? Do she want your child too?"

Dini rubbed his temple and closed his eyes. "Of course, she does. Mama, of course."

His voice sounded strained and he knew his reply did not convince her. There was a long period of silence between them.

Then Mama sat straighter and looked at him. "I get solution to the problem."

Dini waited for another long moment for her to continue. He feared she had compromised him in some way.

"I have find virgin, who will give you child—"

Dini sprung off the bed with such force, Mama leaped off too. He paced the room like a wild animal, shaking his head frantically.

"No, Mama. Never! I will never take a second wife. Do you know what

you are saying? Can you imagine what—what's this, Mama? Why are you

doing this to me? Do you want me to run away from you? First is the herb and

now a woman? Who and what gave you the thought that a virgin has any children 'destined' to her? Mama, mama, you're trying my patience! You're looking for my trouble now! I will never come to your house again!"

Mama silently walked out.

He slumped back on to the bed and buried his face in the pillow, unable to control the flow of tears.

"Oh God, please, take this shame from me. Help me, God. Don't give the devil a chance to mess me up. Strengthen me in these times of temptation. Help me to be strong and to remain wholly devoted to you.

"Give me a child from the wife of my youth, oh Lord I pray—" He wept bitterly.

***

He stayed in his room till late in the evening when he became hungry. Sulkily, he went into the kitchen and asked one of the maids to dish some food for him. The young lady gave him bean cakes and pap, which he demolished. He asked after Mama and was told she should be in her room.

Quietly, he sneaked back into his. He wasn't ready to face Mama. He would leave early in the morning to continue licking his wounds. He'd spent the day, weeping, praying and sleeping, and despite himself, he felt rested.

He had declined the offer for warm water for a bath because he didn't want to delay his quick retreat. Closing the door after him, he took his slippers off and kept them under the bed. The bed was a bit rumpled, so he decided to straighten it before going to sleep.

A shadow passed behind him and he stood, thinking it strange. A woman stood tied in a loose wrapper, just at the entrance to his bathroom. She obviously just had a bath, she smelt fresh, and looked a bit wet, not dripping. He hooked his gaze on her face and gasped. She dropped the wrapper to the floor.

Everything about her shocked him.

His throat closed and his mouth went dry but despite his physical reactions he found his voice. "Get out!"

She involuntarily whimpered and picked up the wrapper for cover. It made him bold, and he yelled, "Get. Out!"

She turned back into the bathroom. His knees buckled and he reached for the wall to gain a hold. His hands shook, and anger boiled from the depths of his being. Slowly he walked toward the bathroom, and through the slightly opened door, watched her hurriedly remove her clothes off the hanger where she'd hung them. Her hands trembled, and a piece dropped.

How could she? How could Mama?

He walked on shaky legs to his door and held it open, angry beyond reason. She came out, fully dressed, and ran out of the room. He slammed the door shut.

Dini picked his things like a robot, with angry, jerky movements.

On his way out, he saw the girl crouched on the floor in the parlour, crying. Mama paced, talked and shouted intermittently, calling out his *oriki*, a praise song for warriors to encourage them to battle.

Dini got into his Toyota Tundra, and drove with speed into the night.

CHAPTER 17

Tonbra dragged in a long breath as the car slowed to negotiate the turn to her destination. This important decision has brought her to this point where her hopelessness could yield a miracle to a nagging problem. She lived a dream since last week—a nightmare definitely, where her life now hung on a delicate balance.

And it started that night a week ago—

She'd known Dini's trip to see his mother wasn't ordinary. Though he seemed excited, her intuition had not felt right. Mama knew Dini's busy schedule, and how difficult he found it to take a break from work. Dini worked on a virgin project worth billions of naira. His working hours ran on a 24-hour shift where he was on call day and night. If Mama wanted to see him, she knew she had to come to Lagos. Instead, she had insisted he come, and not earlier or later than that weekend. An emergency didn't have a date or period! Instead, Mama counted ten days.

Exactly ten days after he spoke with her.

She had been fast asleep that night, not expecting Dini earlier than noon the following day. Being a deep sleeper, she had not heard the truck come in. She heard nothing that Saturday night till Dini burst into the room shouting at her, 'Give me a child! Give me a child now!'

She jumped up to a sitting position, clutching her wrapper to her chest. "Dini! What happened? What time is it? Why—?"

He'd pounced on her, tore off her night gown, and raped her that night. It had never happened before. The man who loved her more than anything in the world?

Ready to die for her? He'd pushed her off afterwards, as though she disgusted him, and staggered out of the room.

Tonbra found him in the guest chalet the following morning but could not face him.

What happened in his mother's house? Why did he leave Apoi in the dead of the night, risking his life to return to Lagos? She wished she could ask him but the following morning, he had muttered a curt apology and left for

work, staying there through time for church and all day.

She had not been able to get him to talk about the event since then. Each time she brought it up, he begged her to forget it. But, how could she? He'd been screaming for a child as he raped her!

That was why she decided to make this trip. She couldn't have if not that Dini went on an official trip to China. He would be away for two weeks. It suited her just fine. If need be, she should have recovered totally from the trip by the time he returned.

She had opted for a chartered vehicle instead of using her car and driver to be sure no one in her circle of influence had any information. The cab driver drove into the tight parking space in the compound, their destination, and Tonbra came down, impulsively shoving on her dark glasses.

"Wait for me," she told the driver who nodded briskly.

Nothing much had changed in the city or the house she walked up to. She knocked twice before a voice muffled a reply. A middle-aged, work-weary, average-looking woman opened the door.

"Good afternoon," Tonbra said.

The woman looked her over. "Good afternoon."

She recognized the woman, the doctor's wife but the woman didn't know her. She couldn't be blamed. The last time she visited she had worn an old T-shirt with faded black skirt. Now she wore a black double-breasted shirtdress from Michael Kors and Chloe wedge sandals. She probably resembled no one the doctor's wife could identify.

"My name is Tonbra George Brisibe. I want to see Dr. Finidi." Her name solicited no recognition and she decided to leave it at that.

The woman took a step back to let her in. "Sit here. The doctor will see you in a minute."

Tonbra nodded her thanks and took the seat indicated. The doctor would definitely remember her. She had been dramatic enough to earn the recognition. The clinic had not changed. She looked round for anything new, anything inspiring. None. She dropped her LV bag on the seat beside the one she took and closed her eyes, taking calming breathes.

Dini's voice continued to ring in her head 'Give me a child. Give me a child now!' He had never been violent before. In the five years she'd been married to him, he had never once done anything like this. Even when he got upset. He never raised his voice or hand at her children, on the contrary, he spoiled them.

To think she thought the issue of childbearing had long been settled.

After the second year of their marriage and she still had not taken in, he'd started suggesting he had a problem. She helplessly watched him do all manner of tests. How could she tell him?

Doctor Finidi walked into the sitting area with a wide smile on his face.

He'd not changed in five years.

"Ah, Mrs. George, what brings you? You look smashing," he said. "Widowhood becomes you!"

Tonbra looked at him and narrowed her eyes, but he would not know because she still had her dark glasses on.

"It's Mrs. Brisibe now," she said coolly.

"Oh, really. He must be a good man! You look young and fresh." He gestured. "Come into the office."

Tonbra followed him. The office had not changed, and the memories made her dizzy. What was she thinking?

He went around and took his seat behind the desk and motioned her to one of the two chairs in the office.

Tonbra looked at the bookshelf behind the doctor and then her eyes drifted off sideways to that abominable table she'd lain on several times in the past. No, she had many regrets for knowing this doctor.

"So, how's life? And how are your kids?"

"Doctor, I want you to undo what you did to me!" She hardly moved her lips, cutting off all pleasantries.

Finidi sat up and clenched his fists beneath his chin. "What I did to you, Mrs. Brisibe?"

She pulled off her dark glasses and glared at him. "You know what you did to me!"

"Oh." He arched his eyebrow. "Can you pay now?" He glared at her in return.

"I'll pay anything!"

"Yeah, you can, can't you?" He laughed. "Oh Tonbra! It's good to see you looking all fresh and sweet, but you're still a desperate woman."

She flew to her feet. "To hell with you, Dr. Finidi!"

"I'll schedule your operation for two days' time. It's half a million." He got to his feet as well. His words subdued her.

"Anything."

A slow mean smile twisted the edge of his lips. He sat down and tore off a sheet of paper from a notepad on the desk. He scribbled rapidly and gave the paper to her.

"Go and do those tests and bring the results to me tomorrow. You have money now so City Labs will do it for you express service." He got up again. "Bring the result tomorrow and you get your operation next tomorrow!" She snatched the paper from him. "That's if you have no diseases!" He winked.

She jerked her bag up and slugged her dark glasses back on. "Thank you."

She stomped out of his office, but not before seeing the smirk on his face. She hated the medicine man with a passion.

***

Deborah opened the front door to the guests and greeted. She took the small travelling bag from Mama's hand and led them into the parlour.

"Put bag in my room, and bring water to drink," Mama said.

"Yes ma." The servant lady curtseyed and hurried off.

Mama gestured the young lady with her to a single couch and took another one.

Deborah came back with two glasses and a jug of cold water. She poured the water for both women and left.

The silence in the room was as chilling as the water both drank. They sat, neither saying a word. Tonbra met them this way when she walked in about an hour later.

"Ha, Mama! Good evening, ma." She crouched in front of Mama in greeting and Mama tapped her back.

"Good evening, my daughter."

"Dini didn't tell me you were coming today," Tonbra said. She looked at the other lady and nodded in greeting. The woman nodded in return.

Tonbra hated strangers in her house but didn't have the courage to ask Mama questions. The lady looked polished, pretty in a homely way, and simple but elegant in a Woodin print dress and black pumps.

Mama said nothing in response, and it left her wondering if Dini knew about this visit. If he did, would he not have sent his driver to pick her? It had been a month since that horrible middle-of-the-night incidence, and Tonbra still winced at the thoughts of it. Since then, Dini had not mentioned either his mother or his elder sister. In fact, he had not mentioned anyone in his family.

"What would you want to eat?"

Mama smiled. "Ha, if there is rice and stew. Is okay. You Lagos people no cook real food, do you?"

Tonbra took the slight in a stride. "Ma-a-ma! We still pound yam and make starch if that is what you mean. In fact, I still made *polofiyai* yesterday!"

Mama laughed. "I hope it taste good."

Tonbra gave up and shrugged. "Okay, Mama. But one day one day, I will convince you." She shrugged. "I will get the rice ready now." She turned to the lady. "Excuse me, please." Smiled at Mama and hurried up the stairs.

Once she got into her room, she called Dini. "Mama is here!"

Dini hissed. She could hear the thunder in his voice even before he spoke. "Mama? What does she want? Why did she come? How did she come?"

"One by one, darling. What sort of questions are those? It's your mother we're talking about."

"I don't want to see her. You can tell her to go to Erebi's house!"

"She came with a woman."

Cold sweat broke on her face when Dini went completely silent for what seemed like one full minute. "Dini?"

"A woman," he said softly. "Describe her."

"She's dark. Well-dressed."

"Chubby cheeks?"

"Yes. You know her?"

"I guess so. I met her the last time I went to see Mama—"

Tonbra noticed his voice had changed. She heard fear and anger or some emotion she couldn't describe. His voice trailed off and she wondered what he wanted to say but didn't.

"Of course, it may not be the same person," he said on a heavy sigh. "I'll soon be home anyway."

"Okay darling."

"I've left the office already."

"Okay then. See you soon."

She hung up and held the phone to her bosom. Whatever evil had come home to roost, and she must chase it far from her.

She changed from her Italian tailored grey suit which she'd worn to an evening event of the Ebisine Francis George (EFG) Foundation into a short peasant dress. The comfortable dress made her look sexy. If she was going into battle tonight, she'd better feel good in her own skin. She exchanged her stilted shoes for simple, trendy slippers, and tied her hair in a scarf. Then she took a deep breath and went back downstairs.

Though she had a cook, she decided to make the meal herself. It gave her an excuse not to sit with Mama and the strange woman.

***

Dini came in less than an hour later and called Tonbra to join them in the parlour. She looked uncertain as he motioned her to a seat, which she took, sitting at the edge.

When she looked comfortably seated, Dini turned to her. "Did you meet Oyinemi yet?"

Tonbra shook her head. "I guess Mama wanted you to do the introduction."

"No, Dini. No do that!" Mama sat forward. "You, Tonbra, go up, we want talk!"

"Why would she not be involved in this talk? After all, your plan will affect her!"

"Not so. Go to your room, Tonbra!"

Tonbra looked from mother to son, confused. She stood but Dini's voice stopped her. "This is your house. You will stay here and join in whatever Mama has to say!"

"Dini, please," Tonbra said softly.

Mama pointed at her with her left hand, a bad sign traditionally. "Leave this room!" Tonbra turned and fled, stifling a cry.

"Mama, this fire you are starting will burn your hands! You seem bent on losing your first son finally!"

Mama leaned back in her seat and spoke softly. Her voice trembled as though she would cry, and so low, Dini had to strain to hear it.

"My plan simple, Dinipre, my son. Please hear, before you get angry. Please." When he continued to glare at Mama, she took a deep breath.

Since entering the house and seeing her, sitting on the couch in his parlour, fully dressed, he had not been able to look at her again! What would make a woman like her, an educated woman, stoop so low to accept to do such a disgraceful thing? He shamed for her.

He found a spot by the mantle place and stood poised for battle. He had lost the one to have Tonbra present already. But God help him, it was the only one he planned to lose.

"If you let this girl give you child, your wife will never know. I will keep the child, care for him—"

"I will know, Mama!" Dini snapped at the top of his voice. He wanted Tonbra to hear him. "God will know."

"What do that matter to you?" Mama said softly.

"It matters all. Everything. You're trying to ruin me, ruin my faith in God." He turned angrily to look at Oyinemi Salpon, a woman he'd once considered to be a real wife material. How so wrong! She was pure trash! She returned his gaze with everlasting, soulful eyes. She bit her lower lips. She should be worried.

"Why are you doing this?" he snarled. "Why have you positioned yourself to be used by the devil?" He turned away from her like looking at her hurt his eyes.

Mama continued as though she had not been interrupted, making sure her voice remained barely audible. "You have heir, someone to carry your name! Oyinemi will go her peaceful life, which she leave for you, just to save our family from shame!"

"Do you know, Mama, that this thing you want to do is the real act of shame? You are trying to bring shame to my life, my family. How will I ever face my wife? And my children?"

"You no have children! Dinipre son of Brisibe. You are childless!" Mama's voice though low carried such force she might have been yelling.

"I do. Timi, Pere and Ebisine are my children. And I will have more!" He wondered where the children were, hoped they had not seen this—this person Mama brought into his house.

"How? From your, your—" She waved her hands in the air." Male pawpaw tree! Can he-goat carry pregnancy?"

"I take exception to that, Mama. I take exception to the audacity you have to to bring—her here! To my matrimonial home!" He stood straight and looked at Oyinemi. "You're going back to where you came from, right now!"

"She no go anywhere, Dini." Mama sat forward. "Do I give you second wife? No. Do I say bring child here, no? You just stubborn and foolish, like your father."

"Thank you, Mama." With jerky movements, he pulled out a wad of one thousand naira notes from his pocket. He didn't know how much. He didn't care. "Take. Take and go and find somewhere to sleep tonight. You can go back to Akure tomorrow morning!" He held out his hand with the notes to Oyinemi, but the latter merely stared at her fingers, which she twisted on her laps. "Take!" He flung the money on her. She sucked in her breath noisily but did nothing more.

Mama jerked to her feet and marched into her room.

"Go and get a life, Ms. Salpon. Following my mother will do you no good at all!"

The words of Mama's message to her now made sense. The time is ripe! The time to seduce him. She had sneaked into his room and presented herself as naked as a jaybird. God forbid! Heaven help him if he ever entered Mama's house again.

Mama came out of the room, minutes later, with her travelling bag. "We go go!" she said and looked at Oyinemi who promptly stood, the money Dini flung on her spilled to the floor. Dini refused to react, though he thought Mama leaving like that was gross.

Mama led the way to the front door and the sacrificial lamb followed obediently.

Moments after they had gone, Dini continued to stand at the same spot, gazing into space. How had things degenerated so much? He wanted to pity the girl Mama had chosen to use against him. I have found a virgin to give you a child—what had Mama done to convince a lady like that—an educated lady, a woman of the 21st century! He knew Mama did not go into diabolism but with her chieftaincy title who knew?!

But no, Mama had the greatest power of persuasion he had ever seen. Oyinemi Salpon has not been charmed! She's been persuaded. That realization brought a fresh rush of rage against the two women but most especially, Oyinemi. Erebi would be in on the plan as well, he knew. But this lady, who agreed to come into his life and his marriage, to defile it, could not be forgiven. Despite the fact that he had sent her to school, given her a future—She would repay him by destroying his life.

He slid to the floor in front of the mantle place and gripped his head with both hands. This can't be the end. Mama never gave up. Her resilience was the reason why all her children got educated and did well in life. He'd seen her work herself, literally to sickness, trying to get enough money to send

them to school. Mama had been the backbone of her family. When she put her hand in the plough, she never looked back!

The same strengths he had always admired in her now worked against him.

He heard Tonbra come slowly down the stairs but had no inclination to attend to her. She came to stand in front of him and when he refused to avert his gaze, sat in front of him on the floor and touched his knee. He just stared into space.

"This is a nightmare, honey. And God will see us through it!" she whispered.

Ah, the God factor. He had to keep that close to mind. After five years of marriage, he didn't have his own child and hadn't minded. Maybe because he hadn't minded, God had left it off. Or maybe Tonbra really was now a male pawpaw tree!

"You heard everything." His voice sounded husky, as though he had been crying for a long time.

She nodded. "Your words, at least. I didn't hear a word of what Mama or the—the other person said."

She looked strained. But even when Tonbra was tired, or stressed, she looked beautiful. The first few months of their lives together had been full of high stress. He'd not seen her smile once in those months and she had been so attractive to him.

And she still was.

"But you can guess?"

She nodded.

He shut his eyes at that point. Looking at her brought him pain. Why allow this evil to come between them? He loved Tonbra. He would always love her. She was everything he wanted in a woman.

Another image came to him, a dark-skinned, chubby-cheeked, pear-shaped beauty and his eyes flew open!

"While upstairs, a thought occurred to me." Tonbra became bolder and held his hands off his head, rubbing them reassuringly. "Since I can carry a baby, at least I have before, I—a lady in the foundation recently did an in-vitro—and she's pregnant with twins!"

"In-vitro." His eyes brightened. It never occurred to him. Of course, an in-vitro!

"Yes. I think we should try it."

He sat up and sighed. "It's a brilliant idea." His face tore into a smile. The muscles around his eyes relaxed and he thought he could breathe again. Good to know Tonbra was concerned as well.

"Oh my! Thank God!" She laughed. "I thought you'd not like the idea!"

"Ah, why not?" He thought his mouth couldn't go wider in a smile. "I'll talk to Dr—"

"I have a good doctor. He's in Warri. I recommended him to the lady in the foundation and—" She shrugged. "She's carrying twins now!"

"Are you sure? Warri? If it's Warri then I'd use NSH."

"Trust me. The hospital they used is in Benin, though. And it wasn't expensive. Altogether they spent less than N3m."

"Or we could do this in South Africa. I have a friend who's into medical tourism. He'll make all the arrangements and—"

"It will be sooo costly, honey."

"Do I mind?" He jumped to his feet and noting her reluctance, held out his hand to her. She placed hers in it and stood. "We'll try your doctor first anyway.

You're right, why go to SA when I can have my baby here." He grinned and pulled her into his arms. "Oh, thank you, Jesus!"

"Thank God!"

He moved back a little and looked at her. Since that horrible night he raped his own wife, he hadn't touched her. He felt guilty. He felt bad. "This will put a total stop to all of Mama's nonsense." She nodded and sighed. He touched her face, and lips. "I'm sorry for all my bad behaviour."

"I understand."

"Do you, my love? My only love?" He bent and picked her up in his arms. He nuzzled her neck. "I want to make it up to you, my sweetheart."

He took her up the stairs. She giggled like a kid in a candy store.

CHAPTER 18

"This is very important to my husband and me." Tonbra paused for a beat and added, "And you owe me!"

"I told you the consequences of these procedures you insisted you needed to do. A young woman starts to tamper with her organs—"

Tonbra swore under her breath. "Give me a break, Dr. Finidi! Those decisions are totally mine. I didn't ask for your opinion."

"Exactly my point!"

"So, what will it be?" She swallowed to calm her nerves. "When can we come and see you?"

"I don't know, Tonbra. I really don't know. I have never done or arranged an IVF before."

Tonbra gasped. "But you could. You are a doctor. You have friends. And we will pay!" He had to. She couldn't afford to meet a doctor who would get to know her history and—And know! "What about that massive hospital in Benin?"

"My friend does not actually work there. He simply has contacts."

"Well, can't his contacts do this for him?"

Finidi's voice changed over the phone. He lowered it considerably, as though he hated to say what he had to. "They don't have an IVF facility in that place, Tonbra."

"But I told my husband a friend did hers there."

"Well, you lied. They don't have the facility."

She wanted to cry. She let out a sigh that ended in a sob. "We are in this together doctor, please. Hey! What am I going to tell him now? Look, if I go down on this, you will too, I hope you know!"

Finidi's ringing laughter told her the truth. He couldn't be bothered. He knew how to cover his tracks.

"Surely Tonbra, you don't believe that. All my dealings with you are perfectly professional." He sighed on a smile. "And I gave you all the options. And told you you're choosing the worst of them all."

"But those are your words against mine!"

"Oh Tonbra, let's not go that way, okay? You'll just lose out. You signed my legal documents, didn't you? It's stated clearly that you were properly briefed on all the options and choices! I thought you read through before signing."

A strangled shriek escaped from her lips before she could stop it. "I hate you!"

"Tonbra, Tonbra! Let's talk about how you can get your IVF. I know you can get it in Abuja."

Tonbra took three deep gulps of air and shifted the phone from her right to her left. The cool air from the air-conditioner did nothing to help the sweat pouring off her skin pores.

"Abuja?" she said weakly. She wiped off the tears trickling down her face. "Do you know the doctors?"

"I can make findings for you. After all, you believe I owe you. It's the least I could do." He paused again. "With your condition, they'll need specialists who'll fetch the eggs from your ovary—" His voice trailed off.

She lowered herself to the edge of her bed. "What do I tell my husband now?"

"Huh, give him my number. Let him talk to me."

She sprang to her feet. "No way!"

"Client confidentiality, Tonbra. If I spill your beans, sue me," he said it with such quiet confidence, she believed him.

"Bye, then." She hung up before he said another word, and slowly sat down on the bed. The walls were closing in, and she feared she would not be able to hold up any longer.

She remembered the light that came on behind Dini's eyes the moment she mentioned the in-vitro. Had she missed something?

Dini had always been so crazy about, and content with his life, his children and his beautiful wife. Till Mama came with her meddling. Now their lives were in a total mess. All her careful plans shot to hell by Mama's interference. She looked around her. She deserved this life of luxury. Ebisine's children attended the best schools. Probably she should have allowed Ebisine Jr. to bear Dini's name but, how could she? She would be cheating a dead man who could not defend himself.

"Oh God, help me out of this one, please God!"

She couldn't come this far to lose everything she had worked and lived for. She opened the door at the back of her closet, the hidden place, and brought out Ebisine's picture, a studio shot. She smiled at it as she had done a million times in the past five years, amidst her tears.

She wished she could have celebrated his death every year, but Dini would not hear of it.

He'd given her money to do his grave and that was all. But of course, she visited that grave every year. With her children. It was their secret. She had warned them never to tell daddy about the excursion they took to Isaba yearly.

"What do I do, my love? How do we get out of this?" She hugged the picture and sobbed. "Why did you leave me? Why? I was happy with our life. I was ready to wait till you got your breakthrough. Why did you leave me?!"

Several minutes later, she brought out other pictures. She stored his pictures like treasures, memories that dated back to their early years together. She'd met him shortly after her secondary education at a family occasion. At just eighteen, and he, a university student, they had fallen in love at first sight.

He was her first and only love.

They had many lofty dreams. How they would travel the world together, and he would give her a good life. Well, he had not done a tenth of it. Life with him, especially after he started his crusading, had been a nightmare. They experienced constant mockery and embarrassment from creditors, constant ravage by sickness and hunger.

She took the pictures with her to the bed and spread them out. If only they could come alive.

Dini must never find them. He'd tried to wean her of Ebisine George. Tried and failed. He thought he had succeeded though. She never talked about her late husband. Never disclosed in any way her continued loyalty to their love. Never once gave off the fact that she had no intention of having any children for anyone else apart from Ebisine George. Never talked about her tied tubes—Thanks to Dr. Finidi who had made a mess of it.

That procedure had gone south, and even the corrective procedure had not been successful! Yet she couldn't allow Dini to know any of this. If they did the IVF in an independent hospital, the report would show her messed up reproductive system. Dini would know she had done those things after her last baby – an obvious malicious act against their marriage.

He would never understand she had nothing against him as a person. That her love for Ebisine George drove her beyond reason. Well, that and the gifts Dini bestowed on her, the good life he promised if she married him.

And her sacrifice was for the sake of Ebisine's children. She could sell her soul to provide for them. They were the only valuables her sweet husband left for her.

How would she have been able to explain the conflicts of those days, coupled with her grief? She has never been able to cope with Ebisine's death. Grief for him enveloped her, overwhelmed her daily, yet, she could only grieve when Dini was at work or out of the country.

Her phone rang, jolting her. She picked up and snapped, "Hello."

"My angel," Dini said softly. "What's for lunch?"

"Lunch? Huh—" Lunch? He wanted to come home for lunch? Her eyes flew to the pictures on the bed. "I'd have to ask Deborah, sorry, ur the cook.

Do you have any preference?"

"Yes. Italian." He chuckled when she gasped. "I'll pick you in two hours."

She laughed. "Okay, my love. I'll be ready. Thank you."

"I love you."

"I love you too."

"Er, did you call the doctor?"

"Yes. He asked that I give you his number. I'll text it to you just now."

"Okay love. See you in two hours. Look special."

"Okay." She giggled and hung up, and like a mad woman, packed all the pictures on the bed.

At ten o'clock she hadn't done anything but mope and cry and mourn all morning. She didn't want to have any other child for two reasons. First, she didn't want to have more children and end up being a widow a second time, but now with four or more children. Second, she had vowed to have all her children for only Ebisine George.

Well, both reasons no longer seemed good enough.

Over the years, she'd saved from what Dini gave her. She now had so much money she could care for six children on her own, if the need be. She would never marry another man if Dinipre Oyinkuru Brisibe died now. Besides, Ebisine's foundation was making a lot of money from donations, and she fixed the monetary gift from Ebisine's award in an account for her children. She could never be broke in her life like when her first husband died.

On the other hand, she could willingly give one child to Dini Brisibe if that would keep her marriage. The man deserved that much anyway. He had been good to her.

With Mama breathing down their necks and having the audacity to bring in another woman for her son, she couldn't afford to shift in her position as Mrs. Brisibe, not even for a moment.

She wasn't ready to give up her current lifestyle. She drove a jaguar, had her own staff; driver, cook, housekeeper, and a fat personal allowance apart from housekeeping! She could go anywhere she wished in the world, chose locations for vacation every holiday with her kids—No way was she giving it up because of one baby!

She wasn't ready to face Mama in a battle either. Even Dini could not face his mother. The best thing to do was to find that child and give them, God helping her.

She picked the personal portrait she hugged every day and pressed it to her lips for a long time. "Let it work for our good again, my love. I love you. Will always do."

She didn't even like Dini or the short, and fair-skinned type of men. She liked tall, dark and handsome like Ebisine. Living with Dini at all only showed her life with him compassed many sacrifices.

"Let it work for us, O God."

CHAPTER 19

The beautiful sun set to the west and provided piles of golden clouds just peering above the horizon, a delightful sight. It however provided Erebi little repose as she crossed and re-crossed her hands in her laps. She wanted to say the right things. A wrong word could shatter their fragile balance. A misunderstood statement would take them back to square one, and she didn't want that.

They had come a long way. But she thanked God things started looking up again. On a lovely, sunny afternoon as she tidied up on her class work in the staff room, Dini walked in with a huge smile on his face, bringing to an end, several months of cold silence.

Erebi had let out a gasp and excused herself to attend to him. He was full of apologies, begging her to forgive and forget. He'd gone to see Mama to apologize as well, and to call a truce.

And to give the good news. Tonbra was pregnant!

She had been so glad and excited. What more? All their concern had been for him and he'd acknowledged that fact. Their relationship had budded and once again, they were like twins, sharing everything in their lives together.

Then this. He'd called her and asked to meet at a sit-out close to his house. He'd sounded so distraught, she couldn't help but oblige him.

A wistful smile lightened her brooding face. "A miscarriage, I believe is something no one plans for. And she will recover quickly in Jesus' name."

Dini looked at her with hooded eyes. "The doctors put her on bed-rest. Still."

She reached out across the table and grabbed his hands, rubbing them gently. "It will be alright."

He slid his hands from hers and gripped his head with both of them. "I spoke with her doctor, and he said she had an ectopic before her last baby." He stared hard at Erebi.

She lowered her hands and clasped them around her glass of cold juice. How come? "An ectopic?" She gasped.

He nodded and swallowed. "She never told me about it. Both her tubes were destroyed due to the ectopic. And so, they had to harvest the egg from her ovary—I think that complication must have—"

She took a quick drink. Her throat had just gone dry. "How many ectopic did she have?"

"One. The doctor said she almost died. Her tubes were destroyed—" He bit on his lower lip, hard. "To think I was offshore while she fought for her life and she never told me!"

"Dini, a woman has two tubes. If there was an ectopic, only one tube is destroyed. Her second tube will be fine." She shrugged. "Unless of course, she had lost the first tube earlier."

A strange expression filled his face. "I don't know about these things. I'm just repeating what her doctor said. Both her tubes are burnt off!" He quivered around a sob. "That's what the doctor said." He dragged his hands over his face and his shoulders vibrated as he sobbed.

Erebi became agitated. The information she just got didn't add up. She knew very little about the medical implications of an ectopic pregnancy and made a note to make enquiries from the doctor in her school infirmary. Still, she knew that one ectopic pregnancy took out one tube not both. Could Tonbra have had two ectopics? One before, and one after delivering Ebisine? These important questions needed answers. But she never got pregnant after Ebisine.

She watched Dini weep for a while and then he let his breath out and looked at her. The veins in his temple throbbed, and his eyes had turned red.

"I'm so sorry about this, Dini. All the money you spent—"

"She did get pregnant. But the doctor said her womb may have been stressed and wasn't ready to hold a child."

"I'm so sorry." She shook her head. "After all the money."

"The money is irrelevant."

"So, what does the doctor say now?"

"I don't know. I don't know, Erebi."

He looked so dejected. He swallowed hard twice, fighting the tears and struggling to speak besides the emotions. Erebi's heart broke and tears sprang to her eyes.

"I was so sure. So glad! I was so looking forward to the baby." His sobs overtook him. They wept softly together for a while. Then Erebi sniffed and looked at him sharply.

"Her doctor is just one person. I think you should seek a second opinion. I'm not sure about the tube thing but if they got her pregnant the first time despite the tubes, they can do it again. Maybe you should try doctors here."

"I have a doctor friend in South Africa who can help. I'll call him."

"And have faith, Dini! There's nothing impossible for God. You know that!" He nodded and sniffed. "How's she though? How did she take the news?"

"She fainted." Dini shook his head. "We had to rush her to the hospital. She went to ease herself in the night and screamed—I think she saw blood."

"That's sad. So sorry. But I know there are better days ahead. You have to be strong for her!"

"I will be." He stood slowly. The night had settled in and fancy lights now lit the garden scene of the sit-out. More people arrived, and took seats in the garden drinking and eating, and dancing to the music blaring from the speakers.

Erebi stood as well. "I'll check her in the house later."

"She's at a hospice. We felt it was good for her to rest away from home."

"I think it's a good idea." She picked up her bag. "I'll check her when she returns home."

"Maybe it will be good if you can check her at the hospice."

"Okay."

He scribbled an address on a small card he withdrew from his wallet. "Here."

She took the card and looked at the address. She recognized the area and nodded. "I'll check on her right away."

Dini shoved on a pair of Ray Ban dark glasses. "Thanks a lot for lending your ears, sis." He pulled her into a tight hug.

"Thanks for trusting me." And she really meant that.

She'd betrayed him once in a bid to help him, and things had gone awful between them. She missed what they had and vowed not to betray his trust again. She was glad he could still cry on her shoulders.

They walked quietly to the car park. Erebi stood by hers and watched Dini open his car, wave at her and then got in. She did the same. She knew he would want her to leave first and she did. He followed her up to the junction, and then took the turn to his house.

Erebi found the hospice on a small, beautiful, inconspicuous turn off Marinho close in Victoria Island. The location fitted the business of the place perfectly. Two other fenced compounds sandwiched the hospice, while a no-trespass green area faced it.

The management took security seriously and needed some convincing before Erebi was allowed to see Tonbra. She had to produce Dini's call card which he'd scribbled the address on, and then call Tonbra to know if she wanted to see her.

Erebi found the environment of the hospice calming, as it should be. Light blue and soft butter cream colour combinations were used for the walls and floor tiles. Everywhere looked clean and soft music played in the background. It felt like a good hospital without the psychological dreariness.

Tonbra's room interior design with a combination of pinks and yellows left you feeling relaxed. Erebi found her propped with pillows against the

wall, watching an old edition of Time Out with Tee-A.

Her face relaxed into a smile when Erebi knocked softly and entered. Erebi smiled, not because she felt like it, but because she wanted to encourage Tonbra.

"How are you, dear?" she said.

Tonbra nodded and despite the smile, tears collected in her eyes. "Hello."

"Hello, darling. How are you?" Erebi perched on the edge of the bed, clutching her handbag.

Tonbra looked small and fragile. Her naked face looked thinner and her eyes were hollow. She clutched a huge teddy bear to her chest, but her arms were mere skin and bones.

"You've been through a lot, poor girl."

"I lost my baby."

"I know. Dini just told me. I'm sorry." She scooted forward and hugged Tonbra.

She had been warned by the nurses not to do or say anything to upset Tonbra and she didn't plan to. Tonbra burst into tears. Erebi rubbed her back till the emotions subsided, cooing gentle words of comfort.

"How's Dini? I've not seen him today, though the nurses said he came while I was asleep."

"He's strong," Erebi lied. How could she describe the true picture?

"Oh, thank you Jesus! I was so worried for him." Tonbra sniffed. "I didn't know he was that desperate for a baby. I thought he loved our kids—" She swallowed hard.

Erebi leaned back and looked away from Tonbra. Did she just say that? "You know Dini loves your kids like his own." She couldn't saw the edge off her voice. She turned to look at the frail woman. What she must have suffered, and for no fault of hers. Maybe.

Erebi couldn't help herself. She couldn't help but yield to the strange nudging to probe the questions raised in her conversation with Dini.

"We stopped seeing them as my kids the day we got married."

"I know, but a man will feel cheated without his very own," Erebi said softly. There was a lot of love lost between the two of them. She tried to push it behind her. "Human beings are just so—complex."

"If I could have this baby for Dini now, if I were God, if only God would—"

Erebi stared at Tee-A for a moment. Involuntarily, she laughed. "This guy is just a very funny person."

Tonbra turned to the screen and after a few seconds, smiled weakly. "He's good. He's just so good with his jokes."

"I'm glad you've smiled a little at least," Erebi turned back to her. "Laughter is truly the best medicine."

The conversation was awkward, she knew. She and Tonbra had spoken very little in the last few months.

"How far gone were you?"

"Three weeks or so."

"Wow. It had not even started the journey. I know Dini should be the one talking about this, but I believe there should be a next time." Erebi shrugged. "Keep trying, don't give up!"

"It's just so expensive. I feel bad about that—and I'm asking, please God, for Dini's sake, do this. Just this once!"

Erebi shifted uncomfortably. "Dini said you had an ectopic."

Tonbra's eyes widened. "He did? Why would he tell you that?" she said hoarse-ly.

Her reaction took Erebi unawares. Did she just leak a secret? "He was just trying to explain—the miscarriage—I guess."

"Even then!"

Erebi shrugged. "He needed to share his thoughts with someone, and I'm his sister. He trusts me."

Tonbra sighed and closed her eyes. Erebi almost didn't hear what she said. "Even then."

"As a woman, I have had many experiences as well. And I know one ectopic is bad enough, not to talk of two—"

"He told you I had two?" This time, the strength that came from Tonbra's voice depicted nothing of her physical state.

Erebi's mouth dropped open but she shut it quickly. "Well, how else would you lose two tubes—and still have a a baby!" She shrugged.

Tonbra's eyes widened so hard, Erebi thought they would come out by the time she was done widening them. Her voice went back to being very hoarse, and she whispered, "He told you all that?!"

"He's grieving, Tonbra. I want you to understand." She stood and picked her bag. "Just tell him the truth about what happened to you. I've known him to handle the truth better than a deceit."

Tonbra flew off the bed, tossing aside the fluffy bear, and blanket covering the lower part of her body. The gesture stunned Erebi, and she gasped.

Tonbra wore a see-through night dress which exposed so much of how she had lost weight. But nothing in her words conveyed her frailty.

"Don't ever come to see me again, you jealous witch. Your plans will never work!"

"What—?" Erebi clasped her mouth with both hands.

"Get out! Get out, you liar!"

Beyond words, and thought, Erebi opened the door, and walked out of the premises. Tonbra's twisted face and words played over and over in her head through her one-hour drive home. What had she said wrong?

Chapter 20

Dini walked into the house, his shoulders slouched. In a rare turn of events, he now played mother and father and the reasons weighed down on him. He loved to do it, but not under the circumstances. If Tonbra was indisposed because of a baby, it would be tolerable. The hospice had told him she would stay for as long as they felt she needed to and that seemed fine by him. Already, she'd stayed over a month.

The clinic used in Abuja had prepared a report to take to South Africa for a repeat of the IVF, whenever Tonbra could muster the physical and emotional strength. The loss of the pregnancy had shaken her beyond his expectation. Up until then, he'd thought she really didn't want to have any children for him.

He stood in the middle of the parlour and wondered at the quiet house. He called out to Timi and got no reply. Then he called Deborah. She ran in, breathless.

She curtseyed. "Welcome, sir."

The children should be home by now. He dropped into a single couch, distracted. "Get me a glass of cold water."

The children's school year would soon end and Dini wanted the whole family to take the trip to SA with Tonbra. It would give her the moral support she needed. He planned to ride on her obsession with the children, by taking them along, knowing it would lift her spirit.

Deborah brought in the water in a jug, with ice.

"Where's everybody?"

"They went to aunty Grace house." Deborah poured water into the glass, added some ice, and turned to leave.

"Thank you." Dini took a sip. "Aunty Grace? Did she come here?"

His question stopped the retreating lady. She turned and faced him. "Yes, sir. She said she will bring them back later."

"But they'll be starting exams in a week! They should be home, studying!"

Deborah stood still, waiting for him to dismiss her. He didn't expect her to have anything to say to that, so he waved her off. She curtseyed and left.

Grace, Ebisine Francis George's older sister, had been a recurring part of their lives.

More recently, she had been involved in her late brother's foundation and worked closely with Tonbra.

Dini hated the idea but tried to let it go. Grace was still not married, and generally in Dini's opinion, a bad influence on his wife and children but Tonbra seemed to trust her. He had never probed the level of their relationship but during the early days, he'd had the impression George's family members hated Tonbra and wanted nothing to do with her. And it seemed the feeling had been mutual.

He stood after finishing one full glass of water and went up the stairs, thinking Timi should have known better than allow her siblings to go out with Grace. Timi at just twelve had written her junior WAEC. He wouldn't have minded if she alone had gone but Pere and Ebisine had promotion exams.

Recently ten, Pere had failed all the entrance exams he wrote and now would have to repeat primary six. That worried Dini a lot because the boy lagged behind in his studies. None of the kids did as well as he would have liked but Pere performed the worst.

He made to open the master bedroom when he heard soft female laughter followed by a deep male one. He stopped short and listened. The sounds came from Timi's room across the corridor. She would soon be thirteen but had recently been displaying a lot of adult tendencies, which Dini worried about, but Tonbra found nothing wrong with, like using make-up and wearing tubes her mother insisted Timi asked her to buy.

Dini moved quietly to the door. A faint smell of cigarette smoke wafted to his nostrils from within. The two people behind the door spoke softly and giggled. When Dini heard a soft moan, he yanked on the door—it opened.

Timi, thank God, sat on her vanity, making her face up. She looked older than her age. Her body now fully developed, rounded out nicely, taking her mother's most attractive features, complexion, figure, and promising height.

A young man sprawled over, half-lying on her bed with his shoes on, smoked a slim cigarette. His dark chocolate skin looked smooth and well-toned, and he had his hair woven into cornrows.

Dini thought he'd go crazy.

Timi jumped at the sight of him but didn't get up. "Daddy!"

The young man flew to his feet, crushing the cigarette with his hand in the same vein.

"What on earth is going on here?" Dini growled. He divided a searing gaze between Timi, who wore a black and yellow polka-dotted half-cut over yellow jeggings, and the boy. He could not be less than sixteen years old or

much older if at all. His jeans sagged so badly, it hung close to his thighs, with his boxers in full view. He wore an over-sized polo shirt and on his feet were a pair of yellow, ankle all-stars.

Dini ran his gaze over him. "Who are you, and what do you want in my house? In my daughter's room?" The boy began to stammer. "Get out. Get out!"

Dini stepped away from the door to let him pass. Timi jumped to her feet and followed defiantly.

Dini's eyes widened. "Get back, Timi. You have questions to answer, young lady!"

"If you're sending him out, I'm following him. We're going for a party!" She snatched her bag off the bed and stood close behind the boy.

"Timi, get back. Don't upset me. You." He pointed at the boy. "Out!"

The boy did not move. Timi hooked her hand around his arm and stood beside him, glaring at the man who'd fathered her for the past six years of her life. The boy, well, kept his gaze on his feet.

Dini stared hard at Timi, then turned around and marched out of the room, slamming the door after him. He couldn't believe what just happened. Timi defying him in front of a stranger? Timi defying him at all. He knew he hadn't been too close to her. He sadly realized he had done little or nothing to be a part of her life! Still, he housed her, clothed her, educated her, fed her, and she called him daddy. He had authority over her.

He called on the two security men at the gate and instructed them to throw the boy out of his house then he went to the entrance of his room and stood to watch.

The boy went willingly with the men. Timi on the other hand struggled with them. She clung to the boy and dragged him with the men, till one of them gripped her by the waist and carried her off the floor while she clawed and screamed and wept and struggled. The security man with the boy back handed him when he tried to fight for Timi, and he groaned, gripping his assaulted cheek with both hands.

Dini watched with narrowed eyes. The other security man tried to put Timi down, but she clung to him, like a wildcat. Dini moved close to them and gave her a hard slap and she went limp in the man's arms.

"Drop her on the bed, and close the door behind you," Dini said. He strolled out and slammed the door after him when he entered his own room.

What on earth? What kind of a father had he been? Of course, Tonbra had shielded those children from him, and it hurt—in return, he'd remained aloof. He loved them with all his life, but he'd helplessly watched his wife take absolute charge of their lives. Now Timi, at twelve, attended parties and entertained boys in her room. What else did she do? He cringed.

He had to talk this over with Tonbra! Did she indulge them like this while he travelled around the globe? What if he had not closed early today?

He wouldn't normally be at home at this time of the day. Some expatriates visited the power plant he supervised and after a business lunch meeting, left. He'd been disinclined to return to the office.

Usually, he returned late in the evening. Most times, he only saw the children in the morning, before they went to school. He provided for their physical needs and ensured they had a family altar every morning but that was it! He didn't even know if his kids were born again!

He blamed himself. The Bible says train a child in the way he should go and when he is old, he will not depart from it. He had left the training off to Tonbra and see what she made of it! A disrespectful pre-teen who made up, wore high shoes, and dressed and behaved like an adult.

Dini undressed slowly and had a shower. He needed to rest his head. When his anger had cooled, he would go and talk to her. Apologize for neglecting her. Talk to her like the adult she wanted to be.

He sat on the bed, thinking about all the sad things happening to him recently. Most especially the loss of the baby. He'd been reassured by Tonbra's doctor the next time would be successful, but he didn't want to take the risk. He would only hope and rely on the report of his doctor-friend in South Africa. That way, he got the second opinion Erebi suggested.

He must have dozed because he jolted when his phone rang. It was Tonbra. He'd planned to visit her after speaking to Timi though he didn't plan to talk about Timi on the visit. It would upset Tonbra.

"Honey, how are you?"

Her voice sounded husky and he wondered if she had relapsed again. The matron had said the physical strain kept coming back when she cried too hard.

"I'm fine. I want to come home."

"Are you sure? Are you alright?"

"It wouldn't matter if I'm here and the house is in chaos!"

"The house is not in chaos. You worry too much."

"I want to come home tonight. Please come and pick me."

"You sound depressed. What does the matron say?"

"I don't care what the matron said. I can't sit here till my house falls on my head!"

"Why are you talking like that? The house—"

"Timi called me." She paused for effect. "She said you barged into her room without knocking while she was dressing up!" Tonbra hissed. "Please come and pick me from here or I'll take a taxi!"

Dini went quiet for a long time. What could he say? He did barge in without knocking. And indeed, she was dressing up—if applying make-up on her face meant that.

He spoke quietly. "What do you make of that?"

"She was hysterical, screaming that she did not want to live in the house anymore! What do you think I make of it?" She had gradually raised her voice as she spoke. By the time she got in her last statement, she was shouting. "Just come and take me from here!"

"I'll be there in a few minutes." He hung up without getting her reply. The conversation stunned him beyond comprehension.

He pulled on his clothes and drove out to pick her up. The nurses on duty protested but the couple insisted on Tonbra's leaving.

Dini drove her home quietly. He'd not seen Timi on his way out, and neither did he see her when he got back in. As Tonbra slowly moved around the room, undressing and wearing a more comfortable house wear, he mumbled something to her about going for a drive.

"Running off to big sis to cry on her shoulder, are you?" she shouted at him.

"What?"

"Remember to tell her what you were trying to do with your own daughter!"

He slammed the door behind him and left the house. He had nowhere to go. He just needed fresh air.

Now his wife accused him of hitting on their pre-teen daughter. Was he a beast?

Chapter 21

Six months after that dreadful day Dini disgraced Oyinemi out of his house, Mama continued to insist she drink her slimy fertility drinks. Six months of living in a balance. She told Tari their marriage had to wait, told him all manner of lies, feeling like the cheat she was—Only her case felt worse because of premeditation.

She picked up the fresh bottle Mama sent the previous week and looked at it closely. As a village girl, she grew up drinking concoctions for her ailments and well-being, so this one meant nothing but—What if she poured this one out? Would there be a difference? Did she care?

Wisdom teaches you not to cross paths with the Iyalode of Apoi. Mama was extremely powerful and as long as she intended to maintain a lifeline with her homeland, she didn't want to be in Mama's bad books. But she feared much more Mama's persuasive skills than excommunication from her village.

When she had visited home shortly after Tari's proposal, it had been to introduce him to her family and to Mama. She never expected Mama to send for her, and to demand for her 'womanhood.' Had Mama forgotten all about Tari whom she just introduced as her fiancé? Did Mama not know the implication of giving her another job? A job that demanded the highest betrayal of the love she felt for Tari?

Yet Mama never came out plainly. She brought in a meal and asked that they eat from the same dish. Then she brought out the traditional wrapper one gave to the mother of her son's children, and the expensive heavy velvet material given to the first daughter-in-law. And Mama begged her, went on her knees, to save her from the shame in the family.

Oyinemi dragged in a long breath and looked at the bottle again. That happened almost eight months earlier. Almost a year of her life, just hanging. No, she had to put a stop to this humiliation. No one could bear this for so long! And all Mama had told her was to wait.

Well, no more.

She walked resolutely to the wash-hand basin in her single-room

accommodation and emptied the bottle into it. Then she opened her wardrobe. She had no other choice but to disappoint Mama. She brought out the wrappers and laid them on her bed. She would not go herself, she couldn't face Mama. She would send the driver Mama normally used to courier the drinks to her.

She threw the bottle in the dustbin and picked up her phone. Afterwards, she would call Tari and tell him she wanted to marry him as soon as possible. Sorry, Mama. I really like your son, but he is married, and may God help him, if God can. I want my life back!

The driver picked up on the second ring. "Hello?"

"Hello, Mr. Taiwo. How are you? It's Oyinemi Salpon."

"Ha, sister. I'm fine. Hope no problem?"

"No, not at all. I wanted you to pick up something from me whenever you're free—for Mama in Apoi."

"No problem."

"Thank you, sir." She hung up before he could reply.

She spread the heavy velvet on her bed and fingered it. The rich purple-coloured fabric came with patterns in gold and red. A royal attire. Mama had told her she bought it when Dini told her he was bringing his wife home, but when she saw Tonbra, her spirit rejected her. Well, Mama could say that now. If things had turned out differently, Tonbra would have tied the cloth on the naming ceremony of her first child for Dini. Mama now wants her, Oyinemi Salpon, to do that, but it will not be possible anymore.

The second fabric, though older and less expensive carried more significance than the velvet. Mama explained that the blue, red, yellow and brown Ankara textile was given to her on her wedding day by her own mother. In her family, the mother of the bride gave one particular material to her daughter for good luck. According to Mama, she had wrapped all her children with that material, and she wanted Dini's child to be draped in it as well. Significant. But it meant nothing to Oyinemi now. She was sending it back.

She worried on what to wrap it with. A nylon bag would demean the importance and Mama could take it as a direct insult. Already, she could count the number of curses Mama would rain on her. And for the umpteenth time, she hated herself for ever getting entangled in this.

To occupy her mind with good things, she called Tari. He picked on the first ring and told her he would call back as he was in a class. She checked the time. Almost ten o'clock. He would call at about twelve when he got off on break, or immediately after the class. The joy of what she would tell him bubbled in her. Her choice made, she laughed out, excited. What joy!

She found a decent cloth-bag given at one of her friends' weddings, and carefully folded each material into it. She then got a wrapping paper. She kept the parcel on her bed and went about preparing herself for work. She would be in by noon.

She finished up marking some scripts and wore her office shoes at about a quarter to twelve. Then Tari called. Excitedly, she picked the call.

"Hello!"

"Hey, my love. How are you today?"

"I'm very fine. Missing you badly."

He chuckled. "I miss you too. And I'm glad you said you miss me."

She'd been so distant. He was a good man to still profess love for her. The conflicts in her life in the past eight months had been so distressing, she had lashed out at him, without reason. Quietly, he'd maintained his position with her, sometimes walking away dejected.

"I'm so sorry love, I've been such a—pain."

"Not at all. I understand we have seasons and pressures. That's why I've been patient. I know you'll come round."

If only you knew, love.

"I've come round, alright!" She laughed and sighed. "Can we meet after school today? I have something important to tell you."

He sucked in his breath. "Don't keep me guessing, what is it?"

She laughed. "After school, love! You're too curious."

She heard a loud knock on her door. "Hold on, please!" She called out and then laughed again as she made to the door. "I have a visitor," she told Tari. "Tonight, after classes."

"Tonight then, my love."

"Bye. I love you."

"I love you more."

She smiled and hung up and jerked her front door open. She fainted.

***

She came to find herself lying on the floor, Mama bending over her. She blinked rapidly for focus, and drew herself up, shrinking away from her nemesis to sit on the bed. What did Mama want in her room in Akure? How did she know where she lived? Well, how didn't she?

Mama stared at her for several seconds before clearing her throat. She wore her traditional regalia, blouse and wrapper made from aso-oke with head tie, and beads on her wrists and ankles and neck. And she carried her official staff.

Oyinemi opened her mouth to speak but words failed her.

Mama placed the beaded staff on the bed beside Oyinemi. "I'm sorry I scare you."

She came to herself and went on her knees. "Mama! Welcome. I wasn't expecting—"

"I know. Rise. Sit down. I no want send you message." Mama stood and began to slowly pace the room.

Oyinemi, for some reason, felt violated by the harmless gesture. She hardly ever entertained in her room. The total space also accommodated a kitchenette and a bathroom, making the bed occupy more than half of the available space. Generally, she lived a solitary life.

Until Tari came along, she had nothing but her job and her family, and her siblings usually in school or in the village, only visited sometimes. The few people she called friends also doubled as colleagues in the school.

She rose from the floor and sat down. Her eyes flashed to the parcel, and she pushed it aside, her heart thudding so fast in her chest, she feared it would burst.

Mama was speaking and she focused.

"I for send that driver Taiwo to you, but this family matter cannot we discuss with stranger."

Oyinemi stared at her. She didn't know what else to do.

Mama walked back and sat on the bed. "You notice I no come for you again after that Lagos issue. Not because I tire." She took a deep breath. "I want give him time. Then he come one day, say his wife get pregnant."

Oyinemi's face lit up. She even smiled. Then Mama's words cut her joy short. "But how can male pawpaw tree bear fruit?" Mama said. "I may be old, and not go school, but that get nothing to do with palm-reading, or knowing star, or seeing future." She clasped her hands together in her laps.

Oyinemi's blood began to pound in her forehead. Her stomach churned. No, O creator, no!

"I decide to wait. And they say she lose baby. And want take her for treatment in foreign land. And I am still waiting.

"But Oyinemi, my saviour, how much long I will wait? I am not getting young. In fact, between me and you, I am dying."

Oyinemi's eyes widened and her hands flew to her mouth. She shuddered at the information. The old woman looked nowhere near dying but who could tell. She thought of Tari and the beautiful meeting she had planned for tonight. A revival of their love! Shot to hell!

Mama sucked in a deep breath. "They say male pawpaw is pregnant only less than one month after my first son Dini disgrace us out of his house. But witch cry yesterday, and child die today! Who no know that yesterday witch kill today child?"

Oyinemi twisted her fingers in her laps, and looked at them, forlorn. Could she bear this any longer? Why succumb to this nonsense anyway? What could be the worst thing Mama would do to her?

"I no wait for God of Dini and Tonbra to perform miracle they cry to him for again!" Mama's voice broke. Oyinemi's eyes shot to her face, but Mama's tears were dry. "Even the prophet of Baal in Bible they carry round

cry from morning till night without answer! They forget from Bible God is no magician. Whatever man sow, he will reap. They have forget that if God be God, every man be liar!"

She sat straight. "Oyinemi, they think I no know way of God they serve, but I know him better." She shrugged her feeble shoulders. "I may not know why or how, but I know Tonbra will never get children again! She has finish the allocation God give her! Maybe she abort half, I no know—"

Oyinemi did not know where her voice came from but she interrupted before she could stop herself. "I cannot, Mama. Please don't ask me to go back to to this plan. Please." She cried. "I want to get married and have a life of my own. I want to move on, Mama, please."

She slid to her knees. "You know I would have done this for you, and for for your son, at least to repay him for sending me to school, and for helping my family—but I can't try again. He—he doesn't want me. Please, Mama—"

She crawled to Mama and put her head on her laps. "Please find someone else. There are many women who would be glad to do this for for your son. So many. Please." She sniffed, pulled herself together and sighed. "Please."

"Where I go start from?" Mama whispered.

Her hand went to Oyinemi's head and she massaged her hair with work-worn roughened fingers. "Dini like you. I see it for his eye when we go his house. He no want face you with anger. No want talk. I know he like you."

She lifted Oyinemi's chin up, and tears trickled down her weathered face. "You think I no know sacrifice you are doing? You think I no feel your pain?

"I feel your pain, Oyinemi, and I no want allow you to shame again." Her fingers cleaned the tears off Oyinemi's face, ignoring the one on hers. "Our people say way you dress to visit in-law will make them know if to ask you to pound yam for lunch. I fail in giving you two times, and I no want fail, again! Trust me, my daughter. Trust me."

Doubts beset Oyinemi's lonely and daring soul. Could she?

CHAPTER 22

Things went from bad to worse. Eventually, Dini moved into the guest chalet.

Leading up to that, several incidents happened made Dini distraught. After the episode with Timi, she became distant, and when he called her and tried to talk through everything, she presented a stone-wall. Tonbra didn't help matters. She became grouchy and cranky and Dini realized something else, lack of interest. He knew he had to do something to guard his home from degenerating.

Though the boys didn't know what, they knew something was terribly wrong. Invariably, they became cold and unyielding, especially Pere. Their exam week approached and with the tension at home, Dini doubted they'd do well.

In order to snatch them out of the quagmire, one day, he drove home when he knew they'd all be out. The boys would be in school. Being a Tuesday, he knew Tonbra and Timi would have gone to the headquarters of the EFG foundation where Tonbra devoted two days a week. Since Timi had finished her junior WAEC, she followed her on those days.

He wanted to surprise them. Get their passports and the visas necessary and then present to them. He'd taken his family to Europe and America, Dubai and some African countries but they'd never been to SA though they'd heard so much about the beautiful country. He saw his chance to level the ground between him and them.

So much tension had built up in the house. Tonbra did not feel well enough to handle conflicts so he'd not bothered her with the details of the fiasco with Timi. He preferred to leave her thinking the worst about him till the storm in their marriage calmed, which he hoped to achieve on the trip to SA. Timi's issue could not be swept under the carpet. They both needed to work together to help her from ruin. There had to be unity between them to battle the decadent path Timi seemed to have chosen to follow.

Since that day, his daughter had maintained a distant and hard profile. At just twelve years old? How could a child that young be so—cynical? At her age he was his parents' puppet.

He never dared do anything they didn't ask of him. He never dared raise an eye at his father or mother.

The house was as quiet as it ought to be. Deborah met him in the sitting room and after a brisk welcome, disappeared into the house to continue with her chores. Dini took the stairs two at a time, feeling a rush of excitement. The heat in his home had worn him out. He missed the loving environment and warmth of family.

He walked to his wardrobe where he kept a safe that contained all his important documents. After bringing out all, including his passport, he didn't find Tonbra, or any of the children's passports. He searched all over again, sure all the passports should be in one place.

His first impulse was to call her. He brought out his phone and started to dial. Then stopped. Why did she remove the passports for her and the children, leaving his alone? Did she have plans to travel without his knowledge? A bout of anger seized him.

He turned round and headed for her closet. Tonbra's closet was some other people's bedroom. When they'd bought the house, she had insisted she wanted a room of her own. Instead, Dini had opted to carve out a large walk-in closet for her.

It did not materialize immediately until a few weeks before the IVF, he got an architect to design something satisfactory for her. But he never bothered to see what had been done there as long as she liked it.

The heady scent of her perfumes hit him first. Tonbra sure knew how to smell good. He looked round, wondering where to start from. Her shoes occupied racks on two of the four sides of the room, floor to ceiling. Drawers, so many small ones, lined one side and then her vanity, just by the door, next to a full-length mirror. A long-cushioned bench, in the centre of the closet, divided the room. Where did she hang her clothes? No clothes in sight, in fact.

He started opening the drawers one by one. Clothes, clothes, clothes, lay neatly folded in all the drawers, except for four which had her lingerie and under wears. Dini felt like an intruder as he lifted clothes in search of the passports. What if he found them, how would he tell her he went in search of them? When we get to that bridge—

He lifted her underwear gingerly, feeling a longing in his loins. It had been a while since he had his wife! Succumbing to a carnal urge, he lifted a bunch and pressed them against his face, dragging in a long breath.

"Oh." He replaced the under wears and slowly closed the drawers.

Where now? He would have left with the thought that she probably kept them in her office at the foundation, instead, he sat on the bench and looked round again. He hadn't found her hung clothes, skirts- and trouser-suits.

He hadn't seen her jewellery either.

Then he noticed two handles in the middle of one side of the wall, obscured from view by the shoes. A closet behind the shoe rack? He went for it and almost laughed when he walked into a walk-in wardrobe. Her clothes hung on one side, and more drawers built in on the other side. He tried to open the drawers, but they were locked!

"Oh my!"

He'd just have to ask her when she returned. He started to close the hidden closet and noticed a lone nail with two small keys hanging down. He seized them, pleased. One of the keys opened all ten drawers. Several of the drawers held Tonbra's jewellery. Some held her head gears and expensive traditional wears.

One held all her documents, including the passports—and land documents he knew nothing about, car documents he knew nothing about, and check books he knew absolutely nothing about! When did she build this private world? When you were busy making all the money for her!

He quietly withdrew the passports. What a mess? She had a life he knew nothing about!

He started to leave, hanging the two keys back, but his spirit failed him. He stood for a long while, feeling dizzy. Sweat broke out on his forehead despite the central air-conditioning in the room. On impulse, he picked the keys and returned the passports the way he found them. This was a whole mistake, intruding—trespassing her—violating her privacy.

He decided to go back to his office as though nothing had happened. He was wrong to be in her closet without her knowledge, touching her...things. He swallowed hard and marched out of the inner closet. But the reality left him dazed. He looked round the outer closet. At the glamour, the beauty, the lifestyle.

"You'd better not deceive me, Tonbra!" He slumped on to the bench and held his head with both hands, characteristically, staring at nothing in particular.

This couldn't be true. Did Tonbra plan to leave him?

He didn't know how long he stared but he soon realized he was staring at another lock. This, a tiny one partly hid by the heel of a shoe.

If he hadn't been staring, he wouldn't have seen it. He had no doubt the second key he'd seen in the inner closet would open it. Dini walked back in, took the key, and with all confidence turned it in the lock. It opened and swung inwards.

He pushed it further and came face to face with the life portrait of Ebisine Francis George Snr.

***

The visitor entered Mama's sitting room and took a seat without being asked. Mama sat in her highchair, the one she used to receive visitors in her capacity as the Iyalode of Apoi.

Grace Layefa George greeted in the traditional way, her knees bent to the ground, and then went back into her seat. "You sent for me."

"You owe me," Mama said, looking stern. "And I want call the favour now."

Grace's lips twisted into a half-smile. "You have done so much for me, Iyalode. Anything for you is not too much."

"It is very simple. Come close."

She leaned forward and Mama whispered her needs. They exchanged words for a while, the two being alone to hear what they talked about.

A fuller smile lit Grace's shrewd face. She returned to sit and looked at Mama. "That is easy enough. There is an occasion coming up.

Prepare your person and give me the date. I will influence it."

"They must no any mistake. The party cannot—"

"Mama, I know. I know. Just give me a date and get your person ready."

"You cannot fail."

"I will not fail." The smile on Grace's face became chilling.

***

Dini's knees gave way under him, and he went down. His head became light and he thought he would faint. A wave of nausea followed, and he took large gulps of air to control it. When he thought he could, he slowly stood and stared at the handsome dead man smiling at him.

He'd been living in this house for the past four years. Had this ghost been sleeping in the same room with him all along? Dini looked round, unable to fully process the sight.

Light shone brightly in what Dini could only describe as a shrine. The sweet smile on the dead man's face spooked him. The live portrait made it look like Ebisine George stood facing the door to welcome visitors.

Pictures hung on the walls flanked the portrait. Family pictures, old pictures, burial pictures—the children's pictures at different ages till date. The room had only enough leg space for nothing more than two people with no place to sit. Tonbra obviously didn't come here to relax. She visited, updated and did whatever anyone did with a—ghost.

Dini retraced his steps out of the space and locked up. He managed to return the key and leave the closet altogether. Back in his room, he rushed to the bathroom and opened the tap over his head. His stomach heaved till the heavy nausea subsided.

By the time Tonbra returned in the evening, Dini had moved to the guest chalet. She probably thought he had taken his sulking over Timi to the next level.

CHAPTER 23

A bright light shone in their dreary situation when upon returning from South Africa, Erebi invited the family for her first daughter, Bodi's matriculation party.

The trip to South Africa had been dreadful, though the children enjoyed themselves fully. For Tonbra, she spent all of the month in the hospital, and later, recuperating. Dini tried to be as supportive as possible through it all. They made up their differences and tried to be happy for one another's sake, but things didn't run smoothly. The operations yielded nothing and Timi's issues silently disappeared from the radar.

She said, "Let sleeping dogs lie."

He said, "Let by-gone be by-gone."

At the end of the trip and after spending in excess of five million naira, Tonbra and Dini once again agreed they should focus on pouring their lives into their children. They agreed anyone probing the child issue planned to break up their marriage and they needed to fight the person off.

On his own, Dini decided to be more available around his family. He delegated more of his duties in the office so he could have family time. He pushed his ordeal in the closet as far back as possible and tried not to cringe each time Tonbra walked in there to dress up. He didn't know what to do about it yet but vowed he would do nothing till he knew for sure, it was the right thing.

Bodi had gained admission into the esteemed University of Lagos and Erebi and Tobi had promised to throw a party for her.

Meant to be a Christian party, and so supposed to be over before night, no one prepared for the jamboree it turned into. After the ceremony on campus earlier in the day, their family and friends went home to commence the party. With abundant food and excess drinks, parents gathered with their friends and family members inside the house while the younger generation clustered, ate, drank and partied on the well-manicured grounds.

Contrary to what Erebi expected, the guests kept coming and going till late in the night. Then someone brought palm wine or palmy as they called it, from Apoi, a special gift from the Kalasuwea of Apoi himself, in congratulating his Iyalode on the ceremony for her granddaughter. Mama had been unable to come but sent lots of her love, and a live goat, which quickly turned to barbecue.

At about 9pm, with *suya* and palmy disappearing fast through a remnant of guests and family members, Dini stood to leave. Tonbra had excused herself at about seven and gone home with the children. Andrew, Dini's distant cousin encouraged him to stay. The young man, about Dini's age, had taken so much palmy, he was tipsy, and his speech slurred.

"I have service tomorrow morning, Andrew." Dini wagged a finger at him. "You should go home too."

"The wife—is—sick!"

Someone pushed a glass of palmy into Dini's hand. He shook his head with a smile. "I don't take alcohol."

The lady pressed it into his hand. "Just a sip," she said. "It's special. It's not fermented. To God!" She swore.

"Take—something—Dini!" Andrew said.

"You—know—how—we—used—to—"

Dini laughed. "Gone are those days when we were stupid." He looked at the lady with the palmy. She carried a big bottle in one hand and the glass in the other. He shook his head and laughed again. "Drinking to stupor and competing over who recovered first. No way!"

"Here—put—" Andrew held out his glass and the young lady filled it, laughing throatily.

Dini suspected she was drunk as well. He didn't recognize her. She would be in her thirties though so she couldn't be Bodi's friend. Maybe one of the ladies who came with the other relatives. Couldn't be Erebi's friend because of her outfit. She wore a tube dress that left little of her heavy bosom to the imagination. Her make-up was loud, unmatched to her profile. Women like her looked better without make-up but they somehow never knew it. And her false lashes seemed too—fake.

He looked round for Erebi and her family. The sitting room still had a lot of people, more than twenty if he counted, but he knew most of the faces. He saw Tobi at the far end of the room with one of the men from Ijaw Youths Association, just before the lady pressed not only the glass, but her body against his.

She giggled wildly. "Bro, be a man!"

He took the glass from her, laughed, gulped the whole drink, and winked at her. She laughed again. The drink hit the bottom of his belly and his head went light.

That drink could not be fresh palm wine, Dini thought. He lowered himself to his seat and tried to focus. He belched several times and smiled at Andrew whose face looked about ten times bigger and spun in an outrageous way. He reached out to him and thought he could touch him but couldn't.

"What's wrong, bro?"

Dini could feel his environment but couldn't connect with it.

"Here, water." A cool glass touched his lips and the cool water trailed a path down his throat, giving such a soothing effect. He looked at the person holding the glass. Blur.

He couldn't control his movements. He heard Andrew laugh out at him and say something about being weak. He leaned his head back, his eyes rolled up and he tried to rise.

"You can't go anywhere," a female voice said. Erebi?

"You're stoned." A man laughed. "Man, you're weak!"

"Help me up." He heard his own voice as though from a distance.

He felt Andrew's arms lift him and then dragged him. Erebi came forward at some point. She sounded concerned. Dini said he'd be fine if he only could rest for a while, but he didn't think they heard him. Mostly the conversation revolved in his head.

A door opened and he felt the coolness of sheets under him, a welcome relief. He didn't have a headache, yet. But he felt light and heavy at the same time. Stoned, Andrew said. It felt like it. Stoned.

Someone pulled his shoes off. Voices sounded as though in a far distance. A little rest would do. A little sleep. Someone's face came close to him. His eyes felt so heavy he didn't know whether they were open or not because he couldn't see anything. Yet his sense of touch seemed to be working for all his other senses. A cool hand touched his forehead. A conversation went on for a while, but he didn't quite comprehend and then he heard the door close.

He closed his eyes, and then opened them, or the other way around.

The door must have opened again, or they had not all left. H could feel a cool body lay beside him. He turned but his eyes must be closed. He lifted his hands, but they didn't move.

"What's wrong with me?"

"Nothing."

The whispery voice calmed him beyond expectation. A woman. Okay, so his throat worked now. He tried to sit up and succeeded until he felt her hands over him. She was taking his clothes off. He thought she seemed in a hurry. He lifted his hand, but they seemed too short to reach her, and the effort took too much energy. The lights had been turned off but a reflection from beyond the windows wafted in through drawn curtains. He couldn't see her face but she—woman—

"What are you doing?"

She did not reply. And then he knew.

***

She stumbled off the bed, landed on the floor on her backside and rolled as far away as possible. He snoozed, cuddled like a satisfied child. He'd slept off on top of her and she had to use all her energy to push him off. She had to get away. Now. But she had to catch her breath and control the pain searing through her body. She sat against the wall facing the bed and drew her trembling knees up, close to her chest. He didn't snore. He slept like a baby.

What a—beast.

As soon as he knew what she was up to, he had taken over. They'd told her he would. A sob escaped her lips and she clasped her hand over it. She couldn't wake him up now. Silent tears ran down her cheeks—she swiped it off with annoyance. They had coached her on what to do—to set him off. And like clockwork, everything had gone according to plan.

What she hadn't planned was the hunger with which he attacked her. Or the length of time it took. They'd simply told her it would not last more than ten minutes. It lasted two hours! Unless the wall clock didn't work. He'd just kept on and on and on.

She crawled to where her clothes had been shed near the door, and with hands that refused to stop shaking, got dressed. A car should be waiting for her outside, if the time had not lapsed. A sob broke from her lips and her hand flew to stop it.

She'd come in through the kitchen and ought to go out the same way. She hoped the car would still be there. She'd been told all would be fast— For the first several minutes, it seemed he tried to discover her, touching places, giving off pleasant feelings, and then he had devoured her, rushed her, caused pain! The remaining time, she was too numb, and scared to feel anything. In that, they had lied to her. They said she would enjoy it! What would she do if the driver had left after waiting so long and not seeing her?

She saw the taxi parked on the road, at the same place she'd been dropped. The driver dozed. She hadn't taken time to see what car she came with because of nerves. She knocked on the window of the taxi, and the driver jumped, winding down quickly.

"Sorry, u don wait for long?"

"No," she whispered.

He opened the back door for her, and she got in. She hardly knew anywhere in Lagos. Everything had been planned for her. She could never forget that day she met a lady who introduced herself as Chikito.

Chikito had been contracted and had a plan for her. She would be taken to a hotel in Lagos that Saturday morning and would be there till Chikito came for her. She would go into the room they'll describe for her, undress,

and excite the 'stoned' man on the bed the way they'll show her. The plan had gone as planned, except that no provisions had been made for the rotten way she felt.

She would be back in Akure first thing in the morning.

Oyinemi had wanted to know if the man would recognize her. She had insisted on knowing before ever leaving Akure. Chikito had been modestly convincing. The man comprehended nothing except for the manner his body moved him! Poor animal. Would he ever know?

The taxi driver stopped in front of her hotel and she stumbled out, muttering her gratitude. The driver shook his head, much the same way she shook her head when she saw prostitutes along some roads on G.R.A in Akure. Well, she wasn't a prostitute, if it mattered any more. She had paid the ultimate sacrifice. She had sold her soul to the devil.

The hotel room repelled her, but she needed the rest it would give. First, she needed a scrub. Her privates felt tender, yet she spared no part of her body the vigorous cleansing.

Afterward, she wrapped herself in the large duvet and wept till her strength finished.

She had given up everything to get pregnant for Dinipre Oyinkuru Brisibe. After she arrived at the hotel, she'd been asked by Chikito to watch countless X-rated movies to prepare her for what lay ahead. She had been disgusted but what choice did she have? She had chosen this path!

She closed her eyes tight, refusing to look at this dreary place. Of course, Chikito could not be anyone's real name, being a slang commonly used for high-class and beautiful ladies, so who was she? Someone being paid or another victim of Mama's imposed influence. Someone who owed on a favour like her?

She prayed she would never see the lady again. Wished she could wish even Mama away.

But all for no use because even as she wished it, Dinipre Oyinkuru Brisibe's seed probably swam to destiny in her womb.

*
*
*

Dini came to, at first disoriented about his environment, and then with poignant realization, flew off the bed. He landed on his feet and doubled over. If he didn't know the layout of the room, he would have missed the bathroom and thrown up on himself. When he felt better, he staggered to the room, and found his clothes on the floor. He checked the time. 3.15a.m.

God.

This couldn't have happened to him! He felt like a complete fool. Of course, he remembered everything. He had taken laced palmy. Laced with

what, he didn't know. An overdose of Viagra, maybe, because he had never felt such an urge in his life—and the woman!

Who did this to him? Erebi? Why would she do this to him, set him up? He held his head for a moment to keep steady. He didn't have a hang-over, really, just—disgust. He should have gone home with Tonbra and the kids. Should have known that a responsible believer didn't succumb to a glass of palmy. Should have discerned his season of trials and temptations. Should have understood the signs of the times!

God.

He walked slowly out of the room, feeling able to drive now. His head was clear, and his eyes were sharp, though he felt—sated—after the night with the woman—

He found Andrew sprawled on the couch in the parlour, snoring and oozing off a thick alcoholic smell. Dini walked past him. Who knows if he was part of the plan? He'd not seen Andrew in years, and the guy had just clung to him throughout the party, encouraging him to stay back when he could have gone with Tonbra, teasing him into taking the glass— He groaned in frustration. No. No going quietly or being quiet about this. There had been a woman with a glass of palm-wine, already laced with a deadly sex-drug. They hadn't planned for him to sleep or die. The drink was meant for— He shook Andrew roughly. The latter jumped up.

"Dini! How do you feel now?"

He narrowed his eyes and took a deep breath to control the storm threatening to burst within him. "Someone drugged me."

The words made Andrew come wide awake, giving Dini the impression, he probably knew nothing about it.

"It's not true! Why?"

"I don't know. But I'm going to find out before I'm done!"

Andrew sat up and rubbed his eyes. "Can you drive? I can take you home if you want, and hike back in the morning."

Where did Andrew live?

He discarded the question immediately it crossed his mind. He didn't care at this moment. They'd talked all evening about the country, and sports and nothing about their personal lives. Well, no thanks. He wasn't taking up any more offers tonight!

"I'm fine." He headed toward the front door.

"Dini!"

"Yes?"

"I don't think you were poisoned. Maybe because it's been long since you took those stuff."

Of course, he was drugged. He knew. The woman would know too. Could it be the same woman who gave him the drink that came back to—? That dirty-looking woman?

God.

"See you, Andrew."

Chapter 24

When he got home, he went to sleep in the guest chalet. He couldn't imagine going to his wife though he'd moved back to his matrimonial room on the family's return from South Africa.

His stomach still turned and during a long shower in the bathroom, he threw up again, this time feeling eternally better. He hadn't been able to sleep back. Instead he stretched out on the bed and gazed at the ceiling. He knew he had to push the guilt aside to chronicle the events. He had failed God.

How could he have fallen so easily? So accessible to such a foul play. Next time, it could be death, and then he would be dead by now, and go straight to hell. Was he to fear eating and drinking in his own sister's house? Well, Erebi had to answer that! And he had to check his own urges for forbidden food and drink.

Beside the angry thoughts at his foolishness came the erotic thoughts about the woman, which he struggled to resist.

He closed his eyes and sprang them open, turned from side to side, yet he couldn't get it away. There were things about that woman— She could be beautiful. If it was the same one who gave him a drink, she looked okay, at least. His body had fitted hers perfectly. Well. He'd plundered her. He blanched at the thought of his lack of control. That he remembered so well horrified him. What had they mixed in that drink?

The planners knew him well. They knew his love for *palmwine*. If another alcoholic drink had been used, he would likely not have fallen for it. They knew the potency of their drug too. He didn't become sick, just overly horny. Charged to the point of no control. He didn't go unconscious. He knew, saw, and acted according to their script.

His throat went dry and he tried to swallow. With the realization came the fear of the consequences. Who was she? What was the plan? Where would she take this experience to? Could it have been to compromise him at work? Or to compromise his marriage. Or— He hadn't remembered she gave him protection!

The child thing.

Could Mama and Erebi have planned this with that—that Salpon girl? But was she the one he slept with? He didn't know. He didn't know if women could be easily differentiated in the dark. Of course, he knew Tonbra's body so he could know her just by touch.

Ah, Tonbra. How would he tell her? He had never cheated on her. She on the other hand, cheated daily, with a ghost! But he hadn't been able to bring the topic up, despite his anger and pain, and plain old disgust. He'd told her he wanted the whole family to go to SA for the vacation, while she did the IVF. And asked her to send their passports to his corporate affairs department, which settled the issue. She didn't have a clue he'd discovered her 'second' life. Could he keep this from her as well? Would it be possible?

Dini taught a class in Sunday school. But rising from the bed of adultery, he decided not to go near that responsibility. Taking the class became a huge burden. He had first-hand experience of not knowing how God would feel, with him in front of the people and telling them God loved them and hated sin. He couldn't.

At the Sunday school teachers pre-fellowship where teachers prayed together before classes commenced, he felt a strong urge to hand his class over to his assistant. It was the proper thing to do. But the coordinator would expect him to give a reason why he couldn't teach. He couldn't lie about that. And he couldn't confess either. So he sat quietly, till the meeting ended and then wished he'd lied when the coordinator assigned him to take the summary.

He wouldn't be standing all defiled in front of his class of about hundred people alone, he would face the 2,500-strong congregation. He stammered a response and the teachers dispersed.

The topic on the pride of Lucifer would continue from the previous week. It had been fulfilling to teach on the attributes of Lucifer. They had highlighted the characteristics of Lucifer and what made him proud. What turned his 'good' pride to a 'bad' one.

From scriptures, they established pride could be bad or good.

For instance, Paul, 'magnified' his office, and 'boasted' in the Lord. Lucifer was beautiful, rich, and full of talents. And many believers had these same attributes.

"Today, we're concluding the topic on the pride of Lucifer." He looked round the class, unable, for the first time since his first day as a teacher, to look into the members' faces. "Who can remind us of all the things in our lives that can make us proud?"

Several hands went up and people enumerated them: beauty, a good job, power, influence, affluence, talents, gifting, a good background, good education, intellect and so on.

Dini inhaled. "We're all correct." God please sorry.

"The pride of Lucifer began when he started to realize his many endowments with all these attributes. He noticed he was more beautiful, more gifted, more endowed, and had more influence than the other angels. In fact, he started feeling God had nothing he did not have! Let's go back to our texts, Isaiah 14:12-20. Ezekiel 28:2-10."

Two different people read the two scriptures and Dini delved with considerable ease into expatiating on the word of God.

"There is danger, when you start feeling self-sufficient. Our sufficiency is of the Lord. 2 Corinthians 3:5. Many people feel they can handle things on their own. Can anyone tell us in what areas people feel self-sufficient?"

Hands went up again. A man stood. "In choosing a life partner." The class cracked with laughter.

Dini felt light. And then tensed. That hit too close to home. He never prayed for one day about the choice of his wife. "You are very correct. Many people even misconstrue the scripture that 'he who finds a wife finds a good thing!' Our finding should be through the help of God." He looked round and picked a lady raising her hand.

She stood. "When we have a good job, we stop trusting God for our daily needs."

"A very good one too. Once your salary can carry, you only plan, and forget God may want you to spend that money of yours differently. Any other?" God was hitting hard on him. Oh God, please, please. Sorry, Lord!

Someone else stood. "There are things we know how to do, and because of our knowledge, we feel we don't need God."

"O-kay. Like what?" Dini said. I'm hearing, God. I'm sorry.

The man who had spoken, half-way back on his seat, stood again. "For instance, if you have a good voice and can sing in the choir, you only work on your skills, and leave prayer out."

"Good one. Which other things do we do based on our secular knowledge?"

"Education too. Some people are very smart. They read and forget to pray."

"Okay. Anything else?"

"Vocations like sewing, cooking, driving—"

"Very true."

"Going into business. Some people just know a business is good, or in vogue and they just go into it without asking God."

Dini nodded profusely. "That's correct. It goes into all other decisions we make too like course to study in the university, person to marry, and so on. So does anyone want to tell us any other area of self-sufficiency?"

"When you have someone who can help you, you tend to focus on that person and forget to rely on God."

"Beautiful!" Dini smiled and nodded at the lady who had spoken.

"Uncles and parents, even your spouse or friends at times. I hope we're learning something and discovering ways to repent." Several people nodded.

"Now, how do you know your pride is no longer a good pride? You know last week, we said pride can be good when it is in the Lord. God wants His children to pose for Him and for His sake. But when does our boasting become the kind of pride Lucifer had?"

After a pause, a man raised his hand and Dini called him. "I think when your focus changes."

"In what way?"

The man groaned. "Well, when your priorities change."

Dini laughed. "Okay, help us." He looked at an elderly woman who now raised her hand.

"I believe this is when you focus on God and not other people before and giving the glory to God. And then that changes. You start feeling you are the one doing what you're doing, and not God helping you."

"Thank you very much, ma. You nailed it. You're both right. That's why the Bible says if you think you are strong, take heed, lest you fall. 1 Corinthians 10:12.

"The moment you begin to feel it's me, or it's all about me, you are on the brink of a fall.

If we go back to our main text in Isaiah, you'll see Lucifer started comparing his abilities to that of God's. You become so self-consumed in yourself you no longer see God in the things you do.

"And this happens in a very subtle manner. It doesn't come in one day! Some people even become arrogant in their humility. What I mean by that is you start taking the glory for your humility." Some people laughed, others nodded with serious faces. "We need to be careful. The moment you start saying in your heart, 'men, I'm good!' you're looking for trouble." He checked his watch. Fifteen minutes more!

"Let's move fast. Reading our texts in Isaiah and Ezekiel, do you see the evil that will befall a proud person who has chosen to raise his head against God? Can we check those things out? Isaiah 14. Let's look at it from verse 15. What's the first thing there?"

There was an incoherent chorus.

Dini's voice rose above the murmur.

"Casting down. A bringing down. That position will be taken. That thing that makes you proud will be taken. You can imagine a rich man becoming poor. A beauty turning ugly.

Knowledge becoming extinct. Let's move on. What's the next one?"

Another chorus.

"People will see it. You will not be disgraced secretly. It is not our portion in Jesus' name." A loud 'amen' went up.

"Okay, the next one is similar to the first one. We have to hurry now. Do you see it? When people are enjoying, the proud man will be suffering. Okay. Let's go quickly to the last segment of our manual. How do you come out of pride, or how can you help someone who is proud to come out of it?"

Someone stood. "I think only God can help a proud man, because no matter what you say, he thinks he knows more than God Himself."

"So, the only thing to do is pray that God will help the person?"

"Yes, deacon. Only prayer."

"So, is it possible for a proud person to be restored back to God?"

The elderly woman stood again while some rumblings of disagreement went around the class. "It is possible for a proud person to be restored. God can humble him."

Dini laughed. "So, it is still God who has to humble him."

Some nodded but some shook their heads. Dini called on one of the people shaking his head.

"I believe God does not forgive pride. That is the ultimate sin. It is Lucifer's sin. He was not forgiven, and God does not forgive it."

A woman stood without being called upon. "What if the person asks for forgiveness? Look at Nebuchadnezzar?"

The man nodded. "Yes. But proud people don't ask for forgiveness! Even Nebuchadnezzar was turned into an animal before he realized himself! Look at Judas! Pride made him not to ask for forgiveness!"

The class went up in a roar. People started arguing. Dini clapped his hands till the class quieted.

"Our time is up. We can ask our questions during the summary. Let's bow down our heads."

While a man prayed, Dini quietly thanked God for helping him during the lesson, and not take his last night's sin into account.

During the summary, another question came up. A young man in probably his twenties or early thirties, from another Sunday school class stood.

"We see all these proud people still excelling. This their punishment is it for after their death alone? Then what is the use now? They marry the prettiest women, drive the fastest cars and live life to the fullest. At the last minute, they become born-again, die and go to heaven. Is this fair?"

Dini clapped. "Praise the Lord! Praise the Lord," he said, to calm the uproar caused by the question. "You have raised a good point brother but consider this. There are several inferences in the Bible about God being a just God. There is the parable of the hirelings in Matthew 20:1-16. This talks about God calling people at different hours of the day, symbolizing different seasons of life. When you get home, you can read it. The Bible also says you are not to envy the wicked. Find that in Psalms 37:7-9 and verses 35 to 38 of the same chapter.

"Now to answer your question, proud and arrogant people are everywhere around us. They may drive the best cars, but you don't know the problems that cruise with them in those cars. Air-conditioned cars but the heat in their lives may defy any external cooling.

"Their houses may have twenty rooms while you're managing two rooms with your wife and four kids, yet you snore while they're roaming the rooms, worried the alarm system may not be working!"

He looked round the now-still auditorium. He had their full attention.

"Their wives may be prettier than yours but does that guarantee they would rather not marry an ugly woman who would not cheat on them." He began to count off his fingers, suddenly realizing an overwhelming anger rising in him. His statement hit hard on him. "A woman who would give them beautiful children, make them happy! Submit to them, satisfy them—a beautiful woman is just a window dressing!"

He stole a quick glance in the direction where the ministers and their wives sat. The head pastor nodded profusely. His wife had travelled but her seat beside him remained unoccupied. Tonbra sat in her pretty and ladylike way, her hands clasped on her knees, her legs crossed at the ankles. Her face, expressionless.

"So, when you envy an unhappy man, you are trying to slap God in the face. Do we get that?" There were nods and murmurs. "I have a beautiful wife, a lovely home, a good job and I serve God. The day I start thinking I got these because 'the boy is good', I'll start going down, no doubt!" He couldn't say he had lovely children much as it was on the tip of his tongue. The owner of the children lived in an inner closet in his room!

"Another angle to this question is that God knows the heart. He looks at our hearts. Sometimes, people make innocent mistakes. Why do some proud people go scot-free, as you say, and some like Judas and Nebuchadnezzar suffer the consequences? The difference is the heart. So only God can judge that. The Bible says even the lawful captives shall be delivered. Isaiah 49:24 and 25. Why? The heart.

"So, in conclusion, love God and serve Him, honour mankind and be true to yourself. And leave God to sort the rest. And God will help you, in Jesus' name. Amen." A thunderous chorus of 'amen' followed his.

"Let's rise up and pray concerning what we have learnt today. Remember Lucifer's tragedy. Pray that God will deliver you from it. It is so easy to get carried away by the good things of life."

He prayed softly. The coordinator of the service walked up to the altar and he handed over the service.

The head pastor nodded at him and he reciprocated respectfully. He took his place beside Tonbra and discovered he had tears in his eyes as he took the prayer point he'd given. He didn't think his life made much sense anymore.

***

The service closed right on time and Dini walked up to greet the head pastor, Pastor Flo.

"That was a brilliant response to the question in Sunday school, Deacon Dini," the fifty-something year old man of God said. "Thank you."

Emotion clogged in Dini's throat and he nodded. "Thank you, sir." He couldn't help the tears that pooled in his eyes.

Pastor Flo frowned. "Are you alright?"

Dini nodded. How could he be appreciated by this clean and holy man of God after last night? He opened and then shut his mouth. He couldn't talk about it. Not now, and definitely not here. "I will have to see you—"

"We should talk sometime soon, Deacon. Call me." The man of God said, as someone else took his attention.

"Definitely, sir." Dini gave a small bow and stepped back.

Usually, he got to church earlier than Tonbra and the kids and left later. But today, he couldn't be around people. He mumbled an excuse away from the ministers' prayers, and post-service fellowship, and left church.

He couldn't go home either.

Chapter 25

Dini's office was on the tenth floor of the Power House on Marina. His organization was straddled with the task of solving the national power problem and as the energy engineer in charge, and head of the technical team, his office was a mini workshop with models and sample materials covering most of the 80sqm space.

It was also his haven. He lived here more than he lived at home. He could articulate his thoughts better here. And right now, he had a lot to think about. He switched on only the air-conditioner and sat in the dark room.

If the Sunday school hadn't gone so well, he would have felt better. But God had covered his shame. Or perhaps God would not allow His work to fail for the sake of His people. That had to be the reason.

He slumped into his seat and allowed the tears to fall. He needed to let out the steam. "O God, I'm sorry. I'm sorry." He wailed. He could never have done this in his right senses.

Commit the abominable. Adultery. He faulted his lack of caution and insensitivity, no excuse of ignorance or foul play. If he'd not stayed back when his wife left, or if he hadn't taken the palm wine— God gave him signs and he missed them!

He needed to find who planned this. He sucked in his breath to calm down. He needed to have a clear mind to solve the puzzle. One thing was clear to him. The lady had wanted sex. She had gone straight for it, provoking him in the most unbelievable way.

The drink he took had been mixed to disorient him, irritate his system even, but not to knock him out. He needed to be alert and sexually charged. And he had been!

Dini dragged his hands over his face and swallowed a sob. Okay. So, she wanted sex, and he gave it to her. The drug worked in a potent way, and she didn't back down. He didn't even know when she left. She came to drain him of his seed and did.

He focused his mind on the events as they happened. Painfully, he had to play back the sex. He wanted to feel what he felt again. Know, with a clear mind, what had happened. Try and recall what she felt like, it was the only way he could try and piece together everything. And probably guess the identity of the perpetrator.

He had a suspect. Oyinemi Salpon.

While taking his bath, preparing for church, driving to church, praying, teaching, singing, looking, wondering, crying—every single free moment in his mind, he thought about her. Who else could it be? What other plan? What other reason? It had to be Mama behind this.

Now he had to run through the ordeal to know if Miss Salpon again submitted herself to be humiliated in the most disgusting way he could think of. If he wanted anyone to be the mother of his children, then not such a shameless woman, for goodness' sake.

She was dark. She blended with the darkness in the room. He squeezed his eyes shut and made himself feel the—sweetness of her body. She was sweet, he had to accept that. And—and a virgin!

He leapt to his feet and paced around the leg space of the dark office. Mama had talked about a 'willing virgin' who would give him a child. He needed to know if Salpon was the one or Mama had found another virgin. Despite his torturous reminisces, he still could not come to a conclusion. He would have to see Oyinemi again. Some things he would see and know! Parts of her he'd touched and remembered—

But if she happened to be the one, then what?

He would demand an explanation. And an apology. Then what? He couldn't demand that she go to a clinic to flush. If she got pregnant, he couldn't deny or claim the child. If she didn't get pregnant, he couldn't bear to know he hadn't been able to—

He felt miserable and conflicted in the most impossible way. And the way his body reacted just at the mere thought of the woman, he felt betrayed. He was a child of God. A married man. A family man—who shared his wife with a ghost!

Back in UT, he had a fraternity who believed in 'keep digging till you find, 'cause only then can you have a life!' That philosophy rang true for him now. He needed to do some findings.

He picked the key to his truck where he'd flung it on his desk and marched resolutely to the door.

But courage failed him. He slid to the floor at the door and sat there till dangerously late in the night.

***

Miss Salpon did not expect any more visitors. She had had two already and given the report they needed. She had no control over the next course of

events. Nothing more to do than to wait for two weeks. And she'd politely told them she would contact them as soon as she had any news.

As she closed the door after Mama, and began to prepare for work, she also closed the door to the things her body, soul and spirit experienced in the last forty-eight hours.

She had made a pact with Mama, and she hoped to God the old woman didn't play any tricks on her. If she got pregnant, she would have the baby and raise the baby on her own. She begged that Mama not try to take the baby to Dini to rear. If at all he was interested, she would take the child to Mama's house where Dini could visit for a weekend or holiday, and then she would return and pick her child. She would not be expected to visit Dini with the child or for Dini to visit the child in her house. She wanted nothing more to do with him. And if she didn't conceive, good. She wasn't doing any more business with Mama. The old woman'd have to take her merchandise elsewhere!

She had already given more than any sane woman would. If she did have a child, it would be the ultimate gift. The gift of a life. What she had lost was more than she could bear.

Her man, Binatari Ekiye. And her innocence.

That evening she planned to fix a wedding date had turned out to be a terminal date for her relationship. Both of them had wept like babies, but Oyinemi had remained resolute. She could not see Tari again. He deserved better, and that was the only explanation she would give. He vowed never to let her go but she knew that in a few months, he wouldn't even want her.

And that hurt more than anything, the shock he would feel when he saw her bulging stomach, and the pain from the disgrace.

She opened the teachers' room in SECA at just about 12.30p.m. A young school leaver called Sade, who had been employed to work the earlier hours from 8a.m to 3p.m as a receptionist, after the previous receptionist, Yemi, got another job, told her a visitor waited for her in a particular classroom. She dropped her bag on her desk and walked to the classroom to meet the person who Sade said refused to leave a name.

In Oyinemi's thinking, it was Tari. He'd called on her several times in the past weeks at odd times, hoping to jolt her out of the nightmare he accused her of throwing them both in.

The classrooms in SECA had been improvised and partitioned because the building had been originally designed for residence. Each classroom accommodated twenty students. Ten desks joined two-seater chairs, arranged two each on four rows, with the extra two placed in such a way that they faced one another at the two ends of the class.

Because of this awkward arrangement, the teacher's desk was closer to the penultimate row, so the odd seat at that end was closest to the teacher's desk. Both sides of the classrooms were well ventilated with large windows that showed the street on the one side, and the corridors on the other side.

Oyinemi walked toward the back of the man. He wore black trousers and rumpled lilac shirt, which hung out, and black shoes. He dug his hand deep in one of the trouser pockets and the other supported his posture as he leaned over the odd desk and stared out.

The unkempt back view convinced her the visitor was Tari. She had a clearer and stronger resolve now. After Saturday night, Tari was better off without her, even if she didn't conceive. She felt disgusted with herself. She couldn't bring herself to tell him the truth, but she could and would send him off once and for all.

The man turned and Oyinemi stopped short, swallowing hard. She thought she would faint. What was he doing here? Who told him about her? They promised they would not let him know. The room had been dark, and he was tipsy. Or else she would never have agreed to it. Not again. She couldn't face him! She felt betrayed. Mama had promised her he would never know!

She took an unsteady step back and turned to run from the room. Great mistake.

Dini moved fast, getting to the door before her and slamming it shut. His hand connected with her upper arm and he flung her against the teacher's desk, forcing her into the armless chair at the desk.

Oyinemi glared into the angriest set of eyes she had ever seen in her life. She knew she could scream, and Sade would come to her rescue. But fear held her still. What could he do to her anyway? Whatever he did, she deserved.

***

Dini Brisibe had leaned over the awkward desk and looked out the window. When he heard footsteps, he'd turned to look at the person approaching, and knew. She was the one. The hair. He'd combed his hand through it so thoroughly, he had his giveaway.

The hair was woven in short stretches with extensions so long, it reached her waist. On Saturday night, she had freed it. Now she held it together with a blue ruffle, which matched the light blue and grey skirt and blouse she wore.

With her imprisoned so to say in the teacher's chair, Dini tried to control his rough breathing and he leaned into her. Her lips trembled with fear. She should be scared. He felt like strangling her. He felt like kissing her too. He jerked back and put distance between them. What sort of a demon was this? How had he gotten himself so entangled?

The only thing he trusted himself to say. "Why?"

"You know why."

"I didn't ask you to help me! Do you know what you have done to me? What you did to me?" His breath caught in his throat. He shoved his hands in his pockets to control their shaking. How could she sit there looking all innocent and tell him he knew why!

"I did what I had to do!"

He paced. This woman was a demon designed to destroy him. He had to tread carefully.

"Do you believe in God, Miss Salpon?"

Maybe she really did not understand the import of her actions. Maybe she needed to be educated. For a split second, he entered the cliché – maybe God designed this so he could minister salvation to her. He left that quickly, as soon as it came up.

"In God?" She looked around as though she needed someone to explain it better.

He reined in his temper. "Yes. God. The almighty one."

"I guess so."

Oh. "What does that mean? Do you go to church?"

"I don't go to church."

"Really?" He nodded. So maybe the cliché was it then. He sat on a rickety desk across from her and looked at her with scrutiny. "No wonder. That figures. You and my mother fit perfectly."

He tried not to be sarcastic but couldn't help it. She had intruded on his life. And he wondered if anything would be the same again.

"I have to ask why, again. Why did you drug me, go to all that length? Come to Lagos, just to have sex with me?"

"I did what I had to do!"

That line drove him close to the edge of insanity. He jumped off the desk and glared at her. "What did you have to do? Why did you have to do it? Were you paid or what? What is the catch in this for you?" He put his face as close to hers as he deemed safe and yelled at her.

Contrary to his expectation, she didn't cringe or move.

Her voice sounded thin but composed. And she looked right back into his eyes. "There is no catch. Nothing. Mama gave me nothing."

He didn't know what came over him. But he bent and kissed her. He thought she would struggle, a little at least. She didn't. She didn't respond either. He raised his head and looked into her beautiful eyes, drawing him. Dragging him.

A Godless woman from the pit of hell had finally taken his soul.

He leaned his forehead on hers. "Oh. Who are you? Oyinemi? Do you know I am married? You made me commit adultery. The ultimate sin against my body, my wife. Against God!"

"I had to do it," she whispered.

He stepped back and stared at her. "You keep saying that."

"Because I didn't want it just as much you didn't. And yet I wanted it just as much as Mama!"

What a strong woman. Her confident words stunned him. They stared at each other for a long moment, and then he laughed nervously.

"How do you expect me to understand that?"

"Mama fired the flame to encourage me. You did nothing to discourage me."

"Nothing! Sending you away twice meant nothing?"

She looked away, and twisted her fingers in her lap. "That—was very humiliating," she said, her voice, hoarse.

Sade knocked once and opened the door. She peeped in and said, "Mama Onresi is here, do you want to eat anything?"

Oyinemi shook her head before she spoke. "No, thank you."

They both must look worse for wear because Sade looked at them alternately and then settled on her. "Are you alright?"

She nodded.

Sade didn't seem convinced though she shrugged and left the door wide open after her.

He dragged his hand over his face. "Is there somewhere private we can go? I want to talk!"

"There's a Mr. Bigg's—"

"I said private. Where do you live?"

She flinched before responding. "Next door."

"Good. We're going to your house to talk!" He led the way, stopped and ushered her to go in front.

At the reception, she told Sade she didn't feel too well and that her 'cousin' was seeing her to the house.

"I said it. You looked sick even when you came in," Sade said. "Sorry." She eyed Dini but said nothing to him. "I'll take excuse for you. Just go and rest."

Oyinemi smiled weakly. "Thank you."

They walked to her room in tensed silence. She opened the front door and allowed him in before locking the door. She went to the windows and began to draw back the curtains so some light could seep in.

"Leave it," Dini said.

He was in the lion's den, to die this death. He closed in on her and pulled her into his arms. His kiss was fevered. Desperate. He pulled off the constraining ruffle on her hair and dug his hands in. This time, she responded.

And thus, Dinipre Oyinkuru Brisibe substantiated his adultery.

Chapter 26

Tonbra, in her nightwear and dressing gown, and cuddled up on a single couch with a tall glass of iced tea, which she sipped, looked at Grace.

"I haven't heard from him, Grace. What am I going to do?" She shook her head. "I called his office three times already and they said he hadn't come in today!"

Grace George checked the time. "It's a few minutes to 7. But you people were in church together yesterday. He didn't tell you where he was going?"

Tonbra shook her head. "You know the way Sunday is for him. But I knew he wasn't himself that yesterday. He was just different. He came in so late on Saturday. At about 3a.m!" She took a long sip from her drink. "And he avoided me through service."

"But you sit together, don't you?"

"We do, but he was very quiet. I think something was eating at him. Some form of guilt. Though he spoke well during Sunday school, but I've discovered my husband preaches better when he's not prepared to do it! Something must have happened to him in that party."

Grace arched her eyebrows. "Like what?"

"Maybe he took beer. That kind of thing will make him feel guilty." She stood and went to the window. She looked out briefly and returned to her seat.

"It's your driver."

Grace checked her designer watch again and gasped. "What was I thinking? I have to get to mainland tonight." She shifted forward in her seat.

"What should I do, Grace? He's not picking his calls and hasn't replied even a text!"

"Did you two have a quarrel?"

"Yes and no. Not a recent one at least! Oh no!" Tonbra covered her face with her hands.

The front door opened and Pere and Ebisine rushed in and went to hug their mum. She hugged them in return and asked them to go on up and

prepare for the night. They didn't spare Grace a glance.

Timi and the yellow all-stars boy followed them in. This time around, he wore heavy orange snickers. He draped one hand over Timi's shoulders, and they bumped into each other as they walked in. He did a small bow and greeted the two women, and Timi greeted as well.

"Is Dad back from work?" Timi said.

"No. He—"

"Isn't back yet. Go on up, you two," Grace said.

The two women watched them walk up without any further comments. When Tonbra was sure they were out of earshot, she looked at Grace.

"Are you sure this is right? Timi has turned into something else. She's so mature now and Dini doesn't approve of this boy in the house.

What if he comes in?"

"Leave Dini! Do you know what he's doing too?"

"No. But I trust my husband."

"Ice cannot melt in hell."

"What do you mean by that?"

"Let's talk about your daughter who is more important. She's 13 now, isn't she?"

"Just turned 13."

"Ah. She's mature enough. When will she start to learn about men? When she's 30? And this boy is responsible. His father was a senator. He was schooling abroad just a few months ago!"

"You didn't tell me that? You only said he's the son of one of our sponsors when he came with you to the centre."

"He is. Very generous sponsor too. His son being Timi's friend is an added advantage!"

"She's just so young. You said he's 16? They're both too young!" Tonbra lowered her voice. "Do you think they'll be—sleeping together or something?"

Grace burst into laughter. "Spare me, Tonbra." She got on her feet and picked her bag. "Call me when you hear from Dini."

She stood as well. "You're so casual about this, Grace."

"The best thing to do when you can't do nothing." Grace said, badly mimicking a Yankee accent.

"What if he still doesn't show tonight? He may need help." They walked to the door together. "I should call the police—"

"Call the police tomorrow morning then. Or call me, and we can go and make the report together. Forty-eight hours after is the standard for reporting a missing adult." Grace hugged her. "And don't worry yourself."

"I'll try."

***

At about midnight, Dini pressed his face into the pillow, trying to blot out every thought. The woman smell around him didn't help. Finally, he had no other excuses. When he'd entered his truck on Sunday night and driven to Akure in the dead of night, he had been on a suicide mission, to kill his marriage vows.

Since then, he had died many deaths in the arms of Oyinemi Salpon. And he had reached a point where only the worst lay ahead. He had committed adultery, over and over again, satisfying a hunger he knew would be the doom of him.

He looked at the woman who cuddled in his arms. She could no longer be solely responsible for his sin. They were both guilty now. And she didn't know God. That made him the adult in this sin.

As though he couldn't help that, he pressed his lips against her forehead. They had talked at length in the night. He discovered she had wanted him long before now—teenage crush that refused to go away, she'd told him.

So much as she knew she was doing the wrong thing, her desires had gotten the better of her.

And she had Mama's soft and persistent persuasions, goading her on. She told him Mama talked about dying. That scared him more than he cared to admit. He would have to take it up with Mama.

They'd made love through the afternoon, after which she had left him to sleep and gone to work. When she returned in the night, she'd prepared dinner and they'd eaten, and then committed the ultimate sin again. When he'd thought he'd had enough of her!

Holding her in his arms afterward, on her narrow bed, he'd demanded an explanation.

She gave him a breakdown of the plan as she knew it, starting with Grace, the traitor. Poor Tonbra thought she had an ally, but her jealous sister-in-law was destroying her life right under her nose. And then the stranger who used 'Chikito' as a cover-name, whoever that was. She had organized the execution of the plan, chosen the drink and drugs—

Oyinemi didn't know her take in the whole plan, if she was paid or not.

She'd spelt out her part in detail. She didn't know how they managed to get him into that room. All she knew was that they made her watch ex-rated films, so she'd know what to do to him. Grace had coached her afterward.

He couldn't say a word. What would he say? It looked like a tale from another continent.

Initially, she'd rested her head on his chest and spoken softly but when she finished, she lifted her head and gazed at him. But what could he say? He'd been had. And instead of being mad, he'd come here and made love to her again. And again.

"That's what happened," she said after a while.

He held her gaze, looking into those beautiful eyes he couldn't resist, and leaned down and kissed her mouth. When he gently rested her head back on his chest, she had murmured, "I don't regret it happened."

For now, he couldn't think of being anywhere else other than here. He had fallen. Everyone would be disappointed in him. His pastor would probably disgrace him openly, and suspend him when, and that was a sure when, he confessed. Tonbra may leave. She was poised for it anyway!

He wanted to know what the Bible said about marrying two wives. "Oh God, Dinipre, don't sell your soul!" he moaned.

The woman in his arms shifted, and then went back to her slumber. How could he want, love this woman? He was a believer, a deacon. He had succumbed to the lust of the flesh. He was no longer justified before God.

Idly, he stroked her back. She lived in a humble place. The room had only a four-and-a-half by six feet bed, which made the cuddling more fun now. But naturally, the bed was small by his standards. She covered the floor with a brown and pink plastic carpet that matched her curtains and bedspread. A table by the wall contained much of her cosmetics and a table top fridge, a 14" TV set and a small record player. Two wooden ladder-back chairs were tucked into the table. She had a small wardrobe and a customized hanger.

Her bathroom had a shower and toilet. And her kitchen was just as narrow as the bathroom. Yet she had asked for nothing in exchange for giving him a child. Mama could have given her a lot of money.

"I'll take care of you, Oyinemi. I promise." He closed his eyes and dozed off.

***

He didn't open his eyes until 9a.m. He heard Oyinemi move around the small kitchen. The smell of fried eggs wafted into his nostrils and his eyes fluttered close as he dragged in a deep, satisfying breath.

He sat up and rubbed his eyes. He found his phone on the floor by his trousers and picked it up. He hadn't been in touch with his wife in almost forty-eight hours. There were over twenty missed calls from her, amongst others. About ten text messages as well. He felt bad about that. She would have been so worried, but he was too distraught on a destructive path to think straight.

He sent a text to her, apologizing and telling her he was alright. She called immediately.

He struggled with whether to pick up or not. Was he ready to speak to her just yet? He allowed it to ring out and stood. He got into his trousers as the phone began to ring again. What did she want? He picked the phone and stared at it till it rang out. And then began to ring again.

Better now then, he thought wearily. "Hello, Tonbra," he said softly.

"Hello." Her voice so loud and panicked changed his demeanour. "Hello, Dini! Where are you?"

"Akure. Why? What's wrong?"

She began to sob, and someone took the phone from her. "Hello, Dini. This is Grace. Where are you?"

He panicked. "Why? What is wrong?"

"The plant—one of the plants." He heard Grace drag in a breath. "There was an explosion—"

"Explosion!"

Oyinemi ran out of the kitchen and came to stand beside him. "Calm down. At the power plant. There was—"

"I'm coming home right now!"

"Wait. You need to know the police are involved. The—five are dead—it doesn't look good—"

"I'm on my way." He hung up and looked frantically for his shirt.

Oyinemi picked it from one of the chairs. "What happened?" She helped him into it.

"There was an explosion in one of my power plants." He pulled her into his arms and pressed a kiss on her forehead. "I'm sorry, I have to go!"

"I understand. Please drive carefully."

He found his shoes and jerked the door open. He couldn't make any promises to her. He walked out without a backward glance, but he heard her soft sobs.

CHAPTER 27

Dini drove straight to his office. With the traffic and bad roads, he didn't make it in till close to 2pm. He took a back gate into the office premises and rode on a private lift to the tenth floor.

Only NGEC occupied the 10th floor and so, the amount of activity going on there amazed him. People milled about. Police officers too.

No one noticed him at first. He headed for the main office. The staff members agitated and crowded the secretary's office. He changed his mind at the last minute and went to the DG's office. He didn't even know which power plant blew up. An explosion, good God! He hoped it wasn't Ogere.

The plant at Ogere had been undergoing several tests and harboured all the engines recently purchased. All the new machines were being tested at Ogere. If anything happened there, then all would be lost. The other two power plants only had the building and generators. Nothing massive!

They had spent the past three weeks test-running the newly installed plants at Ogere. There had been sparks the first day and they had been regulating, and testing. The tests required a tedious, 24-hour surveillance by skilled personnel. The engineers working with him were trained and smart. And they alerted him whenever anything suspicious happened.

Had they tried to reach him without success? He had been so consumed by his self and the lust, he had not wanted contact with anyone. He had put his phone on silent! Could he ever forgive himself? Five men dead! It explained why his right-hand men had not called. Were they dead?

The DG's office was contrarily calm. The DG's secretary, Mrs. Coker, a prim and smart-looking forty-something year old woman, sat at her desk, answering a call. Dini signalled to her to cut it, and she did, after promising to call back.

"Which plant?" Dini barked.

"Ogere."

"Oh. My. God! What happened? Where's DG?"

"He's gone there. I don't know what happened—"

Dini barged out of the office and ran down the corridor, pushing people aside. He needed to get to his office and then to the site. His phone began to ring, and he checked it. Tonbra.

"I'm in the office," he said impatiently, slowing down to a fast walk.

"I was worried. The—"

"I'll call you. Please." He hung up.

He stopped in front of his office and fumbled with his bunch of keys.

"Dr. Brisibe?"

He swirled round. "Yes?" Two plain-clothes policemen came into his direct line of view. Several others in uniform came into his blind sight.

"Zone 2, police headquarters." Both men flashed their badges simultaneously and chorused names he didn't pick. "We need you to come with us."

"I'm sorry. There's an emergency at the—" The uniformed men closed in. Dini looked at them nervously. "What's this about?"

"You'll know when you get to the station."

"I can't possibly leave—"

"Are you coming voluntarily or not?"

Dini looked up and down the corridor and saw some of his colleagues had come out of their offices to watch. The accountant and the accounts staff were next to the next door to him on the right. The office next to his was locked. It belonged to the technicians working with him.

He reckoned they would be at Ogere. Human Resources shared some space with accounts. Research team used the office to the left, with logistics next to them.

Dini looked at the policemen. They came to arrest him? For the explosion? "Does this have to do with the explosion?"

The second plain-clothes officer spoke impatiently for the first time. "Dr. Brisibe, we have a job to do. Are you coming or not?"

Dini nodded and stepped away from his door. The two men, much to his surprise, grabbed and hand-cuffed him. He began to protest, and stopped, fuming with fury that threatened to burst. His truck keys and phone were pried from his hands. He swallowed hard, deciding there and then that he would not allow the policemen to ridicule him.

He walked slowly, forcing the officers to slow their paces as well. Wisely, they also refused to be infuriated by his gait. In front of the DG's office, he slowed even more. Mrs. Coker had come to stand by her door to watch, empathy etched around her eyes and mouth.

"Mrs. Coker," he said. "Please call Tonbra. Tell her they've taken me to zone 2, Obalende. Please."

Tears pooled in the woman's eyes, and she nodded.

The policemen took him out to a marked van and made him sit in the open back like some of the common criminals he'd seen in the despicable

black vehicles. They would pay for this, he swore under his breath. These useless policemen! But then again, they couldn't be acting on their own. This didn't look good.

Obalende, the name of the area the zone 2 federal police headquarters in Lagos was situated, had become synonymous with the police HQ. And dread as well. Only cases of federal interest got here. What did they charge against him? With his phone taken away, he could only rely on Mrs. Coker to communicate with Tonbra.

At the police HQ, two uniformed men took him to a small interrogation room, where his wallet, shoes, leather belt, and Rolex were taken away.

He felt helpless through the humiliation.

"You guys have a lot of explanation to do for—"

The police officer slapped him hard. "Shut up!"

White light burst at the back of Dini's vision. It couldn't have been a normal slap. It felt more like a punch on the side of his head. He went quiet and still after that. His handcuffs remained secure and the policemen walked out without another word.

He didn't know how long he stayed there, but it must have been for a long time. The small square window allowing a little illumination no longer gave it. The single bulb in the room, obviously being controlled from elsewhere because there was no switch in the room, hadn't been switched on, making the room now pitch-black.

Dini deduced the room must be at the far back of some place. He heard little noise from anywhere. Deceptive calm. The room, bare and dreadful, made Dini more frustrated. He couldn't wait to be out of here. He knew his rights. He knew the police had infringed upon it. He hoped to God Mrs. Coker had called Tonbra. And for all his life's worth, he prayed Tonbra will do what's right.

The throb from the hit on his head escalated and his head pounded, the pain reaching to the back of his eyes. Several times he sat down to still the pounding—to no avail. He knew he ought to be hungry. He hadn't eaten since last night when he took rice with Oyinemi.

Oyinemi. To be continued...

His stomach grumbled, and his heart ached. He wished for a glass of water and something to ease the pain in his head. This could be torture ahead of his interrogation. This was so wrong. To be shackled like a common criminal, his arms twisted to the back, and handcuffed. His arms ached, the pain now a dull numb feeling. To be held without charges. To be hit on the head. To be left in a small interrogation room for endless hours without contact, in pitch darkness without ventilation—

He heard the jangling of keys and raised his head from the table where he'd placed it. The single bulb came on and he felt such relief to see Dayo Dickson walk in. Dayo had a scowl on his face, which please Dini.

Dayo and Dini had met during their service year in National Youth Service Corps (NYSC) camp. Dayo had graduated with distinctions, in fact, the best student in his faculty of law at the Obafemi Awolowo University. He was smart, apt and had the instinct of a hunter. Their friendship had coagulated over the years. Dayo, as much as his wit, intimidated with a tall, dark, and handsome profile. His wife, a fellow lawyer, and best graduating student of her time as well, worked part-time in his chambers, and full-time taking care of their two daughters.

Dini had never needed the services of his good friend, though he knew Dayo excelled as a trial lawyer.

"God! What happened to your face?"

"I got punched by a policeman."

"What? Assault." Dayo brought out his iPad 2 and jotted furiously, and then he took several shots of Dini from different angles.

Dini blinked uncomfortably. "Is it that bad?"

"Tell me what happened." Dayo finished with the iPad and took the second chair in the room. "Tonbra called me. She was hysterical. Said you were brought here."

"I heard about the explosion and rushed to the office. They took me from there."

"Have you told them anything?"

He shook his head gently to minimize the pain. "No. I didn't even know why I was taken." Dayo frowned. "What is it? Just tell me!"

Dayo leaned back and folded his arms across his chest. "After Tonbra's call, I came here and gathered some information. Much of it is guess work right now. I would have come earlier but I was trying to get you bailed. That will be done tomorrow."

"I'm not going to sleep here, Dayo!"

"Tonight, you will." Dayo said bluntly. His bluntness made him one of the most sought-after.

"What did I do to be here?"

That question jumped back at him and before Dayo could speak, it seemed he heard the real truth in his spirit. Guilty on three counts of adultery.

"Nutshell, government is putting the blame on you for the explosion."

"Is that a criminal offence? To not be at the site when an accident occurs?"

"Well, that is it exactly, Dini. They're saying it is not an accident."

Dini's eyes widened, and he gasped. "What? I've been working on this project for the past year—travelling, leaving my family, working extra hours—"

"Calm down. Those will be looked into tomorrow. For now, I want to get you unshackled. This is a crazy country. They have no right to tie you like this." He jumped to his feet. "Tonbra is here. They'll allow her to see you

briefly. I think she brought food too."

"Will she be allowed to feed me?" Dini snapped.

"Reserve the energy, Dini. I'll just call her in now."

"They took my phone and watch, and my keys, my shoes, my belt!"

Dayo walked out of the room and came back shortly with Tonbra and a policeman. The policeman loosened the cuffs. He asked Tonbra to eat from the food she brought. She did and took a sip from the bottle of water.

The man left then and Tonbra dropped the food flask on the table and walked into Dini's arms, sobbing loudly. He simply held her, unable to say anything. He had messed up. What would have happened if he'd followed her home after church on Sunday? He shut the last forty-eight hours out of his mind. He couldn't afford even a thought.

After what seemed like an age, Dayo and Tonbra left. Dini couldn't eat the food and only drank water. They took him then to a cell with three other men in it. The criminals took turns beating him till almost sunup.

Chapter 28

Dayo came in before 8a.m the following morning and had impressive news. First, he managed to get Dini out of the depressive cell but not out on bail. Dini got an empty cell where he could conference with Dayo, who was more anxious to talk about the prosecution lawyer, than the case itself. He'd discovered Tonye Sigha would work the case from the office of the attorney general.

"I've heard of him," Dini said casually.

"Tonye Sigha lobbied for this job. He knows it is high profile and he needs it badly. Dini, you must be ready for battle."

"During my days in FUTA, he used to come around a lot. He was the national president of Junior Rotary or so?"

"Yes, and many other things. He is highly ambitious. Has the ears of the president and is looking to take his boss's job—"

Dini afforded himself the luxury of a smile. "He wants to become attorney-general?"

Dayo narrowed his eyes to die-hard stilts. "Yes, Dini. This is election year. Less than seven months to go. This explosion has happened at a very bad time. The president was looking to use these power plants to campaign! Can you imagine how potent the campaign will be if we have uninterrupted power supply? Even for a month!" He sighed. "I don't need to tell you this government is so far the worst we've ever had. They needed the success of the power plant to leverage on their stiff opposition."

Blood drained from Dini's face. His mouth drooped open. Before Dayo said the words, he knew it.

"Yes, Dini. I see you are getting the point!" Dayo paused and typed on his iPad briefly. "They plan to prove this was not a result of their carelessness at all. That the man they put on the project, the best engineer in the field in Nigeria, and one of the best in Africa, Dr. Dini Brisibe, has been compromised by the opposition."

"No!"

"Yes, Dini." Dayo glared. He pressed his lips together grimly, displaying dimples that made him the lady's man when he smiled. "They have put a pit-bull on the case. This is not funny at all."

"I didn't think it was, Dayo!"

"Tonye Sigha is unethical by all means. And like I said, he has the ears of the president. He is highly intelligent, good at what he does, ambitious to hell, and engaged to the president's daughter. The battle for Aso Rock is as much his as is the president's." He spoke rapidly. "I was awake all night, making calls, investigating, and all. I have gone to the site—"

"How bad is it?" Dini whispered, afraid for what he would hear.

"Very bad." Dayo placed the iPad aside. "Five dead. There were sparks from the newly installed machines. The gas pipe had not been turned off at the proper time. The sparks connected with the gas." He snapped his fingers. "Boom!"

"Oh, my goodness."

"Figure for the loss not yet determined but the plant is very much gone. Firemen could not contain the fire. It burned out!"

"Oh, my goodness."

"Let me start by saying you have been denied bail. This cell is being paid for as well, otherwise, you'll be in the other one."

"Thank you, Dayo."

"I think you need a doctor." Dayo examined his friend. "Your face looks very bad."

"I'm fine." Dini hadn't seen himself, but his left eye and his lips felt like they weighed a ton.

Dayo stood. "I have a lot of work to do. When I have more facts, I'll come back. Tonbra is here with breakfast."

"I can't eat anything, Dayo. How could I?"

"You need to eat." He pushed on the cell door which had been left open. "We'll be back."

Dini stared after him and then at the door till they came in. Again, a policeman escorted Tonbra in and ensured she tasted the food and tea she brought in his presence. Dini forced himself to eat. He hadn't had a bath since the previous day and he stank. After taking a picky bit of the food and a full cup of tea, he pushed the food away.

"Can I have a bath?"

"I'll arrange for it," Dayo said casually. "Tonbra wished to have a few minutes with you." He stepped out and stood at the door without waiting for Dini's consent.

Tonbra sat on the edge of his four-spring bed and stared at him. He averted his gaze. He hated himself for it but what else could he do. This was daytime horror.

"I just wanted you to know the children and I are praying for you." She spoke falteringly. Her hand reached out to touch his.

He felt angry. Infuriated by her words. He sat stiffly, wondering why? He had offended this woman, yet he felt offended. He couldn't bear to look at her, couldn't mutter a word. He maintained a stoic gaze that remained stationed above her head.

"The storm will soon be over. I believe it."

She squeezed his hand, wept softly, and then stood, and packed the food flask. She walked out of the cell. Dayo closed the door after her, and they both left. A policeman locked the cell.

Dini refused to let the tears drop.

He got his bath later in the day.

Tonbra brought lunch but he ate none of it. She didn't hesitate. She promised to bring dinner for him, and a change of clothes. He remained mute.

She came back with Dayo in the evening, gave him food, and left him with Dayo.

"She's a good woman, Dini. This must be very hard on her," Dayo said softly.

"I don't know how to console her. I've completely let her and the children down!"

"She was hysterical when she called me. I felt such pity for her."

Dini looked blank. He had nothing to say to that. He was living through a nightmare for the first time in his life, and he didn't know the rules of the game.

"Well, let's get to the business of the day." Dayo opened his iPad. "No charges have been put forward yet. In fact, there's nothing on you now. You are just being held, for heaven knows what. That's officially," Dayo said. "Unofficially, I have gathered you are going to be charged with sabotage of a federal project—"

Dini flew off his thin mattress. "Sabotage!"

"Yes, exactly. Conspiracy to commit a federal offence. And voluntary man-slaughter." Dayo remained expressionless. "Those are the ones I have now, from the grapevine."

"I can't believe this, Dayo. This can't be true."

"They are still gathering facts, evidence, and witnesses. So far, the damage is in excess of N20bn."

"More accurately N15.25bn," Dini said hoarsely. "Actual figures. Excludes the other half the cankerworm ate."

Dayo chuckled. "Bad-mouthing won't help you now, Dini." He shrugged. "I guess if you deduct the storage to the installations and recurrent expenses, you could have that."

"That is what it is. That's the figure." He hissed. "Another ten or so billion was taken off the treasury for the plant but we never saw it on this
side!"

Dayo stared at him for a beat. "You'd better not let anyone hear you say that!" He punched it into his iPad. "Okay. I've been allowed to visit the site again today. I went with my own team of investigators. That's good. I was scared they won't let me in there before the prosecution is done." He looked directly into Dini's eyes. "Did I tell you this will be a long haul? I don't usually ask, or want to know if my clients are guilty—"

"I'm not, Dayo, you know me."

"Yeah, I know you. You're my good friend. I also knew a woman who shot her husband in the back of the head. Her name was Mary Winkler and her husband was a pastor!"

"Dayo—?"

"All I ask, my friend, is that you answer my questions truthfully. I'm not going to ask if you're guilty or—"

"I am not!"

"The charges are going to be very sticky. Unethical of me to say but I doubt you'll get away with this. Sigha is going to demand for life imprisonment. He's going to call you a traitor. He's going to make this look like a coup d'état. Like treason." He nodded as though to convince himself as well. "He's gonna fight you from every angle. I am yet to get the names of the people who died. I will need their profile and will want to know your relationship with them."

Dini clenched his teeth. "Okay."

"I want to know how far gone the project was as well."

"We're more than 70% completed. Why would I want to work so hard and then jeopardize everything with less than 30% to completion?"

"Because this is the last leg of the elections. Because the primaries are less than two months away. Politicians are spending all their money right now. This is the market-day period. Period."

Dini shook his head furiously just as Dayo closed his iPad and stood. "Tomorrow, we start questioning you, Dini. It's going to be extensive. I intend to overturn every stone of your life. Anything I suspect Sigha's going to be interested in. Rest tonight as much as you can. You'll need as much energy as you can garner." He looked at Dini closely. "Are you alright?"

Dini nodded. His face weighed half a ton now.

Dayo patted his shoulders. "You're a man of God, pray about this."

Dini looked at Dayo's face. There was not an iota of deceit in the lawyer's eyes. For the first time, Dini truly felt afraid for himself. All along, he had been cock-sure his innocence would be easy to prove. Not a born-again Christian and in the past when Dayo referred to Dini as a 'man of God', he intended it as a tease, but now he looked grim. He pressed his lips together again, revealing the sweet dimples.

Dayo headed for the door. "Do you need anything? A kind of food, drugs, clothes?" Dini shook his head. Dayo pushed the cell door back.

Dini's head jolted up as Dayo stepped out. "One thing, Dayo."

"Yes?"

"Stop Tonbra from bringing food." He looked away from the surprised look on his friend's face. "I can't bear to see her—I—It's—I can't take it anymore. I'm sorry." He brought his gaze back to Dayo who stared at him. "We can buy food."

"I'm sorry, Dini. I can't imagine what this is like. But what do I tell Tonbra?" He left without getting more than a shrug from Dini.

CHAPTER 29

The days droned by after that.

Dayo's interrogations were long and detailed. He unfolded Dini's life before him, year by year, especially after he came back from UT. The investigations had gone far and become a national issue. Overnight, the media paraded Dini as a suspect in a major national conspiracy. Dayo fought the media war like his life depended on it, crying foul with all his legal strength. Most major cases were won in the media before they got to court and he battled if not to win this, to play a draw.

Two weeks after the arrest, Dayo came into the cell with a woman. Oyinemi Salpon.

Dini was shocked to see her. There had been no hint of a plan to bring her. Since that morning he left her, he had made no effort to contact her. He had been refused all rights to contact the outside world anyway, held like he was a botched coup plotter.

Oyinemi had a slack expression and wet dull eyes, though she still managed to look pretty and innocent. Her scandalous hairdo had been changed. She now brushed short natural hair to the back, parted at the side, and styled in soft finger-waves.

"They refused her entry. I met her at the gate and she persuaded me to bring her in." Dayo explained at the look of shock on Dini's face.

In the last week, Dayo had come less frequently, spending more time on preparing the case, if it would get to that. Dini had still not been charged but Dayo had told him Sigha would be coming in to question him in a couple of days, and then they would start the legal procedure that would lead to one of three things: trial, a release, or settling out of court.

Oyinemi sat on the edge of the bed without being invited to do so. Dayo stepped out of the cell much as he did whenever Tonbra needed to talk privately with her husband.

Dini glared at her. What did he feel now? Warm indifference, or cold anger? He couldn't afford anything else.

He stood at the entrance of the cell and folded his arms across his chest. Leaning against the wall he stared at her, refusing to feel. "Why would you come here?" he said softly. "You're not through with your deceit, Oyinemi, your manipulations!"

"I had to—"

He looked away from her and sighed. "Oh, give me a break. Those things you had to do drive me crazy."

Her eyes pleaded. "I needed to see you, to apologize and encourage—"

He turned to her. "No. You don't regret anything, do you? You don't need to apologize."

"I know if you had not been—"

"I don't want to hear this, Oyinemi." He lifted himself away from the wall and stood arms akimbo. "Please leave. Who told you where to find me anyway?"

"It's in the papers. I saw the news and—"

"Yes, I get it. You can go now."

She sat there, looking small.

He didn't, couldn't raise his voice at her. Didn't understand the complicated feelings he had toward her. "Leave."

She stood. "I came also to—" She faltered.

Dini's dour gaze encouraged her to forget what she had been saying. "Goodbye. Forever. I don't ever want to see you again."

She held his gaze, took in a deep breath.

"So be it," she whispered.

He stepped aside and watched her walk out. Dayo walked in as soon as she left.

Dini's anger burst. "She found me from the papers, Dayo! What if she is an assassin? You let her in, you—"

"She called your mother. She said your mother sent her! I spoke with your mother. Do you think I'm daft?"

It floored Dini. He covered his face with his hands. His mother hadn't come to see him. "I'm sorry. Well, I don't want to see that lady again.

"No problem."

"I don't like that someone can from the media know where I am!"

Dayo nodded profusely. "We'll do something about that. It's either we move you or doctor the report on your whereabouts."

Dini closed his eyes.

"So now, I have tidied on all the loose ends. I will bring you up to the tee shortly, and then we talk about the last day before the explosion.

Sigha is coming tomorrow."

"Tomorrow."

"Yeah, he likes to jump people, but I know it's his style. Now, let me talk." He pinched the bridge of his nose and scrolled on his iPad. "Ur, that

woman who just left, she upset you real bad?" He looked keenly at Dini.

"Forget her."

"Okay then, just checking to be sure you're here."

"I am."

"Let's start from the good news. First, the men who died are all part of your trusted men. Bad news they died, but good for your case. We have people who will witness to the level of trust you placed in those men. You won't sacrifice them, just like that."

Dini stared like a statue. He had wept like a child the day he learnt of the names of the casualties. Three of them were technicians. One was an engineer. The last, a watchman who had three of his children on Dini's scholarship scheme.

"Second, your bank accounts have all been investigated. There is nothing suspicious. A major plus is the fact that the leakages in this project are absolutely zero. It establishes you were not stealing from the project. Money is definitely not your motive and that's a strong point for sabotage."

Dini's face sagged. "They investigated my accounts?"

"Yes." Dayo paused and looked at him. "Is there something they must not discover?"

Dini's voice was barely a hoarse whisper. "Tonbra has—secret accounts. I never bothered to ask her about them. I—oh my my—"

"Does she know you know about them?"

"No."

"Do you know the bank?"

"Banks. I saw four different check books." Dini took a deep breath, but it didn't help. "Oh, my father."

"Can you remember them?"

Dini nodded and mentioned the four different banks. "It kept haunting me. Several times I've wanted to ask but then I let it go."

"It's not in her name or the names of your children. That's all been searched. I will have to find a way to check this out." Dayo made notes.

"Now to the bad news. And it's very bad." Dayo looked at Dini. "I told you they have one of your engineers as an accomplice. They also have a signed confession. I got to know the name of the engineer just this morning."

"And?"

"Engineer Sylvester."

"That's my second in command. He confessed? To what?"

"I'm working on it. Trust me. I am going to get that confession." Dayo sighed. "I know how it works so don't worry yourself."

"I didn't plan anything with Sylvester."

"There's another bad news. And this makes me mad at you."

"What?"

"I told you not to lie to me, Dini. You did."

"I didn't lie to you."

"People saw you in church. But where did you go after church on Sunday?"

"I came to the office."

"Then went where?"

Dini stared at Dayo. The lawyer held his gaze till he looked away. "I can't talk about that, Dayo."

Dayo flared. He flew to his feet. "You said you went home."

The police had grilled him, and he'd told them he went home. Obviously, they'd exchanged notes with Dayo.

"Your wife told the police she didn't see you from after church till when she came with food to the station. From after church on Sunday all through Monday and half day Tuesday. Where were you?"

"I didn't go home, okay? God, it's complicated."

"This is ridiculous. Do you know what this has done to the case? It has changed everything. What's your alibi? Who were you with? Where did you go?"

"I can't—" He choked on his words. "I'll need to talk to my pastor about this."

"Your pastor? Are you insane, Dini? I am your lawyer, talk to me."

Dini dropped his head into his hands on to his laps. Dayo spoke for almost three minutes non-stop, telling him the kind of person Tonye Sigha was. Reminding him he would be made the president's scapegoat and they would roast him. When he mentioned Dini's career, Dini's temper flared as well.

"The career is gone, isn't it? For goodness' sake! I'm thinking of coming out of this in one piece, you're talking about a career."

"I thought your career was important to you." Dayo shouted. "I thought you were gunning for that DG job in about five years."

"Well, whatever, Dayo! I need to speak to my pastor." He opened his mouth and gulped in air.

Dayo turned away, and laughed, a short, sharp sound that cut through the tense atmosphere. "You are not allowed any visitor except your wife and your lawyer."

"You brought in that woman today. Dayo—"

"I'll send your pastor then. Today!" Dayo barked. "If he's not in town, it's your bad luck, Dini. Or if he can't come in today, it's over. You face Sigha tomorrow and have a taste of what the hell ahead would be like."

Dini dropped his head back on his laps. Dayo left the cell, muttering angrily.

What could he have told anyone? He hadn't thought about the alibi. Hadn't thought to plan for one with Tonbra. He couldn't have anyway. The police had gone to his house to search for him, and she had told them she

was worried sick about his whereabouts! Well.

He stretched out on the spring bed and closed his eyes. He wasn't going to start telling Dayo or Sigha anything about an alibi. He had none. Where was he between those hours? Hell. If they wanted to confirm, they could ask the devil. Before he finished forming the thoughts, he cringed. Dayo would die from anger, and Sigha would throw a party. A criminal without an alibi was dead meat.

Well, Dinipre Oyinkuru Brisibe was dead meat.

***

Dayo got the pastor to come in late in the afternoon. He warned Dini they had just ten minutes and he had to catch up on the preparation with Sigha the following day. He had confirmed it would be a pre-trial hearing in a judge's office at the federal high court, though only the lawyers and Dini would be in attendance.

Pastor Flo, a tall, dark-complexioned man, had been in ministry for over thirty years. He had built a congregation from scratch, advancing a message of holiness and love which had since become unpopular. Sin was a reproach in his congregation and he was as stern as Jesus might have been with 'thieves in the temple' but well-loved and respected, even amongst crowd-gatherers.

He walked into Dini's cell, and gave a small bow to Dayo, as the latter exited. Dini's heart cut into two at the look on his pastor's face. How could he have let this hard-working, God-loving, sin-hating servant of God, down? If he'd thought about his pastor, he wouldn't be here today.

Pastor Flo sat at the edge of the bed beside him and looked at him. "Deacon, I'm sorry about what happened to you. How are you?"

Dini couldn't take any more of it. He burst into tears and wailed like a woman. Pastor Flo drew him into his arms and cuddled him like a child.

When the storm calmed, he exploded. "I am sorry, Pastor. I have sinned. Oh God, I have sinned! I am suffering for my sin!"

Pastor Flo, being a patient man, patted Dini's hand. "Tell me everything."

Dini started from the beginning. As he spoke, he composed himself the more. He told Pastor Flo everything, from the day he met Tonbra to the day Mama brought the herbs.

Every detail. When he finished, he couldn't look up. He went on his knees, sobbing again.

Pastor Flo kept quiet for a long time and then muttered, "I knew something was wrong that Sunday." He sighed. "You know of course, you will be suspended. And it will be announced in church." Dini nodded, eager to face retribution. "The details will be told to only the circle of ministers, of course." Pastor Flo sighed again, and shocked Dini when he cracked up and cried as well.

It triggered the kind of emotion Dini never knew he possessed. He fell flat on his face on the dirt cement floor of the police cell, and wept.

His pastor pulled himself together after a while and took a deep breath. "I will pray for you," he said. "But before I do, let me ask you this. Do you love that strange woman?"

Dini did not hesitate. "No. I don't. I knew the moment I saw her today. She is sin to me—I almost hate her!"

"Do you love your wife? Do you love Tonbra?"

Dini kept quiet for a long time. How would he answer this question? He thought he loved her. He thought it had been love at first sight. Over the years he'd seen her vanity, fought to stay with her even in her deceit. He didn't hate her. But did he love her?

"She's still in love with her late husband." Dini shook his head. "How do you compete with a—a ghost?"

Pastor Flo sighed. "I think it's more of guilt. She didn't mourn his death before you married her. Maybe," he shrugged. "If you had let her mourn for a year or two—"

"The children know I'm not their father. That hurts."

"It will." Pastor sniffed. "So how do you feel about her?"

"I don't know. I'm just numb."

"She's going to get to know about the adultery when I address the ministers." Pastor paused and looked at him where he now sat on the floor. "Do you want to tell her first?"

"No."

"The woman may be pregnant for—"

"I don't care, Pastor. I'm not going back that way."

"Let me tell you this—you are special to God. The way things have happened proves it beyond doubt. Many believers dabble into sin for years without consequence, but people like you step out and the serpent bites immediately. The devil has been waiting for you to make the wrong move. You are a prize captive, but know this, even the lawful captive shall be delivered.

"Don't grieve what has happened. Rather celebrate what is ahead. Because you are coming out. You have this case ahead of you, and believe me, focus on Jesus and he will walk you out of this fiery furnace. Do you understand me?"

"Yes, Pastor."

Pastor Flo gathered him close and prayed with scriptures of comfort, grace, forgiveness, and victory.

Chapter 30

Pastor finally left after more than an hour.

Dayo walked into the cell, his face set, his lips pressed together. "I hope you feel better now. You have made your confessions to your priest."

Dini refused to be stung by his sarcasm. He stared into space, his hands clasped between his knees where he still knelt on the floor by the bed.

"Can you sit up, and talk to me?"

Dini sat on the edge of the bed, but his body remained rigid. "What do you want to know?"

"Where were you on Monday night while the explosion was happening?"

"I told you I was at home—"

"Dini, don't—"

"Will you let me finish?" Dini snapped. "I was not, but this is the last time I'm talking about it."

Dayo's mouth fell open. "You have an alibi and you're not going to use it?" He threw his arms up in the air.

"I don't have an alibi. An alibi means a witness. I'm not bringing anyone into this."

"A woman?" Dini pressed his lips together. Dayo continued. "Oh. Because of Tonbra? I understand but don't you think Tonbra would rather have adultery exposed than you go to jail for the rest of your life?"

Dini narrowed his eyes and looked at his lawyer and friend. "At this point, I don't care what Tonbra or anyone thinks—"

"Good. You're becoming a man!"

"I'm doing this for me. I have done enough wrong. I'm not going to drag anyone into anything that concerns me anymore."

"Did you discuss this with this anyone?"

"No."

Dayo drew in a long deep breath. "The way I see it, she wouldn't mind. If Tonbra—"

"My integrity is standing trial. I won't drag it further in the dust by telling everyone I was—somewhere while my plant was burning to the ground!"

The veins on Dini's temples throbbed painfully. But his gaze remained steady on Dayo's face. No chance in heaven or on earth would he change his mind. The two men locked gaze for a moment. He sensed Dayo about to change tactic and he sat up, geared for the new attack.

Dayo lifted his hands in surrender and began to pace the small space. "What do we tell Sigha? He already caught you in the lie." Dini shrugged and Dayo smiled. "I wish we could shrug it off."

"This is my life, right? It's all messed up. Watch me if I care now."

"My thoughts exactly. So, what difference will an alibi make?"

"None to me. That's why I'm not bringing it up. It will ruin someone completely. I can't afford to have another life entangled with mine anymore." Dini stood. "Someone who lives in a protected world. It matters to me what interferes with—with—Look, I have no alibi!"

"I lied that I was with my wife because I was in a place I could not account for. There. You have my answer to Sigha. He can take it to hell if he wishes."

Dayo's jaw hung down.

***

Tonye Sigha was every inch the upward-mobile professional he claimed to be, and a worthy son-in-law to-be to the president of Nigeria, with his good looks a fine mix between the macho of RMD and boyish handsomeness of Desmond Eliot. He cut his hair so short it framed his head tightly. He had a moustache but otherwise a clean shave. His white shirt sparkled, under his hand-made, figure-hugging, black Italian suit, and fitting black shoes. Tonye Sigha, couldn't be more than thirty-two years.

Dini despite himself, admired his well-toned male body clad in the expensive suit. He was light-skinned, a shade or two darker than Dini. His eyes glowed like that of a lion sure of a fat prey when he entered the judge's office at the Federal High Court.

Dayo did not look intimidated by the young, arrogant lawyer. He had often told Dini from experience that in his career, a good platform didn't necessarily make a good lawyer. Dini hoped Sigha was about to learn this and in a hard way too.

The two lawyers shook hands firmly, and then Sigha turned to Dini with a smile he was sure had stolen the heart of the president's daughter, and shook him as well, his grip firm, intimidating.

Sigha nodded. "We finally meet, Dr. Brisibe."

Dini nodded in return. "My pleasure."

The three men sat comfortably on the couches in the office. A young

lawyer named Kuye came in to join them and Sigha introduced him as an intern in his office.

"Let me formally open this meeting with introductions," Sigha said. "The charges facing Dr. Brisibe, I believe, were read to him in his cell this morning?" He looked at Dayo who returned the gaze steadily. "One count of sabotage of a federal project, one count of conspiracy to sabotage a federal project, one count of malicious neglect of his duty, one count of malicious arson, five counts of voluntary manslaughter."

He opened a fancy-looking iPad but didn't look at it as he spoke. "The essence of this meeting is to um, have an informal pre-trial session where both sides can have the full case blown apart and decide either to go on to trial, or agree to settle out of court.

"I definitely will vote for an amicable settlement out of court. I'm not ready to go into a long trial, and then end up where I started from."

"Sigha, this is still introduction," Dayo said.

Sigha laughed, a soft bubbly laughter. A rich man's laughter, not rowdy and nervous. "I get carried away so easily. So. I understand Dr. Brisibe is pleading not guilty on all charges. So, let's go into the details of that plea."

Dayo took Dini through all the questions already prepared. Sigha sat easy, just looking into Dini's eyes. Dini had never seen anyone so self-contained. It made him want to walk out.

When Dayo finished, he signalled to Sigha.

Sigha sighed and scratched his temple with nice, manicured fingers. "Dr. Brisibe, tell me why I should drop the charges against you."

Dini maintained a steady gaze with the man. "I'm innocent."

"Facts show you're not. You knew the machines were not working properly, yet, you neglected the plant. You had a pattern for testing and yet you changed strategy just the day before without informing your staff. To cap it off, you disappeared when you could have been on site to salvage the situation. You knew how best these machines operated. And on top of all the indicting evidence against you, you lied. You can't account for your movements on the night of the explosion!"

"We'll take it one by one, Sigha." Dayo looked at Dini. "Let's talk about the machines."

"On that site, I had deaerators, generating plants, advanced aeroderivative gas turbines, and a host of highly sensitive equipment. The machines are made in China. They are designed to work round the clock. We started off with the initial design but it failed. So, I set them for eighteen hours, and then twelve. We were still testing—" Dini swallowed and sat forward. He still couldn't make direct reference to the explosion. "My team is fully aware. We have schedules printed out daily so those who may 'forget' are reminded!"

Dayo brought out a stack of sheets of paper. "The current one got burnt but they are in the office server. These are the printouts dating back to the

day the machines arrived fourteen months ago. Every single day. Dr. Brisibe

was paranoid about it. He had a copy pasted at the plant, and one pasted in his

office at the Power House."

Sigha arched his eyebrow. "I believe I have something like that?" He looked at Kuye who nodded. "Move on then."

"My disappearance is as a result of common egomaniacal behaviour. I was mad about something." Dini shrugged. "I went to remove it from my shoulder."

"You were away, let me see." Sigha moved things around on his iPad. "Fifty hours precisely from the last time you were spotted in church to the time you showed in your office." He looked at Dini. "This ego-whatever thing you have, how often do you get it?"

"It's rare."

"How often do you experience it and how long does it last?"

"Cut the tricks, Sigha. Dini answer directly," Dayo cut in.

"Someone has egomaniac for fifty crucial hours, I want details, Dayo. You should give me that." Sigha was being condescending and it left Dini with a burning sensation down his throat.

"Look, I lost a few nuts right, I went into hiding."

"Who was in the hole with you?" Sigha glared at Dini with as much mutual irritation. "A woman, Deacon Dr. Brisibe? Who was she?"

Dini breathed in. "You want me to spell it out? I had no alibi."

Dayo almost jumped out of his seat. Sigha's amused look stopped him. "Let's move on. So far the score's a draw."

Sigha rested back and assessed Dini. "We have all your financial records."

"You can't find anything there."

"You're right. But I'm still digging. So far, so good for you, but I doubt it will stay so. There must be stacks somewhere. Do you want to help us out? It might help you if we end up on a bargaining table."

"Sorry, Barrister Sigha, I have nothing to declare," Dini snapped.

"Don't hang in there, Sigha, move it ahead." Dayo had been very nervous about Tonbra's secret accounts and had instructed Dini to get the details the minute he stepped back into his house.

"Your wife's foundation is being investigated," Sigha said.

Dayo had instructed Dini not to make comments on statements. 'Answer questions only.' So, he merely returned Sigha's level gaze.

"Do you have anything to declare there?"

"No."

Sigha leaned forward and looked penetratingly at Dini. It felt as though he had a hook on him, about to fish something, and Dini knew this could hit hard but he managed to keep his breathing normal.

"Dini," Sigha used his first name softly. "I respect you a great deal and I hate what's happening to you right now. All off records," he said, "you're the

best energy engineer Nigeria has produced so far, we don't want to lose you. But hey, you're messing with the wrong guys here, and they'll cut you lose before you know where you dropped—"

"Is this part of this meeting?" Dayo said impatiently.

Sigha turned from Dini to him, and back. He slid back into his relaxed posture and smiled. "Let's talk about Sylvester, your assistant."

Dini didn't know he had been holding his breath till he released it.

"Your assistant has pleaded guilty on lesser charges and has been slammed with ten years. He's going to testify against you at trial." Sigha frowned. "What do you say to that?"

"Nothing. He can't lie under oath."

Sigha laughed out right, exposing a perfect set of even, white teeth. "You seem so sure about that." A smile lingered at the corners of his mouth. "I like you, Dr. Brisibe. It would have been great to meet at the polo club or golf club and not here."

Dini almost commented. Instead, he glanced at Dayo who remained mute, his lips pressed together, his eyes aflame. Sigha was losing ground and they all knew it.

"What was your relationship with Sylvester like outside of the job?"

"We had no relationship. He wasn't competent. He had been thrust on the team because of some influence from some politicians in power. I gave him very little to do."

"You hated your assistant."

"Is that a question?"

"Is it true?"

"I didn't hate him. He was not in the way of the team's progress, so I had no hard feelings about him." Dini wanted to add that if they used Sylvester against him, he would tear the man into so many pieces, their case would disappear before it even started but he said nothing more.

"Why would he want to willingly testify against you?"

"You'd have to ask him that, Sigha, I don't know how Sylvester's brain works. But one thing I know is that he does not make a credible witness against me—"

Dayo's hand went up in the air to stop him and he nodded.

"There goes Engineer Dr. Deacon Brisibe a true patriot with no guile." Sigha's tone dripped of mockery. "I'm going to make you an offer."

Dayo sat forward. "Are you done with that session?"

Sigha sighed. "If I'm about to make an offer, Dayo, I guess that's what it means." He looked and held Dayo's gaze for a moment and then looked at Dini. "Twenty years."

The words hit Dini in the bottom of his belly. His jaw dropped open and his eyes went wild.

"You're dropping all charges, Sigha," Dayo said calmly. "And you know why. Your case is a bottomless pit. You can't even argue one point through."

Sigha smiled again. Dini noted involuntarily that he had a beautiful smile. He was a beautiful man and at the same time, a macho-man.

"I don't want to lose you, Dini. If you take twenty years, you may end up doing only five," Sigha said. "You have no alibi. You have a secret account that will prove you were paid to jeopardize your project—"

"Which you can't prove anywhere," Dayo said.

"And your assistant has a lot to say on that," Sigha said. "Take the offer. Who knows, you may end up with only two years!"

"You need him behind bars till the elections end, and it won't work. The explosion was an accident. It was going to happen sometime." Dayo's voice pitched. "Dini advised government several times on the specifications for the machines. Half of the funds needed were provided, and his recommendation ignored. Those machines were sub-standard, and I have proof he complained. He was only trying to make the best of a horrible situation, testing those machines for weeks on end. Imagine," he gesticulated toward Sigha. "This machine should work through twenty-four hours a day without feeling it, but they couldn't even make it through twelve hours.

"You purposely left out the fact that the gas tunnel was not shut off, which is Sylvester's direct responsibility. The only direct responsibility he had. Whether the machine is on or not, shut the gas at a particular time! And he couldn't even do that for whatever his reasons were. See," Dayo leaned forward. "The best bet right now is hold on tight to your scapegoat, Sylvester. Let him do the ten years or whatever. I hear his godfather is in trouble with the party anyway."

Sigha jumped to his feet. "My offer has a 24-hour mandate. You may want to take it, Dr. Brisibe. Five years against all that loss in life and property is only fair. Let me know."

Dini and Dayo stood as well. "We are not taking it. You don't have to wait for twenty-four hours," Dayo said. "We demand immediate release."

Sigha walked to the door and looked at the two men. "You'll hear from the office of the attorney-general." He exited without pleasantries. His intern followed closely.

A strange silence ensued. "I think we won this one," Dini said softly.

"Yeah." Dayo put his documents away. "But I have a strange feeling about something. I think he's under some form of pressure to nail you. Sylvester is not a big-enough fish." He looked at Dini with narrowed eyes. "How do you give Tonbra money?"

Dini frowned. "What money?"

"Any money? I'll sleep easy if I know what those Tonbra's secret accounts say. If there are chunky deposits, you may not twist out of it."

"I give her cash most of the time in bits. They won't find chunky deposits in it. I write a check if I need to give her more than two hundred and fifty."

"They will find chunky deposits if she stacks before paying in. Get more on that account for me. Sigha played around it. I don't like that. He's going to keep digging till he finds. And I think he's upset right now."

"Wouldn't you be?"

"He's not upset about the result of this meeting. There's something else. He must have wanted something more before coming here."

"Money?"

Dayo shook his head. "No, not money. I think he was waiting for some information. You'll notice he didn't want to dig in on Sylvester quickly."

"He probably knew the facts about Sylvester."

"Probably not." Dayo sighed. "I trust my hunch, and something is not right. Sigha is petty, and he's full of himself. He seems desperate, and I hate desperate people." He looked pointedly at Dini. "You're not off yet so the rule remains. Don't talk when you're not asked to."

Dini nodded. They both left the office. Policemen on guard took Dini back to his cell. He was freed on bail the following week by order from the attorney-general's office, after Dayo put all the pressure he had the ability for. The order had been to free him on bail. The charges were not dropped so further investigations could be carried out. Dini was ordered not to leave Lagos without the knowledge of the police. He was also suspended at work, indefinitely, without any benefits.

His personal possessions were given back to him intact. Dayo took him home.

CHAPTER 31

Tonbra sat rigidly through the short announcement by Pastor Flo.

The pastor had had the good mind to call her into his office and inform her before facing the ministers, and workers, and eventually, the congregation. Deacon Dinipre Brisibe broke his marriage vows and will be on suspension till further notice. The pastor encouraged everyone to pray for Deacon Brisibe in this period. He did not give details but putting two and two together, Tonbra knew people would soon connect the lawsuit Dini was facing as a direct judgement from God.

He deserved it, didn't he? It hurt her to her deepest bone. Of course, sex between them had been much of nothing. From the very start! In recent times, it had been non-existent. If she counted well, almost three months now. Well.

She blamed it on herself. She just still couldn't give herself to any man fully. Ebisine still had her. He had been her first and only, up until Dini came along. She wished she could exonerate Dini, forgive even, but she couldn't. He had openly disgraced her. That was not tenable.

A few people walked up to her and hugged and greeted her after the announcement came up just before service started. After service, more people came. She smiled at first but slowly bitterness crept into her face and soul, till she ground her teeth so she would not scream.

She hated Dini. And she despised Pastor Flo. He had known about this for at least three days and he didn't call to tell her, or better still, as Dini's leader, command him to be the one to tell her. One of the ladies who came to sympathize with her called Dini a shameless dog. But calling him names hurt her more than the lady could imagine, rather than make her feel better.

She was a beautiful woman. More so since she married Dini and got the means to take care of herself. Why do men do this to us, one other lady frowned and hugged her. Was she not good enough for him?

When they'd first got married, Dini had been all over her. Over the years, they'd both settled into a comfortable complacency. They hardly derived joy

from their intimacy and now focused more on companionship. And raising their children. Even though in that they had drifted apart. Each time Dini tried to discipline the kids, it hurt Tonbra so much, gradually, Dini had left it off for her. She felt better that way. She couldn't stand him hurting Ebisine's children.

That was not fair. But once she said it, Dini backed off. She couldn't deny he loved them, but can you love another man's child as your own? Dini tried but it wasn't enough.

This adultery now defeated her more than anything else. A disgrace. It challenged her feminism! A small voice reminded her he might have done it for the sake of getting a baby. Maybe it was the same woman Mama had brought—but she discounted that. Even then! He married her. He took vows he would remain true to her alone through thick and thin. For better for worse.

When she got home after church, she tried to fathom the reason why she felt so numb. She didn't feel like crying. She was just so angry with him, with herself. She, for the umpteenth time cursed her reasons for marrying him.

She didn't plan to go and see him in the cell anymore. In fact, she felt like disappearing, leaving right then with her children. She could if she wanted to. She could pack and leave, just like that. And he would never find her.

Instead she changed from her church outfit, ordered her driver to take the children anywhere they wanted, and went into her closet. She wore the same dress Ebisine bought for her on her last birthday before he died. It was a cheap taffeta and chiffon caftan. She would not be caught in such an outfit these days except in here, where she lived her life with the spouse of her youth.

She did her normal ritual, dusted the framed pictures and then went to stand in front of the portrait. She rested her head on his chest for a while. She kissed him for a long time. Then she brought him up-to-date on the things happening in her life. She talked about the children. She even asked him for advice on what to do about Dini. She felt cheated, disgraced, violated. What would people think of her now? She would be ashamed to go to church, the wife of the cheating deacon.

She talked about her plans and about the foundation. Things were going so well. His name was fast becoming internationally recognized. She was raising a discipleship for him in the world of journalism. The Ebisine Francis George School of Journalism had received approval finally. She was excited.

Then she took the pictures and talked about them. She remembered all their good times together. She stared long and hard at the one on the beach when they travelled together to Port Harcourt. She laughed and laughed and laughed. Then she started asking him why he left. It had been seven years now, and she still could not recover from her loss. She missed the things they did together, the places they loved, and the things they ate—she missed his

huge body as it swallowed hers up.

Then she started the crying ritual. She cried till she slept off. This ritual lasted several hours.

***

Dini came home on a scorching Wednesday afternoon. Mid-week service held on Wednesday, and he planned to be in attendance. He had been told by Pastor Flo, who sent the message to him through Dayo, that his suspension was indefinite, while the church prayed for him and rehabilitated him. He had assignments to do while on suspension, and one of them was to attend every service as often as possible.

He found the house empty except for the servants, and this pleased him. He wished he could move out of their room again. But he didn't want the children to notice just after returning from detention. Deborah welcomed him back without any reference to where he'd been. Better.

Dayo hugged him before leaving, and told him to relax, and focus on the things that made him happy. As though there was any such thing as happiness in his life anymore, with nothing to do, other than just sit and stare.

He walked slowly up the stairs. He had lost tremendous weight in three weeks and felt weak. But food was not going to be panacea. His soul bled. His heart ached. All in less than a month, he had hit something deep within him that amazed him it could even exist. He had prided himself to be a good man, a man who feared God. Now? He didn't even know himself anymore.

His suspension at the office did not bother him at all. He knew he would be cleared. The loss in lives weighed heavily on his soul. He had lost the best men he had in that fire. The suspension in church moved him in a different way. He didn't care what people would say.

What bothered him was him!

Had he been purged of the mad desire he exhibited in Oyinemi's arms, not once but thrice in quick succession? Where did that come from? He hated her now, for sure but what brought it on? He had been a man of tremendous caution and control. Could she have bewitched him?

Was he so prone to losing all restraint? He held his emotions on a tight rein. Before. He'd been tempted by women on several occasions. He'd held himself. He prided himself of the rigid control most men could not boast of.

Would this suspension help him to overcome this new re-packaged demon that had fallen him in battle? Oyinemi who didn't go to church, who spoke timidly and softly, a virgin! Spiritually, he was the Goliath, she was David. One stone was all she had needed to hit him but like the proverbial David, she also had four other stones. She could hit again, and he was sure who would win because the feeling had overwhelmed him again when he saw her at the cell!

That was what he needed to work on and be worried about. Of course, he had one weapon, to flee. It was the only one he had confidence would work. He may need to go away. Take Tonbra and the children to another country. Avoid Akure and Apoi like the plague. He felt like punishing Mama for all this!

He could actually go away. He had several job offers he'd turned down over the years. He had contacts in more than twenty countries of the world. And he could always return to the states and teach. He would be running from a woman he had reluctantly accepted defeat from but that was nothing new. Great men fled from women all the time. For example, Elijah fled from Jezebel! And the few who dared stay, suffered dearly like Samson!

He opened the door to his room and stopped short at the sounds behind him. It came from across the corridor. Precisely from Timi's room. A mad rage overwhelmed him and before he could stop himself, he stomped across the hall and yanked on Timi's bedroom door.

The door was locked from inside. He moved back, and with all his strength, kicked the door. They had not put locks on the children's room doors for all the reasons they thought best, so he knew Timi must have put a form of barrier behind the door. Or did she now have a lock?

He was right. Her vanity stool tumbled on impact from the kick on the door, and Dini pushed it, just as 'the boy' scrambled off the bed, grabbing his trouser, which lay on the floor by the bed. His naked body did not get much of a chance from Dini's pummelling punches. He wasn't interested in the hard hits as much as getting his trousers on. Dini didn't give him a chance.

Timi leapt off the bed, pulling the bed sheet off to cover herself. She screamed hysterically for Dini to stop. When he didn't, she ran out. Moments later, Deborah came running up the stairs with her. Dini stood over the slumped frame of the boy, panting. Blood came out of his nose, mouth, and eyes, while one hand weakly held the trousers dangling from mid-thigh.

Deborah, sobbing, shame-facedly carried the boy's shirt to cover him. She bent over him and touched him neck.

Dini stepped back. "Throw this trash out of my house!"

Timi screamed and lunged at him. She punched him, but he handled her easily with a slap across her cheek. She staggered and fell on the edge of her bed.

"You should be ashamed of yourself!" Dini couldn't control the tears that sprang to his eyes. "You're not even fourteen yet, Timi!"

"I'm leaving this house! I hate you! I hate you!" Timi screamed.

Dini looked at the boy. For a moment, he panicked. "Is he breathing?"

Timi jumped up and went to kneel beside the boy. "You've killed him, you wicked man. You've killed him!" She wailed.

Deborah sniffed. "He'll be alright, sir."

Dini stepped out of the room. She wasn't even fourteen yet! How had he failed so? He found his phone and called Tonbra.

"Where are you?"

"Good afternoon too. Are you still in jail?"

Dini scowled. "I'm home. I need you to come immediately."

The tone must have gotten to her. "What happened?"

"Nothing serious, but Timi was with a boy, in her room! They were—having sex!"

Tonbra kept quiet so long, he said, "Tonbra, did you hear what I said? Did you know the boy before? How could Timi—when did—?" He breathed hard. "Where are you?"

"I'm in the market. I'm shopping for furniture for the Ebisine Francis George School of Journalism." It was his turn to go silent. She knew he hated that name with every thread of sanity in his body. He had displayed it more in recent times.

"I think you should come home. Timi is hysterical."

She raised her voice. "What did you do? Did you barge in on her again?"

"Is that the point? She's not even fourteen and she's sleeping around!"

"She got it from you, I guess! Is that not what you've been doing too?"

"Tonbra!"

"Go to hell!" She hung up.

Dini walked back into his room and went into the bathroom. His head ached. Maybe he should have let it go. Maybe he had finally lost the essence in his own life. Timi was having sex at thirteen! He'd failed in fathering her.

He stripped and stood under the cold shower till it became hazardous to his health. He stepped out and looked around him. His own house depressed him. He wore a simple long caftan and went back to be sure the boy was okay. He was just a boy anyway, probably wasn't much older than Timi. Seventeen at most.

Deborah had cleaned the boy up, and he was dressed when Dini came back and stood in the corridor in front of Timi's room. The boy shrunk visibly and walked with a limp toward the stairway.

Dini pointed his index finger at him and barked, "Don't ever come back here!"

Dini turned back to Timi, but the teenager pushed the stool out of the way and slammed the door in his face. All well, he thought. Her mother would soon come home, and they needed to talk seriously.

Tonbra came home shortly afterward and went straight to Timi's room. The girl was furiously packing her clothes into a big travelling bag. Tonbra tried to pacify her as she threatened to leave. Dini watched for a while with disgust as Tonbra soothed and pleaded with her spoilt daughter not to leave.

He walked back into his room and waited for her to join him. They had to talk about everything their lives had turned into. An apology for his

adultery was in place and he planned to give one, and to explain his dilemma at work to her. If he needed a loving woman, it was now. He needed his wife to face this storm. He felt like crying but held himself.

He didn't know how long the petting and patting lasted. He lay on the bed and closed his eyes and didn't open it until Tonbra stomped into the room.

He didn't remember the assignment Dayo had given him until Tonbra walked straight into her closet.

The accounts!

She was out in a few minutes, changed from her skirt suit and into slacks and a small blouse.

"I'm taking her to Grace's. I won't let you kill her!" she said, vibrating with rage. "I have had enough of your nonsense. I may be leaving as well. Because this is just getting too much." She marched toward the door.

Dini couldn't hold the tears any longer. "Please—"

"Ebisine would never cry in front of a woman," Tonbra muttered. She slammed the door after her.

Chapter 32

Erebi had been in touch through Dayo previously, first because the prison didn't allow her to visit and, second because his attitude toward her changed.

Dini knew things had gone really bad between him and her, but his sister had been mature about it. He had not told her about what happened in her house. He withdrew completely from her, became distant and rude, and though no one spoke about it, Erebi knew something was terribly wrong.

He'd sent an enquiry about Mama's health and when he got a clean report, become more infuriated against Oyinemi. Over the weeks after his release, he built a garrison of hate around her and all the things that concerned her. It was the only defence strategy he relied on. Thoughts about her were forbidden like those thoughts you curse as soon as they cross paths with your mind. His hatred prospered.

A few days after his release, Erebi visited. While he leaned against the mantle-place, and waited for her to make conversation, she sat easy in a couch in the parlour and looked at him. She wore her typical light-coloured skirt-suit, a sign she had been at work, crossed her legs at the ankles, and tucked them under the couch as far as they could go, the posture stretching her upper body to a sit-up position.

"When are we going to ever talk about what is eating at you?" she said softly.

Dini crossed his arms and bare feet and arched his neck. His first instinct snubbed her. But then, he missed her. In the last few weeks, the only people who'd been concerned about his well-being, emotional or otherwise, were Dayo and

Pastor Flo. It was good to see Erebi. Even better that she had disregarded his cold and rude attitude and come out of her way to see him. Everyone had their own challenges, and he knew she wasn't any different.

"I've been through a lot, sis. What can I say?"

"But between you and me. I don't know what I've done to offend you!"

She could feign innocence, and it annoyed him, but he won't be dragged into any game of words.

"I've been going through a lot, Erebi. I'm not myself."

"I know. And I understand. But we used to be close. We used to share our problems—"

He clenched his teeth. "I was in a police cell shortly after the last time I was drugged in your house!"

"I told you the lady who gave you that palmy said she was Grace George's friend—Grace wasn't even at the party. The lady was so drunk herself. By the time Tonbra contacted Grace on the issue, Grace said she didn't know any such person." Erebi straightened even more. "How can you think I planned to poison you with palmy? I was so surprised you took it at all!"

Dini allowed her to finish. It would make sense if he believed the things Oyinemi told him in the middle of the night, cuddled in his arms! But events that followed this period were so overwhelming, he hadn't the opportunity to check out the facts. Erebi had said something about finding the lady who gave him the palmy, dead drunk, sprawled outside the house, sometime later. He could pursue that now. He didn't have a job. He had time to chase Grace down.

"That's easy to believe anyway. You know I stopped drinking."

"I just got the news someone Mama brought here is pregnant for you." Erebi sat forward. "I didn't know anything about it, Dini! I just got the news today and began to put it together. You probably thought I was in on it from the start—"

Dini jerked forward, his head light for a moment. She was pregnant? Erebi continued to talk. Exonerating herself of any knowledge about any plot or any woman and the *palmwine* occurrence. She wanted him to be sure she knew nothing about it all. Didn't know that palmy girl from Adam. Didn't know the girl had planned to drug and sleep—

"She was used." Dini didn't recognize his own voice. The demon was pregnant. They have won. Mama has won!

"How? I don't understand." Erebi walked to him. She placed cool hands on his face. "You've been through so much, dear."

He allowed her to pull his head to her chest and massage his shoulders. In his grief, he blurted out the plan. He confessed everything to her, just as he'd known it. And as Oyinemi had filled in the parts he didn't know.

"I think Mama took it too far," she whispered into his ears. "She knew I wouldn't have agreed to such a horrible plot." She stepped back and looked at him.

His eyes were clear. Hers were wet. She dragged him to sit with her.

"What sort of creature is this Grace George?" Erebi shook her head. "Why would she agree to do that, after all you've been to her?"

"She has nothing against me. She's after Tonbra. But Tonbra would not hear about that. She's my wife's confidant. These days, Timi stays with her. She's the real family!"

"Why would she be after Tonbra?"

"Jealousy, maybe? Or revenge. I don't know." Dini shrugged. "I believe at the beginning of our marriage, she wanted Tonbra to ask me to help her in some way, and Tonbra shunned her. She went to Mama for help. And Mama asked me to give her the money she needed, which I did." He didn't want to talk about Grace. "So, who told you—the—girl is—is pregnant?"

"I went to visit Mama. Our monthly thing. She was in very high spirits. Apparently, the girl just got tested." She sighed heavily. "I sympathize with Mama on her desire, but I don't agree with this kind of intrusion on your marriage."

Dini didn't know what to say. She was pregnant. She was carrying his baby. He was full of hate, yet he had never had such conflicted good-bad news in his life. He was married. He was still serving a disciplinary action taken against what had brought this pregnancy.

Oyinemi Salpon is pregnant. He was elated!

Erebi sighed. "Does Tonbra know any of this?"

"Yeah. I'm on suspension in church and everyone knows why!" He laughed a short sound that came out like a harsh bark. He stood and went back to lean against the mantelpiece. He placed his head on the cool marble and closed his eyes.

"What are you going to do?" The concern in Erebi's voice provoked a contrary angry reaction in him but he swallowed before telling her to leave him alone. After all, Erebi wanted to help. He knew that.

He took a deep breath and turned to her. "Nothing."

"I mean about the girl and the pregnancy."

"I mean nothing. Mama wanted my child, now she has it. Let her worry about it."

Erebi's jaw dropped. "I know how you feel, I really do, but it's not right to just do nothing."

"What do you want me to do? Marry a second wife? Wait till she delivers and bring the child to my house? Or send my wife away to marry her!" He shouted at her much as he wished he didn't.

"This is your child! Unless you dispute it, the child is your responsibility! More so, you don't have any other child."

It sounded lame even in his ears as he spoke. "I have three lovely kids." Erebi started shaking her head but he cut her off with a huge swipe of his hand over the space between them. "I don't plan to talk about this anymore. I have enough reason to go crazy in my life right now."

After the storm with Timi, Dini and Tonbra had settled into a cold reality. They couldn't find even the companionship they'd held dearly before. Their relationship now journeyed toward taking another comfortable shape –

cordial roommates.

Dini had gotten Tonbra's secret check books out, though he hated every second he spent inside the despicable closet. To his surprise, he discovered two more, of banks in South Africa and the UK. The previous four were personal accounts with names Dini did not recognize. He wrote out the details and gave them to Dayo.

They didn't hear anything from the office of the attorney-general for a while, though Dayo investigated the accounts Tonbra kept and discovered they were harmless. Two belonged, from his findings to Pere and Ebisine. However, he made little progress on the foreign accounts.

About a week after his release, Dini decided to take the bull by the horn, and visit Timi in Grace's house. The siblings now virtually lived at Grace's as well. And though there was calm in his house, Dini hated the disunity. Timi had performed badly in her junior WAEC and had been virtually pushed to the next class after Tonbra went on to plead and 'appreciate' the staff of the 'way over the top' expensive school Timi attended.

The meeting with Timi in Grace's house went bad and Dini slapped the teenager again. He knew that would seal their relationship for a long time as she told him she hated him. Again.

"Dini!" Erebi's voice jolted him back. "At least you can give her money. I understand she's a teacher as well. Her income can't—"

"She chose to do this, Erebi! She's not a victim. Mama convinced her and she agreed." He turned away from her. He had difficulty breathing. "I refuse to feel any guilt."

Erebi left after that. He knew his words and attitude upset and she had a right. He didn't have any other child anywhere. This was the only responsibility directly his. Well, he had a wife. One sin too many had been committed. Enough was enough.

CHAPTER 33

One full month after his release, Dini began to get really restless. Nothing changed. Both the suspension at the office and in the church remained. Christmas and New Year came and went uneventfully. He still couldn't leave Lagos and had to report at the zone 2 police headquarters every week. Sigha remained aloof and ever arrogant.

Tonbra took the children for vacation in South Africa and visited her doctors again. Despite their strained relationship, it pleased Dini she wanted to follow-up on the last failed IVF. It gave him some conscience-massage that he had bluntly refused to be a part of Oyinemi's life or pregnancy.

The silence in his home, and life, during the festive season helped him to coordinate his thought process. He had come a long way. All his life, the weathers had been ridden off easily. Now things have changed.

Though it was not officially acknowledged and Tonbra had not been told, by him at least, another woman carried his child. She would be the mother of his child. She would always be a part of his life—unless he bluntly refused to publicly acknowledge her or the child. But he would always know. His morals and status may compel him to deny she existed, but his conscience wouldn't.

He would bear the cross all his life. The nature of punishment meted out would be the knowledge that would forever haunt him. Knowing as he had failed in raising another man's children, someone somewhere would raise his child as well, and probably do a bad job of it.

A scar he would bear on his conscience forever.

At the watch-night service, Pastor Flo asked all to name the year, and everyone gave the year the name they wanted. He then admonished they prepare because the devil would fight that name, which is a prophecy.

Seems the devil was eavesdropping on Dini's thoughts when he named the year, his year of peace and calm. By middle of January, Dini got two mind-blowing calls. At the end, he didn't know which of them was more shattering.

The first call came from Dayo. He didn't know what but apparently,

Sigha had found something on Dini. The prosecutor wanted to meet urgently but Dayo was taking his son back to school in the UK and he had to shift the meeting forward by three days. He told Dini to prepare for a bad day with the prosecutor. In the weeks leading up to the call, Sigha had made public statements in favour of exposing a grand conspiracy to sabotage the power plant project for political reasons. The comments were subtle in relation to Dini, but Dayo had been around long enough to smell a rat!

While Dini pondered and commenced his three-day wait, he got the second call from his doctor friend in South Africa. He hadn't known the Namibian was in Nigeria. They had met in a world conference in Namibia and forged a relationship. When his friend, Dr. Paul, moved to South Africa, they had maintained contact.

Paul was in Nigeria for just two days, attending a conference at Sheraton Hotel. He wanted to meet with Dini urgently. He didn't want his friend to come with anyone, and most certainly not his wife. That set Dini off.

Paul, a gynaecologist, had shown a lot of interest in their case, and had been personally involved in getting the best available personnel to operate on Tonbra.

The conference had a one-hour break during which Paul requested to see Dini. Dini had a bad feeling about the meeting from the start. When Paul smiled tentatively at him before giving him a strong hug, he knew it was not going to be good at all.

On the last trip to South Africa, again, the medical cost had been crippling. Dini didn't mind the cost. Only that this time, Tonbra had not used Paul or the previous hospital.

The doctor took Dini to his room and did not say a word until he had closed the door behind him. What he told Dini afterward almost crushed him, so much he could not let him go home just like that. He had to spend time to speak and convince Dini not to take any action about what he'd heard. After spending the entire one-hour break together, the men hugged each other again, and Dini took his leave.

Acting on his friend's advice, he didn't call Tonbra. Much as he itched for answers, he waited till after dinner when the children had gone to bed before he produced stacks of medical records he hadn't believed belonged to his wife.

Even as he brought them out, he didn't believe what those records stated. Would Paul lie against his wife? Of course not. These records were confidential reports spanning the last eight years of Tonbra's medical history. Paul would go to prison if ever the leak was traced to him.

Tonbra finished her facial rituals and wore a transparent night gown that showed off her beautiful body, but Dini had ceased to see beauty in his wife, especially whenever she stepped away from her closet. In the weeks after his adultery, he discovered he was not in the least interested in being intimate with Tonbra and refused to ponder on the reason. Not that Tonbra did anything to attract him either. Sometimes it seemed to him she had no interest at all as well.

He needed to be calm when he brought this up, according to Paul's advice, and so, he sat on the bed, propped against the wall by two pillows. He placed the folder with his facts in between his legs.

"When last did you talk to Dr. Finidi?"

Tonbra walked to her side of the bed. He watched her intently and couldn't help but be impressed she didn't even pause in her stride.

She spared him a glance and shrugged.

"Can't remember. Before August I think."

It amazed him how much she had changed. When he first met her, she was scared of living. Her husband just died, and they owed on everything from school fees to house rent. Her job was corporate slavery redefined. He had picked her up, loved her, cleaned her, and virtually changed her life around. Then she was timid, afraid. Now she was strong, confident, changed.

"Before you took out your womb. You called to quarrel with him for messing your reproductive system up." Because he spoke as though discussing the colour of her transparent night gown, she stopped just at the edge of the bed and looked at him.

Their gazes clashed with steam. She looked like a cat caught in the glare of a car's headlights in the middle of the night. Yes, caught red-handed.

She stammered a reply and chuckled. He wished he heard what she said. It didn't matter.

"You knew you couldn't have a child, yet you made us spend all that money." He couldn't even be mad at her at this point.

She folded her arms across her chest in a combat stance. "I don't know what you are talking about!"

Her reply drove the nuts out of his brain. He sat forward and slapped the folder in between his legs. "Of course, you do. I have all the facts. Here. Right here!"

"What facts? First, you go cheating with some strange woman, disgracing me in church and now you're looking to score a point, talking rubbish!"

"More than ten million naira, three operations, anxiety, disappointment and all that risking life is what you call looking to score a point?"

How on earth did Dr. Paul think he would not get upset about this? Even if she was begging, he would be upset. All that money. All that time. All the lies. All the hope and expectation and anger and pain of disappointments! How could she compare that waste to his adultery? Or even more, this arrogant denial in the face of glaring truth.

He swung his feet off the bed and carried the folder with him. He stopped himself before standing up. He had never hit her before, but he couldn't trust himself now. He hadn't known he could hit his precious Timi,

or despise her. Neither had he ever thought anything could make him desire, not to talk of sleeping with a woman who wasn't his wife. No, he would not add wife-battery to the degenerated person he had become.

"You are going crazy, and I am not talking to you on my medical situation!"

Tonbra was bold. He had to give it to her. She climbed the bed and pulled the sheet over her shoulders. She even turned his way so he could see the bland expression on her face. He didn't know this stranger. This was not the woman he married.

"Tonbra, this attitude is not going to get you anywhere! You don't even feel remorse!"

She continued to stare at him. Or this was the real woman he married, he just hadn't known her. Pastor Flo said he rushed her. He hadn't allowed her to mourn. That was true. He was discovering another painful fact – he hadn't courted her. He hadn't had time to find out and discover this extremely selfish creature.

Strangely, the thought soothed him. Okay, so this was his wife. He stared at her as though he was seeing her for the first time. She stared right back with a smirk.

"You know I could kill your doctor's career with what I have here?"

She shrugged and blinked. Yes, he married a witch, though that sounded cliché. He'd heard every man at some point in their married lives either believed they had married a witch or was it a fable? He'd thought it was. Still did. The first five years with Tonbra had been a fairy tale, and then the child-talk had begun. Maybe if he'd killed it then, all this would not be happening.

Definitely, Tonbra would not be looking for how to untie her tied tubes, and then discover the failed abortion she had when Ebisine died, had damaged part of her organs, and then discover her tubes had been compromised. And then when they tried to fetch the eggs from the ovary for the IVF, Finidi had further compromised her chances because he wasn't good. And hadn't gotten a good doctor to do it and had further made mistakes.

She had gotten infected and that finally sealed the fate of her fertility. Much of the money he thought went for the IVF after the first time actually went to cover the truth from him. The supposed second IVF had actually been to remove the womb completely. And this last time was just a total rip-off. Tonbra had shared half of the money and scattered the rest into her accounts or whatever she used the stolen money for. Someone with a conscience in Finidi's office had called Paul and spilled the beans. Paul had carefully gathered his information and finally gotten the opportunity to get it to him.

"You don't care what happens to your doctor, do you? Do you even care what happens to anyone? Do you have any scruples at all?"

"You don't care what happens to me!" She lifted her head a bit. "I went through all that horrible, painful procedure because you wanted a child. And all I get is accusations."

"Why didn't you tell me you tried to abort Ebisine? And then tied your tubes right after delivering him?" he snapped, pulling tightly on the reins of his temper.

"Because it was none of your business."

"None of my business, Tonbra. You are my first and only wife. Did you think I would not want children?"

She sat all the way up and continued to look at him. "We had children. Was that not enough for you?" She shouted. "Until your wicked mother came, we were fine."

"We were not fine." He shouted. "I was not fine. If you had told me about all this rubbish, we would have been fine. I could have dealt with it."

"You wouldn't have. You would have been upset and unhappy and make me feel unworthy. At the end, you would look for another woman—like your mother has helped you find."

"I didn't fall for it, did I?" He winced at the indirect lie. He lowered the folder to the floor at his feet and sat on the edge of the bed.

"Well, whether you fell for it or not, the deed is done. Ebisine wanted not more than three kids, and he got it."

Dini saw red. "Oh, so I get the cut for what your dead husband does or does not want?" he growled. "He was always a part of this marriage, wasn't he?"

She reacted just as angrily. "Don't you dare refer to him as dead." Her body jerked toward him and for a moment he thought she would hit him but she crouched on the bed and sneered.

"He's been dead for eight years, sorry." Dini's stomach tightened. The pain that coursed through her face gave him momentary pleasure. Then he remembered the closet, and the pleasure went sour. Good God! What was he dealing with here?

"Well," she purred, her eyes looking sleepy. "It's your loss, Dinipre. As for your foolish allegations about my medical records, you can do as you like with it. But let me tell you this. I didn't change. Thank God my records show I've had no scruples, as you say. But who changed? You."

She rose to her knees and pointed at him. "You said you loved me, that you would take care of me. You changed. You never raised your hands or your voice before, now you hit Timi. Not once but three times. You pretended to care for my children that it didn't matter if we didn't have any more, but you went to sleep with other women to look for children." She paused, letting her words sink in. "You are the pretender. And I hate you!"

Then she slowly rested back on the bed, pulled the sheets over her shoulders, and closed her eyes. But when she spoke again, her voice was still

strong, and loud. "Do your worst. Divorce me. I'm going to sleep." That was it.

Dini stood like a statue and watched her sleep. He was in trouble. His life just took a plunge in another direction.

"If you want a divorce, now's the time to get one. I'm down, almost out. I may go to prison if Sigha has his way. Yeah! The time is just right. Then you can go and mourn your dead husband and love him all you want."

She was quiet for a long time, he thought she had fallen asleep. He picked the folder and leafed through the horror story in it. She had tried to abort her last baby. Then right after delivery, had two procedures of tubal ligation.

The first was compromised so she had a second. Then sometime after she started talking about having a child for him, she had another procedure to reverse the tubal ligation, which failed. Then the first IVF which failed. Then a hysterectomy to save her life. Then nothing. All at his expense.

The last two, he'd thought he was paying for IVFs. Paul told him Dr. Finidi insisted the patient's file was to be with the strictest confidence. They were admonished to talk to him alone. The crook! If not that Paul had stumbled across the information about that hysterectomy, he wouldn't have bothered to sneak around to gather what he had.

His informant from Finidi's office had said she was his wife. And she had mailed photocopies to him. When he saw the horror story, he was convinced his friend didn't know about it.

"You're not half the man that he was," Tonbra said with a clear voice. Dini turned to look at her. She had sat up again. Obviously, she'd been watching him as he flipped through her records. "Look at you." She waved at him. "Short, ugly, yellow pawpaw like you."

Dini glared at her. He had never seen such disgust on anyone's face before. For the first time, he thought she was ugly.

"I don't even know how I could stand your filthy hands touch me. Every time you did. You couldn't satisfy me half the way he did—"

Dini guffawed, the ironic reaction to pain. "Then go lie in his grave with him for your five minutes of pleasure."

She let out a high screeching sound that took Dini back. Again, he thought she would hit him, but she didn't.

She gripped the sheets covering her. "I hate you! I will forever hate you. You will never get what you want from me. And I will never leave you. Try the divorce and see where you get to. I am your nemesis, as you are mine."

She leaped out of the bed.

"Thank you." Dini shouted after her. "I'm short and yellow but my strength is in my brain. Your husband with all his muscles and tall dark handsomeness had no brains. He ended up dead, *dinn e?*"

She stomped into her closet.

Dini shook with fury. He couldn't stay, knowing she was in there. He clutched the folder to his chest and walked out of the room. He went to sleep in the guest chalet.

CHAPTER 34

—◦—

"Am I a short, ugly, yellow pawpaw?"

"Ask your wife."

"She thinks I am."

"Then you are." Dayo chuckled. "You are amazing, aren't you? You're facing a definite jail term and you're bothered about the way you look."

"If the foundation is destroyed, what can the righteous do?" He took a deep breath and handed the folder in his hands to Dayo. "I want to prosecute this doctor."

"Talk to Sigha."

It was Dini's turn to laugh. "Wouldn't that be so ironic?" He dropped the folder in front of Dayo. "You'll find the facts interesting."

"You gave me the facts already. What does it matter? You won't be asking for divorce, will you?"

"No, of course not. She doesn't want a divorce anyway. She thinks we're both serving punishment as we're married. Which probably soothes her guilty conscience." Dini looked at his lawyer. "What's your take on polygamy?"

Dayo's gaze snapped to his and he shook his head. "You're not considering that, are you? You're not even in the right state of mind to talk about such important issues."

"No, just asking." Dini played with the ring on his finger. He'd never given it a second thought before all this. "You know, Dayo, I never told you outright but the night of the explosion—I was with a woman." He sighed.

"I thought as much." Dayo looked at him. "You want to marry the woman? You were ready to stake your freedom to protect her identity."

Dini shrugged. "I'll never marry her. My faith forbids polygamy. I am a leader in church."

"Was she the one who came to see you in the cell, during those early days?" Dayo arched an eyebrow when Dini nodded. "I thought she was pretty."

"She is. Very." Dini studied his ring for a while and then looked at Dayo.

"I'm thinking—if such a lady is pregnant, what do I do about that?"

"Is she?"

"I'm just wondering."

"I think she is or you won't be talking about polygamy."

"If she is, what do I do?"

"Right now, nothing Dini. I'm sorry but you won't be a free man for much longer to consider what or what not to do." Dayo stood and shoved his hands in his pocket. He went to stand at the window of his office, which overlooked a busy street.

"Is that what you can tell me?"

Dayo swung round. "I'm trying to help but I also have a difficult case to argue, Dini. Tonbra has done more harm to you than good, and I'm sorry to say that. I'm not in the habit of criticizing another man's wife but this one could get you locked away for years. If I can scale it down, I'll be glad." He walked back to his seat but didn't take it. "This woman, is she pregnant?"

"Don't bother." Dini gripped his head with both hands. "How long can you argue for me?"

Dayo made to say something and then kept quiet. He took the seat and faced Dini. "Six to twelve months."

Dini shrugged. "I'll be away from it all."

Dayo picked a piece of paper from a pile on his desk. "We go into session in three hours. Is there anything you want me to say on your behalf?"

"No."

Dayo stretched the piece of paper to him. "You might want to keep this."

Dini looked at it. His termination letter. "You keep it. It's not going to help me out of jail or when I come out, will it?"

Dayo dropped the letter back on the pile. "I wish I could encourage you. Tell you to have a better attitude but I guess this indifference will do for now."

"What does a man do when he's down and out?"

"You're down, but not out."

Dini laughed. "I'll keep that in mind."

Dayo looked at him, shook his head and excused him.

At the meeting with Sigha, three days after the one with Dr. Paul, they had been informed there was enough evidence Dini had received monies from unknown bodies, proven beyond a reasonable doubt he passed un-banked monies to his wife who owned more than ten accounts and stashed the monies there.

Dini was shocked to discover Tonbra's siblings, who had never been a part of their nuclear family, all had bank accounts Tonbra constantly credited. Her mother had virtually disowned her when she married Dini. Even Ebisine's mother, who had supposedly cursed the union, had an account as well. Dayo knew Sigha would dig things up. Knew it was not good at all for

their case. But to his surprise, Sigha pressed the suit in another direction.

After all the investigations, Sigha pitched his tent on harmful neglect. The big one would not work. The sabotage and manslaughter charges became secondary. However, the government desperately needed to break the head of the civil servant in charge of the project, Dini. His contract clearly stated he was meant to be on call 24/7. He had neglected his duty, and his whereabouts could not be accounted for.

There was no need to argue the airtight proposition. Dayo advised him to plead guilty to the charges. In law, the maximum sentence was five years. Since he was a first offender, they could plead for him to as little as six months.

Dini was tired of the whole ordeal. He'd been out of sorts for so long, even a jail term seemed welcome. Everything warred against him and he remembered the saying that when a small problem makes you to fall, big problems come climbing on your head. One by one, things had fallen apart. The only thing he held on to now was his sanity. Picking issues as they came, one at a time.

Family was filed in one way. He would not lose his temper anymore. He was conditioned in his mind not to be surprised as well. His job was gone now and filed far away. He wouldn't be thinking about earning a living or maintaining a family for now.

In the sane moments after his madness over Tonbra's fertility, he had had the Christian mind to apologize for whatever had gone wrong between them, and he'd made plans for their upkeep from his estates, in case things went bad, and he lost his job. He had properties in Akure and Lagos which he leased. He also got dividends from stocks in different companies.

Then there was Oyinemi and her pregnancy. No-go area. Case closed. Not to be considered for any action though it haunted him sometimes. His question about polygamy had shocked him as much as it had Dayo. He knew the Bible never categorically condemned polygamy, except for anyone willing to be a leader in the church. Bishops and deacons were to be the husband of one wife. His Christian mind saw polygamy in the same light as adultery, divorce and all the other things God hated.

He'd been on suspension since the beginning of his problems, and he doubted he would get his position back. Even then, he could step down as a deacon. But then what did that do to his Christian testimony? Just like the drinking of wine, polygamy brought more controversy to a Christian's life, than otherwise good. No, he wasn't going to marry a second wife, nor would he divorce the one he had. He had married her. He had chosen, howbeit, hurriedly.

Perhaps he wouldn't have married Tonbra if he had courted her. Had he sought God's face before marrying her? Not particularly. Had he courted her? Not for a week. The onshore visits couldn't count for courting, he had learnt

nothing about her. Did he investigate her background, her marriage or her family? No.

But what did God think of these things? His word clearly states he expects us to take responsibility for our actions. What you sow is what you reap.

Besides, if he was going to continue to be mentored by Pastor Flo, he couldn't marry a second wife, and he couldn't divorce Tonbra. That was the role of a good shepherd, to keep the sheep away from trouble.

Then Tonbra. And the children she bore for Ebisine George. Those he kept in his new storeroom for onward desperate work of rehabilitation and reunion. He wanted to try again. He missed having a happy home and a happy family. This was what he had, and he had to make the best of it. He'd been wrong in many ways too. He hoped to make changes, keep his promises to love and care for them. He hoped to rebuild the broken walls in his relationship with Timi, be a true father to her and the boys, be a loving husband to Tonbra. That was important to his future peace and happiness.

Oyinemi's child. Blank. He didn't know where to put that yet, but he still had till the child was born at least.

His career weighed heavily on his mind. He could get a job with the government whenever he was free. It would not be in the same capacity as before, but did he want to work with government anymore? He toyed with setting up a consulting firm, but he didn't have enough years of experience. One escape route remained though, teaching. It would have to be seriously considered.

Dayo returned to fetch him an hour later. The deliberations were slated to hold in the same judge's chambers where the previous one had held, but this time, with the judge present. Dini sat quietly as the heated arguments went back and forth. Sigha passionately fought to get the maximum sentence.

The judge was reasonable. He gave Dini two years with a clause it could be reduced to nine months if he behaved well.

The judge ordered his immediate imprisonment at the maximum-security prison, Kirikiri, and took his leave after that. Dini remained seated, staring into space. He had expected the worst anyway.

Sigha stood as Dayo tidied his files and muttered to his assistant. "I think the judgement was fair." Sigha looked in between Dini and Dayo.

"I have this doctor I want you to prosecute for me," Dini said with a clear and authoritative voice. Sigha gasped and his eyes widened, his brows arched.

But just for a moment. Sigha gave a soft laugh. "Dr. Brisibe, you are a remarkable person." He looked questioningly at Dayo who shrugged.

"This has nothing to do with Dayo," Dini said. "I have this file on the doctor's actions. I want you to look at it and see what you can do. You'll be working for me. I'll pay you."

Sigha's amused look faded. "I am not interested in prosecuting someone on your behalf, Dr. Brisibe."

Dini frowned. "Why not?"

Dayo finished up and looked at Dini. "Finish up with Sigha. The policemen are waiting to take you to prison," he said casually.

Their whole manner seemed to stun Sigha whose jaw dropped.

Dini looked at Dayo. "Dayo, pass the file on Dr. Finidi, will you?" Dayo did so.

Stupefied, Sigha took the file Dini shoved into his hand. "You know where to find me, Sigha, if you feel you want the case."

He followed Dayo to a small room where he was handcuffed. They rode separately to the premises of the maximum-security prison.

Dini thought he was prepared until he saw the gate open and shut behind him. He began to shake as he was led into the entrance hall where his credentials were taken, and he was given a number. He would be taken to the changing room where he would get his prison uniforms.

Dayo could not follow him beyond the entrance hall. "Do you need anything?"

Dini shook his head. "This is it, right?"

"You'll be fine." Dayo patted his shoulder. For the first time, the lawyer seemed panicked. He avoided Dini's gaze and his voice trembled when he spoke. "Ah, this is never easy." He turned a full three sixty degrees.

"Thanks for everything." Dini turned toward the exit. A prison warden waited to take him on.

"Dinipre!"

Dini turned to his lawyer and friend.

"That woman—" Dayo took two steps toward him and stopped. "If she really is pregnant for you, well, I would think it's proper for you to show some form of responsibility." He spoke rapidly. "I could marry her and keep her outside of my home but as a Christian that you are, that would not be appropriate, right?"

"Right."

"So, I'd think you commit yourself to her in some financial way." He shrugged. "It's only right. Regular stipend or something. I could handle that for you if you give me details—"

"Maybe, Dayo. Thanks for the offer." Dini walked away.

Thus began the incarceration of Dinipre Oyinkuru Brisibe.

Chapter 35

—·—

She was so sick those first three months she could hardly work.

From the moment she returned from the rejection Dini gave her in Lagos, she took ill. She had hoped to tell him about what happened. Had hoped he would be glad to hear the news. Of course, she knew he would feel some conflict. He had tried to have a child with the woman he married without success, and then she now had the privilege.

And he hadn't chosen her. That one truth would stay with her forever. In fact, she wasn't too surprised he blatantly rejected her. She had only wished and hoped that after the nights they shared together, he would feel something for her. But no. He saw her as a problem in his life. It only proved further that men differentiated sex and love in clear terms. She serviced his body but didn't touch his soul or spirit.

Well, she didn't regret her decision for one day. She was strong and willing to carry the stigma, and willing to care for her child as well.

She had a good job. In fact, she wished she could disappear with her child and live quietly and peacefully. Even if Dinipre Brisibe didn't want her, she wanted him, and if all she would have of him was his child, then it was enough for her.

The moment she informed Mama however, all thoughts of vanishing disappeared. Mama

began visiting her every weekend. She took heavy gifts of clothing and expensive wines to her parents, signifying interest in marrying her. Several times, Oyinemi had the impression that even after having one child for Dinipre, Mama would have another assignment for her. And she vowed she would never do it a second time. Except Dini married her.

She hurt at the way she saw him last. She realized she loved him deeply. She wished the love could be returned but as a married man, she had conditioned her mind she may never get reciprocal love. She wished she could comfort him though and help him out of his predicament. Especially because she felt partly responsible.

He had been with her during the explosion he could have prevented if he was in Lagos.

She followed the case and during those early weeks when she was sometime so sick, she couldn't walk, or prepare food for herself, she made sure she caught up on the case. For months, all went quiet, and then she heard he had been arrested a second time, and this time, sent to prison.

That evening when she listened to the news, she wept like a child. The man she loved was going to Kirikiri! She knew she couldn't visit him there. He would never let her. But if he heard about her baby, would he not want to see her? His mother would tell him all about it.

Mama had been happy and sad from the start of their ordeal. The good news the plot succeeded, and then the sad news he was in trouble and then the good news of the baby, then the sad news Oyinemi was sure would have reached her now.

Watching the news and footage on his arrival at the prison, it amazed her how composed and relaxed he looked. His lawyer looked tenser and confused. Oyinemi just fell for him all over again. He was such a handsome, strong man. She felt proud of him. He had been brandished as a saboteur, a

traitor, and a wicked man moved to deceit by greed. All through it, he had maintained his innocence, his dignity and his integrity.

He'd refused to use her as his alibi.

That would have blown the case wide open, vindicated him to some extent. It could have brought him some sympathy from 'cheating' husbands like him, made him more human than the monster the media painted of him. It would have exposed her as well. She was a small city woman. The vultures would have dug out her dirty linen as they'd done for his wife. He had protected her identity.

Her love for him increased on this account. She was willing to forgive him, even if he never looked upon her again!

Through the three months of her extreme nausea, vomiting, weakness and loss of appetite, Binatari Ekiye stood with her like a cedar tree. He never questioned the kind of sickness as though he knew. She was weak, needy, and he was available. She knew he never suspected she was pregnant. And no one ever told him.

Four months into her pregnancy, though not showing yet, she realized Tari seemed to think he was back. He didn't know she was pregnant. No one knew, not even her colleagues at work. She lied she had typhoid fever and that was acceptable enough. The only people who knew were the people back at home, her parents and his mother, and most likely, gossips.

Tari stopped over at her house daily to help with whatever she needed to do. He'd happily told her he now had a job with the Federal Scholarship Board, which was a much better job than he previously had. Because of the new job, he had been able to move from his one-room accommodation to a two-bedroom apartment. He'd also stopped work at SECA to focus on the

new one.

"How are you?" He dropped his bag on a chair and looked round. "Were you able to go to work?"

She'd stopped working late and he knew. So he would drop in at about 8p.m. "Yes, thanks." She walked into her kitchenette and served him some yam porridge with vegetable soup.

It was getting cosier with them and she knew she had to break it. She had chosen her path. She would be the single mother of Dinipre's child. If Dinipre was interested, she would be glad. But if he showed no interest, then it was her cross to bear.

She sat on the bed while he took the chair by the table.

"Thank you. Aren't you eating?"

"No, I ate a little."

"I'm happy your appetite has improved." He took a mouthful and groaned from his belly. "So sweet. You're such a good cook." He smiled at her. She looked away, and he lowered his fork on to the plate. "Something wrong?"

Oyinemi shrugged. Everything is wrong, she wanted to say. "Finish your food first."

"This sounds like real trouble." He put the plate on the table and turned fully to her.

She stood. "Finish your food while I tidy the kitchen." She walked away before he could stop her.

She stayed in the kitchen, rearranging it. There was nothing to do. Nothing to say to him. Since he started coming back around her, she hadn't been able to talk freely with him. She accounted it for the guilt she felt but then what could she say. All their previous times, before Mama brought up her proposition and gave her the symbolic cloths, they had had their whole future to talk about. Now there was nothing in her future with him. And she had to make that clear.

She startled when he stood at the entrance of the kitchen and spoke to her. "I finished eating. What's on your mind?"

"I'm done here too." She walked past him and went back to sit on the bed.

On other times, they'd talked about her health, and the weather. Both avoided talking about the status of their relationship.

He followed her and resumed his seat at the table.

"I don't know how else to tell you this but to come out in the open about it." She turned to him and looked into his eyes. "I'm pregnant." She wondered how the Virgin Mary may have told the brutal news to Joseph—except she was no longer a virgin.

Tari snapped into a straight posture as though someone had hit the middle of his back.

His mouth dropped, his eyes widened. His voice was hoarse when he spoke. "How?"

"I'm almost four months gone now. It's the reason why I've been so sick. I know I should have told you from the beginning but—"

"Wait. Just wait a minute, what are you talking about? Pregnant, how?"

"Please don't ask how or who. I'm sorry I didn't tell you earlier. It's the reason I called us off earlier and I notice you're trying to come back and I don't want to lead you on only for you to discover because it's bound to show soon—"

Tari stood and walked out of her room, slamming the door shut behind him.

It showed sooner than she thought. By the time she clocked four months, her stomach was protruding.

CHAPTER 36

He got one visitor a week from his immediate family, and lawyer. Dayo secured the visitors' permits from the prisons' authorities. In Dini's first week, Pastor Flo visited him. After that, Erebi visited. One or two other friends got to visit in subsequent weeks. Gradually, Dini settled into a pattern.

For him, prison was like the belly of a great fish. He took the opportunity to focus on his inner strength and discover the man within through prayer and fasting. Prison food was nothing to write home about, but he decided to fast every single day of his stay in the prison. He took only dinner. The lifestyle took a toll on his health, and several times, he had to be hospitalized, but when he got back in the cell, he resumed his fasted lifestyle.

Close to the elections, Dayo came to visit once, and informed him he was leaving the country. There were threats on his life, and he didn't want to take chances.

"I leave tonight, Dini. My family has already gone."

"What is the matter?"

"Your reports. I have tried to talk to some trusted people here in the prison to protect you as much as possible. If I could steal you out, I would." Dayo fidgeted, his eyes darting here and there, something Dini had never seen before. "The reports you made on the power plants is now in the hands of the opposition. It is a lethal weapon against the incumbent president. You know what those reports say."

He wrote the report and knew how lethal. The prosecution had avoided a trial in his case and twisted their case around getting him incarcerated without a full trial, just because of that report. Sigha insisted they destroyed all incriminating documents, but Dini made duplicates, which he gave to Dayo, and Mama. Of course, Mama had no idea what it was. He'd given her the suitcase with the documents and asked her to keep in his wardrobe in Apoi. The suitcase also contained duplicated CDs of documents and scanned receipts. Evidence of his innocence.

The documents reported his research on the power plant machines, and correspondence with government, and manufacturers. At the end, Dini had been side-lined and some contractor given his recommendations and asked to purchase the machines. Dini had travelled to China to purchase and had. The contractor had stayed to tidy up the negotiations, pay and ship.

Alas, when the machines arrived, the specifications were sub-standard. The contractor had cut almost half of the cost off. Dini had sent his reports to the appropriate authorities, rejecting the supplies. But someone who had the mouth and enough power to counter him did so. He had been advised to 'make do.' Dini had reported saying he could not be held responsible if the machines failed.

The machines had not failed. They had exploded during testing. Well, better than to have problems after they had been commissioned. Government had been looking for a scapegoat. Dayo had advised him to play dead.

"Why would you give the opposition such a thing?" Dini yawned. If Dayo left, who would take over his case, though he couldn't really be bothered?

"That's the future of the country you're talking about, Dini. This incumbent is roast. Anyway, I'm out of here."

"Who takes my case?"

"I've made arrangements for you. Right now though, nothing is happening. Everyone is going on the campaign trail." He stood. "Your visiting rights have been stipulated. Your pastor and Erebi are going to be regular. If you want anyone else, you'd have to write. But that won't be a problem, right?"

Dini remained seated. "Right."

"Watch your back. The opposition hits the media with your facts tomorrow. From then, you can't be so safe."

"You're a bastard, Dayo! You sold that stuff."

"Quarter of a million dollars. I won't be around for much longer anyway." He turned at the door. "I wish you well. You're a good man."

He was gone before Dini could say more.

The elections were stiff. And bloody. The opposition was desperate. They hit the streets with facts and figures. A few of them died in the hands of the incumbent. Twice, attempts were made on Dini's life. Once while asleep, a pillow covered his face. The weight behind the pillow was massive. Dini knew he had little or no chance. If he fought back, the attacker would win. If he played dead, he would actually die.

He held his breath, and feigned death, and prayed in tongues. The person paused and he found strength to hit in between the man's legs. The killer groaned aloud and then all went quiet. Dini had opened his eyes slowly and discovered his three cellmates were all fast asleep!

He had reported. And his cell was changed.

There were no attacks until after the elections and the opposition won landslide. It was the biggest defeat in the history of the country's politics. A week before the swearing in, someone drew a knife on Dini in the bathroom.

He would have died straight if not that his soap fell to the cement floor, and he bent to pick it up, the same moment the stabber struck out. The knife would have been lodged in Dini's neck.

Someone growled and he fell to his knees. The stabber's knife had gone into the cheap cement wall. He swore aloud and pulled it out. By which time Dini had crawled and run out of the bathroom.

This time, nothing was done to prevent a reoccurrence and Dini had to depend on the power of God to keep him. He spent his days, praying, preaching and teaching.

One day, shortly after the new government came in. He had an unexpected visitor. The young man wore dark clothes, a face cap and dark glasses.

It was Tonye Sigha.

"I can't be seen visiting you." He pulled off the cap but left the dark glasses on.

Dini was amused. "Why is that? You are now the opposition, and I've been labelled to support the opposition."

"Dr. Brisibe, I came in connection with the file you gave me."

Dini leaned forward. "What file?"

"On your wife's doctor."

Ah. "I thought you were not interested," Dini sat back, and folded his arms across his chest. It had been six months since that day in the judge's chamber. Dayo had disappeared about two months earlier.

"I wasn't because like I said, I couldn't be seen doing anything for you or with you."

"So, what changed?"

"Me. Something inside me snapped. I saw the reports you made on the power plant and I snapped."

Dini laughed. "You saw those reports before you started scheming on how to get rid of me."

"Look, Doctor. I didn't come here to argue. I want to work with you. I want to be with you."

"I can't believe this. You want to be with me in the prison—"

"I want to work for you."

"I can't pay your legal fees." Dini shook his head. "Don't know what I was thinking when I gave you that file."

"You paid your lawyer till he ran away."

"Oh, so that's it. You're broke."

He pulled off the dark glasses and glared at Dini. "I don't need your money."

"I'm sure you don't. But how much do you think I can afford? Dayo definitely didn't think much of my fees, or else he would not have run."

"You don't know what you're talking about."

He shifted on his seat and Dini thought he would leave. But he didn't. "Okay, so you want to take my wife's case—"

"Before we go into that, I want you to understand I'm not here because I want your money. You inspire me."

"Good to know. Thank you."

"And your faith is a great challenge to me." Sigha lowered his voice. "I know—who ordered your hit and I'm—I need what you have."

Dini wiped off the sneer on his face and sat forward. "I understand that," he spoke softly, and proceeded to minister salvation to Sigha. To his surprise, Sigha was broken, and wept like a child.

When the tide was over, the two men laughed and spoke about everything in general. Dini discovered a friend in Tonye Sigha.

After what seemed like a long time, Tonye Sigha stood. "I have to go. The case, I'm doing it on my own."

Dini shook his head and smiled. "I appreciate that, you know."

"That doctor should be hung on a pole and I'm going to see to it."

"Take it easy brother." He stood, and the two men hugged. A smile of satisfaction spread on Dini's face as he walked back into his cell.

Chapter 37

Two other memorable visits impressed deeply on his heart, before his release from prison thirteen months after his incarceration. At the president's New Year speech, Dr. Dinipre Brisibe made the list of the prisoners granted amnesty, though he didn't get home until two months later.

But before then, he got a visit from Erebi. It happened to be the last visit from his sister, and it came about six months before his release.

Erebi had taken advantage of every opportunity she had to visit. Once, Mama visited instead but it was so emotional for both of them, Dini asked her not to come back.

As soon as she walked in, Dini knew the visit would be different. Erebi wore her heart on her sleeves. In those days when they were young, Dini hated to have her in on their mischief. She couldn't keep a secret.

She jerkily took a seat in front of him and after brisk pleasantries, sighed heavily. "I know you know I have news." She made sure she held his gaze. "Oyinemi gave birth to a set of twins."

Dini had thought about it a couple of times. He'd even tried to calculate the date without success. His stomach dropped and his heart heaved. Twins! Oh what, how could—What. God!

"Twins?!"

"Boys. Identical."

"When?" His voice was so hoarse he doubted Erebi heard him.

"Three days ago. Mama sent for me to tell you."

He went still and stared into space. What would he do now? How was she? He stood and hooked his hands into the pockets of his prison's trousers. Twin boys! His flesh and blood. He wanted to shout with joy! But their mother was not Tonbra. Their mother was not his wife and could never be.

"Mama expects that you send a name for them."

"Twins have the name God gave them. I have no name for them," Dini said.

This was his day of joy, yet he could not rejoice. Tears sprang to his eyes and he turned away from Erebi before she would see it.

She let out a soft cry and covered her mouth with both hands. "You didn't say that."

Dini could not allow her to see his face. "What did you want me to say? You know how I feel about all this from the beginning."

"But all that is history now. She needs you and your boys need you."

Her words penetrated through skin and muscle into marrow. She was right. The way she said 'your boys' made him go light in the head. He thought he would faint. His boys!

He half-turned to face her, taking care to hide the pain and anger on his face. "They have Mama. She started all this."

Erebi shot to her feet and moved round to face him. She grabbed his two arms and looked into his eyes.

"Don't you care?" She shook him. "What has come over you, Dinipre Brisibe?" She saw just in time as two huge tears dropped from his eyes.

"I cannot care, Erebi. Oh my." He covered his face with both hands and sobbed.

She stepped back from him. "You have a financial obligation toward them."

He took a deep breath in an effort to control his emotions. "I cannot be a part of their lives."

Erebi's eyes widened. "Why?! What's wrong with you? I don't understand this, Dini. I can never understand this. I thought you wanted a child, children of your own. I—"

"Yes! But not like this." He spread his hands out in front of him as though in supplication. "You're a Christian, Erebi, can't you see what this means? I'm in trouble. It won't just go away—illegitimate children. Why would she be pregnant? Why would this sin not go away?"

Erebi kept quiet. She held his gaze and what he read in it pained him to his marrow. "Is this how you see all this? Sin. Something that should just go away?" She sighed. "It was wrong at the beginning but now what can you do?"

"I can't marry her—"

"No one is asking you to marry her!"

"I can't see her. I can't send money to her."

Erebi despite the force behind her voice, spoke softly. "Why?!"

"I can't, Erebi. I just can't."

She picked her bag from the seat where she'd kept it. "I can never understand that. Never. That girl went through a lot of stress doing this—"

"She chose to. She wanted to do it, no one forced her. On the other hand, I was forced into this mess. Tricked! Drugged!" He raised his voice despite himself. "And see where it's got me. Did it not ever occur to you for once, that I'm in prison because of all this mess you people trapped me into?"

"I thought you wanted a child," Erebi whispered but with as much intensity. "I thought Mama was helping."

"She was not." Dini glared at her. "Now, just go. Thanks for bringing the news but no thanks."

"All the money spent on hospital, clothes, all the money, was spent by that girl. She refused our charity."

"I'm sure she'll refuse mine too. They're her children."

"Dini!"

He lowered his voice. What a mess. He couldn't afford to see that woman or send anything to her. Hearing this would take all the energy he could summon not to want to see her. Prison today but free tomorrow, how would he be able to resist her? How would she call to thank him for the money, and he would not go looking for her again?

"I'm sorry, Erebi. I don't know what to say. I have to go back to my cell."

He walked away despite himself. The last look on her face, of pain, anger and disappointment, and then shock, just broke his heart. It took all his strength and control to grief quietly in his cell, and not wail down the walls of Kirikiri.

He wondered what his sons looked like. Erebi had said they were identical. He was fair, she was dark, what did they look like? He didn't care who they looked like. He would be pleased all the same if they looked like him or their mother, it didn't matter! God, he couldn't afford to think these thoughts.

He wanted Oyinemi. God help him, but he wanted that woman.

Pastor Flo visited the following week. Since Dayo disappeared, Erebi and pastor had rotated the weekly visits. Tonbra also had her weekly visits but she didn't come since she was permitted to call once a week. But she never called. Since his imprisonment, she never brought any of the children to see him, with the excuse she didn't want them to see him in prison uniform. Well.

The past week had been full of conflicting thoughts and feelings and he welcomed the refreshing visit from his pastor. Despite his tight schedule, Pastor Flo had devoted that once–in–two-week's visit to him, ensuring his wife visited when he couldn't. He spent the time encouraging Dini. They shared the word and prayed together. Sometimes when pastor had a relevant message, he would bring the CD and the prison authority would provide a player so they could listen or watch together.

Pastor's nurturing greatly helped Dini's growth. In prison, everyone referred to him as 'deacon.' He ministered to prisoners, making it his duty to be their resident pastor. The remaining time, he used for study, prayer and meditation. Though he had become lean in prison, spiritually he was fat.

Pastor Flo brimmed when Dini walked in. He always showed such optimism around him that Dini could not help but be infected. But today was different. There were important thoughts on his mind, and he needed to bring them to the fore.

He summoned the strength to go through the pleasantries and then looked pointedly at Pastor Flo.

"What does the bible say about polygamy?"

Pastor Flo paused for a moment and stared back. "A deacon must be the husband of one wife," he said simply.

"What if I am not a deacon? I can resign, right?" He sounded edgy, harsh, uncaring, and really, he was. He'd hardly slept for days, thinking about this, studying the word on it.

"Anyone can do anything, deacon but Paul says that all things may be lawful but not all things are expedient."

"Expediency aside, pastor, it is not a sin to marry two wives as a man." Dini shook his head. "I looked through scriptures. The polygamy argument is just hinged on the rank of leadership. What God frowns against is divorce, not polygamy. As long as I can provide for my family, which God specifically says I am worse than an infidel if I can't, there is no direct charge against polygamy."

"And you are a leader."

"Only if I continue to lead. I am a leader only if I assume the duties of a leader. I can step down."

"You are called, Dini. You'll throw your call away so you can marry a second wife?"

Dini shrugged. He was ready for pastor. He knew the man of God would try to dissuade him, but he had his arguments all ready. "One is as important as the other."

Pastor Flo smiled. "You know it amazes me the way God works. Some people get away easily with some things. Some don't get even a single privilege, not even once." Dini stared blankly at him, waiting for him to finish so he could press his point. "You're one of those people God does not joke with. You don't get away so easy when you make mistakes because God loves you in a special way."

"You said that before, Pastor, and I know it for myself."

"I'm not going to let the devil have you this time, Deacon. The last time, I saw it in your eyes something was wrong and I postponed doing something about it. Not again. Watch me fight for your life."

Dini laughed though he didn't want to ridicule his pastor. "There's a puzzle, Pastor. I'm sorry I laughed but you don't need to go into battle for my life if you can solve the puzzle."

"You've been here for seven months and I've visited you regularly through this period. Tell me what's new."

"The Bible is silent on polygamy."

"As well as many other issues like smoking, abortion, masturbation, wife-battery—are those things any more acceptable than polygamy? David said once have you spoken, twice have I heard that power belongs to God. It is not for a deacon to marry more than one wife and you are a deacon—"

"What about ordinary members? If it is good for ordinary members, then it is not a sin."

"Some people were polygamists before they came to the light. These ones God overlooked their days of ignorance, and allowed them to continue in their lifestyle, but they could not be made bishops and deacons.

"Now first, Deacon, let me remind you that the kingdom of God is not in meat and drink but in righteousness, peace and joy in the Holy Ghost. What is the Holy Spirit telling you about this second woman?" He scooted forward in his seat and looked penetratingly at Dini.

"Anything not clearly spoken in the scriptures is the jurisdiction of the Holy Spirit. He's the comforter, the helper. The teacher. If you can convince me the Holy Spirit is willing to give you a second wife, you can go ahead. But beware of lying against the Holy Spirit. It's what people are doing these days, and many will perish because of it."

Dini didn't want to win or lose an argument, he wanted answers. "Why would the scriptures be so silent on the issue?" He shook his head.

"Second, if your meat will offend your brother, then don't eat meat. The Bible wasn't talking about the flesh we eat alone but about the controversies around us, like polygamy. What will your testimony be? That once upon a time, you were a deacon but because of another woman, you left everything?"

"She's not just another woman. She's the mother of my kids!"

Pastor Flo could not hide his surprise. His nose flared, his ears flattened. "Kids—I don't understand."

Dini narrated everything all over again. "I love her, Pastor." He sobbed at the end. "How am I going to ignore her? I can't stop thinking about her. I've fought with every iota of strength in my body. I can't stop thinking about her! What am I going to do? I've been committing adultery over and over again in my heart. I can't seem to have any control over my feelings for her."

Pastor Flo sat still for a long time, just staring at the broken person in front of him. The confusion of the situation was mirrored on his dazed expression. Dini continued to sob for a while and when he finally stopped, he looked up at the pastor's face.

"You told me once that even the lawful captive shall be delivered, Pastor!"

"But shall we continue in sin so that grace may abound?" Pastor Flo said softly. "God forbid!"

"She delivered a set of twin boys for me, Pastor—"

"Oh creator!" Pastor Flo lowered his head on to his laps. For a moment, Dini thought he was weeping but when he looked up, his face was dry and

strong and determined. "I'm going to enter warfare on your behalf, Deacon. My wife and I are going to fight for your faith. The devil will not have you," Pastor Flo said. "The devil is trying to sieve you, but I will pray for you."

Dini stared at him unable to speak, his chest heaved rapidly.

"Polygamy is not the meat of the children of God. The Bible says a man will leave his father and mother and cleave to his wife. Not wives. And the two, not three or more will become one. You have no business taking a second wife and the love you have for her must die—"

"I married the wrong woman, Pastor! I've told you the hell I'm in."

"Yes. But you married her." Pastor Flo paused. "I'm sorry you're in a marital mess but there's nothing prayer cannot do." He leaned forward and took both of Dini's hands in his. "If Tonbra accepts to care for the twins—If she apologizes, gets rid of the inner shrine of her late husband—If she becomes the woman you married at the first, would you still want this second woman?"

Dini pondered. Oyinemi was a beautiful woman. Her body satisfied the way no other woman had. She was the mother of his sons.

"No, Pastor. I won't want her."

"You once told me you almost hated her, now you say you love her. Are you sure that if things begin to work between Tonbra and you, you will forget about this woman?"

"What she did to me, my body, my heart, frightened me. I never thought another woman could move me like that." Dini sighed. "I want to be married to only one woman, Pastor. If I had a choice, I'll pick the mother of my children. But I don't. I will stay with Tonbra. Even if she doesn't accept the kids. I must decide to stay with her. It is my cross." He lowered his head and allowed the tears to fall.

"You're here now, and I believe it's a shelter for you, against the future you must definitely face. I want you to take advantage of this time. You've been here now for seven or so months. You have two years altogether. Dedicate it to prayer and fasting, studying and worshipping. There is nothing God cannot do. There is nothing prayer cannot solve. And I will join in and pray for you. I will pray for your heart to go right."

"Thank you, Pastor."

"I am going to give you some scriptures to study. And prayer points till we see in two weeks' time." Pastor Flo opened his bag and brought out his pen and paper. He wrote a list of scriptures and prayers and gave him.

"I want to pray with you, Deacon."

Both men went on their knees in the open visitors' room of Kirikiri federal prison and prayed like they'd never prayed before.

CHAPTER 38

On the day Dini was freed, Sigha picked him from the prison and took him to his house.

"I wonder what you'd want to do today. Pastor Flo did say he would come to the house to pray with you."

Dini sighed. "He did. I'll do that, and then sleep for two full days."

Sigha shook his head. "I can only imagine."

Sigha had not come back since that day he visited, and Dini knew they had a lot to talk about. The man didn't even live in Lagos, but Abuja, and they'd spoken on phone just once. When Dini's name was announced for freedom, Sigha had called to ask about his plans and offered to pick him up. Otherwise, he would have walked out of the prison gate and hiked home.

The house was quiet when Dini walked in. He'd pressed the bell and Deborah had opened, screaming with joy when she saw him. She rushed off to get a glass of water and asked what he would eat. He didn't have an appetite but asked her to prepare something light like boiled yam or noodles.

Sigha took a seat and looked at him. "Your wife will be greatly amazed to see you."

Dini dropped into the couch. "She will be." He felt dirty, sure he didn't smell so good. "I think I want to take a shower." He sighed and stood.

He'd called Tonbra to inform her he was coming home and asked to be picked. She'd declined based on a meeting of the foundation with some sponsors. Mighty important. He'd initially rejected Sigha's offer but had to call him. Just on a moment's information, Sigha caught the next available flight from Abuja to get him. Well.

"You need it."

"What are your plans?"

"What are yours?"

Dini scratched his temple. "I told you. I'm sleeping for forty-eight hours. Then I start to think and plan. I need another job."

"Well, I guess I'll hang out with friends for forty-eight hours while you sleep, then bring you up on what I've been doing on your case."

"Oh yeah, the case." He headed for the staircase. "Hang around for the prayer as well.

Pastor Flo should be here in the next hour."

"Okay, doc."

Dini smiled as Sigha brought out his iPad. He walked tiredly to his room. It was well after school hours and he wondered where Tonbra had taken the children to. She knew he was coming home today. Well, he would not start worrying now. One of the things he'd learnt in prison was patience. He could wait for many things now. He would wait for Tonbra to love him. He would wait for her to get over Ebisine Francis George Snr.

He opened all the doors in the house as he went along, feeling the texture, and the smells and the sights of his own home. It was good to be back. Finally, he went to his bedroom.

Nothing changed.

On the way from the prison, Sigha had graciously stopped at a boutique and bought the outfit he wore, shirt and trousers and shoes. He doubted his old clothes would size him now, but he wasn't going to stay so thin. He opened his wardrobe and stood looking in for several minutes, struggling not to weep. It felt so long ago. Tonbra had not touched his clothes.

Everything was as he left it.

He closed the wardrobe and walked into the bathroom. He needed a hot shower, and he got one. He couldn't soak just yet but he would, before he started the sleep. As he'd thought, he was at least a full size smaller. All his shirts were too big, so he opted for simple native attire, which looked big as well, but not too much.

Pastor Flo arrived as planned with his wife and children, and a couple of the ministers from the church. They had a long session of praise and worship, soaking in the freedom of the presence of God. While the singing was going on, Erebi came in with her family. Andrew and his wife came as well, and a few of Dini's old friends. Good news spread fast.

Afterward, Deborah served the guests with drinks. There was light conversation about everything and anything, little, pleasant jokes, and then the guests left. Erebi promised to be back the following day for a private visit.

At close to eight in the evening, Tonbra and the kids had still not showed up.

"I guess I should leave now as well," Sigha said as Dini came back into the house after seeing Erebi and her family off. "Are you alright? Looks like you'll need clothes."

"I'll survive, for now." He yawned and stretched. "So good of Pastor Flo to come. He's a real man of God."

"Yeah. I do respect him a great deal. He should come and start a church in Abuja and teach the bunch there how ministry's done."

"Sigha the philosopher." Dini smiled. "Would you like to eat with me before you go?"

"Would."

Deborah served them a meal of boiled yam and stewed fish. It tasted like heaven to Dini. "Ur, Deborah, where did madam say she was going?" Dini said. He'd refused to call since she refused to pick him. Patience. Patience he warned himself.

"To office, sir. And the children are in Aunty Grace house."

"Oh, I thought as much. Thank you."

"Servants see and know it all, boss," Sigha mumbled, and Dini laughed.

"This one has been with us forever. She's the custodian of all that can fall my family."

"If you're serious about that sleep, I'll wait it out or I could come tomorrow morning."

"Come tomorrow morning."

Sigha appreciated Dini for the meal and left. Dini went up to bed to sleep. He didn't know what time of the night it happened but when he woke up in the morning, his family was back home. The kids showed remarkable joy, unexpectedly. Timi even hugged him. They seemed genuinely glad he was back, and it took twenty years off his depression.

Tonbra was guarded. But she soon discovered he had kept no prisoners, not even for her behaviour the day before. Before long, she was showing some excitement and talking freely. It was the first test in a list Dini had to pass.

Sigha came in before noon the following day. He expressed gladness at how Dini was relaxed and refreshed and went straight into business. Dr. Finidi was in court. Though the man had been released on bail, the case looked good for the prosecution, though Sigha couldn't take it farther than a magistrate's court and had to make trips to Warri for the case.

"Would you need me to testify or anything like that? Would Tonbra need to show face?" Dini needed to know.

"Yes. Later though. The doctor's lawyer will call Tonbra as a witness. If she accepts, I'm fine by it. I don't even want her as your witness because then, she would not be nailed as an accomplice."

"Don't go there, Sigha. I don't want you talking accomplice. My wife must not be indicted, or I won't go along with you."

"Implicated not indicted. Her image will be tarnished but not much more." Sigha shrugged.

"It's a local case. Don't worry yourself. I doubt anyone will go to jail. Finidi will lose his license though."

"He should."

"I thought you'd be interested," Sigha said. "I got in touch with Dayo. He's somewhere in Europe, and he sent some details of your work to me."

"Some of my work, how?"

"Your researches and projects. He felt it would be wrong to keep those things you gave him especially now he's not likely to come back soon."

"His party is in power."

"Yeah, but he made a lot of enemies before he ran away. I doubt those people will forgive easily."

"How did you find him?"

"I have my ways. You know I lost out on my relationship with the ex-president's daughter after I gave my life to Christ—Well, the new guy she's with helped me to fish Dayo out. They know where he is. Just that they need to be extremely smart to hit him without traces—"

"Dayo is not as smart as I thought. I wish him luck. Anyway, so—"

"So, he sent your files to me. And I looked at them."

"Can I have my stuff back? Hope you've not mistakenly sold my ideas?"

Sigha laughed. "I'm sure that was a joke. What do you take me for?"

Dini swallowed and closed his eyes for a second. "I take that back. What did you think when you read the files?"

"Of selling the ideas right away." Sigha burst into laughter and Dini joined in. "You're a genius, Dini. And I am your legal counsel for life. Take it like that. I don't want to be paid for it."

"Surprise Dayo didn't sell me out."

"He didn't check what you had there. I was just so curious. I wanted to know everything possible about you. I was crazy about you, man."

They both laughed. "Dayo told me he'd never tried to see what you had in those CDs you gave him since you said they were computer files. I discovered I needed some engineering and architectural software to open some of the files and I went to get them. He wasn't interested, thank God. Your man is a crook."

"I figured."

"He jumped you. For my good." Sigha sat forward. "I haven't done anything yet, of course without your permission but the designs you have for generating power is first class in any economy in the world—"

Dini smiled. "Are you an energy analyst now?"

"Yes, Dini. It's what I've been studying since I got these files of yours about two months ago and I'm glad you're out now. I want us to sell this. It will be patented internationally so no country, not even Nigeria can touch it without you. Then we pitch it to West Africa. I believe the design suits our terrain best."

Dini smiled and nodded. "Yeah. Sure. But I'm not done with it."

"Well, I didn't know that."

"It has to be tested and proved before we can give it to anybody."

"Okay."

"The patent will cost a fortune as well, which I may not have handy for

now. I spent a lot of my savings before going to jail—I've not worked for so long now—I may need to get a job first." Dini sighed. He had promised himself not to worry, hard a task as that was.

"We'll take it one step at a time. I've done some research. Filing for the patent, is not expensive. Only a couple thousand dollars. Then we take it from there. I spoke to one or two lawyers who do this for a living and their fees may be the challenge, but this is what they do so you're sure you'll get your patent." He looked at Dini and nodded. "All I need from you genius, is to get to work. Go back to your lab, or your system or wherever engineers perform their tricks, and get me a sellable design Ghana will not be able to resist or Cameroun or Nigeria, Sierra Leone, The Gambia. Go to work."

"Yes, boss!" Dini saluted. It would take months to get it together but Sigha's optimism was too thick to be ignored.

The two men spent the whole afternoon talking about the renewable energy projects Dini had been working on privately. Energy systems, earth systems, and power systems. He'd been doing researches and conducting tests on ways to convert waste to energy in order to generate power. He had broken a lot of grounds in his research and would have given the piece to NGEC had the explosion not occurred.

After lunch, they worked for a while separately. Dini worked on his laptop while Sigha worked on his iPad, both working on the technical and legal aspects of the business respectively.

Sigha looked up. "We need a business name."

Dini rolled his eyes and sighed. "Give me one, now."

"Energy Systems Inc.," Sigha said. "I'm going to goggle that right now, let's see if it works." He typed rapidly.

Dini watched him with unreserved admiration. The flashy, arrogant, president's boy had matured and become a focused, intelligent, lawyer who didn't fly on anyone's wings but his own. All the flamboyance was gone. Even his haircut didn't look as brazen as before.

"Hmm. Taken. We'll go for DOB Energy Systems Inc. then."

"What's DOB?"

"Dinipre Oyinkuru Brisibe."

CHAPTER 39

Gradually, Dini settled back to life on the outside.

Sigha worked with him online. Calling on favours was not a problem for Dini. Before his many troubles, he had affected many lives. He was reinstated in the church and got his dignity back. His testimonies from the prison became a landmark of his faith.

Sigha advised him not to take another paid employment so he sought small consulting jobs in facility management, power generation, waste management, and electrical designs. Dini got by.

Then calls came in from three countries. Benin Republic wanted to wean itself from Nigeria's spoon-feeding but could not pay Dini's price. Cameroon was good but Dini couldn't speak French and wasn't inclined to learn. The Gambia had the best option. They were willing to pay. And Dini was willing to sell. Unfortunately, bureaucracy had the proposal hung in between offices in Nigeria.

Fine-tuning his designs and patenting had cost him a fortune. Refusing to take a loan, he had sold his Tundra and bought a small car, his house in Ogba, and the block of flats in Akure, leaving him with just the house he lived in. A major source of income gone, he realized every achiever had to take dangerous risks at some point. At forty, he wasn't getting any younger. He needed to make fast decisions in his life.

Tonbra carved a niche for herself. The EFG Foundation had taken such roots she now worked in the office daily. Dini chose to respect her decisions and live with it. They never argued. Their relationship had taken a snug look to guarantee relative peace and stability for the children. Dini liked it that way. It gave him the time and energy to focus on his life and business. Conjugal rights were, by an unspoken agreement, not exercised at all.

He filed Oyinemi and that angle of his life away. Once in a while, Erebi would attempt to bring it up. Mama visited him only once after he came out of prison and all she did was talk about the twin boys. It took him weeks to fight off the urge to go and visit. If he did, he couldn't trust himself on what

would happen just yet.

Pastor Flo advised him to set aside financial support for them, which he sent through Mama. That was the only reason Mama or Erebi did not get more upset with him, but he warned them not to attribute the money to him. He didn't want to have anything to do with Oyinemi again. One day, he hoped he would meet his children. But not now. Not now he couldn't trust his feelings where their mother was concerned.

Two years down the road, Dini signed a contract with the government of The Gambia. It was initially a five-year contract to set up an energy system based on non-oil earth materials, renewable energy. He was to build the plant, test and work and stabilize it. It meant he would live in The Gambia.

He thought about the children's education first. Timi was sixteen years and Tonbra wanted her to go for A-levels before studying in the UK. Pere was thirteen, and Ebisine, ten. Timi could stay back in Nigeria, but the boys had to come along.

He was sure Tonbra would like the idea. He was wrong.

He travelled to The Gambia with Sigha, an accountant and a business developer, both employed by Sigha for two weeks, and came back with the signed contract. To celebrate, he took his family to Sheraton for dinner. And over dessert, announced his plans.

Tonbra did not wait for them to leave the exotic buffet hall at Sheraton Hotel, before she aired her opinion.

"I'm happy for you, Dini. But just as I didn't follow you to prison, I'm not following you to The Gambia."

Dini gasped. "We'll discuss this when we get home."

Tonbra shrugged. "You just can't drop this on my laps that you got a contract signed to live in Gambia for five years and I will run and follow. I have a life here."

"Of course, I know. I'm sorry I just dropped it like that. I've been working on it for years now, you know, and my last trip to The Gambia is in respect to it. My excitement—"

"No. No." Tonbra shook her head. "You don't do that. No matter what the excitement is." She turned to Timi. "Right?"

Timi rolled her eyes and shrugged. Dini discovered in recent times the two had become extremely close, discussing everything. Good as that sounded, it left him wondering what sort of woman Timi would be in future, a replica of her mother?

"We're talking about one billion USD, Tonbra." He swallowed. "That is mind-blowing in any currency in the world," Dini said slowly. His cream caramel dessert now tasted flat in his mouth and he pushed it aside, leaning his elbows on the space in front of him.

Tonbra shook her head harder and gave him a 'talk to the hand.' "Don't give me that, Dini. I have a life here. EFG is going on air soon with our 'Know Your Journalist' show. I can't just pack and follow you to—to Gambia like that. Huh?" She shrugged. "You're so selfish in everything you do. Did you even consider the kids? What happens to Timi? Don't tell me you'll leave her here with Grace or who?"

"I've thought it all out—"

"To suit yourself alone."

"You never talked about a show going on air before. I'm hearing this for the first time."

"That is a huge lie, Dinipre Brisibe. Hey!" She raised her voice and turned to Timi. "Can you imagine? Can you people hear what I'm hearing?" She looked at the boys. Pere grimaced. Ebisine nodded in agreement and stole a quick guilty glance at Dini.

"We'll talk about this when we get home," Dini mumbled.

Tonbra talked on for a while about how distant Dini had become to his family, how no one knew him, how the prison had turned him into something else, how he needed emotional therapy, and psychiatric counselling. He refused to say a word.

The ride home was a quiet one. For Dini. Tonbra laughed and joked with the children. They chatted amiably as though Dini was a hired driver. When they got home, Tonbra watched TV for a while and then finally turned in.

Dini allowed her to finish her nightly rituals.

"I feel embarrassed the way you carried on at the restaurant, and right in the presence of the kids."

Tonbra sat on her side of the bed. "Don't annoy me, Dini. Please. Was it proper for you to drop plans for the next five years on my laps just like that?"

"I said I was sorry—"

"But you are not. This is not about this night. This is about everything in this God-forsaken marriage. This is about you living your life and me living my life. Me and my children living our lives and you living yours!"

"I do everything to make you and your children happy. I live my life for you—"

Tonbra jumped up and faced him heatedly. "Oh, so you finally agree they are my children."

"Is that not what you just said? What you told them from the beginning? You not me, behave as if this marriage cannot work. You are the one sucking up to Grace, taking her advice on how to make this marriage a punishment for me. Or you think I don't know?" He stood with his arms akimbo. "You flaunt EFG in my face day and night, and you pretend that foundation gives you all the joy in the world. You—"

"Shut your dirty mouth, you sorry excuse of a husband. What is EFG to you? Nothing! Nothing! Do you know what we do there? Do you care? You talk about Grace. She is the only reason why I am still in this marriage, and you should be grateful."

Despite the anger brewing up inside him, Dini laughed. "You're so deceived. Grace is your saviour, right? Did she tell you she arranged for me to be drugged so I could sleep with a virgin who would give me a child? You are so so deceived."

"You're a stinking liar. You just look for things to say when you're wrong."

"And she made several passes at me—"

"Stop lying you wicked brute. Stop lying. If you think your lies will make me hate Grace or change my mind about you, you're joking." She yelled. "Read my lips. I won't. And I'm not coming with you to the Gambia."

"Don't come with me. You know how to cope alone."

"Yes, I do, jailbird! And your malicious words about people who care for me mean nothing."

"Just so you know, Grace has not stopped wanting me, and making passes. And for your information, she arranges men for your stupid little daughter. You have a wonderful life, live it. Wombless creature."

Dini had promised himself he would not exchange words with Tonbra, get upset and hit back, but as he vibrated with anger, he couldn't help but say things he knew he would regret.

"Too bad for you, Dinipre. I'm wombless and that means you aint getting any children all your useless life. If you like, go to Gambia and sleep with every—"

He lowered his voice considerably. "Grace didn't tell you?" The last time he spoke with Grace, she had boasted and threatened. And ranted like the old maid usually did. "Grace didn't tell you I have two beautiful sons born to me by the same woman she arranged?" He worried his lower lip with his teeth. "My goodness, Tonbra. What a sorry case you are."

Tonbra's face fell, and her eyes became teary. She stared long and hard at Dini and he noticed her lips trembled. Dini experienced a form of satisfaction at her pained look.

"To hell with you." She turned around and headed for her inner closet.

Dini followed. "I feel sorry for you, Tonbra. By now, I thought you would be happy on some level. And perhaps I've been wrong in leaving you to do your rituals too long. Well, not anymore."

"What are you talking about, you idiot?" Standing in front of the mirror, she turned to him, the small key to the shrine in her hand.

He picked a pair of scissors from her vanity, snatched the key from her hand, opened the closet and pushed her forward into it, holding her hand firmly with one hand. Tonbra began to struggle to be free but he was stronger. She clawed and punched at him but couldn't prevail.

Ebisine Francis George Snr. stared at both of them with the winning smile on his face.

The small room was surrounded by up-to-date pictures. Dini flung Tonbra against the full-length portrait and jammed the door.

"It ends here, and now, you hear that?" Dini yelled. "Here and now."

He ripped the pictures closest to him off the wall. Tonbra jumped up and rushed at him. He easily pushed her back and she fell on the floor. She screamed curses at the top of her voice and lunged at him again. This time, she struggled to get the pair of scissors, but he was too strong for her. They both sweat profusely as each struggled for control.

Again, Dini won. She scratched and punched and clawed. He tore pictures till there was nothing on the walls, and then he grabbed her at the waist and carried her, her back to his chest, and facing the portrait of her dead husband.

"It ends here. Forever. Bid him farewell," he shouted at the top of his voice. "Tell him goodbye."

With tremendous strength, he stuck the scissors in Ebisine Francis George Snr's face.

The flex was thicker than it looked. He had to dig in a little harder. Tonbra screamed at the top of her voice and fainted in his arms as the scissors ripped across the dead man's handsome face.

Dini lowered her to the floor and made a feast of ripping the flex into strings. When he was done, he opened the door of the shrine wide, and stepped into the room. All the children were cuddled together, glaring at him with hatred, crying. Deborah held them in a circle of her arms. The cook, someone Dini found to be a new employee, a rotund woman in her late fifties, stood close to the door, and wept openly.

"Deborah, clear the mess," he said stiffly, and stomped out of the room.

He slept in the guest chalet that night.

CHAPTER 40

Dini moved out of the house.

The following day, Tonbra asked for a divorce and he refused to give her one. "This marriage is our punishment, remember? You, for not mourning your husband, me for not choosing with God. So there goes. We are stuck."

But he couldn't stand the antagonism all around him, even Deborah, the quiet unassuming housekeeper became hostile. The cook, whom he never could remember her name, hissed and cursed around the house aloud and intermittently. Dini packed his clothes, and important items, and checked into a hotel. He called Sigha to update him and to plan on their move. They'd been given a month for mobilization, but after a week of hostility, he decided to make his move.

"Tonbra is not coming so we can get a staff house for all of us."

"It will be temporary. The accountant is moving with his family. And so's the business developer. I'm getting married too, sometime," Sigha said.

"Do what you think is best, but I'm not coming with no family. And do it fast. I'm leaving this country in one week." He hung up without getting a response.

Tonbra first reported the incident to Pastor Flo who visited the house and tried to broker peace. Again, he gave them assignments to do together, pray, share the word, and share their thoughts. He advised Tonbra to work out a plan that would suit a move to The Gambia. All his advice however left with him as he drove away from the house. A week later, Dini became a resident of a hotel on the other side of town.

After the call to Sigha, he took a trip to Apoi, for the first time since his release from prison. In a bid to show Mama his displeasure over her plot, he discovered he had punished himself as well, by not visiting his homeland. He had tremendous joy and peace in Mama's house. For all their differences, and all her flaws, Dini loved his mother.

They spoke at length about his plans. Again, she talked unendingly about the twins. Her words rang in his brain, but he had no comments. He still

couldn't trust himself to see Oyinemi, especially now Tonbra and he were technically separated. He'd known his resolve would be tested.

Seeing Tonbra and the children after prison had been one test, and he'd scaled that. Facing off with Tonbra was another test, which he'd failed woefully. He'd dreaded the first time he would have a disagreement with Tonbra, had held it off successfully for two years! But when it came down to it, it had resulted in a separation.

He had a new life in The Gambia, at least for the next five years. He was leaving. He'd visited the country a couple of times and he loved everything he saw there. The people, and the city, suited him well. The government was working, and the prospects for launching his energy systems into other West African countries, brilliant. He had it all coming together for him.

It seemed a good time to test his feelings for Oyinemi. If it went bad, he had an escape route – Gambia calling.

He said nothing of it to Mama, but on his way back to Lagos, he stopped at Akure. It wasn't late yet but he didn't know if Oyinemi still worked at SECA. Or if she still lived in her old apartment. He tried the apartment. She wasn't there anymore.

Next door at the SECA building, the receptionist nicely gave him a number to call. It was progress. Dini walked to his Toyota Corolla to make the call. She picked up after only two rings.

"Hello?"

At the sound of her voice, he knew he would fail the test again. She sounded breathless. Was she attending to the boys, his boys? Did she have his number? His heart thudded.

Instinct told him to cut the call and run.

"Hello?"

"Hello." He took a deep breath. "This is Dini."

There was a long pause. She lowered her voice. "Hello."

His heart skipped several beats and then took on a fast pace. "I'm in Akure, at SECA right now. I don't know if I can see you."

She quietly gave him an address and a description. And hung up.

***

He was just five minutes away. Oyinemi stood breathlessly in the middle of her sitting room, waiting. She knew he would come one day. He would have to see his boys one day. Any man would. She had prepared for this day, every single day since she gave birth to his sons, she had prepared for the day they would see again. Especially because of the way their last meeting went. He had been angry with her. The man who had loved her body unreservedly was gone and the old Dini replaced. He had sent her out of the cell and his life, much the same way he'd done before.

She was a woman, a deeply emotional one. She wanted to be ready to face him, the love of her life. She wanted to be able to tell him, all that remained between them were the boys. She had moved on. To her knowledge, he had sent nothing for their upkeep, but she had been ready for that, though Mama gave regularly. There was a possibility he sent the money and gifts through Mama. Of course, that had its implications too.

But he was here now, and she was shaking from head to toe. What did he want? Would he demand to see his sons? Would he want to take them from her? Those boys were her life. She couldn't live without them.

***

Dini stopped in front of the address, a quaint bungalow, one of several like it in an estate of not more than ten such buildings. The environment looked serene, peaceful, and green. The kind of environment you would want to raise kids. He liked that. He liked that she had changed house. A new urge to make up for lost time rose within him like a demon, but again, the voice of reason asked him to turn and leave.

He came down from his car, took a deep breath, and walked up to the door. He pressed the bell once, and the door opened to him. She had obviously been waiting. He stepped into a neat and cosy sitting room. The furniture made of cane and designed with light blue and navy cushions and throw-pillows, matched a Persian rug in the same shade, in the middle of the floor, and cream and light blue curtains.

She walked stiffly to a single chair and took it. He took the loveseat. There were sounds of children splashing water, and his throat clogged. He wore a t-shirt with DOB embroidered on it, and blue jeans with boots. She wore a simple skirt and blouse, and dressy slippers.

After several moments of silence, he cleared his throat. "How are you?"

"I'm fine." She folded her hands on her laps and summoned the courage to look at him. "I watched on the news when you were released. I thought you'd come then."

He sat forward, his gaze fixed on her face. "I couldn't. So many things happened, and I couldn't bring myself to come at the time." He sighed. "I'm sorry."

"It's alright. I understand."

"You stopped working at SECA?"

"No. I only go in the evenings now—because of the twins."

He scratched his temple. "Oh yes. Of course. How are they?"

She smiled softly. "They're having a bath now. You can hear them?"

Both listened a little and laughed together. He felt so much in love with her. She had not changed one bit. A little plumper than before but she looked smashing! He couldn't stop looking at her. Motherhood befitted her. He'd always known it would. He would not leave today, he told himself. He had to stay with her. He wanted badly to love this woman, feel her.

He groaned inwards. He was still married. He cursed the day again, and his flesh that couldn't resist the instant beauty Tonbra was made of.

"They must be awesome," he said. "Erebi said they are identical."

"They are. They look like you."

His heart swelled with joy and pride. "Really?"

She smiled. "They'll soon run out now."

But he noticed she was tense. Her body language repelled his visit, but she tried to put up a front.

"What about us, Oyinemi?"

She jerked upright. "You're still married?"

He nodded, unable to say more. How could he willingly say anything? He was back in the lion's den, losing the battle of his life.

"Then you know we can't be together again. You know that—"

"Oyin—"

"I won't come between your wife and you again. I know what that was like for me."

"But our boys need—"

The first of the boys ran into the sitting room with a shout. "Mummy mummy!"

Oyinemi stood and caught him in her arms. "Wow, you're clean now, sweetheart. You smell good." She pressed her face against his chest and drew back, smiling.

Dini stood as well and looked at his son with a deep longing. She was right. The boy looked like him, but a shade darker, not as dark as his mother though. She kissed his forehead and he giggled.

"Come and say hello." She handed him to Dini who hugged him tightly. The boy thought it was a joke and giggled some more. Tears sprang to his eyes and he closed them to suppress the emotion.

He looked at Oyinemi. "What's his name?"

"He's the bubbly one so, that should be Tuobowei. His brother is Beleuobowei," Oyinemi said. "We call him T-boy. And his brother, Bowie."

"You mistake them at times?" He looked at the boy's soft features. He was sweet to behold. He had his eyes and nose and mouth. Everything. Except the colour. "You just gave twin names."

"Mama sent the names."

"I'm calling this one Dinipre. His brother is Oyinkuru."

"You're their father. It's your right."

The second twin walked out more slowly, the exact replica of his brother. T-boy wriggled out of Dini's arms and ran to his brother, holding his hand and dragging him to Dini.

Dini laughed. "He sure is outgoing." Dini picked the second twin and looked into his face. "What's wrong, angel?"

Bowie pouted, squeezed his face and in the next minute burst into tears.

Oyinemi collected him from Dini and patted his back. "He's very temperamental especially when visitors are around." The boy stopped crying and Oyinemi went back to sit down, balancing the boy on her lap.

Dini carried T-boy and sat as well. The boy began to fiddle with the embroidery on his t-shirt.

"I like this house and I'll want to continue paying for it from now," Dini said. "I want to be a part of your lives." He looked at her. She began to object but he stopped her. "I want to take up my responsibility. I know what's between us is not normal but please let me start from doing what I should do. School fees, upkeep, accommodation, clothing—" He took a deep breath. "And I want you to know I'm leaving the country."

She jolted. "Leaving?"

"I got a contract in The Gambia. I'll be leaving in less than a week."

Her mouth drooped for a while, and then she closed it and shrugged. "I see."

He reached out his hand to touch hers, but she deftly tucked it in, away from his reach, and smoothed Bowie's shirt.

"Oyinemi, I know how you feel. I do. And I wish I could make it up in any way."

"You can't. I don't even want you to feel like you owe me anything. These boys are a gift and when they are old enough, I'll tell them who their father is—"

A man walked in from inside the house and she stopped talking. Bowie jumped off Oyinemi's laps and ran to him. He caught the toddler in his arms and carried him up. Oyinemi stood and walked to stand beside him. Dini stared at them, hoping it wasn't what he thought.

"Please meet my husband, Tari Ekiye." She looked at the man and smiled tentatively. In a voice slightly above a whisper, she said, "Dini Brisibe, the twins' dad."

Tari Ekiye nodded at Dini. Dini stretched out his hand to him and they shook briefly.

Dini looked at both of them and swallowed. "I have to go. Thanks for your time." He looked at the boys one after the other. T-boy was still in his arms. He moved toward the door and Oyinemi followed him.

At the Corolla, she collected the boy from him. "Thank you for coming."

Dini exhaled, his brows drawn together. He looked into her eyes. "I can never stop loving you." He got into the car and drove off.

***

Oyinemi stood outside till the car had disappeared down the road, watching with mixed feeling. There had been no hope for them, anyway. He was married and not ready to leave his wife. Even if he did, his faith would not permit him to remarry. He couldn't marry her as a second wife. He'd said all that the day they were together. There was nothing they could do more than just that, nothing!

She'd cried when he left because she guessed that was the end. How could love be so deprived? When she got pregnant, she'd hoped it would lure him back. It hadn't. Having the twins hadn't either. Then she knew he would never belong to her.

When Tari came back to her after the birth of the boys, she decided to follow him. For him, his love had never waned. He just wanted to give her time to decide who she wanted.

When the father of the twins did not show up, he decided to come back.

Oyinemi thanked God for Tari. He was a good man. He never referred to or treated the boys like they were not his. He treated her with respect. He loved her, and she loved him, and that was all she ever needed. Dini Brisibe was a semi-colon in her life, not a full-stop. He was just a bend, not the end of the road.

She shifted T-boy Dinipre in her arms. The boys were so big at just two and some months.

She noticed Tari standing right behind her. He had just brought the children home from school when Dini's call came in, and he would have gone back to his office if not that she pleaded with him to wait till Dini left. He'd volunteered to use the time to bath the children, thinking Dini would leave before the task was done. Well.

Tari leaned his head close to her ears. "Are you alright?" he whispered.

She nodded and looked up at him. He was her future. "Yes." She smiled. He still carried Bowie Oyinkuru, who was nodding off on his shoulder.

"Come inside then." He ushered her gently, and they both walked back into their quaint house with their twin sons.

***

Dini refused to think for the first one hour of the drive. As he entered the double-carriage expressway to Lagos, he turned off the air-conditioning and allowed natural air to blow into his brains. He knew he was going too fast.

Oyinemi was married.

Of course, she should be. He was glad someone had agreed to marry her with his twins. What an irony. You reap what you sow, the Bible says. He'd married a woman with kids and now his own children would be fathered by another man. He could have stayed and argued, made demands, but what right did he have? What right could he have?

Now he would have to depend on Tari Ekiye to be a good father to his boys—because he was going away, for good. There was no way around it. He couldn't be married to two women, and she couldn't be married to two men. What a blockage. He remembered a song by his choir once - God blocked it! Well, what an absolute blockade.

He wanted to be happy for Oyinemi. How old was she now, twenty-seven or twenty-eight? She deserved to be married and the man looked kind. He couldn't have made any demands, rock the balance in her life, take the boys from her. He couldn't watch to see her unhappy.

And what had brought that blatant statement about loving her? He didn't know where it came from. It was an impossible situation. She did look happy. The man looked content. Their house was nice and neat, homely, friendly. He hadn't seen any pictures on the walls though and hadn't noticed any rings—He hadn't been looking.

He had proposed a toast for their relationship to continue. She had stalled him. Without telling him she was married, she had made direct inference to his own matrimony. He hated her for a moment. God. He loved her to death.

She had intruded upon his marriage once, and now used the same marriage as a reason to send him off. What an irony. Oyinemi was now married and didn't want him. He had broken his vows with her, and now she wouldn't break hers for him.

He began to laugh. This was not funny at all. He may never see those sons of his again. They would call another man daddy. Just like Ebisine George's children called him daddy. No. He would send money to them, demand to know their progress. He would ask for their pictures and send his.

Oyinemi had not seen the last of him yet.

He'd prayed in prison for God to get rid of her, kill the love. Kill her if possible. He'd been wild and aggressive in fighting his feelings for her on his knees. He'd felt defeated when he couldn't resist the urge to visit her. When he thought he could never stop loving her. But God had been orchestrating it all along. He'd thought God had not honoured Pastor Flo's prayers, answered his cries. But God had. God had given Oyinemi a husband. That had settled the quarrel. She would never belong to him.

He drove off the highway and parked by the side, rested his head on the steering wheel, and wept.

Chapter 41

2016

Grace George drove her new Toyota Prado into the dingy compound near Mushin main market. She pulled up beside an abandoned 1970s Volkswagen Beetle and turned to the young woman seated beside her.

"Are you ready?" Grace said. "Timi, are you ready for this?"

Timi looked at her. "If you're sure, Aunty Grace."

"I am. Your mother used this same doctor several times when she lived in Warri—"

"But you refused to tell Mum and you won't let me tell her."

"You're eighteen, Timi, not a little girl that would go asking Mummy for everything. I thought you were mature by now."

Timi's voice hardened. "I am. But if this doctor was my Mum's—" She shrugged, opened her small purse and took out an orbit spearmint chewing gum, which she popped into her mouth. "What the hell does it matter?"

"My point exactly. But before we go ahead, I want to warn you again. An abortion is not child's play. And I want you never to take risks again. You're young and beautiful. You can't afford mistakes like this."

Timi snickered. "I hear you, Aunty. You had a handful yourself, didn't you?"

"Well, in my days, the prevention options were few."

"Well, let's get on with it before I change my mind."

Grace opened the door, and stepped down, careful to avoid a small, muddy puddle on the ground. She walked to the only story building in the compound which consisted of several dilapidated bungalows.

The first floor had a series of doors on both sides of a dark corridor. Grace switched her iPhone for illumination and walked to the door she sought. She turned and looked at Timi for a second and then knocked on the door.

The door opened as though they were expected. Indeed.

Dr. Finidi smiled at Grace engagingly before shifting his gaze to Timi.

The doctor had hardly aged. Except for a sprinkling of grey hairs at his temple and some wrinkles around his mouth and eyes, he looked pretty much the same.

"Wow! An absolute replica of her mother." He stepped back and they entered a surprisingly well-furnished parlour. "Grace, how are you?"

"I'm fine, doctor. I'm glad I got your new number. I was worried I would not get a discreet operation done, with the rave about the total ban on abortion."

"The Save Nigeria Group is driving everyone nuts these days, banning almost everything. The president being their former leader may well bring the revolution of righteousness this time around. Well, people like us continue to survive." He smiled again. "Timi, right?" Timi nodded. "How far gone are you?" Dr. Finidi smoothly switched to business.

Grace found a single couch and took it. "She's just about 6weeks only."

"That's alright. This way," Dr. Finidi said. "You too, Grace."

He led the way to another room almost as big as the parlour. His consulting room, obviously. A clustered table was at one end, while a long table lay against the wall. "Timi, lie on that table, will you dear." He indicated.

"Grace, feel comfortable." He pointed to a chair in clear view of the table.

Grace took the chair. "Thanks."

He went to his wash-hand basin and picked some surgical equipment, which he dropped into a stainless bowl. "Timi, how's your mother these days?" He took the bowl and put into something that looked like a microwave oven.

"She's fine, I guess," Timi mumbled.

"She travels a lot. For the foundation," Grace said.

"Her husband hired one crazy lawyer who ran me out of the Niger Delta." He barked a short laughter. "But hey, a cat always lands on his feet."

"He doesn't live here anymore."

"Really? Thinking I would send a letter to tell him I just did a little procedure on his little daughter." He bared uneven but white teeth.

"I'm not his little daughter." Timi raised her head, exposing an angry face Grace found adolescent. "I'm nothing to him."

"Be respectful, Timi. He paid for your A-levels and he's paying millions to send you to the UK to study," Grace said. She glanced at Finidi to be sure the doctor got those details.

"And his money is paying the good doctor here."

"He was never there. What do I care?"

Finidi removed the stainless steel from the microwave oven and poured its contents out on to another stainless-steel tray. He pulled on a pair of gloves and took his tools to the table where Timi lay.

"This won't take long. I want you to pretend you're having a massage,"

Finidi said. "Or a pedicure." Timi squeezed her nose. "Take the clothes on your lower body off. All of it."

Grace stood. "I'll wait out at the parlour."

"No, not at all. This won't take a moment. It's a simple procedure."

"A simple sixty-thousand-naira procedure."

"Anyone caught doing it goes to jail for life, Grace. Ten thousand per week's pregnancy is only fair against life imprisonment. Or what do you think?"

Timi absently removed the clothes and the doctor turned to her. "Relax completely. You won't feel a thing."

He filled a new needle with some fluid and looked at Timi. "This deadens you to what I'm doing." He inserted the needle and Timi let out a vulgar expletive.

Dr. Finidi chuckled. "Wow, you got words for a deacon's daughter."

"He's not my father, d—it."

Grace looked at them, uncomfortable.

"And for a deacon he had eyes for the women. He was suspended for so long people forgot he was a deacon—ouch!" Timi's face twisted with pain.

"Suspended for what offence?"

"Womanizing. Or adultery. Some funny reason."

Finidi laughed. "The self-righteous bastard prosecuted me for doing surgeries on your mother. If not that I sign agreements with the patients, I would be roasting by now."

"Still your license was suspended," Grace said.

"I can't practice in Nigeria or anywhere for that matter. That lawyer Sigha or what was his name is an animal. Wouldn't let up. He kept dragging the careless-physician nonsense."

"I hear they call him the pit-bull," Grace said. "He prosecuted Dini before turning around to work for him."

"Really? He is a pit-bull I tell you." Finidi

pulled something out and dropped in an empty waste stainless pan at his ankle. Timi screamed.

"Be careful, doctor."

"She's fine." He looked at his patient. "Pedicures don't hurt."

"This is not an f—pedicure. It hurts like hell." Timi's voice thickened as though she was crying.

Grace shifted forward in her seat. "Doctor, please o. Her mother doesn't know she's here."

Finidi laughed. "Your secret is safe with me."

"D—! Stop, please." Timi groaned.

"There. I'm done." Finidi laughed. "The naughty boy is out."

Grace stood and discovered Timi crying. "Oh my, doctor. I thought it wasn't going to be painful."

"It's in her mind." He deftly cleaned her up and gave her another injection shot. "That's for the pain." He pulled the gloves into the waste pan and gave her a sanitary towel. "Use that. If you feel or see anything abnormal, let me know. The bleeding should stop before night fall. Otherwise, your aunty can call me."

He walked to his desk and wrote on a sheet of paper. He tore it out and gave Grace. "Those will help against any pains or bleeding."

Grace looked at the sheet. "Thanks, doctor." She looked at Timi. "Let's go home before your mother knows what we've been doing." She winked.

***

Tonbra got to know two days later when Timi fainted and had to be rushed to the emergency room of the teaching hospital where the abortion was exposed. Timi had continued to bleed after the first day. She complained to Grace who spoke to the doctor once, and then tried without luck to reach Dr. Finidi the following day. When she went in search of the doctor a few days later, the medicine man's house was locked, and none of his neighbours had seen him.

The doctors fought to save Timi because she had lost so much blood, but they doubted if she would have a normal reproductive system afterward.

Since it was an abortion, the teaching hospital reported it as a criminal case. When she stabilized, Timi was questioned by the police who in turn got Grace arrested. The doctor could not be found.

Tonbra called Dini in her desperation. She needed help in any way. Timi could go to jail for as much as twenty years because she would be tried as an adult. Dini promised to send Sigha to represent Timi but not Grace. She had it coming and that would be her headache.

Timi was charged with maliciously removing a foetus, and Grace as an accessory to the crime. The doctor remained at large. Sigha arrived the day before and saw Timi briefly in the hospital from where she would be moved to a cell when she felt strong enough.

After seeing Timi in the hospital, and hearing of the imminent arrest, Tonbra drove home. The policemen told her to bring food for Timi in the evening at the police station in Panti, where she would see her daughter next. On her way home to do the task, and in broad daylight, weeping and driving, and without her seat belt fastened, she ran into a stationary truck, and died on impact.

Dini travelled home to bury his wife and to take the boys back with him to The Gambia.

Timi got five years in prison.

Chapter 42

2026

Twelve years after Dini left Nigeria, his mother sent for him and he came back.

When Tonbra died, unwilling to go against her wishes, Dini buried her in Isaba, next to the grave of Ebisine Francis George Snr. He had made the trip a very short one. She was just thirty-nine, a few months to celebrating her fortieth birthday. A tragedy if ever one existed. She had lived most of her life celebrating and promoting her first husband. In death, Dini felt he owed her that honour. He had done it promptly and left the country without any social visits.

Tonbra's sons continued to live with Dini in The Gambia, after his five-year contract was extended twice. He sent them to school there and when Timi finished her jail term, and returned as a full-blown woman, she opted to go back to live in Lagos and work for her father's foundation instead of going back to school. Dini didn't want that for her, but again, he had no influence over her. At least, she agreed to live in the Victoria Island house where Deborah, now married to a man who tended the compound, stayed in a redesigned guest chalet.

Grace had gotten away with only three years, and after serving her term, severed all relations with Dini. He never heard from her again, nor did Dr. Finidi ever surface. Dini and Sigha concluded he must have gone to another large city where he could hide, or a remote village. It was anyone's guess.

Mama started complaining about her leg. The pain had taken a new form for weeks and her herbs refused to help. Her pains became so bad she could not move about her daily chores, and she began calling on all her children to visit her one by one.

Dini left instructions that if his mother didn't get better three days after his arrival in the village, he would have to return to The Gambia, and make better arrangements to return and stay longer.

His business had become a phenomenon in the foreign land so much he entered a pact with the government to patent his design with the joint ownership of The Gambia. The government now sold the rights to the designs as part owners, shares they acquired for almost a hundred million American dollars.

In return to accepting to sell, Dini was given an honorary citizenry of The Gambia. To further cement the relationship, several of his Gambian friends and colleagues tried to get him a 'Gambo' wife but did not succeed. Dini was sworn to celibacy. Sigha however did not escape and got married to the president's daughter.

When Dini arrived, he was shocked to find Mama bedridden. At just seventy-three years old, it hurt him to see her so helpless. Mama had been a German machine when it came to activity. She had always been strong, and agile. Tireless. She'd always said the day she couldn't move around, let her die.

On the second day of his arrival, Dini went to sit with Mama, and she began to tell stories of her life to him, mentioning important dates, and events. Dini hurt and rejoiced at the same time for the opportunity to be with her. He could swear those were her last days.

Close to midday, an unexpected guest arrived. It was Oyinemi Ekiye. Mama had sent for her the moment Dini arrived, without either's knowledge. She had come as soon as she got the message.

Mama stretched out her hand to Oyinemi, taking her attention away from a dazed Dini.

She walked into Mama's arms and the old woman began to cry softly.

Her voice was low but as strong as it had always been. "My daughter, you come."

"They told me you wanted to see me urgently. They didn't tell me you were ill."

"I'm dying."

"Don't talk like that, Mama. You're not dying." She lifted herself up and carried Mama with her. "Come on, stand up. Have you checked if they've swept the compound?" She sobbed. "They didn't tell me you are ill. Mama get up."

Dini's throat clogged, and his tears fell as Oyinemi tried to encourage his mother to hang on. She hugged Mama and rocked with her.

"You can't die, Mama. We need you. I need you."

When he couldn't take anymore, Dini separated the two women. Oyinemi fell into his arms and wept. It gave him tremendous pleasure to hold her again. He had thought he'd overcome those feelings. He wasn't young anymore. Some of his friends were getting close to being grandparents. But his body yearned for what his faith would never allow him take.

Oyinemi Ekiye had not changed much. She still had her youthful looks, and though she had added weight, she was still attractive. She looked more mature though. Her chubby cheeks had rounded out with her new motherly

figure and didn't look so chubby anymore, and her cheekbones were more defined. There were faint wrinkles around her eyes and mouth, which made her so cute. She wore a lace boubou with matching scarf, which hid all of her figure. But he couldn't forget what she looked like even if he tried.

He'd changed as well. He'd added some weight. Though more of healthy weight. He had a personal trainer in The Gambia who helped him look stronger, and well-toned. He wasn't young anymore at fifty-two, but he had the strength and agility of a thirty-something. They'd said the new fifty was thirty.

His diet was healthy, his skin firm, and still as 'yellow' though fresher-looking now with proper care. He had a sprinkle of wrinkles on his face as well, and some nice touch of grey hair which highlighted his mature handsomeness.

Oyinemi calmed a little and pulled away from him.

"Let him take care of you, Oyinemi," Mama whispered. "I no fit anymore."

Oyinemi continued to sob. She sat on one side of Mama's bed while Dini took the space on the other side.

"Dinipre, I want tell you story."

Mama slowly talked about the significance of the wrappers she gave Oyinemi seventeen years earlier. When she finished, she smiled and closed her eyes, and told them she wanted to sleep.

For long moments, both sat looking at her, afraid she would die there and then. But Mama did not die that day.

After a while, Dini invited Oyinemi to his apartment. He needed to catch up with her, and their sons. He'd lost touch with her a few years after arriving The Gambia. Her numbers changed, and Tari got transferred to the

Northern parts of the country. To be sincere, he had not been too bent on finding her, for the same old reasons. Perhaps he had been right in that regard, because she still conjured the same old feelings in him.

The house had once again been expanded to accommodate the children's families. The foundation had been reinforced and an additional floor added. The ground floor was now totally dedicated to Mama and her wards.

The first floor was divided into two wings of four-bedroom apartments each and given to Dini and Erebi. The last floor, built as two wings of four-bedroom apartments as well, but designed in such a way that each was subdivided into two-bedroom flats, and shared by the remaining four siblings.

Dini had furnished his to taste in a palatial way. It bespoke his wealth, but it was for him also a reward for his hard-smart work. He felt proud to host Oyinemi in his apartment.

He poured her a glass of chilled juice after asking her to sit, and discovered he was nervous—after all these years. He reminded himself she was married. That meant no-go. He was free, she wasn't, so he led his

conversation away from there. He just wanted to enjoy her company, and comfort her of her grief over Mama.

He perched on a high stool at the bar area, facing the couch she sat on. "You never told me about Mama's wrappers."

She shrugged and delicately sipped her juice. "I don't know why. Maybe I didn't believe it meant anything."

"Mama seems to believe it is everything." He looked closely at her. She wasn't as relaxed as he would have liked. Could this woman be his friend? At least. "She has proved it."

"She's superstitious, you know. Maybe I was too. I don't know."

"She takes you as her daughter. She believes you two have a lot in common."

She dropped her glass on the glass stool beside the couch and stood nervously and paced. "She's dying and I can't believe it." She clenched her fist and looked at him. "Mama can't die. She's been there all the time for us." She heaved a heavy sigh. Tears gathered in her eyes.

He walked gently to her and took her in his arms again. She sobbed into his shoulders and he let her, speaking softly.

"Do you feel what I feel for you?" He said out of the blues. She stepped back jerkily. "I'm sorry. I shouldn't have said that."

"I—" She took a deep breath. "I may have to go back today. I didn't make adequate arrangements for the children."

He stepped away from her, grateful for the gracious way she took him out of the awkward moment. She resumed her seat.

"How are they though?"

Her face brightened a little. "You'll be proud of your boys. They are so tall now. Taller than both of us."

He chuckled. "That's good. Fourteen is the age for boys. They just shoot up."

"They're doing very well in school too. They come top of the class all the time." She smiled. "And they are very respectful too."

"Thank you," he said softly.

"We have Tari to thank most of all."

"Thank him for me. If Mama dies, he should come I guess?" But Dini didn't want to talk about the man who made her happy. She opened her mouth to talk but his question stopped her. "Did you have any more children?"

"Two. Another set of twins actually."

"Really? Wow that's congrats for you there. Well done." He was impressed. "Two girls?"

"A boy and a girl."

"How old are they?"

"Eleven."

"Congratulations."

He wanted to talk about his boys but didn't want to seem too eager. Who could blame him? He'd followed their progress through the years, but complacently. Each time the urge to step in overwhelmed him, he remembered his feelings for their mother. Could he divorce the two, father to the twins and lover to Oyinemi? No. And that made him to back-off.

"So, what do you do now? What happened to SECA?"

"I run an after-hours coaching class in Kaduna, and it's been doing very well." She smiled. "And I run my evening school as well. I hear SECA is still fine, though."

He sipped his juice, looking intently at the glass. "That's good."

She finished her drink. "I must go. I'll come back in a few days." She sighed. "I pray Mama'll still be alive."

"I pray so too. I have to leave tomorrow as well." He sighed. Then his eyes caught and held hers. "I know this is seventeen years belated, but I want to apologize. I didn't live right, then. I was born again and still I lured you into a sin I should preach against. I'm sorry."

"You didn't offend me, Dini. I knew perfectly what I was doing."

"I owe you that apology especially because I never recovered from what we did. What we had." He lowered his gaze. "I'm afraid I'm still tempted to fall into the same error again," he whispered.

"I am a believer now, Dini. I would not have done those things I did years ago if I knew the truth then. But I have no regrets. What happened, happened. We should just move on."

He nodded thoughtfully. "You're right. Thank you." He summoned the courage to look at her. "And I am so glad you are now a believer." She half-smiled. He squeezed his face. "Wonder if it would make sense to preach to Mama—now."

Oyinemi chuckled and tears gathered in her eyes again. "Mama is going to an eternity with Christ, Dini. Haven't you noticed none of the usual rituals associated with her chieftaincy, is going on by her bedside?"

"I thought I'd ask, really." Dini laughed. "That's great news. Thank God."

Oyinemi stood. "I really should go. I'll come back to see her as soon as I can. And as often as I can."

Dini saw her out. "Thank you."

At the door, he pulled her into his arms and closed his eyes, struggling against an overwhelming urge. She stood limply. After a sensible amount of time, she pulled back, gave him a peck on his cheek and hurried away.

CHAPTER 43

Mama died the day after Oyinemi left. On the third day of Dini's arrival. It was as dramatic as her life had been.

The young woman who took care of her in the morning arrived at her usual time by six o'clock and found Mama gasping and asking for Dini. The lady ran from the room, screaming. Dini appeared less than five minutes later by Mama's bedside.

Her eyes were clear, and she had a strange sweet smile on her face. She gasped desperately, trying to say something. Dini knelt beside her and gripped her hands. They were so cold.

"Mama, Mama, it's alright. Just try to breathe, don't struggle." He turned to the lady who, now joined by others wept at the doorway and snapped, "Someone call a doctor or something. Leave this place all of you." They scrambled out.

Mama looked at him with so much warmth he wept. He rested his head on her shoulder and sobbed.

"Good night!" she said softly and closed her eyes.

Dini's head snapped up and he looked at her face. She was gone!

Mama was gone. She looked so peaceful, as though she slept but he knew. His lips trembled, and he gripped her shoulders. "Mama! Mama! Mama!"

The ladies who had gone out all rushed back in and took up wailing. Dini, half lying on the bed, embraced Mama's body. Soon the whole compound filled with wailers. Dini knew Mama's instructions and came to himself when he realized what all the wailing would cost. Mama wanted to be buried not later than twenty-four hours after her death, in a Christian way, and her grave was to remain unmarked till at least one year after.

Dini gave instructions for the gates to be locked, and visitors excused. He was the only one of Mama's children around. First, he called Oyinemi. She was still in Akure, about to leave for Abuja and then on to Kaduna where her family lived.

"I want you to come back—"

"What is wrong? What happened?"

"I—Mama wants to see you—"

"Is she dead? Don't lie to me, Dini. Dini?" She hung up crying.

He pulled himself together and called Tobi. He would know how to break the news to Erebi. Then he called the other four siblings one after the other.

Next he called Mama's doctor who came to confirm her dead and returned to prepare the necessary documentation. He promised to send a nurse to help out with the preparations. A casket was ordered from Akure, and a caterer in Apoi asked to begin preparing the traditional *ekuru*, a bean-meal synonymous with entertaining visitors and neighbours at the death of an elderly person.

Soon the elders in the community would come. They would demand Mama's body for the traditional rites. Mama had specifically said she was not to be cut open by anything for any reason. Not even for embalming. Grave diggers were contracted.

Mama had been a member of the local Methodist Church and Dini quickly prepared and went to meet with the reverend. He was carrying out Mama's instructions and he expected the church to cooperate.

Oyinemi arrived in record time. She had chartered a taxi from Akure. On arrival, she found Dini in front of the house, talking to some young men of the family. She flew out of the taxi before it stopped and ran to him. He caught her in his arms and held her tightly as she wept into him. The two gripped each other in grief, comforting and receiving comfort.

When they calmed, Dini held her in his arm, and left instructions with one of the young men for two of his siblings who lived close by, one in Ondo, and the other in Akure, and were expected to arrive soon. He had fixed the burial for 7pm, approximately twelve hours after Mama slept.

He took Oyinemi to Mama's room where she still looked as peaceful as though she slept. Oyinemi went to kneel beside the bed and place her head on Mama's chest. Dini left her like that to continue with arrangements.

Erebi came in before noon with her entire family. By late afternoon, all Mama's children surrounded her bed. They sang some praises and prayed. Then Erebi chose the same outfit Mama had used years ago for her chieftaincy coronation, and they bathed and dressed their mother, with help from the nurse from the doctor's office.

At 7pm, a short procession filed out to the Methodist church graveyard in line with Mama's wishes to be laid to rest where other dead people lay. Her husband had been buried in the family compound.

The Methodist reverend spoke the blessing over her. In less than an hour, everyone left the graveyard. The children wailed for a while, and then filed back to the house.

They congregated in Dini's apartment and had a family meeting where they agreed to hold a church thanksgiving service in the traditional forty days' celebration. Duties were allocated for who would handle catering, uniforms, and other party logistics. In the meanwhile, everyone was permitted to go back and plan for Mama's party in their own special way.

***

The days flew by and before anyone could actually begin counting, the thanksgiving ceremony was just a few days away. Dini could not arrive till a day to the celebrations. Everyone else arrived at the village before him.

As soon as he arrived, Mama's unmarked grave was visited by her six children, twenty-four grandchildren, and five great-grandchildren, courtesy of Erebi's children who were married.

Dini stole glances at his boys irresistibly.

Afterward, Oyinemi came into his apartment to visit with her four children. As she had said, the boys had grown quite big. They resembled him no doubt but retained close to their mother's colouring. The boys were polite, and respectful. They knew he was their father. She had prepared their minds.

Dini looked at her. "Where are you staying?"

"My mother's house."

"No. Please move here. I have enough space. Pere and Ebisine are using one room. There are still two empty rooms."

"We are actually comfortable where we are—"

"No, I insist. My driver will take you back and bring your belongings. Please." He stood before she could protest further and headed for the door. The driver was at his beck within minutes. "Please," he said when he saw the reluctance on her face.

The four children filed out after her. Tari's children looked like him as well but took Oyinemi's complexion.

He made a note to ask after their father later on when she returned and settled down. Probably he would come in the following day. He did owe him thanks. The man had done a much better job than he did with Ebisine George's children. Of course, Oyinemi was probably a far better wife and mother than Tonbra.

Pere and Ebisine were well-balanced now, and had a direction for their lives, which gave him some satisfaction. Both boys had come back to school in Nigeria. Pere graduated from University of Lagos, went to Law School, did his youth service and now worked as a legal assistant in DOB Energy Systems Inc in The Gambia. Ebisine recently graduated from the same university after studying mass communications. He was waiting to go for youth service.

Timi, well, lost or so. The last time Dini spoke to her, she was doing an online course in business management, which he paid heavily for. The EFG

foundation had fallen apart due to bad management. Sponsors withdrew, and the foundation eventually had to close down, along with the school of journalism.

As Oyinemi and her children left, they met Erebi on the way out. She greeted the party and beckoned on Dini. The siblings walked back into Dini's sitting room.

"I'm sharing the souvenirs I made, first for family. Kitchen towels and trays," Erebi said. "I know tomorrow will be very busy and I may not be able to reach your guests."

"Okay, thanks. You can put them on the dining table."

Erebi did as he said. "But I didn't bring enough. I brought for only your guests. I didn't remember Oyinemi." She sat on the sofa.

"I can share mine with her."

"No, I'll just have to send one of my children to her mother's house when I get back to my room."

"Send it here," Dini said. "I asked her to stay here with the children."

Erebi laughed. "Oh. Good. I was wondering when you'll finally hit on her."

"Hit on her, Erebi!" Dini laughed. "I doubt your Christianity sometimes. Oyinemi may be the mother of my boys but she is a married woman."

Erebi's eyes widened and he wondered what he had said wrong. Then she screeched and clapped excitedly. "Sorry. Sorry."

"What?"

"You don't know she—Tari Ekiye died?"

Dini sat forward. "How was I to know?"

"She didn't tell you?"

He gasped. "Well, we didn't exactly talk about it. I didn't tell her Tonbra died either, so—"

"But she knows Tonbra died." Erebi clapped. "Everyone in the family knew when Tonbra died."

There had been speculations Dini would remarry. He hadn't.

He shrugged. "Tari Ekiye died? When? What happened?"

"He'd battled with sickle cell anaemia all his life. He finally succumbed two years ago."

"What a shame? He didn't look like a sickler when I met him."

"Oyinemi took good care of him."

"Oh, what a pity." He shook his head, pondering. "She never insinuated it. The kids? I hope none is—"

"Oyinemi is AA so their twins are covered."

"Oh, thank God. Wow." Dini sat thinking. Wow. She was free. She was a free woman.

"Her loss is your gain, Dini." Erebi stood. "Even the Bible says he taketh the first to establish the second."

"God must think I'm good for widows." Dini joked and walked her to the door.

Erebi laughed. "Hey, don't see me off. They say that if your parent died and someone comes to visit and you see the person off, the person's parent will die as well."

"So funny, I forgot to laugh, sis." Dini yawned. "You didn't come to visit me, and you don't have a parent anymore." They both laughed and Erebi left.

Her last daughter, Biye, later brought some of the trays and kitchen towels for Oyinemi.

Chapter 44

When Oyinemi returned, Dini was seated alone, much the same way he'd been when she first came in with the children. He couldn't believe his luck. But would she want to remarry, even him? If she was half as attached to Tari as Tonbra had been to Ebisine George, then even he didn't want her. Why hadn't she told him her husband died?

It had been two years already, surely, she had gotten over the mourning—well, one never got over it. Even as bad as their end was, he still missed Tonbra. So maybe she had not gotten over him but at least, she could move on. Or did she have someone already? He couldn't bear the thought. Oyinemi was a beautiful woman. Even after four children, she remained so desirable. She looked none of her age. He felt such a strong attraction for her.

He showed her the rooms and told her about Erebi's souvenirs. She and her daughter took one room while the three boys took the other. She thanked him and he excused her. He went back to his private parlour. He wanted to be alone, and he wanted to think. Should he ask her tonight or tomorrow? If he didn't ask her, he would never know so he had to ask.

She found him about an hour later and placed a night snack on a stool in front of him, with a bottle of water and juice. He mumbled his thanks, noticing with delight she had had a bath. She smelled fresh, tempting. It was close to mid-night and he didn't think she would not go to bed right away.

She smiled warmly and took a seat across from him. His heart thudded in his chest, probably she would tell him now. If she did, he would propose immediately.

"I wasn't even sure if you'd rather eat real food—" She made to stand, but he stopped her. "I brought some food up."

I can't eat anything now!

"No, thanks," he said, and smiled at her. "I'm just too tired. And overwhelmed."

"It's been a day." She yawned. "The rooms here are definitely more comfortable. The children love it. Thank you."

"We thank God. I should thank you for coming as well. You may have simply refused."

They lapsed into a comfortable silence and he wondered what she was thinking. He took a bite of the warm puff-puff she brought. Hmm.

"You made these?" He gestured the snacks and she nodded.

"Yes. There's been some cooking going on in my mother's house. In fact, she didn't want me to come. She released only the children—" She smiled. "My mum can be so funny."

"I hope your mum doesn't see me as the enemy now," Dini said, and smiled. "Taking her precious daughter away."

"She has no choice. She'll get by. She has my siblings with her."

"This is very delicious. I don't usually eat anything this late but this is an exception." He picked another small ball. "So nice."

"Thank you."

"I heard you lost your father—"

"It's been five years now."

"Accept my condolence."

"Thank you." Oyinemi sighed. "Ah, Mama. But we thank God. Tomorrow will be a great day. She will be highly honoured."

"She will be. I hear the first lady of The Gambia will come but I don't want to hope." He finished the puff-puff and drank water.

"That will be a great honour indeed." She smiled. "Mama affected so many lives. She was always looking out for others."

He stared at his toes. *God, give me the words!* "Yeah." He nodded. "She always told me she knew what I need more than I do." He narrowed his eyes and stared at her. "She did."

Their gazes locked. "I need to go in now. Tomorrow will be very busy." She stood and stretched. "Are you through with the snacks?"

He got to his feet as well. "Yes."

"Goodnight then."

She didn't wait. She picked the tray and walked straight out. He slumped back into his seat and held his head with both hands.

***

Not enough words could describe the success of the thanksgiving service. People from all walks of life came to celebrate the life of Mama Brisibe, the Iyalode of Apoi. She had affected so many lives on so many levels, people mourned her death for various reasons.

The crowd gathered represented her diversity.

Erebi had her crowd. Mama's first daughter had retired as the principal of her school, well-respected in her circles. Her husband Tobi sat on boards of several vibrant companies. Her first daughter, Bodi, and Mama's first grand

daughter, now a medical doctor who lived in the United States with her medical doctor husband, Tayo, also came with their three children.

Tokoni, a civil engineer, and Mama's first grandson, married to Toyosi, a pharmacist, both living in Lagos with their two children, also attended. There were Johnny and Biye, who were still unmarried but professionals in different fields. All attended with their circle of friends.

Mama's other four children were successful in various fields as well.

Yinla, a matron at the general hospital in Ondo, married Fred, a medical doctor. The last girl, Tami, a permanent secretary in the federal ministry of education married Rufus, a colonel in the Nigerian army. The two last boys, Wari and Powei were successful businessmen, both married to career women. Wari was a big-time

MTN distributor in Akure, and his wife, Flora, a bank manager. Powei dealt in oil and gas, while his wife, Inimfon, lectured at University of Uyo. All came with their children, family and friends.

And then Dini.

After the church service, a reception commenced at the town square. Canopies erected everywhere, with food and drinks in abundance, a local band entertained so the people of Apoi would enjoy it to the fullest.

Dini entertained his guests in his mother's compound. By derivative, Oyinemi followed suit. A large tent was erected outside and guests got treated to an abundance of food, drinks and good music but Dini entertained the most important guests in his apartment.

As he had been earlier informed, the first lady of The Gambia did attend briefly. Other dignitaries from within and outside the country also graced the occasion with their presence. To his delight, Pastor Flo attended the church service, and preached a moving sermon that found many of the guests giving their lives to Christ. Dini took great delight in introducing Oyinemi and the twins to him and his wife.

By early evening, the guests had thinned out and many gone to the town square where the party had gone beyond the family.

Masquerades performed and alcohol began to flow.

Dini sat in his sitting room with some of the directors of DOB Energy Systems, including Sigha, chatting. Oyinemi came in to serve and to be sure they were alright.

"Oyinemi," Dini said, when he saw she had served the three men with him fresh drinks.

"Come and sit with me. You must be tired." He patted the seat on the couch where he sat.

She shook her head. "If I sit down now, I won't be able to do anything again."

"And if you don't do anything else today, it will not be bad at all."

She laughed but did not sit with him. She took a vacant single couch instead.

The men chatted for a while and she chipped in once or twice, and then, one by one they left. They were all going to spend the night in Akure and didn't want to travel too late.

Dini and Oyinemi saw the guests off, chatted with others in the tent, and returned to the parlour. Oyinemi sighed and laughed.

"What's funny?"

"I was just thinking over the day, and then…Mama, you know. She was just a remarkable person." She shook her head. He stared keenly at her. "I was looking at my album the other day with the children, and we just kept laughing, remembering the good old days when they would visit Mama—"

She wanted to talk about Mama, *yeah right*.

He looked at her, his eyes searching. "Oyinemi. What about us?"

She stopped talking but her mouth remained open. He smiled shyly. He didn't want her to be upset, or to take this so serious she would not be able to answer him right away. Especially when he couldn't but help remember the last time he asked that question.

"When are you going to tell me, you are no longer married?"

She smiled and turned away. "When you tell me, you are no longer married."

Dini laughed. "Oh really! Aren't you smart?" She hadn't given her condolences or something. "As if you didn't know."

He held out his hand to her, and she took it. He dragged her out of her chair and kept pulling till she fell into his laps.

"Dini! Anyone may come in at any time."

She struggled to stand, but he held her tight.

"We don't care." He pressed her head down and took her lips in a gentle, passionate kiss. "Will you believe me if I tell you I've not had a woman since that night with you?" He whispered into her ear before he caught it with his teeth.

"Hmm. Fourteen plus years?" She moaned. "I find it very hard to believe."

"Believe it. I find it hard to believe myself." He groaned. "Tonbra and I were out of sorts till I left the country—and then she died. I was determined to never let sin have dominion over me." He looked at her, searching. "It wasn't easy. I'm over-starved."

She pressed her face into his neck. "We need to be married first."

"I know. We will be married before I leave this village for sure." He winked. "And I want a white wedding too. In the Gambia." He delighted in Oyinemi's gasp. "I never had a white wedding."

"You know," she whispered tremulously, "Mama paid my bride price before she died."

He drew back and looked at her. "You don't say."

She swallowed and traced his face with her fingers. "She did. When our twins were born—"

He caught her hand and pressed it to his lips. His eyes fluttered shut. "She never told me."

"When Tari came for my hand, my father insisted on returning it but you know your mother."

Dini opened his eyes and looked at her, smiling. "Means I don't owe on bride price then."

She laughed. "You don't."

"I love you, Oyinemi." He drew her head down to his again and kissed her lingeringly.

Someone cleared his throat and Dini turned his head toward the door. His personal assistant stood at the entrance, looking at the floor. He lowered Oyinemi to the other part of the couch and smiled at her. She smiled back.

"Isaac, what is it?"

"There is a delegate here to see you, sir. From the presidency. Led by the president's Special Adviser on Power." Isaac kept a straight look on his boss.

"Really? I didn't even know people from the presidency are around." He frowned. "How many people?"

"Six."

"It's a party. Send them in."

The young man gave a small bow. "Yes, sir." And left.

Dini smiled again at Oyinemi and she smiled back.

"I'll go and get refreshments for them." She made to stand again but he took her hand and shook his head.

"Isaac will arrange that." He couldn't stop smiling. And he couldn't stop looking at her.

And she was smiling and looking at him too.

The men came in and introduced themselves.

The SA on Power, also the spokesman of the delegate, excused the late hour of their arrival, saying they had visited the king first. It was close to 10p.m. Dini continued to hold Oyinemi's hand through the meeting. Isaac arranged for refreshments for the guests, a feast.

"His Excellency, President Duke, wants us to ask you to come back home and build the power sector. It's high time Nigeria enjoy what the other countries you've been servicing are enjoying." The man brought out a file and handed it to Dini. "In there is the president's proposal. You have three options. As a private sector operator, or as a consultant, or as a public servant in a ministerial capacity. And it's all clearly written here. When do you return to The Gambia?"

Dini looked at Oyinemi and smiled. "Well, I don't know yet. I'll have to consult—my wife, first."

"His Excellency hopes you'll have a reply before you go back." The SA shared a look between the two of them.

"I should." Dini shrugged. He flipped through the file. "I'll read this tonight. I'm not promising a reply tonight, of course." He looked at Oyinemi and smiled.

"All our contacts are in the file. Please call me anytime."

"I will."

"Please help yourselves to some food," Oyinemi said.

The men were served by two ladies, while they made small talk about the country and the reforms going on through the dynamic new president. Afterward, the SA stood, and his team followed suit.

"Please express my gratitude to His Excellency. I count this offer a great honour," Dini said.

They walked with the men to the door.

As they went back into the sitting room, Dini began to laugh.

Oyinemi smiled. "What's funny?"

Dini related the myth Erebi shared the day before and they both laughed. "The SA and his entourage will soon begin to lose their parents."

"That's if they are still have."

He pulled her back on his laps and looked into her eyes. She wriggled once again but he held her down.

"The children will start coming back anytime from now, Dini." She giggled. "I told them not to stay at the square later than 11p.m."

"As if it matters." He nuzzled her. "If they have any respect, they'll quietly go into their rooms. Pretend they didn't see us." He kissed her neck.

"You're impossible—"

He looked up into her face. "Do you love me?"

"From the first day I saw you—I was only twelve. And you were being sent off to the states."

He chuckled. "Say it."

"I love you, Dinipre Brisibe."

He buried his face in her neck. "I want you to give me another set of twins. Girls this time."

"I doubt if I can muster the strength for more twins." Her speech slowed. "I'm forty, for crying out loud."

He laughed. "And I'm fifty-two. What's in a number?"

CHAPTER 45

THE END

Some stories refuse to end till the very end.

Oyinemi Brisibe buried her second husband, Dinipre Oyinkuru Brisibe after forty blissful years of marriage. It was a state burial, attended by three African presidents and countless dignitaries.

The Brisibe children, two sets of twins, two boys sixteen years older than two girls, were accompanied by their families. The Ekiye twins and the Ebisine George children were also counted as children of the deceased.

Even Timi attended at almost seventy years old, after having lived a fruitless life, and later gone into missionary work. Countless children and families touched by over sixty years of Dini Brisibe's scholarships celebrated a life, a legacy, a heritage.

The president of Nigeria read a tribute at the funeral, of the Nigerian legend laid to rest. A man whose selfless service to his mother country, as Minister of Power for ten full years, and working with several presidents, consulting and mentoring, led to the 30th year celebration of Nigeria's uninterrupted power supply, just few days before he died.

Dinipre Oyinkuru Brisibe would live forever in the hearts of his people.

THE END.

JOIN IN THE FIGHT TO END THE #MONEYWOMAN SALE AND ABUSE OF GIRLS IN BECHEVE LANDS...PLEASE CONTACT THE AUTHOR OF THIS BOOK. THANK YOU!

APPRECIATION:

Tare Osanebi, Sandra Ubong Nta

Biye Filatei Eshofonie, Funkeyi Meeting

Chima Ogbonnah, Priye Noel Kuete

Samsong (Church Boy) for inspiring songs *My Heart Will Trust In You*, and *I'll Depend On You*

ARE YOU SAVED?

All that is written in this book may not be of much use to you if you haven't yet given your life to Christ. We cannot take difficult decisions unless we have the Righteous and Wise One who is greater than the devil to help and choose for us. The Bible says that "greater is he that is in you, than he that is in the world." (1 John 4:4 King James Version) And "we wrestle not against flesh and blood, but against principalities, against powers, against the rulers of the darkness of this world, against spiritual wickedness in high places." (Ephesians 6:12).

This is why I want to encourage you to take this important decision if you haven't yet given your life to Christ. I took this decision almost thirty years ago, and I haven't regretted it even for one day. Please pray this prayer of faith if you are willing to surrender your life to God:

Lord Jesus, I honour you. I praise you, and I acknowledge you that you are Lord. I know I am a sinner, and I ask that you forgive me all my sins. I want you to be my lord and personal saviour. Wash me clean and give me grace to serve you wholly from now on. Come into my heart to reign supreme. In Jesus' name, I pray. Amen.

PRAISE GOD, YOU ARE BORN AGAIN.

Now that you have prayed this prayer of faith, I admonish you to

•Get a Bible and read it every day. (Start from the first four books of the New Testament to familiarize yourself more with your new commander in chief, Jesus Christ.)

•Pray every day.

•Attend a Living Church.

•Introduce yourself to the pastor and seek further teaching. (You can join the foundation class and activity group in church. You are, hence, making yourself available to work for God.)

•Tell others about your salvation.

May God help you in Jesus' name? Amen.

THE NIGERIAN CHILD: MY VISION

Then the LORD answered me and said: "Write the vision and make it plain on tablets, that he may run who reads it." —Hab. 2:2

More than before, it's time for the well-to-do to cater for the less privileged. Over the past few years, the Lord has laid this burden for The Nigerian Child on my heart, and I believe it's time to spread the vision. I have a desire to help and to instigate help for The Nigerian Child. There are currently five areas of help I have been able to identify.

1. The Market-school Project: This vision is aimed at eradicating street and market hawking in the long run. The strategy is to erect schools in marketplaces where children hawking can take a few hours out to learn and then go back to their jobs. It is a long-term project and a highly capital intensive one.

2. The Bread and Milk Project: Bread and milk will be given in the morning to children trekking to school just before school resumes. It can be done once a month, once a week, or every day or as rampantly as the provision is available. It is not very capital intensive, and as little as N50 or $0.35 USD can feed a child with bread and warm milk.

3. The Umbrella Project: This will help alleviate the suffering of children who hawk on the streets (while we work toward eradicating hawking on our streets) by

providing umbrellas, especially during the rainy season. The umbrellas can also be useful during the scorching hot weathers. Umbrellas of different sizes will be given depending on the size of the child. Prices of umbrellas range from N1350.00 to N1500.00 or $2.50 to $3.50 USD.

4. The Sort-a-child Project: This is aimed at helping at least a child in whatever capacity you can. It can be by paying a sick child's hospital bills, buying food and clothing for a child, or paying a child's school fees. It can be as long as a lifetime commitment or a onetime affair.

5. The Student Care Project: This is for secondary and tertiary students who can't afford their school fees. The idea is to help through the bob-a-job initiative.

The Nigerian Child vision is not another nongovernmental, money-spinning organisation. It is service to God and provision for The Nigerian Child. It can be done privately or corporately. The important thing is to help a Nigerian child.

I beg to challenge every church in Nigeria to adopt the sort-a-child project or as the Lord lay it on our hearts.

HELP! Signed
- THE NIGERIAN CHILD

EXCERPT

When he entered the visiting hall, he noticed she was the only one there, and she stood, backing the entrance.

He used the opportunity to drink in her shapely, hippy figure. Clad in black jeans and a black-and-white striped ladies' shirt, he wondered what she would think of him. He felt a strong attraction to her.

She turned, almost as coincidentally as he moved in, and smiled easily. He took note of everything about her. From her oval-shaped eyes, her small nose and mouth, shapely eyebrows, thick wavy hair that was just a little longer than the last time he saw her, to the tiny earrings she wore, with chain and matching pendant resting between her cleavage...

***

Esam followed his eyes to the cleft between her breasts, and heat poured into her face. She knew her dressing seemed suggestive, but she had not done her laundry in weeks, and this was the only thing available. She was paying for her insensitivity.

When she looked up at his face, she met with two deep pools of black emotion. She knew she had ruined the purpose of the visit. She never meant to seduce him, but she could feel that pulse. This man, despite his status, for whatever reason he pleased, was going to use her femininity to destroy her. She'd better be prepared.

"Hi," she croaked after a brief moment of completely losing her voice.

"Hi," he whispered in response, taking a seat opposite her, obviously struggling to control waging emotions.

The warden had already gone to stay at the elevated spot to watch them, unaware of anything between them. Esam breathed in to calm herself and sat down. She was here for business, and though she had least expected what just transpired, she decided not to allow the thudding in her chest to deter her. It was a lesson for next time.

"I'm sorry for upsetting you last time." She stared at him, and he arched his eyebrow in surprise but didn't say a word. "Though you seemed in a foul mood too," she added lightly.

"Prison is a foul place. The environment dictates the mood, most days."

"You seem better today. That's good. I'm glad I came."

"Does your husband not care about you, your being here, especially dressed like this," he growled, startling Esam.

Oh no! She thought.

OTHER BOOKS BY THE AUTHOR

SISTER MINISTER
STRENGTH OF CHARACTER (Devotional & Workbook)
52 WAYS TO PROVOKE GOD (Devotional)
THE DEVIL LIED
NOVELS:
SCENT OF WATER
PEPPER
FRAIL FLESH
TISHA
WAY OF THE UNFAITHFUL
UNDER A RED DELTA SUN
I LOVED A SLAVE
HER LOVER
BLUE DAWN

TRUE DREAM SERIES:
DUMPED
YOUR WISH IS MINE
EVEN THE LAWFUL CAPTIVE
HE TAKETH THE FIRST
THE OTHER SISTER
WHAT'S GOOD FOR THE GOOSE
SERVE A KOBO

JUST LIKE PLAY

SHATTERED

SCATTERED

ÌKA

WISDOM SERIES:

WISDOM FOR MEN

WISDOM FOR PASTORS

WISDOM FOR WOMEN

WISDOM FOR PASTORS' WIVES

WISDOM FOR SINGLES

ISSUES OF LIFE SERIES:

SOMEBODY HELP! I'M IN LOVE

NO IS NOT NEGATIVE

SOME GOD USE, SOME USE GOD